The Investiture of the Gods
Part 1

The Investiture of the Gods
Part 1

By Jeff Pepper

Based on chapters 1 through 50 of the
16th century Chinese novel by Xu Zhonglin

IMAGIN8
PRESS

Published in the United States by Imagin8 Press LLC, Verona, PA 15147 USA. For information, contact us via email at info@imagin8press.com, or visit www.imagin8press.com.

Our books may be purchased directly in quantity at a reduced price. Visit www.imagin8press.com for details.

Written by Jeff Pepper

Based on chapters 1 through 50 of the original 16th century Chinese novel by Xu Zhonglin

ISBN: 978-1959043430
Version 2.0

Contents

Acknowledgements

We are grateful to the original authors of this story and to the scholars who have translated the book into English before us.

In writing this book we have referred to the original Chinese text in *The Project Gutenberg eBook of Feng Shen Yan Yi*[1], as well as an English translation, *Creation of the Gods,* translated by Gu Zhizhong[2].

These books are both available free online. See the footnotes for tinyurl shortcut links to their websites. These shortcut links are safe and do not use any tracking software.

Thanks to my writing partner Xiao Hui Wang, who has translated my English back into Chinese for the books in our *Last King of Shang* series, and has worked with me on so many other fun projects.

Also, many thanks to Yu Jin and his team of artists at Next Mars Media for their terrific cover artwork, and Tzu Yang for her help in translating the poems at the beginning of each chapter.

---

[1] Lu, Xi Xing, *The Project Gutenberg eBook of Feng Shen Yan Yi*, Publisher unknown. 2007-2021. Shortcut link www.tinyurl.com/FengShenBang-01 resolves to www.gutenberg.org/files/23910/23910-h/23910-h.htm.

[2] Zhizhong, Gu (translator), *Creation of the Gods I, II, III and IV by Xu Zhonglin*. New World Press, Foreign Languages Press and Hunan People's Publishing House, 1002. Shortcut link www.tinyurl.com/FengShenBang-02 resolves to journeytothewestresearch.com/wp-content/uploads/2020/05/fsyy-en-cn.pdf.

Introduction

The Chinese title of this book is 封神演义, pronounced *fēng shén yǎnyì*. The first word, *fēng*, means "to grant" or "to confer." It refers to the famous ending of the novel, when hundreds of humans and immortals are given new names and transformed into gods. The second word, *shén*, means "god." The last word *yǎnyì*, means "romance" or "historical novel." So, the closest word-for-word translation would be "Romance of the Naming of the Gods."

Over time, the book has become known in China by a simpler title, 封神榜, pronounced *fēng shén bǎng*. The last word here, *bǎng*, means "list of names," so the English equivalent would be "Naming a List of Gods."

Because these titles are really awkward in English, translators over the years have come up with many different titles for the book. The most common one, which we use for this book, is *Investiture of the Gods.*

Other titles include Canonization of the Gods, Creation of the Gods, The Legend of Deification, The Story of Chinese Gods, and even Chronicles of the God's Order. We have even come up with our own title, The Last King of Shang, which we use for the Chinese language series of books that Xiao Hui Wang and I have written based on this story.

The book is a great example of what is now called shenmo fiction (*shénmó xiǎoshuō*), a genre of Chinese fiction that revolves around mythical deities, immortals, demons and monsters. Shenmo is similar to the sword-and-sorcery genre in American fantasy fiction. *Journey to the West* is probably the best-known example of classical shenmo fiction.

The story is loosely based on the historical events that led to the overthrow in 1066 B.C. of King Di Xin, the 31st in a line of Shang kings going back seventeen generations and six centuries.

The king's name in his lifetime was Di Xin of Shang. After his death he was mockingly referred to as King Zhou, because *zhòu* (纣) is Chinese for "crupper," the rear strap on a saddle that goes under the horse's tail and is most likely to be soiled by the horse. For this reason, some translations refer to him as King Zhou. In this book he's called Di Xin, because the name Zhou (纣, *zhòu*) is confusingly similar to the name of the Zhou (周, *zhōu*) Dynasty that succeeded Shang.

Unlike most of his predecessors, Di Xin was a tyrannical despot. Encouraged by his favorite concubine Daji, he enjoyed inventing creative ways to torture and execute people who displeased him. Not surprisingly, he was despised by his subjects.

According to the concept of "mandate of heaven," heaven gives its mandate to a just ruler, the so-called "son of heaven." If the ruler loses his mandate, the people have the right to overthrow him. In fact, if a ruler is overthrown, that can be taken as proof that he was unworthy and had lost heaven's mandate.

In the case of Di Xin, there were many indications that he had lost heaven's mandate. One poem said:

Heaven has sent down death and disorder;

famine comes repeatedly[1]

This was partly caused by his mismanagement of the kingdom's resources, but also the result of a long-term cooling climate which caused crops to fail.

To make matters worse, there were two disturbing portents in the sky. The five known planets all appeared tightly clustered together in the constellation of Cancer. And a few months later, Halley's comet blazed in the sky. Taken together, many believed that Di Xin had lost the mandate of heaven and needed to be toppled from the throne.

Matters came to a head in January of 1066 B.C., when Ji Fa, the leader of Zhou and Overlord of the West (a title given to him by Di Xin) dispatched a large army which arrived in the capital city of Zhaoge the following month. To defend the capital, Di Xin had gathered 530,000 soldiers and conscripted another 170,000 slaves. But the slaves refused to fight, and many of the soldiers turned their spears upside down or defected to the Zhou side. The Zhou army quickly overthrew Di Xin in the Battle of Muyi, described by a historian as "like crushing dry weeds and smashing rotten wood." Ji Fa became King Wu, founding the Zhou Dynasty which lasted for almost 800 years.

The overthrow of the king of Shang by a mere provincial governor was considered a disturbing precedent by the kings and emperors who followed. They didn't like the idea that their subjects might decide that they were unhappy with their ruler and should take matters into their own

---

[1] Chittick, Andrew (2003). "The life and legacy of Liu Biao: governor, warlord, and imperial pretender in late Han China." Journal of Asian History. Harrassowitz Verlag.

hands. For a local official to presume to go against his king was seen later as "a monstrous crime of insubordination and a violation of Confucian ethics," even though Confucius wasn't born until 500 years after these events.

For centuries, philosophers struggled to resolve this contradiction. The great philosopher Confucius taught that officials should be loyal to their king, just as a child should be loyal to their parents. But what if the king fails in his duties and doesn't care for his people? When the Confucian philosopher Mencius was asked about this, he replied that a king should be benevolent and merciful, but if he is not, then he is not a king but a tyrant, and tyrants must be punished. Referring to the overthrow of Di Xin, he wrote[1], "We heard that the tyrant was punished; not that the king was murdered."

Twenty-four centuries later, Zhu Yuanzhang, the founder of the Ming Dynasty, was also fond of creative methods of torture and execution. He was worried, with good reason, about the precedent set by the popular uprising against the king of Shang. So in the year 1393 he ordered all mention of this historical event deleted from *Mencius*, a classic book written by Mencius and his disciples. This resulted in the erasing of about a third of the book, and what was left became known as the *Abridged Essays of Mencius*.

This story is not just a chronicle the depraved actions of a bewitched king. It also examines the life-and-death decisions faced by his ministers and generals. Should they remain loyal to the king, despite the awful things he does and says? Or should they conclude that the king has lost the mandate of heaven and must be removed? There is no

---

[1] Mencius, *Mencius, Liang Hui Wang* (second part)

middle ground. And as you'll see, each individual needs to decide for themselves where their loyalties lie.

The original novel was published sometime between 1567 and 1619, roughly 2,650 years after the historical events it's roughly based on.

No one knows for certain who wrote the book. The best clue lies in a 20-volume woodblock print of the book that was published during the Ming Dynasty and is now in the Library of the Japanese Cabinet in Japan. On the cover is an inscription saying that the book was carved by Shu Congfu in the Jinkai Bookstore. No author is listed. However, in the second volume it mentions that the book was edited by "Xu Zhonglin, a hermit (or 'leisure man') of Zhongshan." Nothing more is known about him. Since he is referred to as the editor, we don't know how much was actually written by him and how much he collected from other authors and storytellers.

In the book's preface, the publisher claims that the book was purchased in Chu, and that he, the publisher, "daringly continued the writing, by deleting its absurd parts and the vulgar slang... Now the book is finished and it is up to the readers to decide if it is credible or not[1]."

Investiture of the Gods is one of the great novels of classical Chinese literature, along with *Journey to the West, Water Margin, Romance of the Three Kingdoms,* and *Dream of the Red Chamber.* But of these, this one probably has had the most impact on the daily lives and language of the people. Many of the episodes in the book

---

[1] Shuofang Xu and Qiuke Sun, *A History of Literature in the Ming Dynasty*, translated by Li Ma, Springer Nature Singapore Ptc Ltd., 2018.

have become deeply embedded in Chinese culture. Nearly everyone in China is familiar with the main characters of the novel, and there are many popular idioms that come from episodes in the book.

For example, "Jiang Taigong is here, the gods avoid" refers to the power of Jiang Ziya (called Jiang Taigong after he becomes a god at the end) to review the behavior of all the gods and punish them as needed. Traditionally, when Chinese people build houses they put up banners or write the idiom on a wooden beam (see figure below), hoping to intimidate any evil demons and keep them away from the new home.

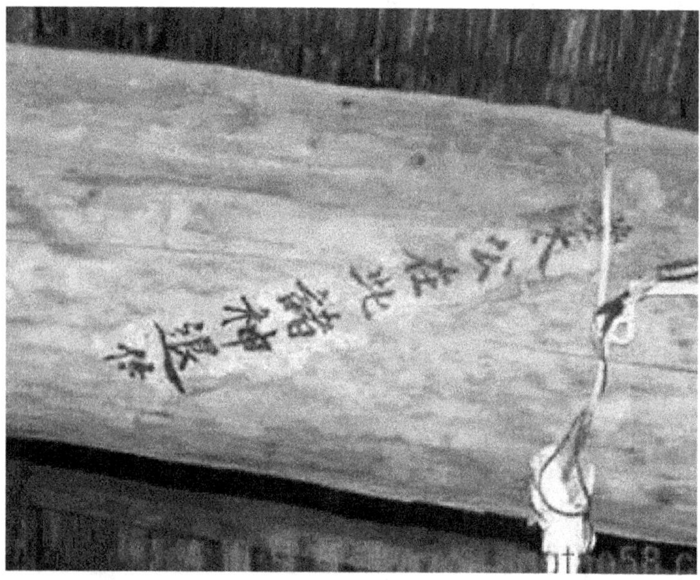

Another popular idiom, "Jiang Taigong fishes, and those who wish to take the bait," is based on the unusual fishing method used by Jiang Ziya in the book. His fishing rod and line were very short, the hook was straight, and he used no bait. He would say, "Fish, if you don't want to live anymore, come and swallow the hook yourself." Today, people use this idiom to describe someone who willingly falls into a trap or ignores the consequences of their actions.

 We've tried to find and squash all errors, but it's unavoidable that some will have slipped through. If you find any mistakes, please let us know by emailing us at info@imagin8press.com. We promise to respond quickly, and we will revise the book to incorporate any changes needed.

I hope you have as much fun reading the book as I had writing it!

Jeff Pepper
Pittsburgh, Pennsylvania, USA
December 2023

Cast of Characters

The original 16th century novel had over 450 different named characters[1]. To simplify things, we have avoided giving names to the minor characters. Here are the important ones who are named in the book. If a character defects from one side to another over the course of the story, they are listed according to their original allegiance. The numbers in brackets indicate the chapter where the character first appears.

<u>Shang Royal Family</u>
- Di Xin – the last king of Shang [1]
- Jiang – queen of Shang, daughter of Jiang Huanchu [1]
- Su Daji – daughter of Marquis Su Hu, the king's chief concubine and then queen, possessed by a fox demon [1]
- Yin Jiao – Crown Prince, elder son of the king and Queen Jiang [1]
- Yin Hong – younger son of the king and Queen Jiang [1]

<u>Shang Grand Dukes and Marquises</u>
- Chong Houhu – the cruel Grand Duke of the North [1]
- Chong Heihu (Black Tiger) – Marquis of Caozhou, brother of Chong Houhu [3]
- Ji Chang – the virtuous Grand Duke of the West [1]
- E Chongyu – Grand Duke of the South [1]

---

[1] For a complete list of all named characters in the original novel, except for characters like Laozi who already existed, see "Creation of the Gods: A Somewhat Less Than Critical Listing of Characters in Order of Appearance" in www.poisonpie.com/words/others/somewhat/creation/text/characters.html.

- Jiang Huanchu – Grand Duke of the East [1]
- Su Hu – Marquis of Jizhou, father of Daji [2]

Shang Ministers
- Bi Gan – Vice Prime Minister, uncle of the King [2]
- Du Yuanxian – Chief Minister of the Observatory [6]
- Fei Zhong – a minion courtier [1]
- Jiao Ge – Supreme Minister [11]
- Mei Bo – Supreme Minister [1]
- Shang Rong – Prime Minister [1]
- Yang Ren – Supreme Minister, later a disciple of Virtue of the Pure Void [7]
- You Hun – a minion courtier [1]
- Zhao Qi – Supreme Minister [9]

Shang Military
- Chao Lei – a palace general of Zhaoge [7]
- Chao Tian – a palace general of Zhaoge [7]
- Chen Tong – commander of Tongguan Pass [31]
- Chen Wu – commander of Chuanyun Pass, brother of Chen Tong [32]
- Chong Yingbiao – son of Chong Houhu, a general at Jizhou [2]
- Fang Bi – Chief of Guards, later a ferryman [8]
- Fang Xiang – Chief of Guards, later a ferryman [8]
- Feng Lin – a general under Zhang Guifang [36]
- Han Rong – commander of Sishui Pass [19]
- Huang Feibiao – brother of Huang Feihu [30]
- Huang Feihu – the head of military affairs [1]
- Huang Gun – commander of Jiepai Pass, father of Huang Feihu and Concubine Huang [30]
- Huang Ming – a palace general, brother of Huang Feihu [8]

- Huang Tianhua – son of Huang Feihu, raised by Master Pure Void Virtue [31]
- Li Jing – commander of Chentang Pass, disciple of Burning Lamp, father of Nezha, Jinzha and Muzha [12]
- Lu Xiong – an elderly general of Zhaoge, led attack against Jizhou [2]
- Mo Lihai – a guard at Jiameng Pass [31]
- Mo Lihong – a guard at Jiameng Pass [31]
- Mo Liqing – a guard at Jiameng Pass [31]
- Mo Lishou – a guard at Jiameng Pass [31]
- Wen Zhong –called Grand Tutor Wen, head of civil affairs for the king
- Xiao Yin – a general at Longtong Pass [31]
- Xin Huan – former bandit chief [41]
- Yu Hua – the Seven Headed General, a sorcerer for Han Rong at Sishui Pass [33]
- Zhang Feng – commander of Longtong Pass, sworn brother of Huang Feihu's father
- Zhang Guifang – a commander at Lintong Pass [18]
- Zheng Lun – a general under Su Hu at Jizhou [3]

Shang-Aligned Gods, Immortals and Demons
- Celestial Lotus – an immortal on Golden Turtle Island [43]
- Cloud Firmament – sister of Zhao Gongming, a hermit on Three Immortals Island [47]
- Gao Youqian – a Daoist immortal, friend of Grand Tutor Wen [38]
- Green Firmament – sister of Zhao Gongming, a hermit on Three Immortals Island [47]
- Jade Firmament – sister of Zhao Gongming, a hermit on Three Immortals Island [47]

- Lady of Golden Light – a Daoist master, friend of Grand Tutor Wen [43]
- Li Xingba – a Daoist immortal, friend of Grand Tutor Wen [38]
- Pretty Cloud – a magician, friend of Shen Gongbao [49]
- Qin Wan – a Daoist master, builder of the Heavenly Destruction trap [43]
- Shen Gongbao – an untrustworthy disciple of Heavenly Primogenitor [37]
- Wang Mo – a Daoist immortal, friend of Grand Tutor Wen [38]
- Yang Sen – a Daoist immortal, friend of Grand Tutor Wen [38]
- Yao – a Daoist master, builder of the Captured Soul trap [44]
- Zhao Gongming – a powerful magician from Mount Emei [46]

Zhou Leaders and Ministers

- Bo Yikao – elder son of Ji Chang [10]
- Ji Chang – Grand Duke of the West, later Prince Wen of West Qi [1]
- Ji Fa – younger son of Ji Chang, later titled King Wu [10]
- Jiang Ziya – Prime Minister of West Qi, disciple of Heavenly Primogenitor [11]
- San Yisheng – Supreme Minister of West Qi [3]

Zhou Military

- Nangong Kuo – a general and minister of external affairs for Ji Chang [10]
- Bai Jian – deceased general under Xuanyuan, brought back to life by Jiang Ziya, builder of the

Terrace of Creation [37]

<u>Zhou-Aligned Gods, Immortals and Demons</u>

- Burning Lamp – leader of all the immortals, disciple of the Buddha [14]
- Deng Hua – an immortal from Mount Kunlun [45]
- Dragon Beard Tiger – an immortal, disciple of Jiang Ziya [38]
- Fairy Primordial – an immortal, master of Nezha, from Qianyuan Mountain [11]
- Grand Completion – an immortal, rescues the Shang King's sons [9]
- Heavenly Master Manjusri – an immortal, master of Jinzha [12]
- Heavenly Primogenitor – the grand master of Daoism, master of Jiang Ziya and Shen Gongbao [15]
- Immortal of the South Pole – a Daoist immortal [15]
- Jinzha – disciple of Heavenly Master Manjusri, first son of Li Jing, brother of Nezha [12]
- Kakusandha – a Buddha [45]
- Laozi – Grand Master of Heaven, founder of Daoism, brother of Heavenly Primogenitor [44]
- Lu Ya – a powerful magician from Mount Kunlun [48]
- Master of Clouds – an immortal from Mt. Zhongnan, raised Thunderbolt [5]
- Merciful Navigation – an immortal [44]
- Muzha – second son of Li Jing, brother of Nezha [12]
- Nezha – third son of Li Jing, a powerful immortal, disciple of Fairy Primordial [12]
- Pure Essence – an immortal from Nine Immortals Mountain [9]
- Pure Void Virtue – a Daoist immortal, master of

Huang Tianhua, from Mount Green Peak [18]

- Thunderbolt – found as a baby by Ji Chang, raised by Master of the Clouds [10]
- Woe Evading Sage – an immortal from West Kunlun Mountain, spiritual master of Li Jing [12]
- Yang Jian – an immortal, disciple of Jade Tripod [40]
- Yellow Dragon – a Daoist immortal [44]

Non-Aligned Gods and Demons

- Ao Bing – Ao Guang's third son [12]
- Ao Guang – Dragon King of the Eastern Ocean [12]
- Blue Cloud Boy – a disciple of Fairy Rock [13]
- Chang'e – the goddess of the moon [26]
- Empress Shiji – a powerful immortal on Skeleton Mountain [13]
- Jade Emperor – the Emperor of Heaven [5]
- Jade Lute – a demon, friend of Daji's demon Thousand Year Old Fox [1]
- Nine Headed Pheasant – a demon, later masquerades as Daji's sister [1]
- Nüwa – the Snail Goddess [1]
- Pretty Cloud Boy – a disciple of Fairy Rock [13]
- Thousand Year Old Fox – the demon controlling Daji [1]

Ancients

- Chen Tang – King Tang, an ancient king [22]
- Gaozong – temple name of ancient emperor Wu Ding [24]
- Shun – an ancient emperor [28]
- Xuanyuan – an ancient emperor [13]
- Yao – an ancient emperor [24]
- Yellow Emperor – an ancient emperor [13]
- Yi Yin – an ancient farmer and minister to King Tang

[24]

<u>Others</u>
- Huang – one of the Shang king's concubines, younger sister of General Huang Feihu [1]
- Jiang Huan – a criminal, servant of Fei Zhong [7]
- Lady Jia – wife of Huang Feihu [30]
- Madame Ma – wife of Jiang Ziya [15]
- Madame Yin – wife of Li Jing [12]
- Song Yiren – a merchant, Jiang Ziya's sworn brother [15]
- Su Quanzhong – son of Su Hu [2]
- Wu Ji (Flying Bear) – a woodcutter, disciple of Jiang Ziya [23]
- Xia Zhao – a young Confucian scholar [27]
- Yang – one of the king's concubines [1]
- Yao Fu – a palace servant [10]

Chapter 1
The King and the Goddess

In the beginning, Pangu split the world in two;
Then came yin and yang, then the stars in the sky
After the sky came the ground, then people;
Youchao taught them to build homes and stay safe

Suiren taught them to use fire to cook food,
Fuxi showed them the ways of yin and yang
Shennong gave them medicine;
Xuanyuan gave them culture and family

Under the five emperors people prospered;
Yu the Great stopped the floods
Xia gave them five hundred years of peace;
But King Jie came and turned day into night

Every day he drank wine and played with his concubines;
Until King Chen Tang came to cleanse the palace
The cruel king lived but fled to the south;
The clouds and rain passed and the nation prospered again

Thirty-one kings later, Yin Zhou takes the throne;
The Shang family breaks like a string
The palace is in chaos, wife and sons are killed;
While the foolish king listens only to his evil advisors

Daji fills the palace with dirt and chaos;
Her snake pit and burning pillar bring pain to the loyal
The Deer Terrace brings pain to the people;
Their anger covers the entire sky

Loyal ministers lose their hearts or die on the burning pillar;
Mothers see their babies die; farmers' feet are cut off
The king trusts evil ministers and forgets to care for the
country;
He fights for no reason and removes good ministers

The ways of religion are forgotten,
Now there is only black magic and trickery
The king's friends are evil, he does not fear God;
He drinks all the time, he is like a wild animal

Ji Chang comes to the capital but is imprisoned in Youli;
His son escapes in a dust cloud and wait for the right time
Even God in heaven is angry and sends disasters
That cover everything like an endless ocean

Life is difficult in the nation, the people cry out;
Then Jiang Ziya appears, a god among men
He sits and fishes, not for fish but for a wise master;
The flying bear comes to him in a dream

Ji Chang brings Ziya back to Zhou in his carriage;

Ziya stays by his side and gives him two thirds of the nation
Ji Chang does not live to see the final victory;
His son takes the throne and works hard every day

Eight hundred marquises come together;
They make a plan to destroy the cruel and evil
At dawn the two armies come together in Muye;
But the king's armies turn and attack Shang

The people kowtow in fear like wounded beasts;
Blood flows like a river and covers the pillars
The new king dons the robe of heaven;
Now the nation is at peace with King Tang on the throne

The war horses return to Mount Hua as the war ends;
The Zhou family begins eight hundred years of rule
The dead king is hung on a white flag;
The souls of the dead soldiers can finally rest

Master Jiang Ziya was born a wise man;
He put everything in the correct place
This is the great story of Shang and Zhou;
It is passed down to this day from parent to child

In the beginning, the King of Shang was a good man.

His name was Di Xin. His father was the twenty-seventh king of the Shang Dynasty. When the old king died after ruling for thirty years, Di Xin became the twenty-eighth king. He did not know that he would be the last.

Di Xin married a beautiful woman named Jiang, who was the daughter of a powerful grand duke. The king also had two concubines named Huang and Yang.

For seven years the country was peaceful. Heaven brought wind and rain at the right times, and the people were never hungry.

The trouble started one day when the prime minister, a man named Shang Rong, stepped forward in court. Shang Rong told the king, "Your Majesty, tomorrow is the fifteenth day of the third month. It is the birthday of the goddess Nüwa. Do you know the story of how she saved our country?"

The king smiled and said, "Yes, but please tell us the story again."

"Many years ago, Buzhou Mountain held up the sky. Two powerful gods were fighting. One of the gods was losing the fight, so he smashed his own head against Buzhou Mountain and destroyed it. The sky started to fall. There were fires and floods. Dangerous animals came to our kingdom and ate the people. When Goddess Nüwa heard about this, she immediately came to help us. First, she cut the legs off a giant tortoise and used the legs to hold up the sky again. Then she used colored stones to repair the sky. But she could not completely repair the sky. That is why even today, the sun and moon move from east to west, and the stars move from southeast to northwest."

"That is a good story," said the king. "What else did Nüwa do?"

"The ancients say that when the world was young, Nüwa was all alone. There were no animals and no people. So on the first day she created chickens. On the second day she created dogs. On the third day she created sheep. On the fourth day she created pigs. On the fifth day she created cows. On the sixth day she created horses. On the seventh day she started creating people from yellow clay. She made the people one at a time. But it took a long time and she got tired. She dipped a rope in yellow clay and swung it around. Bits of yellow clay fell everywhere, and each bit became a person."

"And now?"

"Even now, Nüwa takes care of our people. She brings wind and rain at the right times, so the people are never hungry. You should worship her by going to her temple tomorrow on her birthday."

"You are right," said the king. "We will go."

The next day, the king left the palace through the south gate. It was a warm sunny day. He rode for several *li* to the temple in his royal carriage. Three thousand soldiers on horses rode with him, along all the ministers of the court. Leading the army was General Huang Feihu, the brother of Concubine Huang.

When the king arrived at the temple, he walked into the main hall. He burned incense, bowed low, and prayed to Nüwa. Then he took a little time to look around the temple. While walking around the temple, he saw a statue of Nüwa hidden behind a curtain. Just as he was looking at the statue, a strong wind came in through a nearby window. It blew the curtain aside, and the king saw Nüwa. She was the most beautiful woman he had ever seen. She was more beautiful than flowers in springtime, more beautiful than the moon in the sky.

The king's body became hot with desire. He said to himself, "We have a beautiful queen and we have concubines, but none are as beautiful as this goddess. We must have her!" He told his attendants to bring him brush and ink. Without thinking he wrote a love poem to the goddess right on the wall of the temple. This is the poem:

> *There are phoenixes and dragons*
> *But they are like dirt to us*
> *You are like a beautiful fruit tree in the rain*
> *You are like flowers in the mist*
> *Please come alive, O beautiful goddess*
> *Come to us, come down from your temple*
> *We will bring you to my palace!*[1]

The Prime Minister saw the poem. His eyes grew big. He said to the king, "Your Majesty, Nüwa has been a great friend to our people. You came to her temple to thank her. But now you have insulted her. Please, I beg you, wash this poem off the wall!"

The king replied angrily, "We see no problem here. We saw the goddess and thought she was beautiful. Be quiet. Don't forget that We are the king." And he returned to the palace, to enjoy time with his queen and his concubines.

That evening, Goddess Nüwa returned to her temple after visiting with some friends. She saw the poem written in

---

[1] This may not seem like an insulting poem, but the king's suggestion that the goddess leave her temple and join him in the royal palace made it vulgar, or even obscene, at the time this novel was written.

black ink on the wall of her temple. When she read the poem, she became very angry. She said, "This king is evil. He writes dirty poems on the wall of my temple. He does not know how to show respect to the gods. I will make sure he is the last king of Shang!"

She called for her phoenix and rode it to the capital city of Zhaoge. She was looking for the king. She looked down from the sky and saw the king. But when she saw him, she knew that it was the will of heaven that he would live for another twenty-eight years.

Still angry, she returned to her temple. She told her servants to bring her a magic gourd called the Demon Summoning Gourd. She placed the gourd on the ground. She opened it and pointed to it with her finger. A beam of bright white light came from the gourd and rose into the sky. All the demons in the area saw the light and came to her temple. Dark clouds appeared in the sky. A cold wind began to blow.

Nüwa waited for all the demons to arrive. Then she told all of them to go home except for three female demons: Thousand-Year-Old Fox, Nine Headed Pheasant, and Jade Lute. Nüwa said to them, "Listen carefully to me. I have heard the singing of the phoenix in the west. It tells me that a new king has been born in the province of Qi. I want to destroy King Di Xin, but it is Heaven's will that he will live for another twenty-eight years. So I will destroy him while he lives. I want you three to change into beautiful women. You must enter the palace, and do whatever is needed to stop the king from attending to affairs of state. In time this will end the Shang Dynasty and bring in the new one. Now go!" The three demons turned into winds and blew away.

Back in the palace, the king thought could think of nothing but the beautiful goddess. He did not eat, drink or sleep. He found no pleasure with his queen or his concubines. He did not care about affairs of state. He did not know what to do. Finally, he called one of his ministers, an evil man named Fei Zhong. He knew that Fei Zhong would say anything and do anything to make him happy.

The king said to Fei Zhong, "We cannot think of anything except the goddess Nüwa. We don't care about our queen or our concubines or the affairs of state. What can we do?"

Fei Zhong gave the king a big smile. He said, "Your Majesty, you are the most powerful man in the world. You can have anything you want. If you want a beautiful woman, that is no problem. Just tell each of the four grand dukes to send you a hundred of the most beautiful girls in their region. Soon you will have four hundred girls to look at. I'm sure you will find one as beautiful as the goddess."

The king thought this was a wonderful idea.

Chapter 2
The Rebellion of Su Hu

The Prime Minister in his golden carriage speaks to the king;
In all the kingdom, who is as loyal and wise?

If he knew that the marquises were coming,
He would not have poured ink on sunflower paper

The king was pleased with the report;
He read it and then returned to the palace;

The evening came and then the morning;
The next day, ministers came and praised the foolish king

The kingdom of Shang was quite large. To help him rule the kingdom the king had four grand dukes. Each grand duke ruled about a quarter of the country. Each grand duke had about two hundred marquises, and each marquis ruled a small city or village.

The next morning, the king told his attendants to send letters to each of the four grand dukes. The letters told each of them to bring a hundred beautiful young women to the palace. But Prime Minister Shang Rong heard about this. He said to the king, "Your Majesty, this is a bad idea. Please think about this. Right now, the people are happy in their work and they obey you. But if you do this, they will become unhappy. They will not want you as their king. If you spend your days listening to music, playing with your concubines, drinking wine and hunting, you will not be king for long. I have been a minister for your grandfather, your father, and now you. And I tell you, do not forget the affairs of state and seek only a life of pleasure!"

The king sat quietly for a long time. Then he said, "You are right. We will not do this." He left the hall and went to his chambers to play with his concubines for a while.

The months passed, but the king never forgot about the beautiful goddess Nüwa. The next summer, the four grand dukes and all eight hundred marquises came to Zhaoge. During this time, the evil minister Fei Zhong had become more powerful. He demanded bribes and gifts from each grand duke and marquis. Most of them gave him gifts, but Su Hu, the marquis of Jizhou, did not. Su Hu was a good man, and he disliked Fei Zhong.

Fei Zhong wanted revenge. He waited until the king was not busy. Then he said to the king, "You were right to not ask the four grand dukes to send those beautiful young women last year. But I have heard that the marquis Su Hu has a daughter named Daji. It is said that she is as beautiful as the goddess Nüwa. Perhaps you should bring her to the palace."

The king liked this idea, and started to think about being with Daji. He ordered Su Hu to come to the palace to see him. Su Hu arrived a short time later. He kneeled in front of the king and waited for him to speak.

The king said, "We have heard that your daughter is a fine young woman. We want her to serve us in the palace. If we do this, this will be good for you. You will become part of the royal family. You will also become rich and powerful. How do you feel about this?"

Su Hu replied, "Your Majesty, I think someone has given you bad information. Why would you want my daughter? You already have a lovely queen and many concubines. My daughter is not beautiful. In fact, she knows nothing and has an ugly face."

The king laughed loudly. He said, "You are a fool, Su Hu. Your daughter would be treated like a queen. And you would become part of the royal family."

Forgetting to be careful when speaking to the king, Su Hu stood up and shouted, "You are a terrible king. You care nothing for affairs of state. You spend all your time drinking and playing with women. Change your ways, or your dynasty will end soon!"

The king shouted to his soldiers, "Arrest this fool and throw him out of Zhaoge!" The soldiers took Su Hu away. They took him to the north gate of the city and told him to go back to Jizhou and never return.

Su Hu returned to Jizhou. When he arrived, his ministers asked him what happened during his visit to Zhaoge. Su Hu told them, "That idiot king wanted my daughter as a concubine. What should I do? If I refuse, he will send an army here. But if I agree, he will continue to ignore the affairs of state, and people will say that I helped him to go down that road."

One of the ministers replied, "The ancients say that if a king is bad, his ministers may leave him. Our king only cares for women and pleasure. We should leave him and try to save our country."

Su Hu agreed. He called for a large brush and ink. Then he rode his horse back to Zhaoge. He walked up to the main gate. He held a large brush in one hand and ink pot in the other. He quickly wrote this poem on the wall:

> *You have no respect for your ministers*
> *You have forgotten the five virtues*
> *And so Su Hu, the marquis of Jizhou*
> *Will no longer serve the king of Shang*

A soldier at the gate saw this. He ran back to the palace, kneeled before the king, and told him about the poem on the wall. The king was furious. He called Fei Zhong and told him how angry he was. He said, "It is time to destroy the city of Jizhou. Who should lead our army?"

Fei Zhong thought about this for a few minutes. He said to the king, "Jizhou is in the north. I suggest that the Grand Duke of the North should destroy the city." Fei Zhong knew that the Grand Duke of the North was a cruel man named Chong Houhu.

Prime Minister Shang Rong heard about this. He was worried about what the cruel general might do. So he went to the king and said, "Your Majesty, Chong Houhu is the Grand Duke of the North, but the people do not like him. It may be difficult for him to do this job. Perhaps you should use the Grand Duke of the West, Ji Chang, instead. He is a good man, the people trust him."

The king listened to this. Then he said, "We will send both of them. They will lead the army together."

The two grand dukes, Chong Houhu and Ji Chang, sat down to discuss their plan to attack Jizhou. They agreed that Chong Houhu would lead the army and would arrive first at the city of Jizhou, and Ji Chang would follow shortly afterwards.

Back at Jizhou, Su Hu met with his own generals. They knew that the city of Jizhou was in great danger. They prepared their army to fight against the king's army.

A few days later, Su Hu heard that the king's army had arrived at Jizhou. The king's army had 50,000 soldiers with spears and swords. "Who is leading this army?" asked Su Hu.

"Chong Houhu, the Grand Duke of the North," one of his ministers replied.

"That man is evil and cruel," said Su Hu. "But I will talk with him anyway." He led his soldiers out of the city. The army of Su Hu stood facing the army of the king. Su Hu was in front. He shouted, "Let me talk with your general!"

Chong Houhu came out to meet him. He rode on a big horse. He wore bright golden armor, a red robe and a jade belt. He held a long sword in his hand. Behind him were his son and two other generals.

Su Hu bowed to Chong Houhu. He said, "How are you,

Grand Duke. I'm sorry we have to meet like this. But you know that our king has become a bad ruler. He treats his ministers badly, and he cares nothing for affairs of state. He only wants women and wine. And now he wants my daughter as a concubine."

Chong Houhu replied angrily, "None of that matters. You are a traitor. His Majesty the King has ordered me to kill you. You should kneel before me, but instead, you stand there with your armor and sword." He turned to his men and said, "Who will kill this traitor for me?"

One of Chong Houhu's generals shouted, "I will!" He rode his horse forward and attacked Su Hu. But before he could get close, Su Hu's son Su Quanzhong rode forward on his horse. The two fought, sword against sword, for twenty rounds. Finally, Su Quanzhong killed the general.

Su Hu gave the order for his army to attack. All the soldiers on both sides ran forward, holding their swords high. There was a huge battle. When it was over, the ground was covered with the blood of dead and dying soldiers. Chong Houhu's army was defeated. They fled from the city.

Later that night, Su Hu's army returned and attacked Chong Houhu's army again. They attacked like hungry tigers. Su Hu saw Chong Houhu and shouted, "Chong Houhu! Get down off your horse, I will bring you back as a prisoner to Jizhou!" Chong Houhu saw that his army was losing and that he could not win against Su Hu. So he turned and fled like a dog, as fast as he could.

A few hours later Su Hu's army attacked for a third time. Su Quanzhong saw Chong Houhu and shouted, "I have been waiting for you. Drop your sword, get down off your horse, and prepare to die!" Two of Chong Houhu's generals rushed forward, and all three of them fought with Su Quanzhong. Su Quanzhong fought like a dragon in the sea. He struck the three generals with his sword, killing one and injuring another. Chong Houhu and his army ran away, defeated for the third time. Su Hu's army returned to Jizhou.

The next morning, Su Hu met with his generals and ministers. He asked his son, "Did you capture that dog Chong Houhu?"

"No," replied Su Quanzhong. "Our soldiers fought like tigers. I myself killed one of their generals and injured another. But Chong Houhu and his army ran away. It was dark and I did not want to ride after them."

Su Hu was happy to hear that his army had won the battle. He said, "Chong Houhu was lucky. Now rest, my son."

Chapter 3
Daji is Given to the King

The king ordered Chong to attack the ministers;
But he had little wisdom and could not make a good plan

The failed battle started in the morning;
By evening he had lost and had to flee the camp

From the beginning of time, lust has led to the fall of
kingdoms;
Since ancient days, the evil done by ministers never ends

This is not about the king's lust for Daji;
It is heaven's will that Zhou will rule the kingdom

Chong Houhu and his army fled from Jizhou as fast as they could. Only one in ten of his soldiers survived, and many of those had terrible injuries.

Chong Houhu said to his generals, "We had to fight against the army of Su Hu all alone. Where was the Grand Duke of the West and his army? His Majesty told him to help us, but he did not come. He is a traitor."

Just then, a soldier rushed in and told him that a huge army was approaching. Chong Houhu did not know if they were friends or enemies. He jumped up on his horse and rode out to see. He saw a general leading thousands of soldiers. The general's face was as black as the bottom of a cooking pot. He had a red beard, golden eyes, and wore a long red robe. He rode a fire-eyed monster. In each of his hands he held a golden axe. On his back he carried a strange red gourd. Chong Houhu knew this man. It was his own brother, the Marquis of Caozhou, known to everyone as Black Tiger.

"I heard that your army was defeated," Black Tiger said to Chong Houhu, "so I got here as quickly as I could. It is good to see you again!"

"How many soldiers do you have?" asked Chong Houhu.

"I have three thousand Flying Tiger soldiers, and another twenty thousand are coming soon." The two armies joined together and marched towards Jizhou. They stopped just a few *li* from the city.

In Jizhou, someone told Su Hu that the Black Tiger had arrived. "This is bad," said Su Hu. "Black Tiger is a very good fighter. Also, he has studied magic. I have heard that he can cut off someone's head as easily as taking a stone out of a bag."

His son Su Quanzhong replied, "Father, do not talk like that. You are only making him stronger and yourself weaker. I am not afraid. I will go and fight Black Tiger myself!" Before anyone could stop him, he jumped on his horse and ran out to meet Black Tiger.

Now Su Quanzhong did not know that his father and Black Tiger were good friends, and sworn brothers. When Black Tiger heard that Su Hu's son was coming, he shouted, "My young friend! Please go back and tell your father to come and see me."

Su Quanzhong shouted, "Forget that! We are enemies. Leave this place right now, or you will die!" He attacked Black Tiger with his sword. Black Tiger fought with his two golden axes. They fought for a long time but neither could win. Then Black Tiger turned and rode away quickly. Su Quanzhong rode after him.

As he rode, Black Tiger pulled the lid off his magic gourd. He said some magic words. Suddenly a cloud of black smoke came out of the gourd. A dozen huge eagles came down from the sky. They attacked Su Quanzhong and his horse. Su Quanzhong fought off the eagles with his sword, but the eagles attacked the horse. The horse fell to the ground. Su Quanzhong was thrown to the ground and was taken prisoner by Black Tiger's soldiers.

Su Hu heard this bad news. He said to himself, "My son did not listen to me, and now he is a prisoner. There are many soldiers out there. Soon Jizhou will lose the war. What have I done to cause this? Maybe it is because I have a daughter. If I had no daughter, the king would not want her as a concubine, and my city would not be attacked by the king's army. I cannot let my family be captured by the king's army. It is better that I kill everyone in my family before the king's soldiers come here." He picked up his sword and rushed into the room where his family was.

Daji saw him. She smiled and said, "Dear father, why are you here, and why are you holding that big sword?"

Su Hu stopped. He could not kill his daughter.

Outside the city, Chong Houhu wanted to use all of the soldiers from both armies to attack Jizhou. But Black Tiger said, "Please wait. We don't need to attack the city. Let's surround the city. They will have no food or water, and soon they will not be able to fight. Also, the Grand Duke of the West's army will be coming soon."

The soldiers surrounded the city of Jizhou. Several weeks went by. No food or water could come into the city. The people were very hungry and weak. Finally, one of the generals, a man named Zheng Lun, came to see Su Hu. He said, "Sir, please let me go and fight Black Tiger. I will try to take him prisoner and bring him back here. If I fail, they can cut off my head."

Zheng Lun picked up his two Demon Subduing Clubs, jumped up on his horse, and led 3,000 soldiers out of the city. His soldiers were all dressed in black, making his army look like a black cloud moving across the ground. He got close to the enemy and shouted, "Come out and fight me, Black Tiger!"

Black Tiger came out, surrounded by his Flying Tiger soldiers. "Who is the man who wants to fight me?" he shouted.

"I am General Zheng Lun of Jizhou. You must be Black Tiger. You are holding a prisoner. He is the son of my marquis. Give him to me right now, or I will turn you into dust!"

Black Tiger did not reply. He rode his horse forward, striking at Zheng Lun with his golden axes. Zheng Lun fought back with his two clubs. They fought for a long time, but neither one could win.

As they fought, Zheng Lun saw the red gourd on Black Tiger's back. He knew it was a magic gourd. But he had his own magic. He raised his clubs in the air and said some magic words. Two beams of bright light came out of Zheng Lun's nose. They hit Black Tiger in the face. Black Tiger became dizzy. He fell off his horse. The soldiers grabbed him and tied him up as a prisoner.

Zheng Lun's soldiers carried Black Tiger back to the city of Jizhou. Zheng Lun watched as they threw him down on the ground in front of the gate to Su Hu's palace. When Su Hu saw this, he ran forward. He told his soldiers to untie Black Tiger. Then Su Hu bowed to him. He said, "My brother, please forgive me. Zheng Lun treated you badly. I am so sorry." Then he ordered Zheng Lun and the other generals to come and bow to Black Tiger.

Black Tiger replied, "Thank you, my brother. Please understand that I am trying to help you, not kill you. Let's talk about how we can get you out of trouble and also keep our king happy."

Meanwhile, Chong Houhu was angry that he still had heard nothing from Ji Chang, the Grand Duke of the West. One of Ji Chang's ministers arrived at the camp. Chong Houhu said to him, "Why does your grand duke ignore our king's orders? He rests in his palace while we must come here and fight!"

The minister replied, "My grand duke always says, 'War is a terrible thing, one should fight only when there is no other way.' He has sent me here with a letter for Su Hu. The letter asks Su Hu to stop fighting and give his daughter to the king. If he does that, he can remain the Marquis of Jizhou. If not, he will die."

Chong Houhu laughed loudly. He said, "I think Ji Chang is just afraid to fight. Well, go ahead, give Su Hu the letter, let's see what happens."

The minister left Chong Houhu's camp. He rode up to the city wall of Jizhou. He called out, "Here is a minister of the Grand Duke of the West, with a letter for your marquis." The city gates opened, and he was taken inside.

Su Hu and Black Tiger were having dinner together. They looked up when the minister entered the room. The minister said, "I have a letter for you from Ji Chang, the Grand Duke of the West." Then he handed the letter to Su Hu. It said:

I know you are a good man and you want to serve your king. Please listen to my words. If you send your daughter to the king, you will become part of the king's family. You will become wealthy and powerful. Jizhou will be safe, your family will be safe, your people will be safe, and your soldiers will live. But if you do not send your daughter, Jizhou will be destroyed, your entire family will be killed, and many people and soldiers will also die. You and I are both ministers of the Shang Dynasty. Please think about this and do the right thing.

Su Hu did not say a word. He handed the letter to Black Tiger. Black Tiger read the letter. Then he said, "The Grand Duke of the West is a good man. You should send your daughter to the king as soon as possible. This will show your loyalty to the Shang Dynasty."

Su Hu told the minister to eat dinner with them and stay in the palace overnight. The next day, Su Hu met with the minister. He said that he would bring his daughter to the king's palace. Truly, one letter was more powerful than a hundred thousand soldiers!

Su Hu and Black Tiger drank cups of wine together and smiled. They thought that their troubles were finished.

Chapter 4
The Fox Demon Kills Daji

The world is at war, fighting is everywhere;
The nation is flooded by evil words

The king would not listen to the loyal Shang Rong;
But he listened to the evil minister Fei Zhong

Lust made the king marry the fox and sleep with her;
While cruel monsters ruled the nation and the phoenix flew
away

If the fox can bring down the kingdom,
The goddess will give him a bit of incense[1]

---

[1] "A bit of incense" is a metaphor for a reward obtained in the human world. In this case, it's the reward given to the fox demon by the goddess Nüwa in return for destroying the Shang king.

Black Tiger left Jizhou. He returned to Chong Houhu and told him that Su Hu would give Daji to the king. Chong Houhu said, "Brother, I cannot understand how your letter could win this battle, when my fifty thousand men could not."

Black Tiger replied coldly to his brother, "The ancients say, 'One tree may have both sweet and sour fruit; sons of the same mother may be good or bad.' You should never have attacked Jizhou. Many soldiers have died because of you. I am leaving now. I never want to see you again."

Black Tiger then ordered Su Quanzhong be released and sent back to Jizhou. Then he and his army returned to Caozhou. A day later, Chong Houhu led his own army back to Zhaoge. This was the end of the attack on Jizhou.

Su Hu told his daughter that she would become a concubine of the king. She cried for hours. He told his son Su Quanzhong that he must take care of affairs of state while he was in Zhaoge. He told his wife that he would be gone for a long time. And he said goodbye to his elderly mother.

The next day, Su Hu and Daji left Jizhou and began the long journey to Zhaoge. Three thousand soldiers traveled with them. Su Hu rode close to Daji's carriage to protect her.

After traveling for several days, they arrived at a courier station about halfway between Jizhou and Zhaoge. Su Hu told the station officer to prepare a room for Daji.

The station officer said, "Sir, this is not a good place for you. Three years ago, a demon arrived here. Since then, not a single person has wanted to stay here overnight. I think you should keep traveling and not stop here."

Su Hu replied, "I am a marquis of the king of Shang, do you think I am afraid of a demon? We are not leaving. Prepare the room now!"

When the room was ready, Daji entered it. Three thousand soldiers surrounded the room to protect her. And Su Hu himself sat outside the door to her room. He did not sleep that night. He read a book by candle light, but every couple of hours he looked in Daji's room to see if she was all right.

Around the time of the third watch[1], a cold wind blew in through an open window. It felt like a wild animal had come into the room. Someone shouted, "A ghost! A ghost!"

Su Hu ran into Daji's room and woke her up. "Are you all right, my dear?" he asked. "Did you see a ghost?"

She smiled and said, "No, father, I was sleeping and saw nothing. Please don't worry about me."

Su Hu thought that he was talking with his daughter. But he was really talking to Thousand-Year-Old Fox Demon sent by Nüwa. The fox demon had eaten Daji's soul and taken her body.

The next morning, they continued on their journey to Zhaoge. A few days later they arrived at the capital. General Huang Feihu told Su Hu to leave his three thousand soldiers outside the city, and to come in alone with Daji.

The evil minister Fei Zhong heard that Su Hu had returned. He was unhappy to hear that Su Hu had not been killed by the king's soldiers. He told the king that Su Hu had returned.

---

[1] The night is divided into several two-hour periods or watches. First watch starts at 7:00 pm, second watch at 9:00, third watch at 11:00, and so on.

"That fool!" shouted the king. "We wanted to kill him once, but you told us to let him live. Then he wrote that poem on the wall. We will kill him tomorrow. You just wait and see."

Fei Zhong nodded his head and said, "Your Majesty is right. The laws of the kingdom are for everyone, even marquises."

A little while later, Su Hu came in to the main hall. Instead of wearing his red robe, he just wore the clothing of a prisoner. He bowed and said, "The criminal Su Hu is here. He deserves to die."

The king replied, "Yes, it is time for you to die. We should have done this a long time ago." Then he shouted for his soldiers to take Su Hu away and cut off his head.

But Fei Zhong said, "Your Majesty, please let go of your anger for a little while. Look at Su Hu's daughter. If you are pleased with her, you can take her as your concubine and let Su Hu go. But if you are not pleased with her, then cut off both of their heads. This will show the people that you are strong."

The king replied, "You are right as always, Fei Zhong. All right, bring in the girl."

Daji slowly entered the main hall. She knelt down and said, "Long live the King! Long live the King!"

The king looked carefully at Daji. Her hair was as black as night, her lips were like red fruit, her face was as beautiful as a peach blossom. Her body was as slim as a willow tree. She looked like an immortal from the Ninth Heaven or a visitor from the moon. When she spoke, her breath was like sweet incense. She said softly, "The daughter of your criminal servant wishes Your Majesty to live for ten thousand years!"

The king looked at Daji. He felt dizzy and his soul left his body. His ears became hot, and he could not see. After a minute he was able to stand up. He said to Daji, "Please stand up, our beauty!" He told his servants to bring her to the Immortal Long Life Palace. Then he said to everyone, "Su Hu's family is now part of our family. Su Hu will receive 2,000 piculs of rice every month. He will stay here as our guest for three days. Then five of our ministers will take him back to Jizhou."

Then the king stood up and left the main hall. He and Daji had a long dinner together, with plenty of wine. Then they spent the night together. The next day he stayed in bed with Daji all day.

The king fell in love with Daji. He forgot all about affairs of state. He gave no orders. None of the grand dukes or marquises were able to meet with him. All across the kingdom, trouble started, but the king did not care at all.

Chapter 5
The Master of the Clouds

Colorful spring flowers grow here under a peaceful blue sky;
White clouds and rain fly over distant southern mountains

Purple fog surrounds a golden pavilion;
Youthful immortals drink jade and eat pears

Flowers sing songs of heaven to welcome the gods;
The blue phoenix dances, its green hair flying

This is a place where immortals live, far from the human world;
But then a demonic power breaks down the gates

A Daoist immortal named Master of the Clouds lived on Mount Zhongnan[1]. He had lived there for several thousand years.

One day, Master of the Clouds went for a walk. He carried a flower basket in one hand while he picked medicinal herbs. Looking to the southeast, he saw a dark cloud over the city of Zhaoge. "Ah," he said, "it looks like an ancient fox demon is in Zhaoge. She is probably causing trouble in the palace of the king[2]. I'd better do something about this."

He picked up a pine branch, then he used his knife to make a slender wooden sword. He put the sword in the flower basket. Then he rode on a cloud to the king's palace.

Things were not going well in Zhaoge. The king was spending all his time in bed, playing with his beautiful concubine Daji. It had been ten months since he last came to the main hall. His ministers were becoming very worried. They decided to call all the ministers and generals to a meeting, and invite the king to see them.

The king was lying in bed with Daji, drinking wine and talking. A servant came in and said, "Your Majesty is requested to come to the main hall." The king stood up, told Daji that he would be back soon, then he put on his robe and went to the main hall.

When he got there, he saw that all of his ministers and generals waiting for him. He did not want to talk with any of them. He did not want to read their reports. All he

---

[1] For centuries the Zhongnan mountains, just south of Chang'an (modern-day Xi'an), have been home to many Daoist hermits and Buddhist monks. The Daoist sage Laozi is believed to have lived there when he wrote the *Dao De Jing*.

[2] Fox demons, both male and female, are common in Chinese folklore. They seduce humans with their beauty and sexual skills, then suck the life force from their victims. The older the fox demon, the more powerful it is.

wanted was to go back to bed with Daji. "What is going on?" he asked.

Shang Rong said to him, "Your Majesty, we have not seen you for a long time. Where have you been? We ask you to please take care of the affairs of state, and spend less time with your concubines. If you don't, we are afraid that heaven will become angry and will bring trouble to our kingdom."

The king was not interested in this. He replied, "Everything is fine in the kingdom. We have heard that there is a little bit of trouble at the North Sea, but Grand Tutor Wen Zhong is taking care of that. As for the rest, we're not interested in any of it. You are our ministers. If you do your jobs well, we don't need to do anything!"

While the king was arguing with his ministers, the doors to the main hall opened and Master of the Clouds walked in. He wore a long robe with wide sleeves. In his right hand he held a dust whisk, and in his left hand he held the flower basket. When he walked, the earth trembled. Tigers kowtowed to him and dragons knelt before him.

Master of the Clouds said to the king, "Your Majesty, this poor Daoist greets you."

The king was a little bit unhappy because the Daoist did not bow to him. But he just said, "Sir, where do you come from?"

"I come from the clouds and rivers. My heart is as free as the white clouds, and my mind is as clear as water."

The king smiled. "And where will you go if the sky becomes clear and the waters run dry?"

"When the sky becomes clear, a bright moon appears.

When the rivers run dry, a bright pearl appears.”

The king was pleased by this. He invited the Daoist to sit down beside him. The Daoist said, “You know that there is Daoism, Buddhism and Confucianism. Of these, Daoism is the highest.”

“And why is that?”

“A Daoist bows to nobody and wants nothing. He is not interested in money or fame. He finds happiness in forests and mountains. He sings and dances in the sunlight, he sleeps under the stars when he is tired. He spends time with his friends, he writes poetry, and he drinks wine.”

The king was delighted by this. He said, “That sounds wonderful!”

“The years pass, but he lives forever by understanding *yin* and *yang*. He helps people when he can. He rides on a green phoenix, and he visits with the Jade Emperor himself.”

“And why have you come to see us today?”

“Earlier today I was walking on Mount Zhongnan. I saw a dark cloud over your city. I think there is an evil demon here. So I have come here to help you get rid of the demon. Here is a short poem I have written about it,

> *She is beautiful, she wants to be your lover*
> *But she will drink your spirit and make you weak*
> *If you find her before it's too late*
> *You will save your people from a terrible fate*

The king said, “We don't believe there is a demon in this palace. But if there is, how can we get rid of it?”

Master of the Clouds put his hand in the flower basket and

picked up the pine sword. He gave it to the king, saying, "This is a magic pine sword. Hang it in the main tower and wait. It will kill any demon within three days."

The king ordered his servants to do as the Master of the Clouds said. Then he said, "Thank you for coming here and telling us about spirits and demons. Please stay here and protect us. You will have a high rank, you will wear fine clothing, and you will be famous throughout the kingdom."

"Thank you, but I am a simple man. I know nothing about ruling a nation. I sleep late in the morning and I walk barefoot in the mountains. I have no need of fine robes because I only wear old clothing. I want nothing, except maybe an invitation to the Feast of the Immortal Peaches in heaven. Thank you for listening to me, but now I must go." And with that, he turned and walked out of the main hall.

After the Daoist left, the king had no interest in talking with his ministers. He also left and returned to see Daji and tell her about his meeting with the Daoist. But Daji was lying in her bed. She looked very ill.

"Oh, my dear!" cried the king. "You looked so healthy a few hours ago. Now you are so ill. What is wrong?"

Daji looked up at him, smiling sweetly. She said, "Your Majesty, just now I was outside taking a walk. When I came to the Central Palace Tower, I saw a strange wooden sword hanging there. As soon as I saw it, I began to feel very ill. Now I am so ill that I cannot have sex with you. I'm very sorry, Your Majesty!" And she began to cry.

The king was angry. "That Daoist tricked us! He told us that there was an evil demon in the palace. But instead, he wanted to hurt our lovely Daji." Turning to his servants, he said, "Take down that wooden sword. Burn it immediately!"

The king stayed with Daji all night. The next day she felt better. But the Shang Dynasty's troubles kept getting worse.

Chapter 6
The Burning Pillar

Now the Shang king is killing the loyal and the wise;
So much cruelty, even the gods in heaven know of it.

Loyal and brave warriors are burned to ashes;
Evil demons surround the palace of the king

In the morning, beautiful songs are played on a guqin;
But in the evening, dragon's saliva and green glowing jade[1]

One by one, good people die on the burning pillar;
The souls of old men have no way to return home

---

[1] These are symbols of extreme luxury and decadence. In Chinese lore, dragon saliva was used to create very expensive perfume that would last for decades without evaporating. Green glowing jade was embedded in expensive furniture and other décor.

The Master of the Clouds stayed in Zhaoge for a while to see what would happen. He saw that the sword was burned, and there was still a black cloud over the city. He said to himself, "Now I understand what will happen. The Shang Dynasty will end. The Zhou Dynasty will replace it. And new gods will be created. I must try to tell the people about this." Before returning to Mount Zhongnan, he stopped to write this poem on the wall in the marketplace:

> *A demon cloud is over the king's palace*
> *A new hope rises in the West.*
> *Before many years pass*
> *Zhaoge will see blood and war*

People in the marketplace saw the poem but they did not understand it. Then Du Yuanxian, the Chief Minister of the Observatory, came riding through the marketplace on his horse. He stopped and read the poem. He said to himself, "I have also seen this demon cloud over the king's palace. Things are bad there. I must write a letter to the king."

He stayed up all night writing the letter. Then he gave it to the Prime Minister Shang Rong, asking him to give it to the king.

A little while later, Shang Rong was allowed to enter the king's private chambers. The king was, as usual, in bed with Daji. He had been drinking wine. "What do you want?" asked the king.

Shang Rong replied, "Your Majesty, I have a letter from Du Yuanxian, the Chief Minister of the Observatory. I want nothing for myself here, I am just doing my job as your prime minister. You can cut off my head for doing this, if you want."

The king read the letter. It said:

The king read the letter. Then he gave it to Daji, saying to her, "Du Yuanxian sent us this letter. What do you think about it?"

Daji fell to her knees. She said to the king, "We know that the Daoist is an evil man. Now we know that Du Yuanxian is helping him. You must have him killed."

"You are right, my dear. We must stop Du Yuanxian before other people start listening to him and causing trouble." The king ordered his soldiers to grab Du Yuanxian, take off his fine clothing, and bring him to the palace gate.

When the soldiers were bringing Du Yuanxian to the palace gate, they passed the supreme minister Mei Bo and the Prime Minister Shang Rong. They both saw this, and rushed to see the king. The king was not happy to see them. He shouted, "What do you want? Why do you bother us like this?"

Mei Bo asked, "Your Majesty, may I ask why you want to have Du Yuanxian killed?"

"He is telling crazy stories about a black cloud over the palace. This is frightening the people and causing trouble in the city. He is a traitor to the kingdom."

Mei Bo said, "Your Majesty, you have not been in the main hall for half a year. You drink all day, and spend every night with your concubine. You care nothing for the people or the kingdom. You do not listen to your ministers. Now if you have Du Yuanxian killed, it will be like bringing down a house by smashing its pillars. Please, let Du Yuanxian live!"

The king was furious. He ordered his guards to seize Mei Bo and kill him at once. But Daji stepped forward. She said, "Wait! Your Majesty, I have an idea."

"What is it, my love?" asked the king.

"Mei Bo is not an ordinary criminal. So you should not punish him in an ordinary way."

"What do you think we should do?"

"I have an idea. I think you will like it. Make a pillar of brass, twenty feet high and eight feet across. Put three fire doors in it, at the top, middle and bottom. Strip Mei Bo of his clothing and tie him to the pillar, with his face against the brass. In a few seconds he will die and become a cloud of smoke."

The king smiled at his lover. "That is a wonderful idea, my dear!" He told his attendants to order some workers to build the burning pillar as Daji had said.

Shang Rong heard all this. He wanted to cry. He said to the king, "Your Majesty, I am an old man now, in the evening of my life. I am tired and would like to go home, to spend my last few years with my family. May I go?" The king agreed, and Shang Rong left the palace, never to return.

For the next few days, workers built the burning pillar while the king spent all his time drinking and having sex with Daji. Finally, the burning pillar was ready. Daji looked at it carefully, and said that it was good. The king saw it and laughed. He said to Daji, "My love, you are very smart! Let's use this on Mei Bo tomorrow."

The next day, the burning pillar was brought to the courtyard outside the main hall. Servants put wood inside the pillar and started a fire. Soon the pillar was red hot.

Soldiers brought Mei Bo in front of the king. He was wearing prisoner's clothing. The king said, "Do you know what this is?"

"No."

"You fool. You know how to tell lies, but you don't know what this is. We built it just for you. We will use it to roast you, so everyone will know you are a traitor to your kingdom."

Mei Bo shouted at him, "I am not afraid of death and I am not afraid of you. I have served three kings. Now it looks like the Shang Dynasty will end soon. I am glad that I will not see it."

The king ordered Mei Bo stripped and tied to the red hot pillar. As soon as his body touched the pillar he screamed. Then his body turned to smoke and ash. A terrible smell filled the courtyard.

The king was in a good mood as he left the courtyard with Daji. But his ministers stayed and talked among themselves. Huang Feihu said, "My friends, this burning pillar did not just kill Mei Bo. It also killed the Shang Dynasty. Our nation will become just a cloud of smoke and ash. It will disappear from the earth."

That night, the king ordered a feast for himself and Daji. Music filled the air. The wind carried the sound of music to Queen Jiang's bedroom. She asked her servants, "What is that music?"

They replied, "His Majesty and Lady Su are drinking and eating together."

The queen said, "Get my carriage ready. I must go and see the king at once."

Chapter 7
Fei Zhong Plots Against the Queen

The king loves to have beautiful girls day and night;
He can never get enough drinking and lust;

The moon has gone down, the wine still flows;
The song ends, the guqin starts to play

Becoming even more cruel, he forgets the five virtues;
This brings much killing and great sadness

Loyal ministers cannot turn back the evil;
To this day, it is locked inside the western tower

Queen Jiang arrived at the king's palace. When the king saw her, he commanded Daji to sing and dance for the queen. The queen sat down on the right side of the king. Daji danced and sang for the queen. She danced so beautifully, it looked like her feet never touched the ground. But the queen never even looked at her and did not smile.

When she was finished, the king said to the queen, "My dear, life is short. The years pass by like water. We have little time to enjoy life. Why don't you enjoy Daji's dance?"

She queen replied, "There is nothing beautiful in that woman's dance. And there is nothing good about your rule. A good king cares for his people and stays away from evil ministers. A good king does not drink too much wine and he does not spend too much time with concubines. But all you want is sex and wine. You kill your loyal ministers and you forget about the affairs of state. Change your ways or this will be the end of the Shang Dynasty." She waited for a moment, then added, "I am just a woman, please forgive me if I have said too much." Then she stood up and walked out of the palace.

The king watched her go. He drank more wine. Then he said to Daji, "We don't know what's wrong with that woman. We had you dance and sing for her, but she didn't even look at you. Her words have made us angry. Please dance again, it would make us feel happy again."

Daji replied, "I am sorry, Your Majesty. I cannot sing and dance again for you. Her Majesty said that my singing and dancing will bring the end of the Shang Dynasty. Now I am very worried. I want to serve you, but Her Majesty says I am making you a poor king. I do not want to cause such trouble!" Then she started to cry.

The king put his arms around her. He said, "Don't worry, my dear. We know what to do with that woman." Then they continued drinking and lovemaking.

Daji was very angry at the queen. She thought about this for a few days. Then she sent a secret letter to the evil minister Fei Zhong ordering him to help her get revenge against the queen.

Fei Zhong thought to himself, "This is a difficult situation. The queen's father is the Grand Duke of the East. He has hundreds of thousands of soldiers. He can easily have me killed if I do something against his daughter. But if I don't help Daji, she only has to say a few words to the king while they're in bed, and that will be the end of my life. What can I do?"

He was thinking about his problem, walking back and forth in front of his home. Just then, he saw a big man walking by. He asked the man, "What is your name?"

The big man knelt in front of the minister and replied, "My name is Jiang Huan."

Fei Zhong realized that this man had the same surname as the queen. He said to the man, "What do you do here?"

"I am one of your servants. I work in the gardens. I have been here for five years. Please forgive me for getting in your way."

Fei Zhong smiled and said, "Jiang Huan, I have a job for you. If you do this for me, I will make you a wealthy and powerful man."

"Sir, I do not care about wealth and power. I only want to

serve you." And then the two men began to talk quietly about the job that Fei Zhong had for him.

A few days later, Daji said to the king, "Your Majesty, your love for me has caused you to be gone from the main hall for over ten months. Perhaps it's time for you to go there and take care of the affairs of state." The king agreed and said he would go the next day.

The next day the king rode in his carriage to the main hall. Suddenly a large man jumped out in front of the carriage. He held a long sword in his hand. He shouted, "You are a terrible king. You spend all your days drinking and playing with your girlfriend while the kingdom is dying. My mistress has ordered me to kill you so her father can become king!" Then he attacked the king with his sword. He was quickly surrounded by the king's soldiers. They tied him up and threw him to the ground.

The king's carriage continued on its way to the main hall. When he got there, he told his ministers about the attack. "Who will question this criminal for us?" he asked.

Fei Zhong stepped forward. "Though this servant has no skill, I will do it." The big man was brought to Fei Zhong. After being questioned, the big man said that the queen commanded him to kill the king.

Fei Zhong returned to the king. He said, "Your Majesty, I will tell you what I found out, but only if you agree not to punish me for telling you what he said."

"Of course, we will not punish you," the king replied. "Out with it."

"The criminal's name is Jiang Huan. He is a relative of Jiang Huanchu, the Grand Duke of the East. So of course he is also a relative of your queen, Lady Jiang. The criminal says that the queen ordered him to kill you so that Jiang Huanchu could take your place as king. Thanks to the gods that you were not injured! Now I hope you will discuss this with your ministers and decide what to do with this criminal."

The king said, "Madame Jiang is our wife and the queen. How could she do this to us?" Then he ordered Concubine Huang to judge whether or not the queen was guilty of this crime.

A servant told the queen what the criminal said, and that Concubine Huang would be the judge. The queen rushed to the West Palace where Huang lived. She kneeled before Huang and said, "Heaven and earth know that I did not do this. You know me. You know that I am a good woman. I hope you will tell the king that I did not do this."

Huang replied, "Jiang Huan says that you told him to kill the king, so that your father would become the new king. If this is found to be true, you and your entire family will be killed."

The queen said, "Please listen to me! My father is already a very powerful man. He rules 200 marquises and is a member of the royal family. He has no reason to want to be king. Also, think about my son, Yin Jiao. He is the Crown Prince. If the king dies, my son will be the new king. But if my father takes the throne my son will never be king. Please, tell these things to His Majesty."

Concubine Huang returned to the king and told him everything that Lady Jiang said. He thought about it. He said to himself, "The queen makes some good points." He did not know what to do. But he saw that Daji had a cold smile on her face. "What is it, my love?" he asked her.

"I think the queen told Concubine Huang a fairy tale, and now Huang is confused. You know that Jiang Huan confessed that he was working for Jiang Huanchu and the queen. That criminal did not mention anyone else. I think the queen must be tortured until she tells the truth."

Concubine Huang said, "Don't talk like that, Su Daji. You know that the queen is the wife of the king. She is also the first lady of our kingdom. A queen must never be injured or killed, and certainly she must never be tortured."

Daji replied, "Everyone is the same under the law, even the king and the queen. We all know that the queen commanded Jiang Huan to attack the king. She must confess. If she does not, she must lose an eye."

The king smiled sweetly at Daji and said, "You are quite right, my dear."

Concubine Huang left and returned to the West Palace to see the queen. Crying, she said, "Your Majesty, that evil woman Daji wants to gouge out one of your eyes if you don't confess! Please, save yourself!"

The queen replied, "Sister, how could I confess to something that I did not do? I have been a good woman all my life, now I will not say something that would make my father a criminal. It does not matter if they take out one of my eyes or cut me into a thousand pieces. I will not confess to this."

Just then, several of the king's soldiers arrived. One of them held a dagger in his hand. "Quickly, Your Majesty," cried Huang, "confess!"

"I would rather die!" cried the queen.

The soldiers grabbed the queen. One of them used a dagger to gouge out one of her eyes. Blood ran onto the floor. The queen fainted. The soldiers picked up the eye, put it on a plate, and brought it to the king. Huang followed them.

The king looked at the eye, then he looked at Huang. "Did she confess?" he asked.

"No," replied Huang. "She would rather die than confess to something that she did not do."

The king said nothing for a little while. Then he turned to Daji and said, "We listened to you and removed her eye. Now what do we do?"

Daji replied, "If she does not confess, her father might bring his army here to Zhaoge. He has a hundred thousand soldiers. So we must make her confess. Tell Huang to prepare some burning charcoal. If the queen does not confess, Huang must put her hands in the burning charcoal. That will make her confess."

"But Huang says that the queen has done nothing wrong. If we continue to torture her, I'm afraid that my ministers will become angry. That could bring trouble."

"Your Majesty, we cannot stop now. We are riding on the back of an angry tiger. If we get off, we will be killed and eaten! We must keep going."

"All right," said the king. Then he said to his soldiers, "If she still does not confess, put her hands in the fire."

Huang and the soldiers returned to the queen's palace. The queen was lying in a pool of her own blood. Huang said to her, "Your Majesty! What did you do in a previous lifetime, that you should have to suffer like this now? That stupid king still wants you to confess. If you do not, your hands will be put into burning charcoal!"

The queen said, "I am not afraid of death. And I will not confess!"

The soldiers grabbed the queen's hands and put them in burning charcoal. Instantly her hands burned and were turned into smoke and ash. The queen fainted. Huang fell to the ground, crying.

A little while later, Huang returned to the king. She said to him, "The queen has been tortured again and again, and she still says that she did not do this. Do you think that perhaps someone else is the criminal, and is trying to make it look like the queen did it?"

Before the king could say anything, Daji said, "Don't worry, Your Majesty. Remember that we have the criminal Jiang Huan. Bring him and the queen here and question them both at the same time. That will make the queen confess."

The king said, "That's a very good idea, my dear!"

Chapter 8
Princes Flee from Zhaoge

A beautiful woman brings disaster to the nation;
Thousands die, and many more are sent away

The king obeys his concubine and kills his own wife;
Then he kills his son, ending the line of kings

Great men try to leave but many still die;
The wise ones try to stay out of sight if they can

No one stands with the king, even the army leaves;
They drop their armor and weapons in the dust

Several soldiers brought the criminal Jiang Huan to the West Palace. The queen looked at Jiang Huan with her one eye and said, "Who gave you money to tell lies about me? Heaven will punish you for this!"

Jiang Huan looked at the queen and replied, "You are the one who told me to attack the king. Don't you remember?"

"You are lying!" she shouted.

While the queen and the criminal were waiting to be questioned, a servant ran to the East Palace, the home of the king's two sons, Yin Jiao and Yin Hong. Yin Jiao was fourteen years old, and his brother was twelve. They were playing chess when the servant came in.

He cried, "Your Highnesses, stop your game and come quickly! Someone tried to kill your father the king. The criminal said that the queen told him to do this. His Majesty the king is now very angry. He ordered his soldiers to gouge out one of the queen's eyes, and to burn her hands to ashes. You must help her!"

The two boys ran to the West Palace. They saw their mother lying in her own blood. They cried when they saw her. She said to them, "My sons, look at your mother. Daji told the king that I ordered Jiang Huan to attack him. This was a lie. But the king had me tortured. Please, I beg you, avenge my death!" Then she closed her eye and died.

The crown prince Yin Jiao grabbed his sword and shouted, "Where is the man named Jiang Huan?"

Concubine Huang pointed to the criminal and said, "There he is." Yin Jiao grabbed his sword, ran over to Jiang Huan and cut him in two. Then he shouted, "Where is Daji? I will cut off her head." Then he ran towards the Immortal

Longevity Palace to find Daji and kill her.

As the boy was leaving, Huang called after him, "Wait! I have something important to tell you!" He stopped and turned around. She continued, "Dear boy, you have killed Jiang Huan. Now we cannot torture him to learn the truth. And soon the king will hear about what you have done. You are in great danger!" Yin Jiao returned to the palace.

A little while later, two of the king's generals ran up to the West Palace, swords in their hands. They said, "His Majesty has commanded us to cut off the heads of the two princes."

Huang stood in the doorway. She said to them, "You fools! The boys are not here. I think you just want to come in and look at the pretty concubines. Go and look for the boys in the East Palace. That is where they live."

As soon as the generals left, Huang told the boys to go quickly to the Fragrant Palace where Concubine Yang lived. They ran to the other palace and told Yang everything that had happened. "Come in quickly!" she said to them. The boys went inside the palace.

A few minutes later, the two generals arrived at the Fragrant Palace. Yang shouted, "Stop! You cannot enter this palace." Frightened, the two generals turned around and left. After they were gone, Yang went inside and told the boys that it was too dangerous for them to stay in Zhaoge. She told them to go quickly to the Grand Hall and talk with some of the senior ministers.

The boys left the palace. Yang sat down and cried. She was in a terrible situation. She knew that the king and Daji would soon find out that she had helped the boys. Once they found out, they would torture Yang until she died. She said to herself, "Oh, this is a dark day for me and for the kingdom. The bonds between father and son, between husband and wife, and between king and ministers, all are broken. The kingdom is in great danger, and my life is over." Then she went into her bedroom and hanged herself.

The boys ran to the Grand Hall. When they entered, they saw many ministers and officials. They ran to General Huang Feihu and grabbed onto his robes, crying. Yin Jiao cried out, "Please save, us, General! My father has tortured my mother. I saw her die. Seeking revenge, I killed Jiang Huan with my sword. Now the king has ordered that my brother and I be killed. Please, save our lives so that the Shang Dynasty can live!"

Two ministers, Fang Bi and Fang Xiang, were brothers. They said to the other ministers, "The king has killed his queen. He has tried to kill his sons. He has tortured and killed a good minister with the Burning Pillar. But what do we do? We stand around talking like a bunch of old women in the marketplace. We say that our king should no longer rule our nation. We should all leave Zhaoge and find a new king."

Then the two Fang brothers picked up the two princes. Fang Bi picked up Yin Jiao, and Fang Xiang picked up Yin Hong. They carried the boys out of the Grand Hall and left the city through the south gate.

Huang Feihu said to the other ministers, "There are many ministers here, but only those two have shown true loyalty to the kingdom. If the king sends soldiers after them, they will probably die."

In the Immortal Longevity Palace, the king was angry. "Where are the princes?" he asked his generals.

They replied, "We have looked in the East Palace, the West Palace, and the Fragrant Palace, but could not find them."

The king said, "They must be in the Grand Hall. Go there, find them, and put them to death."

The two generals ran over to the Grand Hall. They shouted, "Where are the two young princes?" Huang Feihu told them that the Fang brothers had taken them out of the city already. The two generals returned to the king and told him.

The king shouted, "Go and tell Huang Feihu to find the Fang brothers and the two princes, and kill them all right away."

Huang Feihu was told of the king's command. He got on his ox and rode quickly out of the city. Soon he saw Fang brothers and the princes walking on the road. He rode up to them and got off his ox. Then he threw himself onto the ground and said to the princes, "His Majesty commanded me to come here and kill you. I cannot do that, but I must obey the king's command. Please, take your own lives."

Yin Jiao kneeled and said, "Oh please, general, let us live."

"I cannot do that. My king has commanded me."

"All right. Then kill me, but let my younger brother live."

Yin Hong said, "No, that is wrong. My brother is the Crown Prince, and I am just a young boy with no talents. Cut off my head and let him live."

The two boys cried and argued, and the three men listened. Finally, Huang Feihu said, "All right, stop crying. We must save our kingdom, no matter the cost. I have an idea, but you must not tell anyone about this. If the king hears about my plan, it will bring death to me and my family. Fang Bi, you take the boys to Jiang Huanchu, he is their maternal grandfather and the Grand Duke of the East. Tell him to gather a large army. Fang Xiang, you go to see E Chongyu, the Grand Duke of the South. Tell him to also gather a large army. Together, they should attack Zhaoge and get rid of this evil king."

Then Huang Feihu turned around and rode back to Zhaoge. He told the king, "Your Majesty, I tried to catch up to the princes, but I could not find them. I asked many people but nobody had seen them."

The king nodded his head. Then Daji said to the king, "Your Majesty, I am afraid that the two princes will meet up with their grandfather and gather a powerful army. You must stop them. Send an army of three thousand soldiers on horses after them right away!" The king ordered Huang Feihu to do that.

Huang Feihu said to one of his generals, "The king has told me to gather three thousand soldiers on horseback. Go and gather three thousand soldiers, but only take those who are old and sick. That will be the king's army."

The next morning, the army of old and sick soldiers started slowly after the two princes. But the Fang brothers and the two princes had already been traveling for two days.

The Fang brothers and the two princes came to a fork in the road. One road went east to the lands of Jiang Huanchu, who was the Grand Duke of the East and the princes' grandfather. The other road went south to the lands of E Chongyu, who was the Grand Duke of the South. The Fang brothers decided that it would be safer for the two princes to travel by themselves. So Yin Jiao took the road to the east, while Yin Hong took the road to the south. The Fang brothers went back towards Zhaoge, leaving the boys to travel alone.

The two young princes had lived their entire lives in the palace. They did not know how difficult it was to walk on a road for days, without a comfortable bed or good food. They both became tired and hungry, and they walked slowly.

Around midday, Yin Hong came to a small house near the road. He walked into the house. Seeing the family eating dinner, he said loudly, "Bring food for the prince!" The family jumped up, led him to a seat, and brought him rice and other food. They asked him his name. "I am Yin Hong, the younger son of the king," he replied. The family all kowtowed to him. Yin Hong ate his meal. When he was finished he thanked the family, then continued walking south. As nighttime came, he was in a place without any houses or inns. But he saw an ancient temple in the forest. He pushed the door open, lay down, and quickly fell asleep on the floor.

Meanwhile, his older brother Yin Jiao was walking east. He was also very tired and hungry. When nighttime came, he saw a large house. He opened the door and called out, "Is anyone home?"

"Who is there?" said a voice from the darkness.

"I am a traveler, just passing through. It is getting late. Would you please let me stay here for the night?"

"Your voice sounds like you are from Zhaoge. Is that true?"

"Yes sir, I am from Zhaoge."

"Come in, come in."

Yin Jiao walked into the house. He looked into the darkness and saw an old man. Looking closer, he saw that the man was none other than Shang Rong, the prime minister. Shang Rong saw Yin Jiao. He immediately knelt down before the prince. He asked, "Why are you here, Your Highness? Why are you traveling all alone?"

Yin Jiao told him about the torture and death of his mother, the king's order to kill the two princes, and the other terrible things that the king had done. Shang Rong listened to his story. When the prince was finished, Shang Rong said, "That king has broken the bonds between husband and wife, between father and sons, and between king and ministers. He must go. Your Highness, I will return to Zhaoge with you. I will ask the king to change his ways, before the kingdom falls."

Back on the road, the three thousand soldiers finally reached the fork in the road where one road went south the other went east. The generals knew that the army was traveling too slowly to catch the princes. So one general took fifty of the strongest soldiers and went on the east road. The other general took another fifty soldiers and went on the south road. The rest of the soldiers were told to wait there for the two generals to return.

Chapter 9
The Death of the Prime Minister

The loyal minister speaks to the king to help the nation;
Wake up, he says, and rule your kingdom wisely

He does not want to join the others in death;
But he thinks, is this my last day on earth?

His mind cannot be moved, it is like gold or stone;
Even the gods in the jade capital are listening now

But he does not succeed and his head is smashed;
The others see it, their tears flow like rivers

The two groups of fifty soldiers headed east and south in search of the two princes. They marched all day and into the night without stopping. In the middle of the night the eastbound soldiers came to the ancient temple where Yin Hong was sleeping. They entered the temple. In the torchlight they saw the sleeping prince. The general cried, "Your Highness! Your Highness! We are here to take you back to the palace!"

Yin Hong replied, "General, I will go with you, even if it means going to my death. But I am so tired that I cannot walk." The general helped the young prince onto his own horse, and he walked beside the horse. They marched back to the fork in the road.

Meanwhile, the eastbound soldiers came to the home of Prime Minister Shang Rong. The general entered the home. He saw the Prime Minister sitting with Yin Jiao. The general said, "Your Highness! Prime Minister! His Majesty the King asks that you return to the palace."

Yin Jiao looked up and saw the general. He said, "All right, I will return to the palace with you. But I have little hope that I will live much longer. Perhaps my younger brother will live longer than me, so he can avenge the death of our mother."

The general said to Shang Rong, "Prime Minister, I will take Yin Jiao back to the palace. You should wait a little while before returning, so nobody thinks that we were planning something together." He kowtowed to the Prime Minister, then he left with Yin Jiao.

The group of soldiers with Yin Jiao marched back towards the fork in the road. There they met the group of soldiers with Yin Hong, and the rest of the three thousand soldiers who were waiting there. Together they all returned to Zhaoge.

When they came to the gates of the royal palace, the two young princes saw General Huang Feihu and a large group of ministers standing there waiting for them. Yin Jiao said to them, "Ministers, General, you all know that my brother and I have done nothing wrong. Please help the Shang Dynasty and save us from death!"

"Don't worry," said the ministers. "We will speak up for you."

The two generals who had brought back the princes went to see the king. They told him that the two princes were now back in Zhaoge. The king said to them, "We don't need to see them. Just cut off their heads and bury their bodies."

"Your Majesty," said one of the generals, "how can we kill them without a written order from you?"

Without saying a word, the king picked up a brush and ink. He wrote on a piece of paper, "Kill the princes." He handed the paper to the generals.

The generals returned to the gate, carrying the king's order. But when they got there, one of the ministers grabbed the king's order and tore it to pieces, saying, "The king is doing terrible things, and you fools are helping him! Do you really plan to kill the two princes right here at the city gate? That would be a disaster. Let's all go to the Grand Hall. We will ask the king to come and talk with us about this matter." They all walked to the Grand Hall. As they walked, several of the generals surrounded the two princes to protect them.

When they all reached the Grand Hall, the ministers struck the bells and banged the drums to tell the king that they wanted to meet with him. In the Immortal Longevity Palace, the king was with Daji, drinking and talking. They heard the bells and drums. The king said to Daji, "The ministers want to talk with us. They probably want us to let the princes live. What should we do?"

Daji replied, "Order that the princes be killed today, and that anything else can be discussed tomorrow." The king picked up brush and ink. He wrote, "Kill the princes today. If you have questions, we can talk about it tomorrow." He handed the order to a servant, telling him to carry it to the main hall.

But the two princes were not fated to die that day. An immortal named Pure Essence was from Taihua Mountain. Another immortal, Grand Completion, was from Nine Immortals Mountain. The two immortals had nothing to do, so they were traveling together. They were just passing through Zhaoge when they saw two bright red beams of light coming up from the princes to the sky. Looking more closely, they saw a dark cloud of death over the royal palace. They understood that the Shang Dynasty was going to end soon, but that the two princes needed to live. Grand Completion said, "Let's save the two princes."

The two immortals brought a great wind. The wind picked up dust and moved rocks. It blocked the sun and turned day to night. Darkness fell over the palace. Thunder and lightning filled the sky. All the ministers in the Grand Hall fell to the ground, covering their heads with their arms. When the wind stopped, they looked around. The two young princes were gone.

The ministers said to each other, "Heaven will not harm those who have done nothing wrong. And earth will not cut off the life blood of the Shang Dynasty."

Around this time, Prime Minister Shang Rong arrived at Zhaoge. He walked into the Grand Hall. He said to the other ministers, "My friends, I have been living a quiet life in the forest. I did not know that the king would kill his wife, try to kill his sons, and spend all his days playing with his concubine. While this is going on, you have been living the good life and have done nothing to help the nation!"

"What could we do?" they replied. "The king spends every day with Daji. We never see him."

Shang Rong said to them, "I will go and see the king, though it will surely mean my death. I will tell him the truth. That is the only way that I can face the kings of ancient times when I meet them after I die." Then he told the guards to strike the bells and beat the drums, to call the king.

The king was angry when he heard the bells and drums, but he got up and rode in his carriage to the Grand Hall. Walking into the hall, he saw a man kneeling on the floor. "Who is that man?" he asked.

"The man once called the Prime Minister dares to give you my report," said Shang Rong. And without looking up, he handed his report to one of the ministers, who put it on the desk in front of the king.

In the report, Shang Rong started off by telling the king that in the beginning, the king served the people and the nation well. But, he said, recently the king has listened to traitors, spent his days drinking and playing with concubines, tortured and killed his own queen, and ordered the death of his own children. He told the king that it was time for him to change his ways. He must kill Daji and the other evil ministers. This, said Shang Rong, was the only way to return the nation to health and happiness.

The king turned red with anger. He shouted to his guards, "Take this fool out to the palace gate and beat him to death with a golden hammer."

As the guards moved towards Shang Rong, the old Prime Minster shouted, "I have served three kings. I have taken care of this nation as if it was a motherless child. Everyone can see that this dynasty will soon fall. What will you say to your ancestors when you meet them after you die?"

"Kill that old man at once!" roared the king.

"I am not afraid to die!" said Shang Rong. "What about you?" Then he threw himself against a stone pillar. His head crashed against the stone. Blood poured from his head as he fell to the ground and died.

The ministers watched this but dared not speak. The king ordered that Shang Rong's body be taken out of the city and thrown into a field.

Chapter 10
Ji Chang Finds Thunderbolt

Heavenly mist surrounds Mount Qi;
Thunder in the southeast is carried on the morning wind

The sound of thunder awakens dreaming butterflies;
Lightning comes from the shadows and stirs up the dust

Three of five show the way to Qi's success[1];
Now a hundred sons are in the Zhou capital

The dynasty has little time left, soon dragons and tigers will
come;
They will kill the old king and bring the new days of Zhou

---

[1] "three of five," or three fifths, often refers to something powerful, influential, or significant. Here, it is the discovery of Ji Chang's hundredth son, Thunderbolt.

One of the ministers, a man named Zhao Qi, stepped forward. He said to the other ministers, "My friends, I am willing to give up my life and join the Prime Minister in the underworld." Then turning to the king, he said, "You are a criminal! You have killed your wife and the Prime Minister. You don't listen to your ministers or dukes. You only listen to Daji and the evil minister Fei Zhong. Your rule is like a tree without roots. It will fall soon!"

The king shouted at him, "How dare you say this to us!" Then turning to his guards, he said, "Put this criminal on the Burning Pillar!"

Zhao Qi said, "Death is nothing to me, because I have lived a good life. But you are a criminal. You will lose your throne and will suffer for ten thousand years!"

The guards had already started a fire inside the Burning Pillar. Now it was red hot. They took off Zhao Qi's clothing and tied him to the Burning Pillar. In a few seconds he was turned to ash. A cloud of smoke was all that was left of him.

The king turned and walked out of the Grand Hall. He got in his carriage and rode back to the Immortal Longevity Palace. There he sat down with Daji and drank a cup of wine with her. He said to Daji, "Today Shang Rong killed himself, and we put Zhao Qi on the Burning Pillar. But no matter how many of these fools we kill, the rest of them still insult us. Also, we are worried about Jiang Huanchu. When he hears of his daughter's death, he might bring an army and attack us. How can we stop this?"

Daji smiled sweetly and said, "Your Majesty, I am only a woman. I know nothing of these things. Perhaps you should ask Fei Zhong, he always has good ideas."

The king called for Fei Zhong. After the king told him what

happened, the evil minister knelt and said, "Your Majesty, you are right, the four dukes could start trouble. Perhaps you could bring all of them to Zhaoge and cut off their heads. Then the eight hundred marquises will be like a dragon without a head, or a tiger without teeth."

The king was delighted to hear this. He sent orders for the four grand dukes to come to Zhaoge.

One of the messengers came to see Ji Chang, the Grand Duke of the West. He handed the king's order to the duke. Ji Chang read the order and thanked the messenger. Then he said to his eldest son, "My son, I have been ordered to go to Zhaoge. I have divined that I will be there for seven years. This is the will of heaven. Do not try to visit me. While I am gone, you will rule in my place. Take care of the people, always follow the law, and listen to your elders. I will return after seven years."

Then he said goodbye to his mother, his wife, his concubines, and the rest of his ninety-nine sons. He set out on the road to Zhaoge with fifty men.

After they had traveled about seventy *li*, Ji Chang said to his men, "Find a safe place for us to stay during the rain storm."

The men said to each other, "The sky is clear. How can it rain?" But a few minutes later the sky grew dark, there was thunder and lightning, and heavy rain began to fall.

After a few minutes the rain stopped and a bright light appeared in the sky. Ji Chang said, "A bright light after a rain storm means a great warrior has arrived. Go and find him." The men did not understand this, but they did as he ordered. They heard a baby crying. Coming closer, they saw it was a baby boy. They picked up the baby and brought it to Ji Chang.

Ji Chang said, "I have ninety-nine sons. If I make this boy my son, that will be one hundred."

As he looked at the baby boy, a tall Daoist appeared. He said, "My name is Master of the Clouds. I am looking for the great warrior who just arrived." Ji Chang bowed to the Daoist, and told his men to give the baby boy to him.

The Daoist said to Ji Chang, "This baby's name is Thunderbolt. Please let me take this baby to Mount Zhongnan. I will be his teacher. Later, I will give him back to you." Ji Chang bowed his head. The Daoist turned and walked away, carrying the baby boy.

Ji Chang and his fifty men traveled for several more days. They finally arrived in Zhaoge. Ji Chang met with the three other grand dukes. None of them knew why they had been called to Zhaoge. They sat together for several hours. They talked, they drank wine, and they argued. After a few hours Chong Houhu was tired so he went to bed. The other three stayed there, talking. Around the second watch, they heard one of the attendants quietly, "Tonight you are drinking and laughing, but tomorrow your blood will be on the ground."

Ji Chang said, "Who said that?" None of the attendants said anything. Ji Chang asked again, but still, none of the attendants would speak. Angrily, Ji Chang called to the guards, "Take all of them outside and cut their heads off!"

When they heard this, the attendants all pushed one of them, a man named Yao Fu, forward. Ji Chang told the rest of the attendants to leave. Then he turned to Yao Fu and said, "Why did you say that? Tell me the truth and you will be rewarded. Otherwise, you will lose your head."

Yao Fu replied, "Sir, I work in the home of a royal messenger. The messenger told me that after the king killed the queen, he was afraid of the four grand dukes. Daji told the king to bring you all here, so that he could cut your heads off. Watching you drinking so happily, it hurt me to think of your deaths tomorrow."

Jiang Huanchu asked the attendant how his daughter, the queen, had died. Yao Fu told him about the torture. Jiang Huanchu fell to the floor, crying. "I will go to see the king tomorrow!" he said.

Back at the Immortal Longevity Palace, Fei Zhong told the king that the four dukes were in Zhaoge. He said to the king, "Tomorrow the dukes will come to give you their reports. Don't bother reading the reports. Just tell the guards to tie them up and cut off their heads."

The next day, the four dukes came to see the king. Jiang Huanchu was the first to give his report to the king. The king did not even look at the report. He said to the duke, "You and your daughter planned to kill us and take our throne. This crime is as great as a mountain." He said to his guards, "Take this criminal out and cut him into a thousand pieces!"

As he was dragged away, Jiang Huanchu shouted, "You fool! I have been a good servant of the nation. But you are an evil tyrant. You killed the queen and even tried to kill your own children. You listen only to your evil concubine and your evil ministers. I am not afraid of you or of death itself!"

Chapter 11
The Deaths of the Grand Dukes

How can you tell the secrets of heaven,
When the king harms loyal ministers and gives power to evil

If not for the loyal ministers,
We would have seen blood and flesh flying

Remember the ancient king imprisoned for seven years,
He studied the words of Fuxi and gave us the Eight Trigrams[1]

Since ancient times, fate has favored a wise king;
And right now the sun is shining on Mount Qi

---

[1] King Wen of Zhou (1099 – 1050 BCE), a wise and fair king, visited the court of the Shang king Jou the Terrible, who threw him in prison for seven years. While in prison, King Wen reflected on the ancient Eight Trigrams developed by Emperor Fuxi 1800 years earlier. He decided to arrange the eight trigrams to form an eight-sided ring. This arrangement is called the post-heaven Bagua circle.

The three other dukes watched, frightened, as the guards dragged Jiang Huanchu away. One of them said, "Your Majesty, the king is the nation's head but his ministers are his arms and legs. If you kill Jiang Huanchu without even reading his report, it will destroy the bond between king and ministers. Please think about this!"

Then, still frightened, they handed their report to the king. The king read the report, growing more and more angry as he read it. Finally he tore it up, pounded his desk with his fist, and shouted, "Take these traitors away and cut off their heads!"

Fei Zhong was pleased with this, but he did not want his friend Chong Houhu to be killed with the others. He knelt before the king and said, "Your Majesty, all four of the dukes are criminals, but some are worse than others. Certainly, Jiang Huanchu should die for trying to kill his king. E Chongyu and Ji Chang have said bad things to you or about you. But as I see it, Chong Houhu's only crime was in following the others. He has served you well in the past. We beg you to spare him so that he can serve you in the future."

The king agreed to spare Chong Houhu, but said that the other three must die. Then Huang Feihu and several other ministers came forward and knelt before the king. They said that the three dukes were all good men who had served the king well. But the king said to them, "They are all traitors who have planned to kill us or said terrible things to us. How can you ask us to spare them?"

The ministers replied, "Your Majesty, these three dukes have large and powerful armies. If you kill them, wouldn't those armies rise up and start a war?"

The king thought about this. He said, "All right, we will spare Ji Chang. But the other two must die immediately! And if you continue to try to have them spared, we will do the same to you!"

Several guards came forward and dragged two of the dukes out of the Grand Hall. One of them drew his sword and cut off E Chongyu's head. Several others tied Jiang Huanchu's hands and feet to a pillar, and cut him into a thousand pieces. The king returned to the Immortal Longevity Palace. That night, the attendants of the two dead dukes left the city and rode back to their homes as quickly as they could.

The next day, Fei Zhong came before the king. He said, "Your Majesty, you must be careful with Ji Chang. He says one thing but thinks another. If you let him return home, he will join with the armies in the south and east, and we will have war. It will be like sending the dragon back to the ocean, or the tiger back to the forest. Too dangerous!"

The king replied, "We have already spared him. What can we do?"

"Leave it to me," smiled Fei Zhong.

The next day, Ji Chang left the city with his attendants. He rode about ten *li*. There, several other ministers were waiting for him. They said, "We heard that you were leaving today. We have food and wine for you. Please eat and drink with us before you go home."

Ji Chang was pleased to join them. They ate and drank and talked for a while. Then Fei Zhong rode towards them, bringing more wine. The other ministers saw him. None of them liked Fei Zhong. So they quickly said goodbye to Ji Chang and returned to the city.

Fei Zhong sat down with Ji Chang. They drank a large amount of wine together. Ji Chang had already drunk a lot of wine, so he became careless with his words. Fei Zhong said, "Duke, it is said that you can see the future. Is this true?"

He replied, "Of course. I throw gold coins and I read them with the I Ching. This method never fails."

"We both know that His Majesty is having trouble ruling the nation. Can you see the fate of this dynasty?"

Foolishly, Ji Chang said, "The future is dark. I have seen that our king will be the last king in the Shang Dynasty."

"When will the dynasty end?"

"In a few decades, no more."

Fei Zhong nodded. "And can you see my fate also?"

"Yes. Your fate is strange. Some people die from illness, others from the actions of others. But I see your fate is to die from being frozen in ice."

Fei Zhong laughed. "And what of your own fate, duke?"

"I will die happily, in my old age."

They talked and drank for a while longer. Then Fei Zhong said that he had things to do in Zhaoge and had to return. He rode back to the palace and went to see the king. He said, "Ji Chang is a terrible man. He says that the Shang Dynasty will end with your death, in a few decades. He says that I will die frozen in ice. But he says that his own death will be from old age."

The king hit his desk with his fist. He said, "That old fool! We spared him, and now he talks like this! Send some soldiers to bring him back here. We will cut off his head!"

Meanwhile, Ji Chang and his men rode westward. He knew that he had drunk too much wine and said the wrong things to Fei Zhong. Also, he knew that his fate was to remain in Zhaoge for seven years, so it was too soon for him to return home. He looked to the east and saw a general and several soldiers riding towards him. The general said, "Grand Duke, His Majesty orders you to return to Zhaoge immediately."

"I know," he replied. He told his men to continue riding home. He said, "I will return home in seven years. Tell my son to listen to his mother, live in peace with his brothers, and take care of the people." Then he followed the general back to Zhaoge.

The general brought Ji Chang before the king. The king was still angry. "You old fool!" he said. "We spared your life, but now you speak lies about us and the dynasty. We should cut off your head right now."

"Your Majesty, I am a fool. But I know that there is heaven above, earth below, and the king in the middle. How can I tell lies about you?"

"You talked about our fate, but you spoke nothing but lies!"

"I only used the gold coins and the I Ching to see your fate. This method has been used for many centuries. It does not fail."

"Oh? We will show you that it fails. You predicted you will live a long life, but we will have you killed right now. Guards, take him outside and cut off his head!"

But before the guards could take him away, Huang Feihu and five ministers came into the Grand Hall. Huang Feihu said, "Your Majesty, we care only about the fate of the nation. The people love Ji Chang. There will be trouble if you kill him. Also, his method of seeing the future is a good one. Please, order him to see the immediate future and tell you what tomorrow will bring."

The king laughed. "All right. Ji Chang, what will happen tomorrow?"

Ji Chang threw some gold coins on the floor and looked at them. Then he looked at the king. "Your Majesty! Tomorrow at noon the Ancestral Temple will catch fire and burn to the ground. Quick, do something!"

But the king said to his guards, "Lock up this old fool. We will see what happens tomorrow at noon."

The next day, the ministers were all at Huang Feihu's home, watching the Ancestral Temple. The weather was beautiful, without a cloud in the sky. But exactly at noon, a huge bolt of lightning came down from the sky. It struck the Ancestral Temple, setting it on fire. Then a strong wind came and made the fire bigger and hotter. In a short time, the entire temple was turned to ashes.

The ministers rushed to see the king. They said, "Your Majesty, the Ancestral Temple has burned to the ground, just as Ji Chang said it would! Now we all know that he is a great sage. You must set him free!"

The king replied, "All right, we will spare his life. But we will not let him return home to cause trouble. He will stay here in Zhaoge until the kingdom is at peace again. Take him to Youli."

And so, Ji Chang lived quietly for several years in Youli. In his heart he had no anger towards the king or anyone else.

Chapter 12
The Birth of Nezha

A rare treasure is hidden in the cave of golden light;
It was put on earth to help the virtuous

The Zhou Dynasty has started to prosper;
But it's the beginning of the end for the Shang Dynasty

Since ancient days, the will of heaven brings help;
But even so, disasters will come

Time runs in a circle, dynasties rise and fall;
The king, the ministers, the people, all turn to dust

When the attendants of the dead Grand Dukes of the South and East returned home, they told the marquises in their regions what had happened to the two dukes. Soon afterwards, 400 marquises gathered their armies. A huge army of 600,000 soldiers attacked two mountain passes that led to Zhaoge. But the king's soldiers were already guarding the mountain passes and they stopped the army.

A third mountain pass, Chentang Pass, was guarded by a general named Li Jing. He was a Daoist who had studied for many years with an immortal named Woe Evading Sage.

Li Jing had two sons. His wife had been pregnant with a third child for three and a half years but had not given birth yet. Li Jing and his wife thought that because the baby was so late, it must be a demon or a monster.

But one night, Madame Li had a dream. In her dream, a Daoist came into her bedroom and told her, "Hurry Madame, your excellent baby is coming!" Then the Daoist threw something at her. When she woke up, she felt the baby coming. A little while later, a strange baby was born. It looked like a ball rolling around on the floor. Frightened, Li Jing struck it with his sword. The ball split in two and a beautiful baby came out. His face was white as the moon. He wore a gold bracelet on his right wrist and a piece of red silk on his belly. Li Jing picked up the baby and held it in his arms.

The next day, a Daoist came to see him. He said to Li Jing, "My name is Fairy Primordial. I live on Qianyuan Mountain. May I please see the child?"

Li Jing picked up the baby and handed it to the Daoist. The Daoist looked carefully at the baby. He said, "This is no ordinary boy. He is really an immortal named Pearl Spirit, sent down from heaven. You should call him Nezha."

"I will. Thank you very much," replied Li Jing.

"Would you please allow me to teach this boy?"

"We would be very happy."

The Daoist thanked him. Li Jing invited him to stay for dinner, but the Daoist said he had things to do on Qianyuan Mountain. He stood up and left.

Nezha began to study Daoism with Fairy Primordial. Seven years passed. Now the boy was already taller than most men. One day he went for a walk beyond Chentang Pass. It was a hot day. Nezha saw Nine Bend River nearby. He took off his shirt. Then he put the red silk in the water so he could wash himself. Every time he put the red silk in the water, the river water turned red and the ground shook.

Ao Guang, the Dragon King of the Eastern Ocean, noticed that the ground was shaking. He sent a yaksa, a nature spirit, to find out why. The yaksa went to Nine Bend River. He saw the tall boy putting his red silk in the water and shaking the ground. He came out of the water and said, "Boy! Why are you turning the water red and shaking the ground?"

Nezha looked up. He saw a large beast with blue face, red hair, a big mouth, and holding a large axe in his hand. "What kind of beast are you?" he asked.

"Who are you calling a beast?" replied the yaksa angrily. He rushed at Nezha and tried to hit him with the axe. Nezha had no weapons, but he hit the yaksa on the head. The yaksa fell to the ground, dead.

One of Ao Guang's soldiers saw this. He ran to Ao Guang

and said, "Your Majesty! A young boy has killed your yaksa!"

Ao Guang was very angry. He stood up and prepared to go and fight with the young boy. But before he could leave, his third son, Ao Bing, came in. He said to his father, "Relax, Father. You don't need to do this. I will go and catch this criminal for you."

Ao Bing and a group of dragon soldiers rushed out of the palace and towards Nine Bend River. They came to the place where Nezha was standing. Ao Bing said, "Are you the boy who killed my father's yaksa? Tell me your name and where you are from."

"Yes, it was me," replied Nezha. "I am Nezha. I am the third son of Li Jing, the general of Chentang Pass. I came here to bathe in the river. Your yaksa attacked me for no reason, so of course I killed him. And who are you?"

"I am Ao Bing, third son of Ao Guang, the Dragon King of the Eastern Ocean." Then Ao Bing attacked Nezha. But Nezha just laughed. He threw his red silk up in the air. Thousands of fire balls appeared and fell down on Ao Bing. Ao Bing fell to the ground. Nezha went over to him and hit him on the head, killing him instantly.

Nezha thought that he should give his father a gift. So he removed a tendon from the dragon's dead body, thinking that it would make a fine belt for his father to wear. Then he returned home, carrying the tendon in his hand.

The soldiers returned to Ao Guang. They told him that the boy was the son of Li Jing, and that the boy had just killed Ao Guang's third son. Ao Guang was very unhappy and very angry. He changed into an old scholar and went to see Li Jing.

Li Jing heard that Ao Guang was coming. He was very happy, because the two of them were good friends and bond brothers. He came outside to greet his old friend. But Ao Guang said to him coldly, "Brother, one of your sons was bathing in Nine Bend River today. He used a magic weapon to turn the water red and make the ground tremble. Then he killed one of my yaksas. I sent my son to see what had happened, and your son killed him too. Even worse, your son took a tendon from my son's body!"

Li Jing said, "My good friend, this cannot be true. I don't think my son was away from my house today. Please wait here. I will ask him." He went to find Nezha. Nezha told him the story of what happened at the river.

Li Jing cried and said, "Oh my son, you have caused great trouble for me and our family. Come and tell your uncle what you just told me."

The two of them went to see Ao Guang. Nezha said to him, "Uncle, I am sorry I killed your son. I did not mean to do it. I still have the tendon. You can have it back if you want it."

This made Ao Guang even more angry. He shouted to Li Jing, "You have a terrible son! My yaksa was appointed by the Jade Emperor himself, and my son was the god of rain. Your son killed both of them! Tomorrow I will go see the Jade Emperor. He will know what to do with you." Then he turned and stormed out of the house.

Li Jing and his wife cried, thinking that the Jade Emperor would kill their entire family. Nezha kneeled before them and said, "Father, Mother, remember that I am a disciple of Fairy Primordial. I will go and see him right away. He will surely help us."

Nezha picked up a handful of dirt and threw it in the air.

Then he used his magic powers to fly on the dirt to Qianyuan Mountain. He went to Fairy Primordial and knelt before him. He told his master everything that had happened, and he asked for help.

Fairy Primordial said to Nezha, "Come over here. Open your shirt." Nezha opened his shirt. The immortal used his finger to draw an invisibility spell on Nezha's chest. Then he said, "Go to the Palace of Heaven. Find the Precious Virtue Gate and wait there for Ao Guang to arrive." Then he told Nezha what to do when Ao Guang arrived. He finished by saying, "And if you have any trouble, come back and see me. And don't worry about your parents, they will be fine."

Nezha went to the Palace of Heaven. He found the Precious Virtue Gate. The gate had four huge pillars. Wrapped around each pillar was a red-bearded dragon whose job was to gather clouds and make rain. Inside the palace were thirty-six smaller palaces and seventy-two huge halls. Everywhere there were beautiful gardens filled with colorful flowers and grasses. There were many ministers and attendants in the palace, all wearing colorful robes. Pretty birds flew in the sky above them.

Nezha waited there. Soon Ao Guang arrived, but he could not see Nezha because the boy was invisible. Nezha ran up to Ao Guang and hit him on the back. Ao Guang fell to the ground. Nezha raised his fist, ready to kill Ao Guang.

Chapter 13
Two Immortals Fight

Even Shiji can become wise;
Her spirit waited inside a stone for ten thousand years

She took energy from the moon, the stars, and the earth
She spent years learning about Li, Kan, and the Heavenly Stems[1]

Look at the clouds forming, watch the mist rising;
Listen to the songs of dragons and the roar of tigers

Use fire to face disaster and win;
The dark cannot fight against the light

---

[1] Li and Kan are two of the Eight Trigrams, where each trigram is a combination of three solid or broken lines that symbolizes different natural phenomena and aspects of life. The Heavenly Stems are part of the 60-year calendar cycle, said to have been invented by the Yellow Emperor in 2700 B.C.

Ao Guang looked up from the ground. He saw Nezha holding him down and ready to kill him. He said, "So, it's you! First you kill my yaksa. Then you kill my third son. And now you dare to attack me, the god of rain, right here in the Palace of Heaven! You are a criminal, and you will pay for this!"

Nezha replied, "Shut up or I'll kill you too. You don't know that I am an immortal. My real name is Pearl Spirit. I'm a disciple of Fairy Primordial. Heaven sent me to be the son of Li Jing, so that I can serve as a general in the coming war between Shang and Zhou. I was taking a bath in Nine Bends River when those two came and insulted me, so of course I had to kill both of them. Now you want to tell the Jade Emperor about it? He will just laugh at you."

Then Nezha started to pull off Ao Guang's dragon scales, one by one. Blood came from the places where the scales had been. He said, "Now, I want you to forget about talking to the Jade Emperor. Come with me to Chentang Pass, or I will finish killing you."

Ao Guang had no choice. He agreed. Nezha started to let him get up. But then he stopped and said, "I have heard that dragons can become very large or very small. I don't want you to fly away from me. Change into a small snake. I will carry you to Chentang Pass." Again, Ao Guang had no choice. He changed into a small snake. Nezha picked him up and put him inside the sleeve of his robe. Then he flew down to Chentang Pass.

Li Jing met his son. "Where have you been?" he asked.

"I went to the Palace of Heaven to ask my uncle Ao Guang to not talk to the Jade Emperor about me. Here he is." He reached into his sleeve, took out the small snake, and threw it on the ground.

The snake changed into human form. It was Ao Guang. He said angrily to Li Jing, "You son is an evil beast! He killed my yaksa, he killed my son, then he pulled off my scales. Look!" He showed Li Jing where the scales had been pulled off. He continued, "I am going to call the dragon kings of the four oceans. Together we will go and see the Jade Emperor about this!" And with that, he changed to a gust of wind and blew away.

Li Jing and his wife watched the dragon king fly away. They were both worried, but they knew that their son was extremely powerful. His wife said to the boy, "Nezha, please go and play outside for a while."

Nezha went outside. He walked past the mountain pass. He saw a stone tower. Walking up inside the tower, he saw a large bow and three arrows. He said to himself, "My master told me that I will a general in a war against the Shang Dynasty. Perhaps I should learn how to use a bow and arrow." He picked up the bow and one of the arrows, and shot the arrow towards the southwest. It flew through the air, all the way to a cave on Skeleton Mountain.

This cave was the home of a powerful immortal named Empress Shiji, who had two disciples named Blue Cloud Boy and Pretty Cloud Boy. The arrow hit Blue Cloud Boy, killing him instantly. Pretty Cloud Boy saw it. He ran to tell Empress Shiji. Empress Shiji pulled the arrow out of Blue Cloud Boy. Looking at it, she said, "I know this arrow. It is Sky Shocking Arrow. It should be at Chentang Pass. Li Jing must have shot it, killing my disciple."

She mounted her phoenix and rode quickly through the air until she arrived at Chentang Pass. She called out, "Li Jing!

Come out here now!"

Li Jing ran out to see her. He kowtowed and said, "Your disciple kneels before you. What brings you here?"

"Don't say those nice words to me." She showed him the arrow and told him that it had just killed one of her disciples.

Li Jing said, "I know this arrow. This is the Sky Shocking Arrow. This was left here by the great Emperor Xuanyuan. It is a treasure of Chentang Pass. Nobody has been able to use this bow and arrow since ancient times! Please, give me a few minutes so I can find out who did this."

He went back to his house, thinking that perhaps his immortal son was the one who shot the arrow. He called Nezha to come and see him. When the boy arrived, he said, "My son, I think it's time for you to learn how to use a bow and arrow."

Nezha replied, "Yes Father, I want to learn! In fact, just a few minutes ago I found a bow and three arrows in a stone tower. I shot one of the arrows but I don't know what happened to it."

His father shouted, "You unfilial boy[1]! You keep causing more and more trouble for this family." And he told the boy what the arrow had done.

Nezha said, "Father, please don't be angry. Please take me to see this immortal on Skeleton Mountain." The two of them flew quickly to Skeleton Mountain. They were met by Pretty Cloud Boy. Nezha thought that a fight was going to start, so he hit the boy as hard as he could. Pretty Cloud

---

[1] Filial piety is the obligation that a child has to their parents.

Boy fell to the ground. Empress Shiji rushed out of her cave and saw her second disciple lying on the ground. "You monster!" she screamed. Nezha threw the red silk into the air to try to wrap up Empress Shiji. But Empress Shiji just opened the sleeve of her robe, pulling the red silk inside. Nezha had no other weapons. He turned and flew away as fast as he could.

Empress Shiji said to Li Jing, "This has nothing to do with you, you can go home now." Then she flew after Nezha.

Nezha flew to Qianyuan Mountain and knelt in front of his master. He said, "Master! Empress Shiji thinks I killed her disciple. Now she's trying to kill me. Please save me!"

Fairy Primordial replied, "Go and hide in the garden. I will deal with her."

He waited. Soon Empress Shiji arrived at his cave. "Brother," she said, "your disciple has killed one of my disciples and hurt the other one. He also attacked me. Tell him to come out right now."

Fairy Primordial smiled and said, "Sister, please let go of your anger. Listen to me. We both have studied the Way. We know that a great war is coming. The Shang Dynasty will fall soon. The Zhou Dynasty will rise in its place. And an immortal named Jiang Ziya will create many gods. To prepare for the coming war, my Grand Master told me to send all my disciples down to the human world to join in the fight. Nezha is one of my disciples. He will help Jiang Ziya establish the new Zhou Dynasty. Now, I am sorry that your disciple has died. But don't worry, your disciple will become a god when the war is over."

Empress Shiji was still angry. She replied, "Though we have both studied the Way, we must find out who is the stronger."

Fairy Primordial began to tell Empress Shiji why he was stronger. But Empress Shiji would not let him finish speaking. She attacked him with her sword.

Fairy Primordial quickly ran into his cave. He kowtowed towards Kunlun Mountain and said, "Master, please forgive me. Your disciple must disobey your order not to kill anyone." Then he came out of the cave and began fighting with Empress Shiji. They fought with swords for a few rounds. Then Empress Shiji threw her magic handkerchief at him. He said a few magic words and pointed at the handkerchief. It fell to the ground.

He took the Nine Dragon Divine Fire Coverlet out of his sleeve and threw it at Empress Shiji. It landed on her head. He turned and saw that Nezha was watching the fight with great interest. He said to Nezha, "You must go home right now. The four dragon kings have already met with the Jade Emperor. The emperor has sent his guards to arrest your parents. Go and save them!" Then, seeing the look on Nezha's face, he added, "And no, you cannot have my Nine Dragon Divine Fire Coverlet."

Then he turned to face Empress Shiji. He clapped his hands. The Nine Dragon Divine Fire Coverlet caught on fire. Nine fire dragons appeared. They wrapped around Empress Shiji and burned her until she changed into her true form, a large uncarved rock[1].

---

[1] Shiji was a Daoist. In the *Dao De Jing*, an "uncarved block of wood" refers to a person's original nature, unaffected by cleverness. It is the simple and natural state that one should return to. The Daoist classic *Zhuangzi* says, "If you were to meet someone who understands great plainness, who subscribes to nonaction and returns to the simplicity of the uncarved block... you would really be surprised!"

Nezha flew home. The four Dragon Kings were already there, ready to kill his parents. Nezha said to them, "I am the one you want, not my parents. I will pay with my life." Then he used his sword to cut off his own left arm. Then he cut open his own belly. Then he broke all of his own bones.

Nezha died. His soul floated on the wind until it reached Qianyuan Mountain.

Chapter 14
Nezha Returns to Life

Who knows the power of immortals;
They can even bring the dead back to life

Just one grain of cinnabar awakens the dead;
A soup made of lotus leaves heals the soul

Nezha was not of this world, he did not need flesh and
bones;
But he needed incense to become an immortal

From now on he must conquer the land and give it to the
true king;
And help the Zhou of West Qi to expand their empire

Fairy Primordial was sitting in his cave on Qianyuan Mountain. Looked up, he saw Nezha's soul floating towards him. He said, "You cannot stay here. Go back to your home at Chentang Pass. Visit your mother in a dream. Tell her to build a temple for you. If people worship you for three years you will be able to return to human form. Now go!"

Nezha's soul returned home. He waited until night when his mother was sleeping. Then he entered her dream and said, "Mother, it's me, your son Nezha. I am dead. I have no place to rest my soul. Please build a temple for me where people can worship me. Only then will I be able to go to Heaven."

Madam Yin woke up from her dream. She told her husband what she had seen. But Li Jing said angrily, "Forget about Nezha. That boy has caused enough trouble already."

But the next night Nezha came to his mother again in her dream. He came again, night after night. After a week he said to her, "Mother, if you don't do as I ask, I will cause a lot of trouble for the family."

Madam Yin did not want to argue with her husband. So she quietly told a few of her servants to go into the forest and build the temple. It was a beautiful temple deep in the forest, with high white walls. In the center was a golden statue of Nezha surrounded by attendants and guards. People started coming to the temple. They prayed to Nezha, and Nezha always answered their prayers.

Li Jing did not know about the temple. But one day he was returning with his army from a trip to another mountain. He saw a large number of people visiting a strange temple in the forest. "What is this?" he asked some of his men.

The soldier replied, "This temple appeared about six months ago. There is a god inside, and he answers the peoples' prayers."

"And who is this god?"

"God Nezha."

Li Jing was furious. He went inside and saw the gold statue of his son. He kicked it, knocking down the statue and breaking it. Then he went outside and told his soldiers to burn down the temple.

Nezha's soul was not in the temple at that time. But later that evening he returned to the temple. He saw nothing but smoke and ashes. One of his attendants told him that Li Jing had destroyed the temple. "Oh Father," he cried, "How could you do this to your son?" He did not know what to do. So he went to see his master on Qianyuan Mountain. He knelt before his master and asked him what to do.

Fairy Primordial said, "There isn't much time. Soon Jiang Ziya will come. You must be ready to help him." He told one of his attendants to bring him two lotus flowers and three lotus leaves. He tore the flowers into three hundred little pieces; these were for the three hundred bones in the human body. He put the pieces on the ground. Then he placed the three lotus leaves on the pieces; these were for heaven, earth and man. Then he put a little bit of golden elixir in the center and pushed some of his own *qi* into it. Finally, he grabbed Nezha's soul and threw it into the center. There was a tremendous bang, and a human young man jumped up. He was big and strong.

Nezha kowtowed to Fairy Primordial. He said, "Thank you, Master. Now I must take revenge on my father."

"First, come with me to the garden," said Fairy Primordial. They walked into the garden. Fairy Primordial gave Nezha several magic weapons. There was a Fire Tip Lance for fighting, two Wind Fire Wheels for traveling fast, a piece of red silk to replace the one he had lost, a Universal Ring for fighting, and a gold brick. "Now go back to Chentang Pass," he said.

Nezha used the Wind Fire Wheel to return quickly to Chentang Pass. "Father, come out right now!" he shouted.

Li Jing came out and said, "You evil beast! You brought trouble before your death. Now that you have returned to life, you have brought even more trouble!"

"You destroyed my temple!" shouted Nezha, and he attacked his father with the Fire Tip Lance. They fought for several rounds. Li Jing knew he could not win against his immortal son, so he turned and rode away on his horse to the southeast. Nezha followed on his Wind Fire Wheels. He quickly caught up to his father. But just then, they saw a young Daoist walking. It was Muzha, the second son of Li Jing.

Muzha said to his younger brother, "Nezha, stop this now. You must not kill your own father!"

Nezha said, "Elder brother, this is not your fight. You don't know the situation." Then he told Muzha everything that had happened. "So, who is right, Li Jing or me?"

Muzha replied, "Parents are always right in matters of their children."

Nezha said, "That man is no longer my father." This made Muzha very angry. He attacked Nezha. Nezha fought back. After a few rounds, he threw his gold brick at his brother, knocking him to the ground. Then he started chasing Li Jing again.

Li Jing knew he could not move as fast or fight as well as Nezha. He thought that maybe he should just kill himself so he would not have to lose a fight to Nezha. But just then, he heard a voice singing,

Warm winds blow through the forest

Beautiful petals float on the water

Where do I live, you ask

Far away among the white clouds

This was Heavenly Master Manjusri, the master of Li Jing's son. "Save me, Master!" cried Li Jing.

"Go and wait in my cave," replied the master. Li Jing went into the cave.

A few minutes later, Nezha arrived on his Wind Fire Wheels. He saw Heavenly Master Manjusri standing there. "Have you seen General Li Jing?" he asked.

"Yes, he is in my cave. And who are you, young man?"

"I am Nezha, a disciple of Fairy Primordial. Tell Li Jing to come out right now."

"I have never heard of you. Now go away and stop causing trouble here." Nezha attacked Heavenly Master Manjusri, but the master took out his weapon, the Dragon Bound Stake, from his sleeve and threw it in the air. Strong winds blew, fog filled the air, and Nezha began to feel confused. A moment later he found himself tied tightly to a golden stake, with golden rings surrounding his body. He could not move.

Heavenly Master Manjusri called out, "Jinzha!" This was Nezha's eldest brother. "Beat this young man for me." Jinzha began hitting Nezha. After a while Heavenly Master Manjusri said, "All right, that's enough. You can stop now."

A few minutes later, Fairy Primordial arrived. Heavenly Master Manjusri smiled and said to him, "I have been teaching your disciple a little lesson. Now, set him free and bring him here." Fairy Primordial went up to Nezha, waving his hand. The golden rings fell off Nezha's body. He said to Nezha, "Come with me. Kneel down and kowtow to your uncle!"

Nezha had no choice. He kowtowed to Heavenly Master Manjusri and said, "Master, thank you for the beating."

Heavenly Master Manjusri replied, "From this day forward, there must be no anger between father and son." He turned to Li Jing and told him he could leave. Then he told Nezha that he could also leave.

But Nezha was still very angry. He started chasing his father again. Li Jing looked back and saw Nezha coming after him. "What do I do now?" he thought.

Just then, he saw another Daoist. "Please, help me!" shouted Li Jing.

"What seems to be the problem?" asked the Daoist.

"Nezha is coming. He wants to kill me!"

Just then, Nezha arrived on his Wind Fire Wheels. The Daoist turned to Li Jing. He hit Li Jing on the back and spat on him. Then he said, "Go and fight the boy. I will watch you."

Li Jing knew he could not win against his immortal son.

But he started fighting anyway. The fight began. Nezha thought that he would win easily, but his father was very strong and fought very well. "I think that Daoist is helping him," he thought. He turned and attacked the Daoist with his lance.

The Daoist spat a white lotus flower. It stopped Nezha's magic lance. He said to Nezha, "Why are you attacking me?"

Nezha replied, "Because you are helping Li Jing!" And he attacked the Daoist again. The Daoist lifted his arms towards the sky. A beautiful pagoda fell down from the sky and landed on top of Nezha, trapping him inside. A fire started inside the pagoda. Nezha began to burn. The pain was terrible.

The Daoist said, "Now will you make peace with your father?"

"All right, I will," replied Nezha.

The Daoist put out the fire and said, "Call him 'father' and kowtow to him." Nezha had no choice, he did what the Daoist ordered. Then the Daoist said to Li Jing, "I give this pagoda to you. Any time Nezha gives you trouble, you can put this pagoda on him and burn him. Now, the two of you must live in peace together. Forget about the past, and help the Zhou king in his war against Shang. Nezha, you can leave now."

Nezha left and returned to Qianyuan Mountain.

Li Jing said to the Daoist, "Master, may I know your honorable name?"

The Daoist replied, "I am Master Burning Lamp. It is time for you to give up wealth and fame. You must go into the mountains and become a hermit. As you know, the king of Shang is evil and must be destroyed. Soon, the king of Zhou will need your help in the coming war. When that happens, you may leave the mountains and join the fight."

Li Jing kowtowed to Master Burning Lamp. He went home, quit his job as general of Chentang Pass, and became a hermit in the mountains.

Chapter 15
Jiang Ziya Leaves Mount Kunlun

Ziya has returned to the human world;
His hair is grey, he looks like a wild man

He is too old and too slow to work;
He tries to make money but people just see a fool

The river was not in the flying bear dream;
But the river knows that prosperity is coming soon

Soon it will be time for Ziya to begin a new empire;
It will bring eight hundred years of prosperity

Heavenly Primogenitor was the grand master of Daoism. He lived in a great palace on Mount Kunlun.

He was worried about the coming fall of the Shang Dynasty. So he called all the leaders of Daoism and Confucianism to meet with him. They talked for a long time. The leaders decided to create 365 new gods. To create these new gods, they would use people who would die in the coming war between Shang and Zhou. Those people would be changed into gods of thunder, fire, stars, mountains, clouds, rain, and other things.

The leaders needed someone in the human world to select the 365 people and change them into gods. Jiang Ziya, one of Heavenly Primogenitor's disciples, was to be that person.

So Heavenly Primogenitor sat on his golden throne and called Jiang Ziya to come and see him. Jiang Ziya came and kowtowed before his master.

"How long have you been here on Kunlun Mountain?" asked the master.

"Master," said Jiang Ziya, "I came here at age thirty-two. I am now seventy-two."

"The Shang Dynasty will end soon, and the Zhou Dynasty will rise. New gods must be created. I want you to leave this mountain and go to live in the human world. You will help the new king of Zhou as his general and prime minister. Here is your fate:

> *You will be poor for twenty years*
> *While fishing at the river, a wise man will find you*
> *And make you prime minister to the king*
> *You will be a general at ninety-three*
> *Powerful men will create a new dynasty*

Jiang Ziya did not want to leave Kunlun Mountain. He had been studying the Way for forty years but had failed to become an immortal. He still had much to learn. He told his master he did not want to go. But his master said, "This is your fate. You must do this." So sadly, Jiang Ziya picked up his things and left Kunlun Mountain.

He knew nothing of the human world. But he remembered that he had a sworn brother named Song Yiren who lived in Zhaoge. He decided to go see his brother.

Song Yiren was a wealthy man with a large house and many servants. He came out to greet Jiang Ziya. "Brother," he said, "I have not seen you for many years. I am so happy to see you today!"

The two brothers sat down and had a vegetarian meal with wine. Song Yiren asked, "What have you been doing in heaven these past forty years?"

"I have learned many things. I know how to carry water, to care for the trees, to make a fire, and to make magic elixirs."

His brother replied, "Those jobs are for servants. You are no servant. You should start a business. And also, you need a wife."

The next day, Song Yiren went to see an old friend named Ma who had an unmarried daughter. He gave the friend four *taels* of silver as a gift, and the friend agreed to let his daughter marry Jiang Ziya.

Song Yiren went back to tell Jiang Ziya that he'd found a wife for him. He said, "You will like her. She has a good education. She has never been with a man. And she is sixty-eight years old, so she will be a good match for you."

They were married soon after. But Jiang Ziya was really not interested in married life. He kept thinking about his earlier life on Mount Kunlun. He wanted to study the Way and had no interest in his wife or in starting a business.

One day Ma said to him, "We are living a good life here with your brother. But what if he dies? We should have a business, so that we will always have money for a good life."

"You are right," he replied. "But what can I do? I know nothing of business. All I can do is make rakes."

"All right, let's start a rake business. There are many bamboo trees nearby. Cut down some trees, make some rakes, then bring them to the marketplace in Zhaoge and sell them. It's easy. It will bring us a little bit of money, and that's better than no money at all."

So Jiang Ziya made some rakes. Then he carried them thirty-five *li* to the Zhaoge marketplace. He spent all day there but did not sell a single rake. He walked back home, carrying the rakes on his back. He told his wife, "Nobody in Zhaoge needs a rake."

She replied, "You old fool! Everyone needs a rake. You just don't know how to sell them." They started shouting at each other.

Song Yiren heard the shouting. He ran over and said, "Please don't argue! There are other ways to make money. We have a lot of wheat here. I'll ask my servants to turn the wheat into flour. You can take the flour to the marketplace and sell it there."

When the flour was ready and put into bags, Jiang Ziya

carried the bags to the Zhaoge marketplace. He went to several different places but nobody wanted to buy his flour. Finally, a man stopped and asked for a penny's worth of flour. Jiang Ziya put the flour bags on the ground and started to take out a small amount of flour for the man.

But just then, a frightened horse came galloping down the road. Jiang Ziya and the man jumped out of the way, but the horse's legs caught on the flour bags. The bags went flying every direction, and all the flour blew away. The man left without buying any flour, and Jiang Ziya walked home with no money and empty bags.

When he got home, his wife was happy to see the empty bags of flour. "This is wonderful!" she said. But then Jiang Ziya told her what happened. She started shouting at him again, and before long they were arguing loudly.

Song Yiren came over and stopped them from arguing. "Don't worry about a little bit of flour," he said. "I have another idea. I own several restaurants in Zhaoge. One of them is a large restaurant near the city's south gate. You can go there and be the boss."

But that did not work either. People went to Jiang Ziya's restaurant, but they were frightened of him and did not stay to eat any food. He had to return home and tell Song Yiren that he could not be a restaurant boss either.

"All right, let's try one more thing," said Song Yiren. "I'll give you fifty *taels* of silver. Go buy some pigs and sheep. Take them to the marketplace in Zhaoge and sell them. That should be easy."

But that did not go well either. Heaven was angry at the King of Shang, so there had been no rain for many weeks. The king had told the people to pray for rain. And during this time, nobody was allowed to kill any animals. Jiang Ziya did not know this. So when he brought his pigs and sheep to the marketplace, the guards took all his animals. They wanted to arrest Jiang Ziya, but he left the animals and ran away.

He returned home with no money and no animals. Sadly, he told Song Yiren what had happened. "I am a terrible businessman," he said. "I have lost your money. I don't know what to do."

But Song Yiren just said, "Don't worry, it's just a few *taels* of silver. Come, let's go into the garden and have some wine."

Chapter 16
The Jade Lute Demon

Demons keep coming, the fate of the nation is dark;
The will of heaven brings suffering to the capital

Strange energy did not harm the stars in the sky;
It was evil spirits that killed the loyal ministers

A thousand years of work is lost
To gain a single day of happiness

If not for Ziya's wisdom,
No one would see the pipa demon in the fire

Jiang Ziya sat in the garden with his bond brother, drinking wine and enjoying the fine weather. He saw goldfish in the pond, and he heard birds singing in the trees. He looked around. Smiling, he said to Song Yiren, "This would be a good place to build a tower."

"Why would I build a tower here?" replied Song Yiren.

"It will bring you good fortune. If you build a tower here, your family will have thirty-six jade belted ministers and also several gold belted ministers.[1]"

"It's interesting that you tell me this. I have tried to build here several times, but each time I build something, it burns down. I don't even try anymore."

"That's because there are evil spirits here. But don't worry. You build the tower, and I will take care of the evil spirits."

Song Yiren gathered several workers. They started to build the tower. After several days of work, they were ready to raise the main beam. That night, Jiang Ziya sat quietly in the garden, watching. At midnight a strong wind came, sending clouds of dust into the air. A fire started in the new building. Jiang Ziya looked inside and saw five evil spirits in the tower. Fire came from their mouths. The wind made the fire so hot that the earth turned red.

Jiang Ziya drew his sword. He walked through the fire towards the five spirits and said, "Come out, demons! You have already caused too much trouble. Now you must die!"

A loud bolt of thunder shook the earth, causing the spirits to fall to their knees. "Lord!" they cried, "please spare our

---

[1] In ancient China, leather belts with sheets of ornamentation, called *dàikuǎ*, were worn by officials as indicators of their rank. The highest ranking wore jade, and the second highest wore gold.

lives. We used to be animals, but we have studied the Way for many years. Now we are spirits. If you kill us, all of our work will be for nothing. We are sorry we caused you trouble."

"All right," he replied. "Leave this place and go to Mount Qi. Wait for me there. Don't cause any trouble. Later I will need your help with something." The five spirits kowtowed to him, then flew away to Mount Qi.

While he was talking to the spirits, Madame Ma and Song Yiren's wife were watching him. They could not see or hear the spirits, so they thought Jiang Ziya was just talking to himself. "Old man, who are you talking to?" asked Madame Ma.

"Oh, I was just getting rid of some evil spirits," he replied.

"You can talk to spirits?"

"Yes. And I am also a fortuneteller." Just then Song Yiren came to find out what was happening. Jiang Ziya told him the story.

Madame Ma said to Song Yiren, "My husband is a fortune teller. We should give him a shop in the city so he can start a fortunetelling business."

Soon after, Song Yiren gave his brother a nice little shop near the south gate of Zhaoge. Jiang Ziya put up a few small signs. On the left was a sign saying, "Speak only of the Dao." On the right was a sign saying, "Always speak the truth." On the back wall was a third sign saying "Inside the sleeves are the sky and earth, inside the jug are the sun and moon." He opened the shop and sat down to wait for customers. He went to the shop every day for four months, but no customers came in.

Finally, a woodcutter came into the shop. He was a big man who lived in the forest. He dropped his firewood on the floor and looked down at Jiang Ziya. He pointed to the sign on the back wall and asked, "What does that mean?"

Jiang Ziya replied, "It means that I know the past, the future, and everything in heaven and earth. Also, I will live forever."

The woodcutter said, "Big words, old man. If you know the past and the future, you should be able to tell my future. If you are right, I'll give you twenty coppers. If you are wrong, I'll beat you up and destroy your shop."

"This is my first customer, and he is a very bad man!" thought Jiang Ziya. But he said, "That is no problem. I will write three sentences on a piece of paper. You must do exactly what is on the paper. Ok?"

The woodcutter agreed. Jiang Ziya wrote three sentences on the paper. The woodcutter read it:

Walk south.

You will find an old man sitting under a tree.

He will give you 120 copper coins, four plates of food, and two bowls of wine.

The woodcutter thought this could not possibly be right, because nobody had ever given him that much money in twenty years. But he picked up his firewood and started walking south. Soon he saw an old man sitting under a tree. The old man shouted, "Woodcutter! Come over here!"

The woodcutter walked over to him.

"Your firewood looks good," said the old man. "I will buy

all of it for 100 copper coins." The woodcutter was happy to sell the firewood. He was also happy that the man was giving him 100 coppers instead of 120, because he did not want to pay the fortuneteller. He gave the firewood to the man. While the man went in his house to get the money, the woodcutter swept the ground clean.

A few minutes later, a young servant came out. He carried four plates of food, a pot of wine, and a bowl. "Please, eat and drink," said the servant. The woodcutter poured all of the wine from the pot into the bowl, so it would be one bowl of wine instead of two. But after he drank the wine in the bowl, he saw that the pot was full of wine again. He poured that wine into the bowl and drank it too. Then he ate the four plates of food.

The man came out of his house carrying a bag of coins. He said, "I was going to give you 100 copper coins. But I see that you have swept the ground clean in front of my house. So I'll give you another 20 coins. Go and buy yourself some wine."

The woodcutter ran back to Jiang Ziya's fortunetelling shop, shouting, "There is an immortal in Zhaoge! There is an immortal in Zhaoge!"

He arrived at the fortunetelling shop and said to Jiang Ziya, "You really are an immortal, sir! Now the people of Zhaoge will be happy and have no more trouble."

"Fine, fine. Give me my twenty copper coins," replied Jiang Ziya.

"I must do something more for you," said the woodcutter. Then he ran outside and looked around. He saw a wealthy looking man. The woodcutter grabbed the man and pulled him towards the shop.

"What are you doing?" said the man. "I have business in the city and I don't have time for this."

"Come with me. You have to meet this fortuneteller."

"No, I don't. Let go of me."

"If you don't come with me, I will throw both of us into the river and end our lives." The rich man had no choice, so he went with the woodcutter into Jiang Ziya's shop.

Jiang Ziya told the rich man's fortune. He told the rich man that he would collect 103 silver *taels* that day. The man walked out of the shop, laughing and shaking his head. As he left, the woodcutter shouted to him, "If the fortuneteller is correct, you must pay him half a *tael* of silver." The rich man just waved him away and kept walking. A crowd of people had gathered to watch this.

Two hours later, the rich man returned. He said loudly so that everyone in the crowd could hear, "This fortuneteller is truly an immortal sent from heaven! I collected 103 silver *taels*, just as he said!"

This made Jiang Ziya famous throughout Zhaoge. Everyone wanted him to tell their fortune, and they were all happy to pay him a half *tael* of silver. He brought home a lot of silver, and this made his wife very happy.

Jiang Ziya's fame spread far and wide. It even reached the demon named Jade Lute who lived in a graveyard several *li* south of Zhaoge. Jade Lute was one of the three demons who was called by Nüwa seven years earlier. She was a friend of the thousand-year-old fox demon who had killed Daji and taken her body. She would often go to visit Daji at night. Whenever she visited Daji she would stop to eat one or two of the palace maids.

One morning she was leaving the palace after visiting Daji. Flying over the city, she looked down and saw a crowd of people surrounding Jiang Ziya's fortunetelling shop. "I wonder if he can tell my fortune," she said to herself. So she came down to earth, changed into a beautiful young woman, and walked through the crowd to Jiang Ziya's shop. She said, "Sir, can you tell my fortune?"

Jiang Ziya saw her. He knew immediately that she was a demon. "Of course, madam," he said to her. Then he grabbed her hand and would not let go.

"How dare you!" she shouted, so everyone could hear. "I am a lady. Let go of me at once!"

People in the crowd shouted at Jiang Ziya, telling him that he was an old man and should not touch a lady like that. But he said to them, "My friends, this is no lady. This is an evil demon."

She tried to get away from him. Jiang Ziya grabbed a brick and hit her on the head. She fell down and blood ran onto the ground. "The fortuneteller has killed a lady!" shouted the people.

Just then, Prime Minister Bi Gan rode past on his horse. He stopped and asked what was happening. Someone said, "There is a fortuneteller here named Jiang Ziya. A woman asked him to tell her fortune. He grabbed her. She fought back. He hit her head with a brick and killed her!"

The Prime Minister ordered his guards to arrest Jiang Ziya. They dragged him to the Prime Minister, but still he would not let go of the woman's hand. "What are you doing to that woman?" he asked.

"Sir," replied Jiang Ziya, "I am no criminal. This is an evil demon. You know that there is evil in Zhaoge these days. I think perhaps this demon is the reason for it."

Bi Gan said, "I will bring you to the king. He will decide what to do with you." So they all went to the palace to see the king.

When they arrived at the palace, the king was sitting with Daji. The king looked at them and said, "This looks like a woman, not a demon."

Jiang Ziya replied, "Your Majesty, if you put her in the fire, you will see her true form."

The king agreed. So the guards gathered a large amount of firewood. They lit it and waited for the fire to become big and hot. Then threw the woman's body into it. They watched for four hours, but the woman's body was not burned at all. Finally, the king said, "Four hours in the fire is enough. The fortuneteller is right. She is a demon."

Chapter 17
The Snake Pit

The snake pit is full of evil, its spirit fills the sky;
It is filled with palace maids' blood and flesh

So many pretty bones, no place to bury them;
Their smell lingers near their souls

Once they dreamed of home, now they sing empty songs to the moon;
Sad and lonely, they cannot rest

Their air of sadness fills the heavens;
But it also helps to bring the Zhou to power

Jiang Ziya watched the evil demon's body lying in the fire, not burning. He wanted to see the demon's true form. So he brought out magic fire from his mouth, nose and eyes. The magic fire flew towards the demon's body. The demon opened its eyes and sat up. It looked at Jiang Ziya and said, "Why are you doing this to me?"

The king and his ministers saw and heard this. They could not believe that the dead body was sitting up and talking. "Your Majesty," said Jiang Ziya, "please go inside. A big storm is coming." And just then, a huge bolt of lightning came down from the sky. The ground shook. The fire went out. When the smoke blew away, the demon's body was gone. And a jade lute was lying on the ground.

Daji was very angry that her good friend Jade Lute had been killed. She thought to herself, "Sister, don't worry. I will have my revenge on Jiang Ziya. He and I cannot both live." Although she was very angry, she smiled at the king and said, "Your Majesty, I would like to have that jade lute. I can play it for you day and night. Also, it looks like Jiang Ziya is a wise and powerful man. You should give him a job here in the palace."

"Good idea, my love," said the king. He ordered his attendants to put the jade lute in the Star Picking Mansion. Then he gave Jiang Ziya the position of Director of the Imperial Observatory.

The next day, Daji went to the Star Picking Mansion. She picked up the jade lute and moved it to the very top of the building. She knew that if the jade lute gathered qi[1] from heaven, earth, sun and moon for five years, her friend

---

[1] *qi* is spiritual energy.

would return to life and become a demon again.

A few days later, Daji was playing the jade lute and dancing for the king. All the concubines were smiling and watching. But in the back of the room, about seventy palace maids were crying. Daji asked who they were. A servant told her that they were maids of the dead queen.

Daji went to the king. She told him about the seventy maids. She said to him, "Those maids will cause trouble for us. They must all die."

"Of course, my dear," smiled the king. "We will have them killed right away."

"No, please wait. I have a better idea. You should dig a hole in front of the Star Picking Mansion. Make the hole 50 feet deep and 240 feet around. Put thousands of snakes in the pit. Then strip the maids and throw them into the pit."

The king liked this idea, but he did not have enough snakes. So he commanded his people to bring snakes to the palace. All the snakes in Zhaoge were brought to the palace. When there were no more snakes in Zhaoge, the people went out into the countryside to find more.

Jiao Ge, the king's Supreme Minister, did not know why the king wanted so many snakes. He asked the leader of the king's guards what the snakes were for. The guard leader replied, "The king wants all of the queen's palace maids to be killed. They are to be thrown into a large hole in front of the Star Picking Tower. Then the snakes will bite and kill the maids."

Jiao Ge and the other ministers ran to the Star Picking Tower. They saw a group of palace maids standing near the large hole. They were stripped, tied up with rope, and crying with fear.

Jiao Ge went to see the king. He knelt before the king and said, "Your Majesty, these maids have done nothing wrong. But you are going to kill them in a terrible way. No king has ever done anything like this before!"

The king just replied, "These palace maids are evil. We must deal with them."

Jiao Ge said angrily, "The king should be a good father to the people. But you care nothing for the people. You do not listen to your ministers. You killed two of the grand dukes, and you used the Burning Pillar to kill other good people. And now you want to kill these maids who have done nothing wrong. I tell you, stop spending all your days playing with your concubine Daji. Stop listening to Daji and that evil minister Fei Zhong. Only then can you save this kingdom and bring peace to the land."

The king jumped up and shouted, "How dare you speak to us like this! Guards, strip this fool and throw him into the snake pit!"

But before the guards could grab him, Jiao Ge shouted, "You are a tyrant, and death will come for you soon enough." He jumped out of a window and smashed into the ground, dead.

"Throw that body into the snake pit!" roared the king. "And throw the palace maids in after him!"

The king's guards grabbed each of the palace maids and threw them into the pit. The snakes surrounded them, bit them, and started to eat their bodies. The king and Daji watched this for a while. Then the king patted Daji on the arm and said, "My dear, this is really too wonderful for words."

Daji smiled and said, "Your Majesty, I have another good idea. You can dig two more holes. Put trees in one of the holes, then hang strips of meat on the tree branches. This will be the 'Meat Forest.' Fill the other hole with wine and call it the 'Wine Pool.' Your Majesty will be the only one to use the Meat Forest and the Wine Pool."

"Wonderful!" said the king. He told his servants to dig two more holes and create the Meat Forest and Wine Pool. When they were finished, the king and Daji had a nice dinner.

"I have another idea for you, Your Majesty. I think you should have the palace maids fight with the eunuchs. It will be fun to watch. Let the winners drink from the Wine Pool. But the losers should be killed and their bodies thrown into the Meat Forest." The king liked this idea, and ordered his servants to do as Daji said.

Now, Daji had her own reasons for wanting all these people to be killed. She was really a fox spirit, of course. Late every night, while the king was sleeping, the fox spirit changed back to its original form. Then the fox spirit drank the blood and ate the flesh of the dead bodies.

Daji was not finished doing evil things. She still wanted to have revenge on Jiang Ziya for killing her friend, the demon Jade Lute. One day when she and the king were drinking wine, she asked him to build a new building. She wanted it to be forty-nine feet high, with a huge terrace on top. She called it the Deer Terrace. "Your Majesty," she said, "if you build this, it will show everyone how powerful you are. It will be like one of the palaces in heaven. Immortals will come down from heaven to visit with you.

They will kowtow before you and call you 'Great King.' You and I will live together forever."

"Of course, my dear," said the king, who had drunk too much wine. "But who could build this for us?"

"I think Jiang Ziya is the best person for the job," she replied. "He is a wise man, and he understands *yin* and *yang*." So the king called for Jiang Ziya to come and see him.

Jiang Ziya did not know why the king was calling him. So he did a divination and saw that great danger was coming. He said to Bi Gan, "Good bye, my friend. Thank you for helping me. I don't know if we will see each other again." Then he went to the palace.

When Jiang Ziya arrived, the king said, "We have an idea for a new building. We call it the Deer Terrace." Then he showed Jiang Ziya the designs for the Deer Terrace and said, "We want you to build this for us. It's a big job, but we know you can do it."

Jiang Ziya looked at the designs for the Deer Terrace. He thought to himself, "This building cannot be built. Daji and the king are out to get me. I'd better get out of Zhaoge, and quickly!"

Chapter 18
Flight from Zhaoge

Day and night,
the Wei River flows

Ziya sits alone fishing,
his hook above the water

Even before the dream of the flying bear,
he waited at the riverbank

As the sun falls slowly behind him,
he thinks of his white hair

The king showed Jiang Ziya the designs for the Deer Terrace. He said, "We want you to build this for us. It's a big job, but we know you can do it."

Jiang Ziya looked at the designs. The king waited for a few minutes. Then he looked at Jiang Ziya and said, "I want you to build this. How long will it take?"

Jiang Ziya studied the designs for the Deer Terrace. He thought about it. Then he replied, "This is a huge project, Your Majesty. It will take thirty-five years, maybe longer."

The king turned to Daji to ask her what she thought. She said, "Your Majesty, what good is the Deer Terrace if it's not ready until we are both too old to enjoy it? I do not trust this man. He is just a poor magician who knows nothing about how to build anything."

"You are right, my dear," said the king. Turning to his guards, he said, "Take this magician away. Execute him using the Burning Pillar."

"Your Majesty," said Jiang Ziya quickly, "please wait and listen to me. Building the Deer Terrace will need many workers and a huge amount of money. But the kingdom has no money anymore. The people are hungry, the country is at war, and you spend all your time in bed with your concubine. Please do not continue on this path. It will destroy you and the kingdom."

The king was enraged. He shouted to his guards, "Seize this fool! Cut him into little pieces!" But before the guards could grab him, Jiang Ziya ran out of the palace. He ran to the Nine Dragon Bridge, jumped off the bridge, and disappeared under the water. The guards ran after him. When they got to the bridge, they looked down at the water but they could not see him. They thought he had drowned, but in fact, Jiang Ziya had flown away on an invisible water cloud.

A few minutes later, Supreme Minister Yang Ren came to the bridge. The king had named him Supreme Minister after the previous Supreme Minister, Mei Bo, was executed on the Burning Pillar. Yang Ren saw four guards on the bridge looking down at the water. He asked them what they were looking at. They told him that Jiang Ziya had jumped off the bridge.

"Why did he do that?" asked Yang Ren.

The leader of the guards replied, "His Majesty told him to oversee the building of a huge new building called Deer Terrace. Jiang Ziya spoke against the king. So of course, the king became angry. He ordered us to kill him by cutting him into many pieces. That's why Jiang Ziya jumped off the bridge."

"What is this Deer Terrace?" asked Yang Ren. The leader of the guards told him.

Yang Ren was unhappy about this situation. He went to see the king, who was at the Star Picking Mansion with Daji. He kneeled before the king and said, "Your Majesty, our nation has three big problems right now. In the east, the son of the late Grand Duke Jiang Huanchu is fighting against us. In the south, the son of the late Grand Duke E Chongyu is also fighting against us. And in the north, Grand Tutor Wen Zhong has been fighting at the North Sea for ten years but has not won the war yet. Many good people have died in these three wars, and it has been very expensive. We have no more people and no more money. Please, Your Majesty, stop this foolish project."

But the king did not want to hear this. He told his guards,

"Take this traitor out of here and remove both of his eyes." The guards did as they were ordered. They gouged out Yang Ren's eyes, then they brought the eyes back to the king on a plate.

Even though the king took both of Yang Ren's eyes, the Supreme Minister continued to do his job and help the king. In the heavens, a Daoist immortal named Master Pure Void Virtue saw this. He told one of his disciples to bring Yang Ren to his cave in the sky. The disciple flew to Star Picking Mansion. Then he created a big dust storm and took Yang Ren's body while it was hidden by the dust.

The king's servants told the king what had happened. He said to Daji, "The same thing happened when I was about to execute the two princes. It looks like this is happening a lot these days. It's nothing to worry about. But now we need someone else to oversee the building of the Deer Terrace." He selected Chong Houhu, the cruel Grand Duke of the North.

The disciple brought Yang Ren's body to the Daoist's cave. The Daoist poured a little bit of magic elixir into both eye sockets. Then he blew a magic breath. "Rise up, Yang Ren!" he cried. Yang Ren sat up. In each eye socket there was now a tiny hand. In the palm of each hand was a tiny eye. Now Yang Ren could see again, but he could also use his new eyes to see all the secrets of heaven and earth.

He looked around and saw the Daoist. He bowed and said, "Thank you, Sir. Please take me as your disciple and let me serve you for the rest of my life." The Daoist agreed. Yang Ren stayed with Master Pure Void Virtue for several years.

Back at Zhaoge, Chong Houhu brought thousands of workers from all parts of the kingdom. He worked them day and night. Many of the workers, mostly the young and old, died while working there. Their bodies were thrown into the foundations of the Deer Terrace. Many others tried to flee the country.

Jiang Ziya flew back to his home on the water cloud. His wife met him and said, "Welcome home, husband and minister!"

He told her that he was no longer a minister of the king, and that the king had tried to kill him. He said, "We need to leave Zhaoge. Let's go to West Qi. We can wait there until it is time for me to help the new king."

But his wife was not happy. She said, "Husband, you should have obeyed His Majesty and built this Deer Terrace. We would have had lots of money. Why did you argue with the king like that, when everyone else knows which way the wind is blowing? You are nothing but a poor magician, and you are a fool. I will not follow you to Qi."

"A wife must follow her husband. We will have a good life in West Qi, and you will have money and happiness there."

"No, I am a native of Zhaoge, and I will not leave. Our marriage is over. Give me a divorce."

Jiang Ziya wrote a letter of divorce and held it in his hand. He said to his wife, "As long as this letter is in my hand, we are still husband and wife." Without waiting even a second, she reached out her hand and grabbed the letter. He said quietly, "The bite of a snake and the sting of a wasp are nothing compared to this woman's heart."

Jiang Ziya packed up his things and left the house. He traveled west towards the province of West Qi. He crossed many rivers and mountains. Finally, he came to Lintong

Pass. There he saw hundreds of people. They were sitting on the ground, crying.

"Who are you and why are you here?" he asked.

One of them replied, "We are all from Zhaoge. The king has named Chong Houhu to oversee the Deer Terrace project. He has ordered that two out of every three men must work on the project. Tens of thousands have already died. If we go there, we will probably die too. So we left Zhaoge. But now we cannot get through the pass because the commander will not let us through."

"Don't worry," he said, "I will take care of this." He put down his luggage and went to see the commander. The commander heard that an official from Zhaoge was here to see him, so he let Jiang Ziya in. But after he heard what Jiang Ziya had to say, he became angry.

He said, "You are not a court official, you are just a poor magician. The king gave you wealth and power, but you turned your back on him. You say that you want to help these people, but all I see are a bunch of traitors and cowards. The law says that I should arrest you and send you back to Zhaoge. But this is the first time we have met, so I will be kind and let you go. Now get out of here."

Jiang Ziya returned to the crowd of people. He told them what the commander had said. They all began to cry. "Please don't cry," he told them. "I can help you but you must do exactly what I tell you. Wait until night comes. Then close your eyes. You may hear the sound of wind. Don't worry about that. And do not open your eyes. If you do, you will die."

When night came, the people all closed their eyes and waited. Jiang Ziya kowtowed towards Mount Kunlun. Then he began to say some magic words. A strong wind came. It picked up all the people. The wind carried them across Linton Pass, across several other passes and mountains, all the way to Golden Chicken Mountain. Then the wind placed them safely on the ground. Jiang Ziya told them, "You can open your eyes now. You are at Golden Chicken Mountain in the province of West Qi. You can go now."

The province of West Qi was governed by the Grand Duke of the West, Ji Chang. But Ji Chang was a prisoner, forced to live in Youli by the king's order. So the province was governed by Ji Chang's eldest son Bo Yikao.

Bo Yikao took good care of the hundreds of people. He gave them food and homes and jobs. He also talked with the people, and they told him everything that was happening in Zhaoge.

Bo Yikao said to his ministers, "My father has been a prisoner for seven years. Nobody from his family has gone to see him. What good are his ninety-nine sons if we cannot help him? I must go and see him. I will take the family's three great treasures and give them to the king. Perhaps then the king will let my father return home."

Chapter 19
Gifts for the King

The loyal minister's son dies
Because of the king's fox demon

The evil king plays with his concubine
And ignores his ministers

Better for him to die from ten thousand knife cuts
While keeping his honor

History will tell his sad story;
Tears fall like pearls

Bo Yikao said goodbye to his mother. Then he went to see his younger brother Ji Fa and said, "Guard the province while I am in Zhaoge. Don't change anything, and take care of your brothers."

Then he set out on the journey to Zhaoge. He passed quickly over five mountain passes and across the Yellow River. Finally, he arrived at Zhaoge and stayed overnight at a hostel.

The next day he went to the palace. He waited all day but nobody came to let him inside. He did not dare to enter on his own. So he returned to the hostel. He went back on the second, third and fourth days but was still not invited into the palace. Finally on the fifth day, while he was waiting at the gate, he saw the Prime Minister Bi Gan coming on horseback. He knelt before the Prime Minister.

"Who is kneeling before me?" asked Bi Gan.

"I am Bo Yikao, son of the criminal Ji Chang."

Bi Gan got off his horse and raised the young man up, saying, "Please get up, Prince. Why are you here?"

"Sir, when my father offended His Majesty, you saved his life by speaking to the king. My family will never forget this. Now my father has been a prisoner for seven years, living in Youli. We are worried about him. I have come here to ask His Majesty to let my father return to his home. In return, I have brought the king valuable gifts."

"What are these gifts?"

"I have brought four gifts. First, I have brought a magic carriage that comes from the ancient Yellow Emperor. It can go wherever the rider wants to go, without need of driver or horses. Second, I have brought a magic carpet that makes any drunk person sober as soon as he lays down on it. Third, I have brought a white-faced monkey that sings and dances. It knows three thousand eight hundred songs. And finally, I have brought ten beautiful young women for the king's harem."

"These are wonderful gifts, but I'm afraid His Majesty is too far gone to change his ways. In fact, these gifts might make things worse. However, I will tell him and we will see what he does."

Bi Gan went to the palace and told the king that Ji Chang's son had come to see him. The king ordered the young man to enter the palace. Bo Yikao entered, fell to his knees, then he walked on his knees until he was close to the throne. Without looking up from the floor he said to the king, "The son of your criminal minister wishes to speak with you, Your Majesty."

"Speak, young man," said the king.

"Our family is grateful that you have allowed my father to live. I now ask you to let him return to his family so that he may live the last few years of his life at home. If you do this, your kindness will be remembered for ten thousand years."

While he was speaking, Daji stood behind a curtain secretly looking at him. She liked what she saw. The young man was tall, strong and handsome. She came out from behind the curtain and walked until she was standing next to the king. She said to the king, "Your Majesty, I have heard that this young man is a great musician, a master at playing the guqin[1]." Turning to Bo Yikao, she smiled sweetly and said,

---

[1] The guqin is a plucked seven string instrument, similar to a zither, that according

"I have heard that you play the guqin very well. Would you play a song for me?"

Still looking at the floor, Bo Yikao said to the king, "Please, Your Majesty, my father has suffered for seven years. My heart is broken. How can I take pleasure in music at a time like this?"

"Yikao," replied the king, "play us a song. If we like it, we will set you and your father free."

This made Bo Yikao happy. He thanked the king. Servants brought in a guqin. He sat on the floor, put the guqin on his knees, and began to play this song:

> *Willows move in the morning breeze*
> *Peach blossoms glow in the sun*
> *Without care for carriages running east and west*
> *The grass covers the earth like a green blanket*

Music came from Bo Yikao's fingers like the tinkling of jade, like the sound of pine trees in the forest. The king loved the music. He said to Daji, "You are right, this young man plays beautifully."

Daji also enjoyed the music. But what she really wanted was to enjoy Bo Yikao. She though he was very handsome and strong. Then she looked at the king and thought he was old and weak. She said to herself, "I must keep this handsome young man here. I will find a way to get him into my bed. I think he will be a lot more fun than that old king."

She said to the king, "Your Highness, I have an idea. You

---

to legend has been played in China for five thousand years. In 1977 a recording of guqin music was included on the Golden Record that was sent out to interstellar space on the Voyager 1 and 2 spacecrafts.

can let Ji Chang go home, as we have no need for him. But keep Bo Yikao here. He can teach me to play the guqin, and he can play for you anytime you want."

"That is a wonderful idea," said the foolish king, and he agreed.

Daji ordered the palace servants to prepare a feast. During the feast she raised her golden cup of wine and toasted the king again and again and again, until the king was too drunk to even sit up. When he fell asleep, she told the servants to put him to bed. Then she asked Bo Yikao to teach her how to play the guqin.

The two of them sat on the floor, each one with a guqin on their knees. Bo Yikao told her about the guqin: when to play it, when to not play it, how to hold it, how to use one's hands to play the strings, and so on. Daji listened, giving him smiles and warm looks with her eyes.

Bo Yikao knew that Daji was trying to seduce him, but he knew that it would be a terrible mistake for him to go along with her. So he kept his heart like ice. He did not even look at Daji during the lesson.

Daji saw that she was not getting anywhere with the young man. She ordered another feast, and told Bo Yikao to sit next to her. He replied, "I am the son of a criminal. I would not dare sit next to the queen. If I did, I should die ten thousand deaths!" He remained sitting on the floor, not even looking up at her.

Daji had one more idea. She told the servants to clear away the feast. Then she said to him, "Let's continue with the lesson. But you are too far away from me. I cannot learn like this. I will sit on your lap. You can put your arms around me and hold my hands. That way you can teach my hands how to play the strings. I will learn much more quickly."

Bo Yikao was in trouble now. He said to himself, "I think it is my fate to die here. But I would rather be an honorable ghost than a dishonorable man." Then he said to her, "Your Majesty, if I did as you ask, I would be no better than a beast. You are the queen, the mother to the country, honored by all. Please do not lower yourself like this. If the people learned about this, they would never honor you again."

Now Daji was furious at Bo Yikao. She ordered him to leave the palace. Later that night, in bed, the king asked her how the lesson went. She replied, "I must tell you, that young man was not interested in teaching me to play the guqin. He only wanted to use my body for his own enjoyment. When I saw what he was trying to do, I sent him away."

The next morning, the king ordered his servants to bring Bo Yikao back to the palace. He said, "Why did you give the queen such a bad lesson yesterday? She still cannot play the guqin."

The young man replied, "Your Majesty, it takes time to learn to play the guqin."

The king did not want to say anything about the seduction. He said, "Play us another song, young man." Bo Yikao sat on the floor and played this song:

> *My loyalty reaches to the heavens*
> *May His Majesty live forever!*
> *May the rain and wind come at the proper time*
> *May the kingdom be strong and last forever*

The king liked this song and could not find anything wrong with it. When Daji saw this, she said, "Your Majesty, I have heard that the white-faced monkey can sing very well. Let's hear it sing."

The servants brought out the monkey. Bo Yikao gave it two wooden clappers that it could use to play while it sang. The monkey sang a beautiful song. As the king listened to the song, he forgot his anger. As Daji listened, all evil thoughts left her body. She even forgot who she was. The fox spirit floated out of her body.

Daji did not know that the monkey was more than just a monkey. It was a powerful spirit who had studied the Way for a thousand years. It saw the fox spirit. Dropping the clappers, it attacked Daji. The queen jumped backwards. The king hit the monkey and killed it with one blow from his fist.

Daji started to cry, saying, "That young man tried to use the monkey to kill me!"

"I did not do anything!" cried Bo Yikao.

"How can you say that?" shouted the king. "Everyone saw your monkey try to kill the queen!"

"Your Highness, monkeys are wild animals. They do not always do as they are told. This one likes to eat fruit. When he saw the fruit in front of the queen, it tried to grab some of it. Besides, how could a little monkey harm a person? It had no weapons of any kind."

The king thought about this for a while. Gradually his anger left him. He said to Daji, "This young man's words make sense. The monkey was a wild animal."

Daji said, "Your Majesty, you have been kind to this man.

Let him play another song. But if there is any anger or criticism at all, then you must execute him."

"Of course, my dear," said the king.

Now Bo Yikao saw that he could not escape the net thrown by Daji. He sat on the floor to play one more song.

A king is always good to his people
He will never be cruel to them
Hot pillars turn flesh to ash
Long snakes feast on bellies
The sea is full of blood
The forest is full of corpses
The people are hungry
But the Deer Terrace is full
The farms are dying
But the king eats well
May the king remove evil ministers
And bring peace to the nation

The king shouted, "Guards, grab that traitor and execute him!"

But Bo Yikao said, "Wait! I am not finished with the song." Then he sang,

May the king let go of his lust
May he get rid of the evil queen
When the evil is gone
The ministers will gladly obey
When the lust is gone
The kingdom will be at peace
I am not afraid of death
But you must kill evil Daji

Then he stood up and threw the guqin straight at Daji's

head. The queen jumped out of the way and fell to the floor.

"Guards!" shouted the king. "Trying to kill the queen with a guqin is a terrible crime. Throw him in the pit of snakes!"

"Wait," said Daji, getting up from the floor. "Give him to me. I will deal with him." She told the soldiers to nail his feet and hands to planks of wood. Then she ordered the soldiers to cut off his flesh, bit by bit. Bo Yikao continued to shout at her until he died.

When he was dead, Daji said to the king, "I have an idea. Let's cut up the flesh into little pieces. Then we will make meat pies out of it and give them to Ji Chang. If he eats the pies, that means he is just an ordinary man and you can let him go home. But if he refuses, that means that he is a sage, and you should kill him to prevent trouble."

The king agreed. Bo Yikao's flesh was sent to the kitchen, where it was made into meat pies. Then he ordered the meat pies to be sent to Ji Chang in Youli.

Chapter 20
San Yisheng Bribes the Ministers

Since ancient times, evil ministers love wealth;
They harm the loyal and virtuous

To spare a life, they demand that gold and silver be put in their bag[1]

They think only of themselves;
They don't care about the pain of their country

But everything can change in a second;
They don't know that the sword is already coming down

---

[1] In the original Chinese poem, the ministers demanded that coins be put in a *jǐn chán*, a special purse made of rich brocade that was used as a tip jar for performers in ancient times.

During the seven years that Ji Chang was a prisoner in Youli he never spoke in public and never caused any trouble. He spent his time studying divination. He wrote a book that would later be called the Book of Changes (I Ching). He also relaxed by playing the guqin.

One day while playing the guqin, he heard an unhappy sound coming from the lowest string. The sound was like death. He stopped playing and did a divination using gold coins. This is how he learned that his son had died. The divination also told him that the king wanted to give him his son's flesh to eat.

Soon after that, a messenger arrived carrying a plate of meat pies. The messenger told Ji Chang, "His Majesty is worried about your health. He went hunting yesterday and killed a deer, so he ordered the kitchen to make the deer meat into pies for you."

Ji Chang knew that this was a trap. If he refused to eat the pies, the king would know that he was a powerful magician and would have him killed. So he said to the messenger, "How kind is our king! Even though he was tired from hunting all day, he still found time to think of his criminal minister. Long live His Majesty!"

He ate one of the meat pies. Then he ate another, then one more. The messenger watched him eat the pies but said nothing. Then he left and returned to Zhaoge. He went to the palace and said to the king, "The criminal Ji Chang thanked you many times for the meat pies. He ate three of them. Then he kowtowed and said, 'Long live His Majesty!' He kowtowed again and asked me to deliver his words to you."

The king smiled and said to Fei Zhong, "So, Ji Chang has

eaten the flesh of his own son. It looks like he is not a powerful magician at all, just an ordinary man. I think there is no danger if let him return home."

Fei Zhong replied, "Your Majesty, please be careful. I think Ji Chang is trying to trick you. He knew that you would kill him if he refused to eat the pies. It would be dangerous to allow him to return home. There is already trouble in the west, you don't want any more!"

The king said, "No man, not even a sage, could eat his own son's flesh. But maybe you are right. I will keep him in Youli."

Meanwhile, the soldiers and servants who had traveled with Bo Yikao to Zhaoge heard that their master had been killed. That night they all fled back to Qi. When they arrived home they told Ji Fa, the younger brother of Bo Yikao, what had happened to his older brother.

Ji Fa cried and said, "How could the king do such a thing? Even though my father has been a prisoner for seven years we have remained loyal to the king. But now the king has killed my older brother. The bond between king and his people has been broken."

Then one of Ji Fa's generals stood up and shouted, "It is time for us to fight! We must send an army to Zhaoge, get rid of this evil king, and bring peace to our country!"

But the Prime Minister, a man named San Yisheng, stood up and said, "Master, you should cut off that man's head. He is a fool and will cause us great trouble."

Ji Fa replied, "Why should I cut off the head of my general?"

San Yisheng said, "Think of your father Ji Chang. He has

been a prisoner for seven years, but he remains loyal to the king and he is alive. If you send an army to Zhaoge, the king will execute him before our army even reaches the city."

The room grew quiet as the ministers thought about this. Then San Yisheng continued, "You know that Ji Chang did a divination and told us he would be a prisoner for seven years. He told us not to send anyone to save him. But your older brother did not listen, and now he is dead. He should not have gone to Zhaoge. And he should have done things differently. He should have bribed the evil minister Fei Zhong. That way Fei Zhong would have spoken to the king and helped to free Ji Chang. Once Ji Chang was free, we could have raised an army and attacked the king."

Ji Fa said to San Yisheng, "You speak well, Prime Minister. Tell me what should we do now?"

"Send two of your best ministers. Have them wear the clothing of merchants. One of them should give valuable gifts to Fei Zhong. The other one should give valuable gifts to another minister, a man named You Hun. Both of them have the ear of the king. By bribing them both, you will make sure that the king does what we want."

Ji Fa agreed. Two of his ministers were given valuable gifts to bring to Zhaoge. They traveled over five passes and across the Yellow River and arrived at Zhaoge. They did not stay in the hostel used by ministers. Instead, they stayed at a small inn that was used by merchants.

The next evening, one of the ministers went to see Fei Zhong. Fei Zhong said to him, "Who are you and why are you here at this late hour?"

The minister replied, "Sir, please forgive me for coming

here so late in the evening. You have been very good to us and you have saved the life of our master Ji Chang. We are grateful to you. I have some small gifts for you. I also bring a letter from San Yisheng, the Prime Minister of West Qi."

The minister handed San Yisheng's letter to Fei Zhong. It said,

> *Supreme Minister Fei Zhong. I am sorry that I have never met you. But all of us in West Qi thank you for your help. Our master Ji Chang foolishly said some things which angered His Majesty. But because of your help, he is still alive and living in Youli. Please accept these small gifts as our way of thanking you. Also, please think about our master, who is old and sick and wishes to return home. If you could speak to the king about this, we would remember your kindness for ten thousand years.*

Fei Zhong looked at the gifts, which included 2,400 taels of gold and two pairs of white jade coins. "These gifts are very valuable!" he thought to himself. He told the minister to return to West Qi. He said he needed a bit of time to him think about how to help get Ji Chang released.

Meanwhile, the other minister had a similar meeting with You Hun. Satisfied, the two ministers returned to West Qi.

Fei Zhong and You Hun were both very happy with the bribes, but of course they did not say anything to each other about the meetings or the bribes.

A few days later, the king was relaxing, playing chess with Fei Zhong and You Hun. The king won all the games. Afterwards they had a feast. The king said, "I heard that Ji

Chang ate the flesh of his son. So of course, he is no magician."

Fei Zhong said, "Your Majesty, you know that I have never trusted Ji Chang. However, I sent some of my men to Youli to keep an eye on him. They tell me that Ji Chang is loyal to you. He burns incense for you on the first and the fifteenth of every month. He prays for your health and for peace in the kingdom. He has never said anything bad about you in seven years."

The king turned to You Hun and asked, "And what do you think of Ji Chang?"

You Hun had listened to Fei Zhong's words. Now he knew that Fei Zhong had also received bribes. He knew that he needed to do something more in order to earn the bribes that he had just received. So he said to the king, "I have also heard that Ji Chang has been loyal to Your Majesty. In seven years, he has done nothing to harm the country. Moreover, I think that Ji Chang could help us to win the wars that we are fighting in the east and south. Perhaps you could give him the title of Prince and put him in command of the dukes' armies. Once the rebels in the east and south hear of this, they will put down their weapons and go home."

The king was pleased to hear that his two most trusted ministers both agreed on this. He gave the order that Ji Chang be freed and should come to see him. A messenger went to Youli to tell Ji Chang.

Ji Chang said goodbye to the people of Youli and traveled to Zhaoge to see the king. He entered the palace, dressed in white because he was a criminal. He kowtowed to the king, saying, "The criminal Ji Chang should be executed for his

crimes, but Your Majesty has chosen to let me go home to
see my family again. May you live for ten thousand years!"

The king replied, "Ji Chang, you have been a prisoner for
seven years but have never said a word against me. You are
a loyal minister. I am letting you go home. I am also
naming you prince[1], the leader of all the dukes, so you can
use their armies to protect the kingdom. There will be a
great feast in your honor. After the feast, you may parade
through the streets for three days." Ji Chang kowtowed
again.

For the next two days, Ji Chang paraded through the
streets. Late on the second day, he saw a large group of
men on horseback coming from the other directions. He
saw that it was General Huang Feihu riding on his huge ox.
Ji Chang dismounted and bowed to Huang Feihu. Huang
Feihu dismounted from his ox, bowed to Ji Chang, and
invited him to come to his home later that evening.

The two men ate and drank for a while. Then Huang Feihu
said to Ji Chang, "My friend, I can see that you are happy
today. But you must see what is happening! Our king
spends all his days drinking and talking with evil ministers
like Fei Zhong. He spends all his nights playing with his
concubines. He has executed many loyal ministers. He has
thrown people into the pit of snakes. You must do
something about this! Stop parading through the streets.
Go back to Qi immediately and do something to help your
country!"

Ji Chang felt like he had just awakened from a dream. He
bowed and thanked Huang Feihu. He said, "Thank you, my

---

[1] Now that the king has named Ji Chang as a prince, the original book sometimes
refers to him as Prince Wen. But we will continue to call him Ji Chang.

friend. I will leave right away. But how can I get home?"

Huang Feihu replied, "I can help you. Put on the clothes of an army officer. Take these tiger tallies[1]," and he handed him some tallies. "You will be able to go through the five mountain passes with no trouble."

Ji Chang again bowed and thanked Huang Feihu. That night, Huang Feihu ordered his men to open the gates of the city. Ji Chang and a small group of soldiers left the city under cover of darkness.

---

[1] Tiger tallies, called *hǔfú*, were used in ancient China as a way for kings and emperors to authorize and delegate the power to generals to command and dispatch an army. The tiger was a symbol of courage.

Chapter 21
Flight Through Five Passes

Huang saved Ji Chang, he gave him a tally;
This allowed him to leave the king's land

You and Fei asked the king to stop him,
Help came from the clouds for the Qi lord

Good people usually don't live long in this world,
Now the flying dragon brings auspicious news

Ji Chang vomited his son's flesh,
But sweet fragrance remains in his mouth

Ji Chang did not return to his hostel that night. The officials at the hostel waited for him. When he did not appear, they went to tell Fei Zhong.

Fei Zhong went to see the king, but he was very afraid. He went to the Star Picking Mansion and kowtowed again and again before the king. Then he said, "Your Majesty, I must tell you that Ji Chang only finished two days of parading through the city streets. Now he is gone. Nobody knows where he is, but I think he has left the city."

The king was very angry. He said, "You told me that I should name him Prince and forgive his crimes!"

Fei Zhong continued to kowtow. Without raising his head, he said, "Your Majesty, who can understand the human heart? You know the saying, 'When the sea dries up you can see the bottom, but even when a man dies nobody can know what was in his heart.' The criminal Ji Chang has been gone for less than a day. There is still time to catch him. You can send soldiers to bring him back to Zhaoge, then you can cut off his head."

The king sent an army of three thousand soldiers on horses with orders to catch Ji Chang. The soldiers left the city through the west gate.

Ji Chang was in no hurry. He had crossed the Yellow River and was riding towards the first mountain pass. He rode slowly west, enjoying the beautiful weather. Suddenly he heard the sound of many horses behind him. Turning around, he saw a cloud of dust rising in to the air. "Oh no!" he said to himself. "I have been very foolish. That must be the king's army. If they capture me, I will be a dead man." Then he began riding westward as fast as he could, with the king's army close behind him.

Meanwhile, on Mount Zhongnan, the Master of Clouds was sitting outside his cave. He looked down and saw the army chasing Ji Chang. Quickly he called one of his disciples and told him to fetch Thunderbolt. A few minutes later Thunderbolt arrived and kowtowed to his master.

"Disciple," said Master of Clouds, "your father is in danger. You must go quickly and save him!"

"My father? Who is that?" asked Thunderbolt.

"Don't you remember? It is Ji Chang, the Grand Duke of the West. Go quickly to Tiger Cliff to find a weapon, then come back here to see me."

Thunderbolt left the cave and went to Tiger Cliff. He looked around but did not see any weapons. He was about to leave when he smelled something delicious. He followed the smell. He came to a little stream running down the mountain. It was a beautiful place. All around were trees and grasses. Foxes and deer wandered through the trees, and birds flew overhead. Looking up, he saw two red apricots hanging from a tree branch. He reached up and pulled the two apricots off the branch.

"I will eat one and give the other to my master," he thought. But when he ate one, it was so delicious that before he could stop himself he ate both of them.

A moment later, there was a loud "Pop" and a long wing suddenly appeared under his left arm. Then there was another loud "Pop" and another wing appeared under his right arm. Then his body began to change. His face turned a dark blue, his hair turned red, his teeth grew long and his eyes grew large. His body became twenty feet tall.

He stood there with no idea what was happening. Just then,

the disciple came up to him and said, "Brother, our master orders you to come immediately to see him."

Thunderbolt walked back to his master's cave. His head was down and his long wings dragged on the ground. Master of Clouds saw him. "Wonderful, wonderful!" he said. "Come with me."

They walked together to a nearby peach garden. Master of Clouds picked up a large golden cudgel. He handed it to Thunderbolt and started to teach him how to use it. Thunderbolt learned how to move the cudgel up and down, left and right, how to turn like a tiger of the forest, and how to rise like a dragon from the sea. The cudgel flew through the air, filling the air with bright light.

When he was finished, Master of Clouds wrote the word "Wind" on his left wing and "Thunder" on his right wing. Then he told his disciple, "These two words will let you fly through the heavens. Now go quickly and help your father get away from the soldiers. Help him go through the five passes. But you must not hurt any of the soldiers. When you are finished, return here so you can finish your studies."

Thunderbolt flew quickly down to earth. He saw a man in a black shirt on a galloping horse, with thousands of soldiers chasing him. He shouted to the man, "Are you the Grand Duke of the West?"

Ji Chang looked up and saw a huge bird holding a golden cudgel. He was terrified, but he shouted back, "Who are you? How do you know my name?"

Thunderbolt came down to the ground and kowtowed. "Forgive me, Father, I did not mean to frighten you."

Ji Chang had many sons, but none of them looked like this. He replied, "Why do you call me Father? I don't know you."

"My name is Thunderbolt. You found me in the forest seven years ago and made me your son. Now you are in danger. I can help you get through the five mountain passes and return safely to West Qi."

"All right. But you must not hurt or kill any of the soldiers. I am already in a lot of trouble; I don't want you to make it worse."

"Of course. My master told me the same thing." Then Thunderbolt flew into the sky. He flew back towards the army and came down to earth right in front of them. Waving the golden cudgel, he shouted, "Stop right there!"

The soldiers stopped. Some of them turned back. But the two generals shouted, "Attack!" and charged towards Thunderbolt.

Chapter 22
The Grand Duke Returns

Ji Chang returns home after eating his son;
His tears never dry

This do not change who he is;
He is still loyal to his king

No one can say what heaven has written;
But crimes always bring blood and ashes

It does not matter what happens on earth;
Heaven always decides who must leave and when

Thunderbolt saw the two generals coming towards him. He held up his golden cudgel and said to them, "My friends, please stop. My name is Thunderbolt. I am the hundredth and youngest son of Ji Chang, the Grand Duke of the West. He has been a loyal minister for his whole life. He is filial to his parents, he is loyal to his friends, he upholds the law and does his best to be a good subject of the king. But the king made him a prisoner for seven years. Recently the king set him free and allowed him to return home. So why are you chasing him and trying to capture him? My friends, you do not need to show your courage. Go back home and leave us in peace."

One of the generals laughed loudly and said, "You ugly beast! Your words are the words of a fool!" Then he rushed towards Thunderbolt, attacking him with his sword.

Thunderbolt easily blocked the sword with his golden cudgel. Then he said, "Please stop. I would enjoy fighting you, but my master and my father both told me not to hurt your or any of your soldiers. Before you attack me again, watch this."

While the generals watched, Thunderbolt jumped up into the sky. He landed on a side of a nearby mountain. He swung his golden cudgel at another mountain. With a loud roar the mountain split in half. He said to the generals, "Do you think your heads are stronger than that mountain?"

That was all the generals needed to see and hear. They turned and led their soldiers back to Zhaoge. Thunderbolt returned to his father and said, "I spoke with the generals and asked them to go home to Zhaoge. They are leaving now. Now it's time for me to take you home to West Qi."

"Thank you," said Ji Chang. "But what about my horse? He

has been my loyal servant for seven years."

"Father, the horse is not important. Let it go."

Sadly, Ji Chang patted the horse on its head. He said, "I don't want to leave you here, but the soldiers might come back again. Go now and find yourself another master." Then he climbed on Thunderbolt's back and closed his eyes. He felt the wind on his face as Thunderbolt jumped into the sky and flew quickly through the air. After a few minutes they had flown over all five mountain passes and arrived at Golden Chicken Mountain. Thunderbolt came down to earth and said, "Father, we have arrived. I must leave you here. Take care. I will see you again."

Ji Chang looked around. He said, "But son, we are not at West Qi City yet. We are still in the mountains far from the city. Why are you leaving me here?"

Thunderbolt replied, "I must leave you here, Father. My master ordered me to only take you beyond the five mountain passes. You must travel the rest of the way by yourself. I will join you later, when my magic is more powerful." He knelt down and kowtowed to his father. Then he jumped into the sky and flew back to Mount Zhongnan.

Having no horse to ride, Ji Chang turned and began walking west. He walked all day. He was an old man and was exhausted by the end of the day. Stopping at an inn by the side of the road, he ate some dinner and went to bed. But in the morning, he realized that he was not carrying any money. He could not pay for his food and his room.

The clerk, a young man, was very angry. He said, "How can you stay here and eat our food, then not pay for it?"

Ji Chang replied, "I am sorry, young man, but I have no money with me. All my money is in West Qi City. Please let me leave. I will be happy to pay you later."

The clerk said angrily, "You may not know this, but you are in the province of West Qi. Nobody here will steal from another person. The Grand Duke of the West rules with kindness and fairness. Everyone here lives in peace and happiness. Now you need to pay what you owe, or I will take you to see the Supreme Minister."

Just then, the innkeeper came to see why the two people were arguing. He looked carefully at the visitor and saw he was Ji Chang, the Grand Duke of the West. The innkeeper kowtowed and said, "Please forgive us, Your Highness. We had eyes but did not see you. I am the owner of this small inn. It has been in my family for over a hundred years. Please sit down and have some tea."

Ji Chang was happy. He said, "Sir, I am glad to meet you. Do you have a horse that I can ride to the city? I will of course pay you for it when I return."

"Your Highness, we are not wealthy people, we have no horses. But we have an old donkey. You can ride the donkey, and I will go with you to make sure you arrive safely at the city."

Ji Chang was pleased to hear this. Soon he and the innkeeper left the inn and began traveling west. They traveled for several days until they reached West Qi City. It was late autumn. The trees were turning from green to red, and cold winds blew. Ji Chang had been gone for seven years, and he missed his family.

In West Qi City, Ji Chang's mother was sitting at home. She felt a strange wind come in through the window. She did a divination and learned that her son was returning. Quickly she told her grandchildren and the ministers. They all came out of the city and waited in the road for Ji Chang to arrive.

Soon Ji Chang arrived, riding the innkeeper's donkey. His eldest son Ji Fa stepped forward. He said, "Father, you were a prisoner for seven years. Your children did nothing to help you. We are no better than criminals. Please forgive us. We are overjoyed to see you again!"

Ji Chang began to cry. He said, "My friends, my sons, I never thought that I would come home and see you again! I am very happy, but I can't help but feel a bit sad at the same time."

Supreme Minister San Yisheng stepped forward and said, "In ancient days, King Tang was also made a prisoner. He was kept in Xiatai for many years. When he was finally freed, he united the entire country and became the first king of the Shang Dynasty[1]. Now that you are home again, perhaps you will be like King Tang, and your years at Youli will be like his years in Xiatai."

But Ji Chang said, "Your words have no meaning for me. A loyal subject of the king would never do such a thing. I am a criminal, but His Majesty was kind to me and only imprisoned me for seven years. Now he has set me free, named me a prince, and ordered me to fight the rebels. I will never turn against our king. And I ask you to never

---

[1] King Jie was the last ruler of the Xia Dynasty, which was the first dynasty in China. It was said that he drank day and night with his concubines and made a lake of wine large enough to float full sized boats. Chen Tang led an uprising against Jie. Tang was exiled to Xiatai but was later released, He then led an army that deposed Jie and established the Shang dynasty in the 16th century B.C.

speak like that again."

He returned to his home to see his wife and his mother, then he put on his official robes. He rode his coach through the streets, greeting the people of West Qi City. Everyone in the city came out to see him. They sang, danced and shouted his name.

As he looked at the people, he thought of his son Bo Yikao. He remembered eating his son's flesh. He fell to the ground, screaming. His face turned as white as paper. Then his belly made a strange sound. He opened his mouth and vomited up a piece of meat. The meat fell onto the ground. Then it grew four feet and two long ears, turning into a rabbit. The rabbit ran towards the west and disappeared[1].

Ji Chang saw the rabbit run away. Then he vomited up three more pieces of meat. They also turned into rabbits and ran away towards the west.

The ministers took him to see his doctors, who told him to rest for a few days. After resting, he met with his ministers and told them the whole story of his imprisonment, his release by the king, and his escape back to West Qi with the help of Thunderbolt and the innkeeper. "Please make sure that the innkeeper is given a good amount of money to thank him for helping me," he said.

Then Supreme Minister San Yisheng tried one more time to get Ji Chang to rebel against the king. He said, "Master, two thirds of the kingdom and four hundred marquises are now in rebellion against the king. Now you have returned home like a dragon returning to the sea or a tiger returning

---

[1] The *Book of Documents*, one of the five classics of ancient Chinese literature, says that when Ji Chang vomited up his son's flesh, he created rabbits on earth. The Chinese words for rabbit (兔) and vomit (吐) are both pronounced *tù*.

to the mountain. This is the time for us to act."

One of his generals spoke up, saying, "My Lord, we need to act now. We have 400,000 soldiers and sixty generals. We should attack the mountain passes, surround Zhaoge, and cut off the heads of Daji and Fei Zhong. We can name a new king and bring peace to the kingdom."

But again, Ji Chang refused to turn against the king. He said, "You both have been loyal subjects, but now you both speak like criminals. How can you forget that the king is the head of the kingdom? A minister must be loyal to the king, just like a son must be filial to his father. Without thinking I spoke words against the king, and the king was right to punish me as he did. Now I am grateful to the king for letting me return home. I wish that the rebels would put down their weapons. Please stop this talk, and I hope I never hear you speak like this again."

The general replied, "What of your son Bo Yikao? He only went to Zhaoge to help you, and you know what the king did to him. We must have a new king!"

"No, my son caused his own death. I told him that I would be a prisoner for seven years, and I told him not to come and see me. He disobeyed my orders. He did not understand the situation. That is why he lost his life. Now that I have returned, my job is to help the people of West Qi to have a better life, not to start a war."

San Yisheng and the general listened to his words. They kowtowed to Ji Chang.

"Now," continued Ji Chang, "I want to build a new building, south of the city, to be called The Spiritual Terrace. It will be used for divination, to see the future. This will help the people of West Qi. But I'm afraid it will be too expensive."

"Please don't worry about that," said San Yisheng. "You have been good to the people. They are grateful to you and would be happy to help build it. And if want, you can pay them with silver and let them come and go as they wish."

This made Ji Chang very happy. He sat down and wrote the notice that would be put up on the gates of the city.

Chapter 23
Dream of a Flying Bear

Ji Chang is the king's loyal servant;
His loyal subjects are happy to work for him

They build the Spiritual Terrace;
He puts money in their pockets

West Qi stands on a strong foundation;
The king's empire drowns under the sea

No need to discuss the fate of Mengjin;
Everything is in the dream of the flying bear

Ji Chang's notice read:

West Qi is a peaceful land, but from time to time we have had floods and droughts here. We need a way to learn what the weather will be. For this reason, I wish to build a Spiritual Terrace in a place just west of the city. Many workers are needed for this project. If anyone wishes to work on this project, I will pay you one tenth of a tael of silver for each day of work. You may start and leave whenever you wish. If you do not want to work on this project, I will not order you or anyone else to do this.

The people of the city read the notice. They were happy to learn that the Spiritual Terrace would be built, and they were even happier to learn that they would be paid in silver to work on the project. Many workers stepped forward, and in just ten months the project was finished.

After the Spiritual Terrace was built, Ji Chang saw that the *yin* and *yang* were not quite correct. The terrace needed a pool of water on one side. He told this to San Yisheng. A short time later, a group of workers started to dig a hole for the pool. As they were digging, they found a skeleton buried in the ground. They told Ji Chang about the skeleton. He told the workers to go and bury the skeleton somewhere else.

By this time, it was late in the day. Ji Chang ate dinner on the Spiritual Terrace, then he decided to spend that night in a room on the terrace instead of returning to the palace.

That night he had a strange dream. In the dream, a big white tiger flew in from the southeast. It crashed into the room where Ji Chang was sleeping. Then there was a loud "Boom!" at the back of the terrace, and a bright white light shot into the sky.

Ji Chang woke up from the dream. He thought about it but he did not know what it meant. In the morning he asked San Yisheng about the dream.

"Your Highness," said San Yisheng, "this is a very good dream. The animal in your dream was not a tiger. It was a flying bear. This means that a great minister will soon come here and enter your service. The bright white light is the future peace and happiness of West Qi."

Ji Chang thanked him. Then he returned to his palace, thinking about who the great minister might be.

Meanwhile, let's return to Jiang Ziya. After he helped the people who were trying to leave Zhaoge, he went to live in a small hut in the forest. There was a river near the hut. Every day he sat on the ground, his back against a willow tree, and he fished. As he fished, he recited Daoist scriptures, and his mind was always on the Dao.

One day, as he was reciting Daoist scriptures and fishing, he heard a man nearby. The man was singing this song:

> *Over the hills and across the mountains*
> *The air is filled with the sound of my axe*
> *The axe is with me all the time*
> *I use it to cut away vines*
> *Rabbits run across the fields*
> *Birds sing in the trees*
> *I am just a happy woodcutter*
> *I have no money but I don't care*
> *I sell my wood to buy food*
> *I have rice, vegetables and good wine*
> *At night I sleep beneath the trees*

When the song was finished, the woodcutter walked up to Jiang Ziya. He dropped his firewood on the ground and sat down. He said, "Sir, I often see you fishing here. May I have a little chat with you?"

Jiang Ziya replied, "Yes, of course! A chat between a fisherman and a woodcutter, just like in the old stories![2]"

The woodcutter said, "Sir, my name is Wu Ji. Please tell me, what is your honorable name, and where do you come from?"

"My name is Jiang Ziya, but sometimes I am called Flying Bear."

Wu Ji laughed loudly. "My friend, great sages have two names. But you are nobody. You are just an old man who sits and fishes all day. You remind me of the man who waits all day for a rabbit to run into a tree and knock himself out. You don't look like a great sage to me."

Then the woodcutter looked closely at Jiang Ziya's fishing line. He laughed again and said, "My friend, you look old, but you have learned nothing in your years. Look at this fishing hook!" He held up the fishing hook in his hand. It was just a straight needle. "You may fish for a hundred

---

[1] This song is strikingly similar to the song of the woodcutter who Sun Wukong meets in Chapter 1 of *Journey to the West* (see our book, *The Rise of the Monkey King*).

[2] This conversation is very similar to the one between the fisherman and the woodcutter in Chapter 10 of *Journey to the West* (see our book, *The Emperor in Hell*). There are many stories and songs in Chinese folklore about a fisherman and a woodcutter discussing the meaning of life. Education was valued in ancient China, but Daoism stressed the value of living in simplicity and harmony with nature. Thus, educated people may talk at length without getting anywhere, but simple people such as these can quickly get to the heart of the matter.

years but you won't catch anything. Let me tell you what to do. First, make this needle red hot and bend it into a hook. Then put a bit of meat on it. Wait for a fish to bite, then quickly pull the fish out of the water."

Jiang Ziya just smiled at the woodcutter. He said, "You only know half of the story, my friend. I don't care about catching fish. I am waiting to catch a duke, or perhaps a king."

"So, you want to be a duke or a king? You look like a monkey to me."

"Well, I may not look like a duke or a king. But your face doesn't look very good either. Your left eye is a little bit green and your right eye is a little bit red. That tells me that you will kill a man in the city today."

Wu Ji stood up. He said, "We were just having a friendly chat. Why did you suddenly say such a terrible thing to me?" Then he picked up his firewood, turned, and walked away.

The woodcutter arrived at the city. He walked through the marketplace, trying to sell his firewood. Just then, Ji Chang was traveling through the marketplace on his way to the Spiritual Terrace. Guards rode ahead of him, shouting, "Get out of the way! Get out of the way!" Wu Ji turned quickly to get out of the way. He still had his load of firewood on his back. One long piece of firewood had a sharp end. As Wu Ji turned around, the firewood struck a city guard in the head, killing him instantly.

Other guards quickly arrested the woodcutter. Ji Chang stopped his horse. He looked down and asked the woodcutter, "Why did you do that?"

Wu Ji said, "I did not mean to kill that guard. I was trying to get out of the way. My wood swung around and hit the guard."

"I am sorry, but you killed a man. Now you must pay with your life. That is the law here in West Qi."

He ordered his men to draw a large circle on the ground. He ordered Wu Ji to stay inside the circle and wait there until it was time for his execution. This was the custom in West Qi. Since Ji Chang could know everything through divination, nobody, not even a criminal, would dare to try and escape the circle. They knew that they would be captured, and things would be much worse for them.

Wu Ji waited inside the circle for three days. He thought of his mother, who was waiting for him at home. He started to cry. Just then, San Yisheng passed by and saw the woodcutter crying. He said, "Why are you crying? It is the custom in West Qi for a killer to pay with his life. Crying will not change that."

Wu Ji replied, "Please forgive me, sir. I know that I must pay with my life. That is not why I am crying. I am thinking of my poor mother who is waiting for me at home. When I am executed there will be nobody to take care of her. She will die at home and her bones will remain unburied. Thinking about this breaks my heart."

San Yisheng thought about this. Then he said, "Don't cry. I will talk to His Highness about this. Perhaps you can go home, take care of your mother for a while, then come back later for your execution." Wu Ji kowtowed in thanks.

San Yisheng went to the Spiritual Terrace and talked with Ji Chang about the matter. Ji Chang agreed to let the woodcutter return home for a while. Wu Ji was allowed to leave the city and go home.

When he got home, his mother said, "My dear boy! Where have you been? I was afraid that a tiger had killed you on the mountain. I have not been able to eat or sleep for several days."

Wu Ji told her what had happened. He told her about meeting the old man who fished with a straight needle. Then he told her about the old man's divination, and the killing in the marketplace.

She said to him, "My boy, that was no ordinary fisherman. He was a great sage. You must go back to him and beg him to save your life."

Wu Ji thanked his mother. Then he went looking for Jiang Ziya.

Chapter 24
From Fisherman to Prime Minister

Jiang Ziya left busy Zhaoge to rest here,
where green waters surround the hills

He reads Daoist books to pass the time;
Three golden fish smile at him

Birdsong fills the air;
He listens to the sound of the stream

The garden is covered with morning dew;
It waits for the arrival of Ji Chang

Wu Ji went to the stream where he had seen the fisherman earlier. There, sitting under a tree, was Jiang Ziya. Wu Ji walked up quietly behind him. Without turning around, Jiang Ziya said, "Aren't you the woodcutter I met a few days ago?"

"Yes sir," said Wu Ji, "I am."

"Did you kill someone that day?"

Wu Ji threw himself down on the ground and cried. He told Jiang Ziya everything that had happened in the city that day. Then he said, "When autumn comes, I must go back to the city. I will be executed for killing that man. There will not be anyone left to care for my mother, and I fear that she will die soon afterwards. I beg you, please save us!"

Jiang Ziya said, "This is your fate. Fate is hard to change. You killed a man, so now you must pay with your life. What can I do?" But Wu Ji continued to cry. Finally, Jiang Ziya said, "All right, I will save you. But you must become my disciple."

Wu Ji kowtowed and agreed. Jiang Ziya continued, "Now that you are my disciple, I must help you. Go home and dig a hole next to your bed. Make it four feet deep. Sleep in it tonight. Tell your mother to throw a few grains of rice on top of you. That's it. You will have no more trouble."

Wu Ji ran home and told his mother. "We must do as the sage commands!" she said. Wu Ji dug the hole as his master had ordered him to, his mother threw some rice on top of him, and he slept in the hole that night. That same night, Jiang Ziya said some magic words to cover up Wu Ji's star so that nobody could see it in heaven.

The next day, Wu Ji returned. Jiang Ziya said, "I don't want you to spend all your time cutting wood. Every afternoon you must study military strategy. If you do this, you will become a minister. Remember what the ancients say: 'No one is born a general or minister; a person must work hard to get ahead in life.' "

Meanwhile, San Yisheng was thinking about the woodcutter. He said to Ji Chang, "Do you remember that woodcutter, the one who killed the guard? I let him go home to care for his mother. But he has not returned. I wonder what happened to him."

Ji Chang did a divination. He said, "Ah, I see. The woodcutter threw himself into a deep pool of water and drowned. So he is dead. There's nothing else we need to do now."

Winter came and went, and spring arrived. One day Ji Chang said that he wanted to get out of the city and enjoy the beautiful weather. He rode out of the east gate on his horse, accompanied by his ministers and hundreds of soldiers. As they rode, they saw colorful flowers, tall grasses, and beautiful birds. Farmers worked in the fields, and young girls picked tea leaves.

After a while they came to a hill. Ji Chang saw that his soldiers had arrived there before him and had killed a large number of deer, foxes and tigers. The ground was red with their blood. Ji Chang was very unhappy when he saw this. He said to his prime minister, "This is not right. You know that the ancient emperor Fuxi did not eat meat[1]. Fuxi said, 'People eat meat when they are hungry, they drink blood

---

[1] Fuxi is a mythical emperor, the brother and husband of the goddess Nüwa. It is said that he created humanity and invented music, hunting, fishing and cooking.

when they are thirsty. But I only eat grain because I want all creatures to live in peace.' Here we are, enjoying the beautiful weather. How can we enjoy ourselves when animals suffer because of us?"

San Yisheng bowed. He told the soldiers to stop killing animals.

A little while later, they saw some people sitting by a stream, drinking and singing. Some of them were singing this song:

> *Remember King Tang[1] who killed the tyrant*
> *It was the will of heaven and the people*
> *King Tang brought peace to the land*
> *Six hundred years ago*
> *Today we have another tyrant*
> *He loves wine, women and killing*
> *While his people go hungry*
> *Deer Terrace is covered with blood*
> *I wash my ears clean of power and money*
> *Every day I sit by the stream and fish*
> *Every night I study the stars*
> *I will live with no worries at all*
> *Until my hair turns white*

"That is a well written song!" said Ji Chang. "Go find out who wrote it." One of his generals rode his horse over to the group of singers and asked them who wrote the song.

One of them told him, "The song was written by an old fisherman. He lives about thirty-five *li* from here, next to a stream. He fishes there every day. We heard him singing

---

[1] This is Cheng Tang, the first king of the Shang Dynasty and mentioned in Chapter 22. He overthrew King Jie, a tyrant and the last king of the Xiao Dynasty.

the song there."

Ji Chang said to San Yisheng, "Did you hear the words, 'I wash my ears clean of power and money'? It reminds me of a story about the ancient emperor Yao. He had a son but the son was worthless. So he searched for a good man to be the next emperor. One day he found a man sitting by a stream and playing with a golden ladle in the water. He asked the man what he was doing. The man said, 'I have walked away from fame, money and family. I only want to live here in the forest.' Yao said, 'Sir, I am the emperor. I see you are a good man. I do not want my worthless son to be the next emperor. Would you please take this job?' The man immediately jumped into the stream and started washing his ears in the water."

San Yisheng laughed, and the two men continued riding and enjoying the weather. Soon they came to a group of woodcutters singing this song:

> *When dragons rise in the air, clouds appear*
> *When tigers come, the wind blows*
> *But no one comes to see me*
> *Remember Yi Yin who worked in the fields[1]*
> *He waited for King Tang to find him*
> *Remember Fu Yue, poor and forgotten[2]*
> *He waited for King Gaozong to dream of him*
> *Since ancient times, some people become famous*
> *While others remain forgotten and poor*

---

[1] According to legend, Yi Yin was a farmer living in obscurity. King Tang had to ask him five times to join his government. He became a high official in Tang's government.

[2] Gaozong was the temple name of Emperor Wu Ding of the Shang Dynasty. He dreamed that he would meet a sage named Yue, and sent officials throughout the land to find him. Fu Yue was discovered in a woodshed and became Chancellor in Wu Ding's government.

I spend my life here by the stream
Resting under the sunshine
While kings and dukes fall
I look to the heavens and smile
While waiting for a wise ruler

Once again, Ji Chang though this was a good song. He sent his general to ask who wrote it. The woodcutters told the general that the song was written by an old fisherman who lived by a nearby stream.

"We should go and see this old fisherman," said Ji Chang. But just then, a woodcutter came. He was carrying firewood and singing this song:

In the spring, waters flow without end
In the spring, grasses are beautiful
The goldfish have never seen Yinpan River
The world does not know me
They think I am just a fisherman
Sitting by the stream all day

"This must be the sage we were looking for!" said Ji Chang.

But San Yisheng looked at the woodcutter and said, "Your Highness, this is no sage. This is Wu Ji, the man who killed your guard in the marketplace last year."

Ji Chang said, "It cannot be. My divination said that the woodcutter killed himself last year." But he agreed that the man was Wu Ji. He ordered the woodcutter arrested. Then he said angrily, "How dare you run away and try to escape your fate!"

Wu Ji threw himself on the ground and kowtowed to Ji Chang. He said, "Your Highness, I have always been a good man. When you set me free, I went to see an old fisherman named Jiang Ziya. They also call him Flying Bear. He took me as his disciple and let me live and work without fear. Sir, even ants and worms try to live as long as they can. Shouldn't men do the same?"

Ji Chang discussed the matter with San Yisheng. Then he let Wu Ji go and asked him to take them to meet the old fisherman. They all rode to the stream, but when they arrived the old fisherman was not there. They went to his small house nearby, but the servant boy said that the old fisherman was not at home and he did not know when his master would return.

San Yisheng said to Ji Chang, "Your Highness, I think we are doing this wrong. You know that when the ancient emperors went to meet great sages, they did not just go. They selected a good day, they washed, and they did not eat meat. We should go home and do these things correctly."

Ji Chang agreed with this plan. They returned to the city. Ji Chang ordered his ministers to spend three days preparing for their second visit to the stream. On the fourth day, they put on their best robes and returned to the stream. Ji Chang rode in his carriage.

When they got close to the stream, Ji Chang told everyone to stop and wait. He got down from his carriage and walked quietly to the stream. He saw Jiang Ziya sitting by the stream, fishing. Ji Chang stood quietly behind him. Jiang Ziya was singing this song:

> *The wind blows from the west*
> *White clouds fly in the sky*
> *Where will I be at the year's end?*
> *Five phoenixes sing as my master comes*

When he stopped singing, Ji Chang said softly, "Are you truly happy?"

Jiang Ziya turned around and saw the prince. He threw himself to the ground and said, "Please forgive me, Your Highness, I did not know you were here."

Ji Chang helped him to stand up and said, "I have been looking for you. I was here once before, but I was not prepared to meet you. Now I have prepared, and here you are. I am very happy to meet you."

"Your Highness, I am an old man. I know nothing of how to be a minister or a general. You should not have wasted your time coming to see me."

San Yisheng said, "These days, the nation is troubled. Our king spends his days drinking wine and playing with his concubines. He treats his people worse than dogs. He has killed two of the four Grand Dukes. Many of the marquises have risen up against him. My master has come today with gifts, hoping that you will help him rule the nation." Then he put the gifts on the ground in front of Jiang Ziya. "Please," he said, "get onto His Highness's carriage and come with us back to the palace."

But Jiang Ziya would not get into the carriage. He said, "I am a man of low rank, how could I possibly ride in His Highness's carriage?"

Ji Chang and San Yisheng tried to get him to ride the carriage, but he refused. Finally, they asked if Jiang Ziya would ride on the horse that pulled the carriage. He agreed. In that way they all rode back to the palace.

When they arrived at the palace, Ji Chang named Jiang

Ziya prime minister of West Qi. Jiang Ziya was eighty years old when he began his work as prime minister. He did his job well. West Qi was peaceful and the people were happy.

News of Jiang Ziya's new job reached the commander of one of the nearby mountain passes. He sent a messenger to Zhaoge to tell the king what was happening in West Qi.

Chapter 25
A Feast for Demons

The Deer Terrace was built for the gods;
Only demons came to the feast

Ordinary people cannot escape the ordinary world[1];
How can a mortal mind see past the mortal trap?

If you try to trick a wise man,
Your evil actions will only make things worse

Only a fool like this king would obey evil Daji
And kill the virtuous

---

[1] In the original poem, this line reads "Muddy bones cannot escape the muddy world." Muddy bones means an ordinary person, as opposed to a saintly person who is clear and beyond worldly things.

The messenger rode for several days until he arrived at the capital city. He gave his report to Bi Gan, the Prime Minister and the king's uncle. Bi Gan went immediately to see the king in the Star Picking Mansion.

"Your Majesty," said Bi Gan, "I have just heard that Ji Chang, the Grand Duke of the West, has named Jiang Ziya as his prime minister. This is bad. You know that the Grand Duke of the East and the Grand Duke of the South are already rebelling against us. In the north, Grand Tutor Wen is busy fighting rebels there. If Ji Chang also rises up against us, we will be in serious trouble."

The king listened. But before he could say anything, an attendant came in to tell the king that Chong Houhu, the Grand Duke of the North, wanted to see him. The king told the attendant to bring him in.

"Your Majesty," said Chong Houhu, "you ordered me to build the Deer Terrace. I am happy to tell you that after two years and four months, the project is finished."

"That is wonderful!" said the king. "As long as you are here, we have to tell you something. We just heard that Ji Chang has named Jiang Ziya as the prime minister of West Qi. What should I do about that?"

Chong Houhu laughed. "Don't worry about him, Your Majesty. I know that man. He is like a frog at the bottom of a well[1]. He knows very little and he can do nothing to harm us. If you sent your army to fight him, all the marquises would just laugh at you."

---

[1] There is a well known Chinese folk tale of a conceited frog who lived at the bottom of a well. The frog thought he knew everything about the world, but in fact he only knew what little he could see by looking up at the sky from the well.

"You are right of course," said the king. "Now, we would like to take a look at the Deer Terrace. We will take the queen to go and see it. You and Bi Gan may join us there."

A short time later, the king and Daji rode in the royal carriage to the Deer Terrace, followed by dozens of servants and maids. It really was a beautiful building. The towers were tall and covered with blue tile roofs. Inside the building were several halls. Each hall had bright white pearls set into the ceiling, so it looked like a night sky full of stars. Everything in the halls was made of jade and gold.

The king loved it. But Bi Gan thought only about the huge cost of the project, and all the workers who had died building it. He thought, "The paintings on the walls are made from the blood of the people, and the halls are built from the spirits of the dead."

The king ordered a big feast with music and dancing. He said to Daji, "My love, do you remember what you said to us? You said that when the Deer Terrace was finished, immortals would come down from heaven to visit us there. Now the Deer Terrace is finished. When do you think the immortals will come?"

Of course, Daji knew nothing at all about immortals, and she had no idea how to call them. She had just said this to trick the king into building the Deer Terrace. She needed some time to come up with a plan. "Your Majesty," she said to him, "the immortals cannot come now. They will come when the moon is full and the sky is clear."

"There will be a full moon in five days," he replied. "Let's come back then and meet the immortals." He was hungry for Daji, so he took her to their bed and played with her the rest of the night.

For the next four days Daji thought about how to trick the king into thinking that immortals were coming to visit. On the fourth night she gave the king a lot of wine. He fell asleep. As soon as he was asleep the fox demon came out of Daji's body. It flew on a gust of wind to the cemetery where the grave of Emperor Xuanyuan was, thirty-five *li* outside of the city. Dozens of powerful demons lived there.

One of the demons, Nine Headed Pheasant Demon, greeted her. It said, "My dear, why are you coming to visit us here? I thought you were enjoying life in the royal palace and had forgotten all about us."

"My old friend," replied the fox demon, "I have not forgotten about you. The king has built a Deer Terrace and wants to meet immortals there. I would like you and the other demons to change your appearance so you look like immortals. Then come to the Deer Terrace when the moon is full tomorrow night."

Nine Headed Pheasant Demon said, "I am sorry but I cannot come tomorrow night, I have to do some other things. However, thirty-nine of the demons here are powerful enough to change their appearance. They will all come to your Deer Terrace tomorrow night."

Daji thanked her and returned to the palace. In the morning she told the king, "Your Majesty, tonight is the full moon. Thirty-nine immortals will come to the Deer Terrace. If you meet them, you will have a long and happy life."

The king was pleased to hear this. He told Bi Gan to come to the Deer Terrace that night. Bi Gan thought this was a stupid idea, but he said he would come.

That night, the king, Daji and Bi Gan came to the Deer

Terrace, accompanied by dozens of servants and maids. A great feast was prepared. They sat and waited in the cool evening with the stars shining overhead. Finally, the moon rose in the eastern sky. A great wind began to blow, thick clouds covered the sky, and the earth became cold from heavy fog. Then up in the sky, thirty-nine immortals appeared. Of course, they were not really immortals; they were demons. Some of them were hundreds of years old. These demons had eaten the *qi* of heaven, earth, sun and moon, and had the ability to change their appearance. Now they all looked like Daoist sages. They wore robes of blue, yellow, red, white and black.

One of the demons called out, "Today we are honored to come to this feast given by the King of Shang. May his dynasty last a thousand years!"

The king told Bi Gan to walk out onto the terrace and serve them wine. Bi Gan saw thirty-nine Daoist sages sitting in chairs, in three rows of thirteen chairs each. "How strange!" he thought. "They really do look like immortals."

He greeted the demons and offered them wine from a golden pitcher. They looked beautiful. But although they could change their appearance, they could not change their smell. They smelled bad, like foxes. Bi Gan smelled them and thought, "Immortals are beautiful and smell clean. These are beautiful but they smell terrible. I think these might be demons."

He gave each of the demons more wine to drink. The fox demons had never tasted the king's wine before, and it was very strong. As they drank the wine, they became drunk. They began to lose their ability to change their appearance. Their fox tails reappeared and could be seen hanging out of their robes. Bi Gan saw this. "Oh no," he thought, "here I am serving wine to a bunch of fox demons." He finished serving the wine. Then as quickly as he could, he left the Deer Terrace and mounted his horse. Two attendants rode ahead of him, holding red lanterns to light the way.

As he rode away from the terrace, he met general Huang Feihu riding towards him. He told Huang Feihu, "My friend, I was just on the Deer Terrace with His Majesty and Daji. I was serving wine to thirty-nine immortals. But then I learned that they were not immortals at all, but evil demons. I could see their fox tails by the light of the moon. What should I do?"

"Don't worry," replied Huang Feihu, "I will take care of this matter. You go home and go to bed."

Huang Feihu ordered his men to watch the gates leading out of the city. He told them to watch for demons walking or flying away from the Deer Terrace. If they saw any, they were to follow them to see where they were going.

A short time later, the feast was over and the fox demons all left the Deer Terrace. They were very drunk and had difficulty flying. Several of them fell to the ground. They walked slowly, in groups of three and five, back to their home at the grave of Emperor Xuanyuan. The soldiers saw this and reported it back to Huang Feihu.

The next morning, Huang Feihu ordered three hundred of his soldiers to carry firewood to the grave, and to build a big fire at the hole where the fox demons had gone. They lit the fire and watched as it burned. When the fire had burned out, the soldiers pulled out the bodies of the dead fox spirits. The air was filled with smoke and the smell of burned flesh.

Huang Feihu told his men to collect the dead foxes that did not have any burns on them. He told them to skin them and make a fur robe for the king. He thought, "This will make the king happy because it will show that we are loyal. It will also be a warning to Daji."

But there is an old saying, "Mind your own business and you will have no trouble, but your nose into other people's business and disaster will follow."

Chapter 26
Daji Plots Revenge

On a windy and snowy night,
Bi Gan tried to give a gift and change the king's mind

He wanted to remove evil from the king's heart,
But now he is the demon's next target

The heart of Daji's demon is as cold as ice;
People will speak of its evil for ten thousand years

Too bad the Shang dynasty has come to this;
It has become like rain lost in springtime's flowing river

Winter had arrived. Strong winds came from the north, and heavy snow covered the capital city of Zhaoge like a blanket of silver pearls. The wealthy sat around their stoves, eating hot soup and keeping warm. The poor had no rice to eat and no firewood for their stoves.

The king and Daji were sitting together in the Deer Terrace, drinking wine. An attendant arrived, saying, "Bi Gan is here. He wants to see you."

The king told the attendant to bring him in. When Bi Gan came into the room, the king said, "Uncle, it is cold and snowing. Why don't you stay home where it is warm?"

"Your Majesty," said Bi Gan, "the Deer Terrace is so high that it reaches all the way to heaven. It must be cold here. I brought you something to keep you warm." Then he gave the king the fox skin robe. The king put it on.

"Thank you, uncle," he said. "We have never seen such a beautiful robe." Then he invited Bi Gan to have some wine and enjoy the Deer Terrace with him.

When Daji saw the robe that was made from the skins of the fox demons, she felt like a sword had been pushed into her heart. She thought, "I will kill you, Bi Gan, you old bastard." But she did not show her anger to the king. Instead, she smiled at him and said, "Your Majesty, you are a great king, the dragon of this land. How can you wear a robe made from such a low animal as a fox?"

"You are right, my dear," replied the king. He took off the robe and gave it to his attendants.

Daji thought for several days about how to have her revenge on Bi Gan. Then one day she had an idea. While she was with the king, drinking wine, she changed her appearance so that she was not as beautiful as before. The king looked at her with a confused look on his face. Daji looked up at him and asked, "Why are you looking at me like that?"

The king said, "Because you are as lovely as flowers and as beautiful as jade. We want to hold you in our arms and never let you go." But he did not mean these words. He really was wondering why his concubine was now so unattractive.

"Oh, Your Majesty, I am not beautiful. But you should meet my sworn younger sister, Hu Ximei. She is a hundred times more beautiful than I am."

"Oh, I would like to meet her!" said the king.

"She is a nun. She has spent years in a mountain cave studying the Way. She lives at the Purple Sky Nunnery. I remember that she once told me, 'If you ever want to see me, just burn some incense and speak my name. I will come to you right away.' "

"Please, my dear, burn some incense and bring her here!"

"We must do this correctly, Your Majesty. Tomorrow night I will wash my body, then I will put out tea and fruit on a table in the moonlight. Then I will burn the incense."

Later that night, during the fourth watch while the king was asleep, the fox demon slipped out of Daji's body. It went to the grave of Emperor Xuanyuan to meet Nine Headed Pheasant.

When Nine Headed Pheasant saw the Thousand Year Old Fox Demon, she was very angry. "You asked my sisters to come to your Deer Terrace, and I helped you. That night they were all killed! This is your fault."

Thousand Year Old Fox Demon cried with her and said, "I am so sorry, my sister. But don't worry, we will have our revenge." Then she told Nine Headed Pheasant her plan. Nine Headed Pheasant listened and agreed to the plan.

The next day, the king could not think of anything but meeting Daji's beautiful sister. He waited all day. Finally, the moon rose in the sky. He and Daji went up to the Deer Terrace. Daji said to the king, "Your Majesty, please understand that my sister is an immortal and also a nun. If she comes here and sees you, she might be frightened. Please go and wait in another room."

The king agreed. Daji washed her hands. Then she burned some incense and called out the name of her sister. Soon the wind began to blow, dark clouds covered the moon, and fog filled the air. It became very cold. Then they heard a sound like the tinkling of jade. "Here comes Hu Ximei, riding on the wind and the clouds!" cried Daji.

The king waited in the next room, watching through the curtains. The clouds disappeared and the moon came out again. In the moonlight he saw a Daoist nun. She wore a pink robe, a silk belt, and shoes made of hemp. Her face was as white as snow, her mouth was small and red, her cheeks were like peaches. She was the most beautiful woman the king had ever seen. The king thought that Daji was pretty, but Hu Ximei was like a goddess from heaven, like Chang'e come from the Palace of the Moon. His heart beat fast and he felt hot. "If I could sleep with Hu Ximei, I would be happy to give up my throne," he thought.

The two women were talking and sipping tea. Daji ordered a vegetarian feast, and the two of them ate together. They knew that the king was watching and listening, so Hu Ximei did everything she could to increase the king's desire for her. Watching her, the king could not sit still. Finally, he coughed to tell Daji that he could not wait any longer.

"Dear sister," said Daji, "I must ask you something. Please don't be angry with me."

"Of course, my dear," replied Hu Ximei.

"I have told His Majesty of your great virtue. He would like to meet you. But he wanted me to ask you first, to see if that was all right with you."

"Oh, sister," said Hu Ximei, "I don't think I could meet him. I am a nun, as you know. It would be against the rules for me to sit at the same table with him."

"No," said Daji. "You are not just a nun, you are now an immortal. You have moved beyond the rules of the three realms[1]. Besides, our king is the Son of Heaven. He has the right to meet with anyone he wants to. And remember, you and I are sworn sisters, so the king is really your brother-in-law. There's nothing wrong with meeting with a close relative!"

Hu Ximei nodded her head and said, "Then I will do as you ask."

As soon as he heard this, the king came out. He bowed to her. They greeted each other. Then he sat down, giving Daji and Hu Ximei the seats of honor. He stared at Hu Ximei, and she looked back at him, a hungry look in her eyes.

---

[1] The three realms as defined in Buddhism are the realm of sensuous desire (*kāma*), the realm of the material world (*rūpa-dhāt*), and the realm of formlessness (*rūpa-dhātu*).

Daji knew that the king was drunk with desire. She stood up and said, "Your Majesty, please excuse me. I must go and change my clothes. Please keep my sister company for a while."

After Daji left, the king poured wine for Hu Ximei. He gave her the cup. She said softly, "You are too kind, Your Majesty."

The king felt like he was on fire. He asked her to take a walk with him on the terrace. She agreed. They walked out in the moonlight, with Hu Ximei's hand on the king's arm. She leaned her body against him, and he could feel the heat from her body.

"My dear," said the king, "leave that nunnery and live here in the palace with your sister! Life is short, and you will be very happy here. You will have wealth, power, and pleasure." She said nothing, but continued to keep her body close to his.

Seeing no resistance, the king picked her up and carried her to a nearby room. He set her down gently on a bed and took off her clothes. Then the clouds and rain came[1].

Afterwards, as they put their clothes back on, Daji came in. She smiled and said to them, "Well, what have you two been doing?"

"We just made love," said the king. "This was fated by heaven. From now on, the two of you will live here with me." He ordered another feast. After they finished, he

---

[1] According to legend, the lady Yaoji died unmarried, was buried at Wushan and became a goddess. Later, the king of Song was traveling through the area. He dozed off under a canopy and dreamed of her sharing a pillow with him. She left him with this poem: "Dawn is the clouds, dusk is the rain, day and night, under the canopy." Over time, "clouds and rain" became a metaphor for lovemaking.

made love to both of them again.

For days, the king did not leave the room where he lay with Daji and her sister. They spent every day making love, singing, and drinking wine.

But one day, Daji cried out. She fell to the floor, spitting up blood. The king said to Hu Ximei, "I have never seen this before. What is going on?"

"Oh, her old illness has come back. When we were together in Jizhou, she had an illness of the heart. She almost died. The doctor helped her by giving her a special soup, made from a human heart that had seven openings."

"We must do that," said the king. "But where can we find someone who has a heart with seven openings?"

"Your Majesty, I can find out by divination."

"Do it at once!" said the king.

Hu Ximei moved her fingers as if she was doing a divination. After a minute she said, "Your Majesty, there is only one person in Zhaoge with this kind of heart, but I don't think he will want to give it up. It is your minister, Bi Gan."

"That is wonderful! Bi Gan is my uncle. He should be happy to give up a bit of his heart to let my queen live." He ordered Bi Gan to come see him immediately.

Bi Gan was at home when a messenger arrived to order him to come to the palace. "That's strange," he said to himself. "There is nothing going on in court. Why does the king want to see me?" Then another messenger arrived, and another. Finally, when the sixth messenger arrived, Bi Gan asked him what was going on. The messenger explained about the arrival of Hu Ximei, Daji's strange illness, and the divination.

Bi Gan was frightened. He went to say goodbye to his wife. "My dear," he said, "the evil concubine Daji is ill, and the idiot king wants to use my heart to cure her. I don't think you will see me alive again."

"Husband," said his wife, crying, "you have never done anything to cause the king to want you dead. How can he send you to such a cruel death?"

His son came in. He was also crying. He said, "Father, don't worry. Jiang Ziya knew that this would happen. He left a note for you." Then he handed the note to his father.

Bi Gan read the note. Then he burned the note and mixed the ashes with water. He drank it. Then he put on his official robes and rode his horse to the palace.

When he arrived at the palace, the other ministers asked him what was going on. He replied that the king needed his heart, but that he did not understand the real reason. Then he went up to the Deer Terrace to meet with the king.

The king said, "Uncle! Our queen is very ill. She can only be cured by drinking soup made from a special heart, one with seven openings. You are the only one in the kingdom with such a heart. Please give us a small piece of it."

Bi Gan said, "How can I live if my heart is damaged? You are a foolish dog and you are not thinking clearly. Too much wine and too much sex, I think. If you kill me, that will be the end of your dynasty!"

The king shouted at him, "If the king demands your death, you must die. Now do as I command, or I will have my guards remove your heart!"

Bi Gan asked one of the guards for a sword. He said to the king, "When I die, I will meet the ancient kings in heaven. I have nothing to fear from them. Can you say the same?" He kowtowed towards the Ancestral Temple. Then he opened up his official robe. He pushed the sword into his own chest, making a large hole. He reached into the hole, pulled out his own heart, and threw it on the ground. Not a single drop of blood came from the wound.

Everyone stared at him. He stood up straight, closed up his robe, and left the terrace without saying another word.

As he walked out of the Deer Terrace, the other ministers shouted, "Bi Gan, how did it go with the king?" But he did not reply. He walked past them, mounted his horse, and rode towards the north gate of the capital city.

Chapter 27
The Grand Tutor Returns

The dynasty's birth and death are already written;
Nothing can change its fate

One minute the ministers discuss peace,
The next minute the armies start fighting again

Mortals try but they cannot change fate;
The gods decide the direction their lives will go

Evildoers are always punished in the end;
They try to escape but heaven does not listen

Bi Gan rode away from the city quickly, the wind whistling past his ears. After riding for a few *li*, he heard a woman selling cabbages by the side of the road. She called out, "Tasty cabbages, sir. They have no heart!"

Bi Gan stopped his horse. He said to her, "But what if a man has no heart?"

"A man with no heart will die at once!" she replied. As soon as Bi Gan heard this, he cried out and fell from his horse. Blood poured out from his chest. The woman ran away as fast as she could.

What happened here? Bi Gan was alive because of the magic in the note that Jiang Ziya had written. The magic protected Bi Gan from harm, but the magic only worked if Bi Gan believed that it would work. If the cabbage selling woman had said something like, "A man can live even without a heart," Bi Gan would have continued to live. But she said that he would die. He believed her, and he died.

A few minutes later, two generals arrived. They had been sent by Huang Feihu, who had ordered them to follow Bi Gan. They saw Bi Gan's dead body on the ground. They turned around and rode as fast as they could to tell Huang Feihu and the other ministers what had happened.

One of the ministers, a young Confucian scholar named Xiao Zhao, was furious. "That tyrant killed his own uncle!" he cried. "That goes against the law and everything that is right. I am going to see him right now." He ran right into the Deer Terrace, not even asking permission.

The king was in the Deer Terrace, waiting for Daji's heart soup to be prepared. He looked up and saw Xiao Zhao. "What do you want?" he asked.

The young scholar said, "I am here to kill you!"

The king laughed. "I don't think a junior minister is permitted to kill a king."

"Oh, and is a king permitted to kill his own uncle in order to make soup? Bi Gan was your uncle, the younger brother of your father. You and that bitch Daji have broken the law. You are an evil tyrant, and I am going to kill you now!"

He grabbed a sword and ran towards the king. But the king was a very good fighter. He easily stepped aside, and Xiao Zhao's sword only stabbed the air. The king's guards ran towards Xiao Zhao. But before they could grab him, Xiao Zhao ran to the edge of the terrace and jumped to his death.

Meanwhile, Bi Gan's body was brought back to the city. Funeral preparations were made.

At the same time, the great general Grand Tutor Wen was returning to the city, riding his great black unicorn. He had just finally defeated the rebels at the North Sea. As he approached the city, he saw the flags of a funeral procession. "Whose funeral is this?" he asked.

"Bi Gan," said someone.

Grand Tutor Wen entered the city. He looked around. He saw the huge Deer Terrace. He saw the two tall yellow pillars. Then he entered the Grand Hall of the palace and saw the dust on the king's desk. "Everything has changed around here!" he said. "What are those yellow pillars?"

Huang Feihu replied, "They are called burning pillars. They are hollow and made of brass. If anyone does something that the king does not like, a great fire is built inside the pillars. When the pillars are red hot, the prisoner is tied against the pillars, face first. They are quickly burned to ash. In this way, many good men have died, and many more have left the city."

Grand Tutor Wen has furious. He had a third eye in his forehead. All three of his eyes became bright with anger, and a white light came out of his third eye. He shouted, "Strike the bells and ask His Majesty to come to the main hall!"

Back at the Deer Terrace, the king was resting with Daji. She had drunk the heart soup and appeared to quickly recover from her illness. An attendant came in and said, "Your Majesty, Grand Tutor has returned from the North Sea. He wants you to come to the main hall."

The king was silent for a minute. Then he said, "I will come."

An hour later, the king entered the main hall. He said to Grand Tutor, "You have defeated the rebels at North Sea. We are truly grateful to you."

"Thank you, Your Majesty," Grand Tutor Wen replied. "For fifteen years I have fought monsters, demons, rebels and thieves. You know that I will do anything to serve my king and my country. But I have heard that there is trouble here in Zhaoge. I have also heard that several dukedoms have rebelled. This worried me, and that's why I have returned. Please tell me what's going on."

"Two of the grand dukes, Jiang Huanchu and E Chongyu, were working together to kill me and take the throne. So I had them executed. Now their sons have risen up in rebellion."

"Who else heard Jiang Huanchu and E Chongyu saying that

they wanted to kill you?" The king had no answer to this.

"What are those yellow pillars?"

"We use them when ministers are disloyal."

"What is that huge new building?"

"We go up there in the heat of summer. It is cool there and we have a nice view of the city."

Grand Tutor Wen became angry. He said, "Now I understand why the dukedoms are rebelling against you. You have failed in your duty to the nation. You do not listen to good ministers. You spend all your time playing with your concubines and plotting with evil ministers. You have spent the nation's money on foolish projects like the Deer Terrace and those brass pillars."

Grand Tutor Wen continued, "I remember when your father was king. The people were happy and our borders were peaceful. Now there is trouble everywhere. I need to think about this. I will give you a report in a few days."

The king got up and returned to the Deer Terrace. Grand Tutor Wen went to see the other ministers. He said, "Please, tell me everything."

Huang Feihu bowed and began to speak. He told Grand Tutor Wen everything that had happened since Daji arrived at Zhaoge. When he was finished, Grand Tutor Wen said, "This is all my fault. I have been away from Zhaoge for too long and I have allowed this to happen. Now I must do something. In four days, I will give my report to the king."

The ministers all went to their homes. Grand Tutor Wen stayed in his house for three days, writing a memorial to the king. On the fourth day, he went to see the king. He said, "Your Majesty, I have a memorial for you." Then he laid the memorial on the desk in front of the king. The king read it. The memorial started off by discussing the king's failures. Then it made ten proposals:

1. Destroy the Deer Terrace.
2. Destroy the Burning Pillars.
3. Fill in the Pit of Snakes.
4. Fill in the Wine Pool and destroy the Meat Forest.
5. Banish Daji from the capital.
6. Cut off the heads of Fei Zhong and You Hun.
7. Open the granaries to feed the hungry people.
8. Send ministers to the East and South dukedoms to discuss peace.
9. Search the mountains and forests for wise sages.
10. Encourage the people to speak freely without fear.

When the king was finished reading, Grand Tutor Wen handed him an ink brush. He said, "Your Majesty, please sign your name."

The king replied, "We must think about the first item. The Deer Terrace is a beautiful building, and we spent much time and money building it. As for the fifth item, we will not send Daji away, because she is a good queen with many virtues. And as for the sixth item, we do not want to execute Fei Zhong and You Hun, they have served us well and committed no crimes. So, I approve all your proposals except for the first, fifth and sixth."

Grand Tutor Wen told the king that all ten proposals were important. "The people are very unhappy about the Deer Terrace. The ghosts of the dead are weeping because of Daji. And the gods in heaven are angry because of Fei

Zhong and You Hun. You must do all ten of these things, to save the nation."

The king stood up. "That's enough for now. You and I must discuss this again later. I will agree to seven of these proposals, but not all ten of them."

As the king started to leave, Fei Zhong and You Hun came into the room. They did not realize what was happening. Fei Zhong tried to speak to the king, but Grand Tutor Wen stepped in between them, saying, "Who are you?"

"I am Fei Zhong."

Grand Tutor Wen said, "Ah, so you are the one who has turned the king against his own people!" And he smashed his fist into Fei Zhong's face, knocking him to the floor.

"What did you do?" cried You Hun.

"And who are you?" asked Grand Tutor Wen.

"I am You Hun."

"So! The two of you are working together to make yourselves rich and powerful, while the nation suffers!" And with that, he raised his fist and knocked You Hun to the floor. He called to the guards, "Seize these two traitors and hold them for execution!"

The king said, "Those two have insulted you, but that is not bad enough to have them executed. They both will be tried according to law, and we will see what punishment they receive."

Grand Tutor Wen thought that he may have gone too far. He knelt before the king and said, "Your Majesty, I only want happiness for the people and peace for the nation. I want nothing else."

That was the end of the meeting. But shortly afterwards, a messenger arrived to tell Grand Tutor Wen that there was a new rebellion in the East Sea district.

Grand Tutor Wen went to see the king. He said, "There is a new rebellion in the East Sea district. I must deal with this. I need to go there with 200,000 soldiers. We can continue discussing the memorial when I return."

The king was very happy to learn that Grand Tutor Wen was leaving the capital. He quickly approved the plan.

A couple of days later, the army was ready to leave. The king went outside the east gate with Grand Tutor Wen and General Huang Feihu. The king raised a cup of wine to Grand Tutor Wen. But Grand Tutor Wen gave the cup to Huang Feihu. He said, "Let General Huang drink this wine. General, you must take care of the state while I am gone. Don't be afraid to do what must be done."

Then he turned to the king and said, "I hope you will take better care of the nation. Listen to your loyal ministers and don't do anything to make things worse. I will be back in a year, maybe less." Then he rode his horse to the front of the huge army, and they rode eastward.

Chapter 28
Punishing the North Grand Dukedom

The Grand Tutor returns in victory,
But he knows nothing of the evil in the kingdom

The king has failed in his duty;
The nation is broken and falls into chaos

The Grand Tutor offers ten proposals to save the kingdom;
He wants to remove all the evil ministers

The nation should be happy and prosperous;
He makes plans but knows that nothing will happen quickly

Of course, the king was delighted when he found out that Grand Tutor Wen was leaving the capital. He immediately ordered that Fei Zhong and You Hun be released from prison and given their jobs back. Then he ordered a party for himself and invited all of his ministers to come to the royal garden.

It was a beautiful spring day. The garden was filled with flowers and birds. Green water flowed underneath a golden bridge into a blue pool full of goldfish. There was a white stone path through the garden, with two carved stone dragons on either side. Lovely palace maids walked through the garden bringing food and drinks.

The king sat in the library, with Daji and Hu Ximei sitting on either side of him. The other ministers were in the garden. As he ate, Huang Feihu said to the ministers, "I'm sorry but I cannot enjoy this banquet. The country is being torn apart by rebellions, how can I enjoy the flowers? The king must change his ways, or I'm afraid this dynasty will end soon." The other ministers nodded their heads in agreement.

The banquet ended at noon. But when the ministers went into the library to thank the king, he said, "It is such a beautiful spring day, why are you leaving? Stay, and I will come and drink with you." The ministers had no choice, they had to remain.

The drinking, singing and dancing continued. When darkness fell, the king ordered that candles be lit. In the library, Daji and Hu Ximei had become drunk from too much wine. The two women fell asleep. Then the fox demon inside Daji flew out of her body. It flew away on a gust of cold wind, looking for human flesh.

Everyone in the party felt the cold wind. Someone called out, "A demon is coming! A demon is coming!" Huang Feihu was half drunk, but he jumped up. He saw the fox demon coming towards him. In the darkness he saw that it had eyes like golden lamps, a long tail and very sharp claws. Huang Feihu had no weapon, so he broke off a piece of wood from the pavilion railing and swung it at the demon. He missed, and the demon attacked him.

"Fetch my hunting hawk!" shouted Huang Feihu. His guards went and got the hunting hawk, which was large and had golden eyes. The hawk flew up in the sky. It saw the fox demon and attacked it with its claws. The fox demon cried out and dove under some rocks in a nearby hillside.

The king saw this. He ordered his attendants to dig out the rocks to get to the fox demon. They dug down two or three feet into the hillside. They did not find the fox demon, but they found a huge pile of human bones. The king saw the pile. He said, "The Daoist sage told me that there was an air of evil in the palace, but I did not believe it. But now I see that he was right."

That was the end of the party. The ministers thanked the king and went home. Daji was still in bed, but she had bad scratches on her face. In the morning the king saw her face and asked what happened. "Your Majesty," she said, "last night after you left to drink with your ministers, I went for a walk in the garden. I walked into a tree branch and got these scratches on my face."

"My dear, you should be more careful!" said the king. "There are fox demons in the palace." Then he told her the story of what happened. But he did not realize that he was telling the story to a fox demon, and he did not know that he had been sleeping with that fox demon for the past several years.

Meanwhile, Jiang Ziya was serving as the prime minister for Ji Chang. One day he read a report that there was another rebellion against the king, and that Grand Tutor Wen had been sent to stop the rebellion. Then another report came, saying that the king had ordered Bi Gan's heart to be cut out of his body to be made into a medicinal soup for Daji. Then a third report came, saying that Chong Houhu was plotting with Fei Zhong and You Hun, and was making himself wealthy while the people went hungry.

Jiang Ziya went to see Ji Chang and told him everything he had learned recently. He said, "In my opinion, we must get rid of Chong Houhu. If he stays at His Majesty's side, disaster will follow. As you know, His Majesty gave you the power to fight traitors and rebels. Well, Chong Houhu is a traitor. If you get rid of him, you will help His Majesty be a great ruler again."

Ji Chang replied, "Tell me, if we send an army against Chong Houhu, who will lead it?"

"I shall serve you like a dog or a horse."

Ji Chang was happy to hear this, but he was also afraid that Jiang Ziya might be too eager to attack the city. So he said, "Good. But I will go with you, so we can discuss important matters together."

They gathered an army of 100,000 soldiers. Ji Chang carried an ox-tail hammer and a yellow axe, both given to him by the king to show that he had the authority to fight traitors and rebels. The Zhou army left West Qi City with the cheers of the people ringing in their ears.

A few days later, the Zhou army reached Chong City and set up a large camp just outside the city. Chong Houhu was not there, but the city was under the command of his son Chong Yingbao. Chong Yingbao said to his generals, "Ji Chang has decided to attack us. You remember that he fled Zhaoge a few years ago. Now he attacks us for no reason. Well, if he wants to throw away his life, that's fine with me." Then he told his generals to capture Ji Chang and bring him to Zhaoge.

The first fight was between one of Ji Chang's generals, a man named Nangong Kuo, and a general of the Flying Tiger army. The two of them fought on horseback, horses circling and swords flying. The Flying Tiger general was strong, but Nangong Kuo was stronger. They fought for thirty rounds. Then Nangong Kuo knocked the other man from his horse. Some Zhou soldiers ran up and cut the man's head off. They brought the head back to their camp and gave it to Jiang Ziya.

Chong Yingbiao saw this, and he was furious. He hit his desk with his fist and shouted, "Get the entire army ready. Tomorrow we will fight!"

The next day, the gates of Chong City opened and a huge army rushed out. They rushed towards the other army, then stopped a short distance away. They saw an old Daoist riding his horse towards the front lines. He had white hair and a long silver beard. He wore a gold hat and a robe tied with a silk belt, and he carried a sword in his hand. It was Jiang Ziya.

Jiang Ziya shouted, "Commander of the Chong army! Meet me at once!"

Chong Yingbao rode his horse forward. He wore gold

armor over a red robe. He shouted, "Who dares to attack my city?"

"I am prime minister Jiang Ziya. You and your father are as evil as the sea is deep. You have taken the people's wealth like hungry tigers, and you have harmed them like wild wolves. You are not loyal to His Majesty. Now my master, Ji Chang, is doing the job that His Majesty has given him."

Then Ji Chang rode up next to Jiang Ziya and shouted, "Chong Yingbao! Get down off your horse and come with us. We will bring you back to West Qi and execute you and your father. There is no need for your soldiers to die for you."

Chong Yingbao shouted back, "Jiang Ziya, you speak big words but you are just a weak and foolish old man. And Ji Chang, you are a traitor to our nation!" Then he turned to his generals and asked, "Who will remove these fools for me?"

One general from Chong City rode forward, swinging his axe. He could not defeat either of his opponents, so Chong Yingbao sent two more generals into the fight. Jiang Ziya saw the situation and ordered six of his dukes to join the battle. Outnumbered, Chong Yingbao rode forward himself and joined the battle.

They fought for twenty rounds. Two of Chong Yingbao's generals were killed. Seeing that he was badly outnumbered, Chong Yingbao fled back to the city with the generals and the rest of his army. They closed the city gates. Chong Yingbao sat down with his generals to decide how to fight the Zhou army.

On the Zhou side, Jiang Ziya wanted to attack the city immediately. But Ji Chang said, "If we attack the city, jade and stone will be burned together[1]. Many people will die. We have no reason to kill the people of the city; we want to rescue them."

Jiang Ziya thought to himself, "My master is as virtuous as Yao and Shun[2]." So he decided to wait. He sent Nangong Kuo to Caozhou with a letter for the Marquis of Caozhou, the brother of Chong Houhu and the man known as Black Tiger. He hoped that Black Tiger would come and help them. Then he waited.

---

[1] "Burn both jade and stone" is a Chinese idiom meaning to destroy indiscriminately.
[2] Emperor Yao was born around 2717 BC. He was one of the first emperors of China, and is revered for his wisdom and fairness. He had nine sons but did not feel any of them were worthy to take his place, so he selected a brilliant young man named Shun to be the next emperor.

Chapter 29
Death of Two Grand Dukes

Chong Houhu is cruel and greedy;
He takes the people's wealth and makes it his own

He meets the king and wants to control him;
He uses a thousand different tricks to help himself

He works the people almost to death,
Then he makes plans to remove the king

Jiang Ziya has virtue, though his king has none;
He knows the dynasty will fall and many people will die

Nangong Kuo left for Caozhou. He spent the night in a hostel, and the next day he went to see Chong Heihu.

"What brings you here to see me?" asked Chong Heihu.

"My lord, I have a letter for you. It's from prime minister Jiang Ziya."

Chong Heihu opened the letter and began to read.

Dear Chong Heihu,

A minister should be loyal to his king, helping him so that the people and the state will benefit. But if the king is evil, or if the king does things that are harmful to the people and the state, then a minister must not help him. You know that your brother has been doing evil. His crimes are as great as a mountain. For that, he is hated by the gods and the people.

My master, the Grand Duke of the West, has the authority to punish your brother. But if he does this, may people might die. So I ask you to do the right thing. Arrest Chong Houhu and bring him to the Zhou camp.

If you do this, you will be known as a virtuous and courageous man. If not, people will think you are the same as your brother. They will not be able to tell the difference between jade and stone. Please think about this and give us your reply as soon as possible.

Jiang Ziya, Prime Minister

Chong Heihu read the letter, then he read it again. He sat and thought about it. Then he said quietly, talking to himself, "Jiang Ziya is correct. Even a filial brother should know when to do the right thing. If I arrest my brother, I will save the Chong clan from certain death. If this is unfilial, then I will apologize to my parents after my death." Then he looked up at Nangong Kuo and said, "I will do as your prime minister asks. There is no need for me to reply to this letter. Tell Jiang Ziya that I will arrest my brother and bring him to the Zhou camp."

The next day he left for Chong City with 3,000 Flying Tiger soldiers. When he arrived at the city, his nephew Chong Yingbao came out to meet him.

"Forgive me, uncle!" he said. "I am wearing armor so I cannot give you a proper bow."

"Dear nephew, I heard that Chong City is being attacked. I bring 3,000 of my best soldiers to help you defend the city. But tell me, why is Ji Chang attacking the city?"

"I don't know, uncle. But I am certainly happy that you are here to help us!"

At dawn the next day, Chong Heihu led his Flying Tiger soldiers out of the city to face the Zhou army. He was wearing golden armor over a red dragon robe, and he rode a fire-eyed monster. His face was as black as the bottom of a pot, he had yellow eyebrows, golden eyes, and a long red beard. Jiang Ziya saw him, and he understood what was happening. He sent Nangong Kuo out to face him.

"Chong Heihu," shouted Nangong Kuo. "Your brother is a criminal. He has harmed many good people. We have the right to arrest him!" Then he raised his sword and attacked Chong Heihu. They began fighting. The two of them were close to each other, slashing with their weapons. They fought for twenty rounds. Then Chong Heihu said quietly,

"Let's stop fighting now. I'll see you again when I have arrested my brother."

Nangong Kuo slashed at his opponent one more time, then he turned his horse and retreated, calling out, "Chong Heihu, you are too strong. Please don't come after me!"

Chong Heihu turned and rode back to the city. Chong Yingbao had been watching the fight. He asked Chong Heihu, "Uncle, when your enemy ran away, why didn't you use your magic eagle?"

Chong Heihu replied, "My dear nephew, you forgot that Jiang Ziya is a powerful magician from Kunlun Mountain. He would have killed my eagle. But don't worry, we won the fight. Now we must make plans. We need your father here. Please send a messenger to him and tell him to return here immediately."

Chong Yingbao sent a messenger to Zhaoge, telling Chong Houhu of the situation and asking him to return to Chong City.

Chong Houhu read the letter. He immediately went to the king and said, "Your Majesty, we are having problems with Ji Chang. He does not wish to live in peace. He has brought a large army to Chong City and he has attacked my brother. Please, I beg you to help!"

"Ji Chang is a criminal," replied the king. "Go to Chong City right away. Take three thousand men and seize that traitor."

A few days later, Chong Heihu saw his brother approaching the city with his army of three thousand soldiers. He said to one of his soldiers, "Take twenty men and wait just inside the city gate. When you hear me rattling my sword, arrest

Chong Houhu and take him to the Zhou camp." Then he said to another soldier, "As soon as I leave the city, arrest Chong Houhu's family. Take them to the Zhou camp." Then he rode out of the city to Chong Houhu's camp.

Chong Houhu saw his brother approaching the camp. He came out to greet his brother. Chong Yingbao was also there and he came out to greet his uncle. Then the three of them rode back together to the city. As soon as they rode through the gate, Chong Heihu pulled his sword halfway out of its scabbard, then he pushed it back in and gave it a loud rattle. Immediately, twenty soldiers ran out. They seized Chong Houhu and his son Chong Yingbao.

"Dear brother," cried Chong Houhu, "what are you doing?"

Chong Heihu replied, "Brother, you are not a good minister. You have caused the people great suffering. You have made yourself wealthy while the people go hungry. But our Grand Duke is wise. He can tell the difference between good and bad. As for me, I would rather offend our ancestors than see our clan destroyed. I must arrest you."

Chong Houhu and his son were brought to the Zhou camp, where his wife and daughter were already waiting for him. He said to her, "Ah, my brother is so cruel to me. Who would have thought he would do something like this?"

Chong Heihu also entered the camp. He dismounted and went to see Jiang Ziya and Ji Chang.

"Chong Heihu," said Jiang Ziya, "you are a loyal minister. You have placed the well-being of the people above your own family. You are truly a hero."

But Ji Chang looked at Chong Heihu in surprise. He asked,

"What are you doing here?"

Chong Heihu replied, "My brother has committed crimes against heaven. I have brought him here for trial."

"But he is your older brother!"

Jiang Ziya spoke up. He said to Ji Chang, "The people hate Chong Houhu. Even little children hate him. But now they know that Chong Heihu is a virtuous man, and much better than his brother."

Then he ordered Chong Houhu and Chong Yingbao to be brought in. The two of them kneeled in front of Ji Chang, Jiang Ziya and Chong Heihu. Jiang Ziya said, "Chong Houhu, you have committed so many crimes, I cannot list them all. It is time for you to be punished by heaven. Guards! Take them outside and cut off their heads."

Ji Chang was too surprised to say anything. The guards grabbed the two prisoners and took them outside. A few minutes later, the guards returned, holding two heads in their hands. Ji Chang had never seen a head cut off like that. He covered his eyes with his sleeve and cried out, "This is terrible! I will surely die because of this."

Later, after Chong Houhu's family was released, Ji Chang returned to his home in West Qi. He felt sick. He could not eat or drink anything. Every time he closed his eyes, he saw Chong Houhu standing before him, crying out to Ji Chang to give him his life back. Doctors came to see him, but their medicines did not help him at all.

All the lands that were ruled by Chong Houhu were now ruled by Chong Heihu. They became a separate country, not under the control of the king in Zhaoge. The king learned of this and was furious. He ordered his army to go to West Qi and arrest Ji Chong and Chong Heihu.

But his ministers knelt before him and said, "Your Majesty, please think about this. Many people hated Chong Houhu and thought he was cruel and greedy. They are happy that he has been arrested and killed. Perhaps this is not be a good time for you to take action." The king agreed to wait.

Ji Chang's health continued to worsen day by day. He called Jiang Ziya to his bedside. Jiang Ziya came in and kneeled by the bedside. Ji Chang said to him, "I must tell you something important. I am grateful to His Majesty for making me Grand Duke of the West. I should have remained loyal to him. I was wrong to allow the deaths of Chong Houhu and Chong Yingbao. He and I were the same rank, so I did not have the authority to execute him. Now I hear him weeping all the time. When I close my eyes, I see him standing by my bed. I don't think I can live much longer."

He continued, "After I die, you must not rise up against the king. If you do, it will be a difficult situation for you to meet me after you die."

Tears ran down Jiang Ziya's face. He said, "It was you who made me prime minister. I dare not disobey you now."

Just then, Ji Fa came in. Ji Chang said to him, "My dear son, you must take my place after I die. You are young. Do not listen to anyone who says anything against our king. It is true that our king has no virtue, but he is still our king, and we must be loyal to him. Now, kneel before the prime minister and accept him as your father."

Ji Fa knelt down and kowtowed to Jiang Ziya.

Ji Chang continued, "My dear son, remember to love your

brothers, and be kind and helpful to the people. If you do as I say, I can die in peace." Ji Fa kowtowed to him.

Then Ji Chang said, "His Majesty was kind to me. I am sad to think that I will never see his royal face again. And I will not be able to go back to Youli and help the people there." Then he died. He was 97 years old. It was the twentieth year of the reign of King Di Xin of the Shang Dynasty.

After the funeral, Jiang Ziya proposed that Ji Fa become the new Grand Duke of the West, with the title of King Wu[1]. Ji Fa's first order was to increase the rank of all officials by one grade. All 200 marquises and all the tribal leaders came to the city and kowtowed to him.

News of this reached the palace secretary in Zhaoge. He decided that he needed to tell His Majesty that there was a new king in West Qi. He went to the Star Picking Mansion to see the king.

---

[1] This means "The Military King."

Chapter 30
Huang Feihu's Rebellion

When the king tries to play with the minister's wife,
he weakens the throne and lets evil triumph

He listens only to the demon Daji;
he turns away from the wise words of Lady Huang

This virtuous woman stands tall;
while the foolish king brings disaster to all

Now the rebels push against the strong pillars of heaven;
they want the save the kingdom from the king

The king's guards let the palace secretary into the Star Picking Mansion. The secretary kowtowed to the king. He said, "Your Majesty, I have bad news. Ji Chang is dead. His son, Ji Fa, is now calling himself King Wu. This could be a big problem. I suggest that you send an army to punish him immediately."

The king laughed and said, "Ji Fa just recently stopped drinking his mother's milk. What can he do to us?"

"Yes, he is young. But remember that he is getting help from Jiang Ziya, San Yisheng, and Nangong Kuo. Together, they are dangerous."

"Jiang Ziya? He is just a sorcerer, nothing more."

The palace secretary bowed and left the mansion. He said to himself, "This king is a fool. I'm afraid the dynasty will end soon."

Time flew by. Soon it was New Year's Day, the twenty-first anniversary of the start of the king's reign. All the ministers came to greet the king, and their wives came to greet Queen Daji. This is when trouble started.

Lady Jia was the wife of Huang Feihu. She came to greet Queen Daji. When Daji heard that Jia was coming, she thought, "So, Huang Feihu, you sent your eagle to kill me. Now your pretty little wife comes to see me. She will walk right into my trap!"

 Daji's palace maids brought Lady Jia in to see her. Daji said, "My dear Lady Jia, it is so good to meet you! You are a few years older than I am. You should become my sworn sister."

Jia replied, "Oh, Your Majesty, how could I? You are a queen, but I am just an ordinary woman. It would be like a pheasant in the woods becoming the sister of a beautiful phoenix."

Daji said, "Oh no, my dear. I am just the daughter of a marquis. But you are the wife of a prince, a relative of His Majesty."

The two of them sat and drank a few cups of wine. Then a palace maid entered and said, "His Majesty is coming."

"Oh no!" cried Jia. "It is not right for me to meet him here. I am a minister's wife. This would be a violation of the law. Where can I hide?"

Daji smiled and said, "Don't worry, sister. Go there," and she pointed to the rear of the hall. Jia ran and hid in the rear of the hall. Then the king came in. He saw cups and plates on the table.

He said to Daji, "Who were you drinking with, dear?"

"I was sitting and talking with Lady Jia, the wife of Prince Huang Feihu. Have you ever seen her, Your Majesty?"

"Of course not. We cannot visit with the wife of our minister. That would be a violation of the law."

"But Your Majesty, remember that Huang Feihu's sister is your concubine. So, Lady Jia is actually your relative. You may see her without violating the law." The king thought about this. Then Daji continued, "She is really quite beautiful. I think you would really like her. Please allow me to bring her up to the Star Picking Mansion. Then you can go there and surprise her."

The king was excited about seeing the beautiful Jia. So he left to wait. Daji went to find Jia. She saw that Jia was uncomfortable and wanted to leave, so she said, "Sister, please don't leave yet. Come with me to the Star Picking Mansion. You can see the entire kingdom from up there!"

Jia had no choice, so she followed Daji to the top of the Star Picking Mansion. Looking down, she saw a pit. The pit was filled with piles of human bones and thousands of snakes.

"What is that?" she asked.

Daji replied, "That is the pit of snakes. It is difficult to keep evil people out of the palace. So, if we find any evil people here, they are stripped and thrown into the pit to feed the snakes." Daji saw that Jia was frightened, but she just smiled and told the palace maids to bring wine.

While they were drinking, a palace maid came and told the two women that the king was coming. Daji said to Jia, "Don't worry, sister. Go over there," she pointed to the railing, "and wait for me."

The king came in. He sat down next to Daji. Then he looked to where the beautiful Lady Jia was standing by the railing. "Who is that?" he asked.

"That is the wife of Prince Huang Feihu," said Daji. Jia had no choice. She turned and bowed to the king. The king looked at her with desire in his eyes.

"Please sit down," he said to her.

Jia remained standing. Daji said to her, "You are my sister-in-law. There is nothing wrong with you sitting with us."

Now Lady Jia saw the trap. She became frightened, but she said to the king, "Your Majesty, I came here to visit with my sister. Now please allow me to obey the law and leave at once."

The king smiled at her and said, "Please sit. If you don't sit down, we will have to stand up." He poured a cup of wine and handed it to her.

Now Jia saw that she was trapped. She knew that she would not be able to leave the Star Picking Mansion alive. She took the cup of wine and threw it in the king's face. She shouted, "Idiot king! My husband has been your loyal servant. But instead of thanking him, you insult me and violate all the laws of heaven and earth. You and your evil queen will soon meet your deaths!"

The king shouted to his guards to seize Lady Jia. But before they could grab her, she ran to the railing. She shouted, "Dear husband, I will protect our honor with my life. Please take care of our children!" Then she jumped to her death.

Soon, news of Jia's death reached Concubine Huang, the sister of Huang Feihu and the sister-in-law of Lady Jia. She ran to the Star Picking Mansion and went upstairs to find the king. She pointed her finger at him and said, "You damned tyrant! You owe your life to my brother. He has fought pirates on the eastern ocean. He has fought rebels in the south. Every member of my family has been loyal to you. Today, Lady Jia came to greet your queen. But you could not control your queen or your own lust. Now my sister-in-law is dead. Years from now, when people tell the story of our kingdom, your name will be dirt!"

Then she turned to Daji and said, "And you, you bitch. You have poisoned the king's mind and brought chaos to our kingdom. And now you have brought death to my sister-in-law!" She ran over and punched Daji in the face, as hard as she could. Daji fell to the ground. Concubine Huang hit her twenty or thirty more times.

Now, Daji was really a fox demon and could have easily

fought back against Huang. But she knew that the king was watching. She cried, "Help me, help me, Your Majesty!"

The king ran over and pulled Huang off Daji. But Huang, blind with rage, turned and hit the king in the face. "You tyrant!" she shouted, "How can you defend that bitch. I'll make her pay for killing my sister!"

Now the king was angry. With one hand he grabbed her hair; with the other hand he grabbed the front of her robe. Then he picked her up and threw her over the railing. She fell to the ground and died instantly.

The king looked down from the railing. He saw Huang's broken body, lying next to Jia's body. He felt bad about what he'd done, but he did not say anything to Daji.

Lady Jia's attendants were still waiting for her in a nearby hall. A couple of palace maids came and told them what had happened. The attendants ran to General Huang Feihu, who was enjoying a feast with his brothers and generals. They cried, "Disaster, Your Highness! Disaster!" Then they told him that Lady Jia threw herself from the railing of the Star Picking Mansion, and that the king had then thrown Concubine Huang to her death.

Huang Feihu heard their words but could not think of anything to say. His brother, Huang Ming, jumped up and said, "Brother, I think I know what happened. The king saw your wife's beauty and wanted her for himself. Your wife had no choice but to jump to her death. Concubine Huang probably heard of this and argued with the king, causing him to throw her off the Star Picking Mansion."

He continued, "You know that the sages say, 'If the king does not rule properly, the people may seek a new king.' We are all loyal to the kingdom. We have fought for our country in the north, south, east and west. But now we are no longer loyal to this tyrant. We must rebel!" He and the others jumped up, holding their swords in their hands.

Huang Feihu said, "Stop! What does the death of my wife have to do with you? Remember, the Huang family has served the kingdom for seven generations. How can you rebel against the king now, just because a woman has died?"

The others stood still, surprised at this. They did not know what to do. Then Huang Ming laughed and said, "You're right, brother. This has nothing to do with us at all. Why be angry?" Then he and the others went back to eating, drinking and talking.

Huang Feihu was still angry. He said to them, "Why are you all laughing?"

One of the generals looked at him coldly and replied, "To tell you the truth, brother, we are all laughing at you." Huang Feihu was speechless. The general continued, "We all know that you have earned your rank as the top general in the kingdom. But other people, who knows what they think? They might think that your high rank is because the king really liked your wife."

Now Huang Feihu was turning red from rage. He shouted, "Enough! We are leaving Zhaoge!" Then he paused and added, "But where should we go?"

Huang Ming replied, "You know what the ancients say, 'A good man chooses a good master.' The king of West Qi already controls two thirds of the kingdom. He is a good man. Let's go there."

Then Huang Ming thought, "My brother might change his mind. I'd better make sure that doesn't happen." He said to his brother, "We should get our revenge now and not wait until later. Let's fight the king right now."

The men all rode to the king's palace. Huang Feihu rode his ox while the other men rode their horses. They all wore armor and held swords in their hands. They arrived at the palace gate just as the sun was coming up. One of the generals shouted, "Tell the tyrant to come out right away. Otherwise, we will smash the gate and come in anyway!"

The king was sitting alone in the palace, thinking about what had happened the previous night. A guard ran in and told him that Huang Feihu and his men were waiting outside, swords in hand. The king put on his armor and rode out on his horse to meet them.

One of the generals raised his sword and shouted, "Tyrant! You have insulted the wife of your minister!" Then he rushed at the king, slashing with his sword. The king easily blocked the blow. Then Huang Ming rode forward and also attacked with his sword. Seeing this, Huang Feihu rode his ox forward and joined the fight.

The king was big and strong and a good fighter, but he could not win against three opponents. It was like a dragon fighting three wild tigers. He fought for thirty rounds, then turned and rode back through the palace gate. His guards closed the gate and locked it.

Huang Feihu and his men turned around. They rode out of Zhaoge through the west gate. There, they met up with their families, and together they rode towards Mengjin[1].

---

[1] Today, Mengjin (pronounced *mèngjīn*) is a district in the city of Luoyang. In ancient times it was a ferry crossing for the Yellow River. It is believed that King Wu of Zhou and his allies crossed the Yellow River here on their way to Zhaoge, leading to the theory that the original name was actually *Méngjīn*, which means "ferry

The king sat in his court, saying nothing. His ministers came in to find out what was happening. They asked him, "Your Majesty, why did Huang Feihu rebel against you?"

The king replied, "Lady Jia insulted our queen. Then she felt guilty, so she threw herself over the railing. Concubine Huang arrived and also insulted our queen. While they were arguing, she accidentally fell over the railing." He did not explain why he was fighting with Huang Feihu and his men.

The ministers did not know what to say about this. The story sounded false, but of course they could not say that to the king. Then Grand Tutor Wen arrived. He had just returned from the Eastern Sea district. He also asked what was going on. The king told him the same story that he'd just told the ministers.

Grand Tutor Wen said, "I know Huang Feihu. He is a good man, loyal to you and to the kingdom. He and his wife came to the palace because it was New Years Day. But the Star Picking Palace is your private home, not part of the main palace. Why was Lady Jia there?"

The king did not answer. Grand Tutor Wen continued, "Then Concubine Huang must have heard of her sister in law's death and come here. But I think you were angry at her and threw her off the balcony. These deaths were not the fault of Jia and Huang. They are your fault! You know what the ancients say, 'If the king rules badly, the people may seek a new king.' I am not surprised that Huang Feihu rose up against you. Your Majesty, you should forgive him. I will go and find him, and ask him to return."

---

crossing of the alliance."

One of the ministers spoke up. He said, "Grand Tutor Wen, you are right that His Majesty should have treated Madam Jia and Concubine Huang better. But on the other hand, Huang Feihu was wrong to attack the king."

Grand Tutor Wen thought about it. Then he said, "Perhaps you are right. Send messengers quickly to the commanders at the mountain passes. Tell them to close their gates and not allow the rebels to pass through. That will give me time to catch up to them."

Chapter 31
Flight and Pursuit

The loyal and virtuous depart;
There is no rain and the people are hungry

The wise Grand Tutor quickly takes control,
While evil ministers continue to bring misery to the people

Don't even think about crossing the three passes;
The enemy is approaching from all four directions

The enemy chases the army but it disappears in the bright
sun; Don't worry, their fate is already written

Huang Feihu and his men left Zhaoge through the west gate. They passed through Mengjin, crossed the Yellow River, and rode until they were close to Lintong Pass. Huang Feihu heard sounds of shouting and saw a cloud of dust rising into the air. Looking back, he saw a great army approaching. Then he looked to his right and left and saw two more armies coming from both sides. Then he looked backwards and saw that yet another army was coming towards him from Lintong Pass.

He sighed deeply and thought, "How can I fight all four of these armies? All I can do is wait for death for myself and my family."

In heaven, the immortals had nothing to do. In the past, the Daoist masters had enjoyed going to listen to lectures at the Jade Palace. But these days there were no lectures. Everything was on hold until Jiang Ziya finished creating the new gods. So the immortals passed the time touring the nearby mountains and picking flowers.

One of the immortals, Master Pure Void Virtue, was traveling over Lintong Pass when he heard the sounds of sadness coming from a man on earth. Looking down, he saw Huang Feihu and his men surrounded by four armies. "Well," he thought, "it looks like someone needs to rescue these people." He told one of his servants, a genie, to wrap up the men in a flag and hide them deep in the mountains. The genie did as he was ordered.

Grand Tutor Wen led his army towards the place where Huang Feihu had been. He looked around but did not see anyone. He met with the generals who were leading the other three armies, and they said that they had not seen Huang Feihu's men either. Wen thought, "This is strange. I was told that Huang Feihu crossed the Yellow River and was headed towards Lintong Pass. We came at him from all four directions, but he is not here. Where is he?"

Master Pure Void Virtue saw that Wen had stopped. He thought, "I have to make these soldiers go away, so that Huang Feihu can continue through the pass." He took a handful of magic sand out of his robe and threw it towards the southeast. The sand turned into a group of men riding fast towards Zhaoge. Grand Tutor Wen saw them and sent all four of the armies in pursuit. The armies rode all the way to Mengjin, but they never caught up.

When the armies had gone, Master Pure Void Virtue ordered his genie to return Huang Feihu and his men to the road. The men looked around, confused. They saw that the armies had disappeared. "Heaven has surely helped us!" said Huang Ming.

But they still had to get through Lington Pass. The pass was guarded by a group of soldiers led by Zhang Feng, an older man who was a sworn brother of Huang Feihu's father.

Huang Feihu led his men up to the gate of Lington Pass. Zhang Feng came out, leading a group of soldiers. "Listen to me," he said, "Your father and I are sworn brothers, and you are a loyal subject of the king. Do not bring shame to your ancestors. Get down from your ox and let me take you back to Zhaoge. Perhaps some ministers will speak up for you, and you and your family will not have to be executed."

Huang Feihu replied, "Uncle, you know that our king spends all of his time drinking and playing with his concubines. He listens to evil men, he does not listen to his loyal ministers, he ignores affairs of state, and he is cruel to the people. I have done hundreds of things to help him, yet he forgets all that and insults me. How can I remain loyal to him? Please, let us pass through."

When he heard these words, Zhang Feng became angry. "Traitor!" he shouted. He slashed at Huang Feihu with his sword, but Huang Feihu blocked the blow. He struck again. Now Huang Feihu became angry and attacked. They fought for thirty rounds. Zhang Feng was a good fighter but he was an old man. He became tired and could not fight anymore. He turned around and rode away on his horse.

Zhang Feng looked back and saw that Huang Feihu was chasing him. He put away his sword. He reached into his robe and threw a stringed hammer[1] at his pursuer. But Huang Feihu knew about this weapon. As the hammer flew towards him, he slashed upwards with his sword, cutting the string. Then he grabbed the flying hammer with his other hand.

Seeing this, Zhang Feng fled back to the pass. The soldiers locked the gate behind him. He sat down, breathing heavily. He thought for a while about what to do next. Then he ordered General Xiao Yin to come see him.

Xiao Yin came in and awaited his orders. Zhang Feng said, "We cannot beat Huang Feihu in a fight. So tonight, I want you to take three thousand men with bows and arrows. Surround his camp. Then have all your men shoot their arrows at the same time. Kill every one of the rebels, then cut off their heads and bring them to me."

---

[1] This is a small hammer or mallet with a rope attached, making it possible for the user to throw it, then retrieve it afterwards.

Xiao Yin left. But he remembered that several years earlier, he served in the army under Huang Feihu and was promoted to general. He did not want to repay this kindness by killing Huang Feihu and his family. Secretly he went to Huang Feihu's camp and met with the rebel leader.

"Sir," he said, "you remember that I served under you several years ago. You made me a general. I must tell you that Zhang Feng has ordered me to kill all of you tonight with bows and arrows. I cannot do that. It would be a crime against heaven."

Huang Feihu replied, "I cannot thank you enough for coming and telling me this. If not for you, my entire family would die tonight. Tell me, though, is there anything you can do to help us get out of here?"

"Wait a few minutes for me to return to the pass. Then attack as soon as you can. I will open the gates for you."

Huang Feihu immediately gathered his men. They rode towards the pass, shouting and waving their swords. The gates opened and they rushed through.

Zhang Feng heard the sound of galloping horses. He saw what happened, and set off to chase Huang Feihu. But as he passed through the gate, he did not see Xiao Yin standing on the other side. Xiao Yin slashed at him with his sword. Zhang Feng fell from his horse, dead.

"Thank you!" Huang Feihu shouted to Xiao Yin as he rode away. "I don't know when I can repay you for what you did today."

They rode about eighty *li* and stopped when they got to the next pass, Tongguan Pass. The commander of this pass was Chen Tong. This man also knew Huang Feihu. Several years earlier, he had served under Huang Feihu in the army. He disobeyed a command and was sentenced to death. But several other generals asked Huang Feihu to show mercy, so he was not executed. Still, Chen Tong disliked Huang Feihu and was happy to have a chance to punish him now.

He put on his armor and prepared for battle.

When he saw Huang Feihu he shouted, "Hello, General! You used to be a high ranking general, but now you are just another criminal on the run. Grand Tutor Wen told me that you would be coming here. Get down off your ox. I will take you back to Zhaoge. There is nothing else you can do."

Huang Feihu replied, "You are wrong, General. Once you were under my command and I treated you like my own brother. You disobeyed my orders, but I showed you mercy and did not execute you. But even after that, you insult me. Very well. Get down off your horse and fight me now. If you win, I will go with you to Zhaoge."

Then Huang Feihu attacked with his sword. Chen Tong blocked with his own sword, and they fought for more than twenty rounds. Huang Feihu was the stronger fighter, though, so Chen Tong turned, jumped up on his horse, and rode away as fast as he could.

Huang Feihu chased him. But then Chen Tong pulled out a magic javelin. This javelin had been given to him by an immortal. It never missed its target. He threw it. Huang Feihu was struck in the chest. He cried out and fell to the ground.

Huang Ming and another general saw this. They rushed forward to attack Chen Tong. But Chen Tong threw the javelin again and killed the other general. Then, not wanting to fight Huang Ming, he turned around and fled.

The men in Huang Feihu's camp were filled with sadness when they saw the two dead fighters. They had no leader, no plan, no place to go towards, no place to return to.

In heaven, Master Pure Void Virtue was on Mount Green Peak, meditating on his green cloud. Suddenly his heart jumped. He looked down and saw that Huang Feihu had been killed. Immediately he called for one of his disciples to come and see him.

The disciple was a young man, nine feet tall, with smooth skin, bright eyes and a body that was as strong as a tiger. He wore a robe with a hemp belt, and simple straw sandals. "What can I do for you, Master?" he asked.

"Your father needs your help," replied Master Pure Void Virtue.

"Who is my father?"

"He is Huang Feihu, a prince of Shang. He has been killed by a magic javelin. Bring him back from the dead. Then introduce yourself. You will serve together in the battle that is to come."

"I don't understand, Master. How can this man be my father?"

"Thirteen years ago, I was riding a cloud. Suddenly I saw a bright beam of light. I looked down and saw that the light was coming from your head. You were only three years old at the time. I knew immediately that you had a bright future, so I brought you here to be my disciple. Your name is Huang Tianhua."

Then Master Pure Void Virtue gave the boy a sword and a flower basket, and told him how to bring his father back from the dead. The boy kowtowed to his master. Then he picked up a handful of dust, threw it in the air, and rode it swiftly to Tongguan Pass.

Chapter 32
Huang Tianhua Meets His Father

Using the power of the five Dao[1],
You can become like air and be carried far on the wind

You can travel through the lands of the living and the dead,
And fly high over Mount Tai and Mount Mang

Don't fail to save your father even if it is difficult;
Have a strong heart and don't fear the wolves

Father and son meet at Tongguan Pass;
They are both pillars of virtue for Qi and Zhou

---

[1] Daoists believe that everything in the material universe is made from five elements: wood, fire, earth, metal and water. These five elements are associated with the five directions, five colors, five bodily tissues, five fluids, five solid organs, and five hollow organs.

Huang Tianhua flew down from Mount Green Peak. He arrived at the Huang camp around five in the afternoon. Nearby a group of men and horses stood around a lamp. The men saw him and reached for their swords. "Who are you?" they called.

Tianhua replied, "This poor Daoist is from Mount Green Peak. I have heard that His Majesty is in trouble. I can help him. Bring me to him quickly!"

The men looked at him carefully. He had long black hair that was coiled up on top of his head. He wore a long robe with big sleeves that fluttered in the wind. In one hand he held a strange flower basket, and he had a sword tied on his back. He looked like a powerful tiger.

They led him to Huang Feibao, the brother of the dead general Huang Feihu. Huang Feibao could immediately see that the boy looked a lot like his own brother. He said to the boy, "Can you bring my brother back from the dead? If you can, you would be like a father or mother who brings new life into the world."

The boy was led to the back of the camp. There he saw Huang Feihu lying on the ground, cold and dead. His face was white and his eyes were closed. Next to him was another body. "Who's that?" he asked.

"That is our sworn brother. Both of them were killed by Chen Tong's magic javelin."

"Bring me some water," said Huang Tianhua. When the water arrived, he took some elixir out of his flower basket and mixed it with the water. He opened up Huang Heihu's mouth and poured the liquid into his mouth. The liquid ran into the dead man's body, reaching all his internal organs and all 84,000 hairs on his body.

"Now we wait," said Huang Tianhua. They waited for an hour or two. Then the dead man cried out in pain and opened his eyes.

"Where am I?" asked Huang Feihu, looking around. "Is this the land of the dead? Why are you all here with me?" The others told him what happened. Huang Feihu stood up and thanked the boy.

The boy knelt down and said, "Father, don't you know me? I am your son, Huang Tianhua! You remember that when I was just three years old, you sent me away to study with Master Pure Void Virtue on Mount Green Peak. I have been there for thirteen years." His father looked at him and cried with joy.

Tianhua looked around and saw his two uncles and his three brothers. But he did not see his mother. "Father, why didn't you bring my mother with you? If the tyrant king captures her, it will be a terrible day for our family!"

Huang Feihu began to cry. He told his son how his mother had jumped from the Star Picking Mansion to stop the king from dishonoring her. Then he told the boy that the king had also thrown his aunt from the Star Picking Mansion. When the boy heard this, he said, "Father, I will not go back to Mount Green Peak. I will stay here on earth and take revenge for my mother's death!"

Just then, a messenger rushed in to tell them that Chen Tong was outside the camp, calling for a fight. Huang Feihu was so frightened that his face turned the color of ash. But his son said, "Father, don't worry. Go and fight him. I will protect you."

Huang Feihu put on his armor and rode his ox out to meet Chen Tong. Chen Tong was surprised to see the man who he thought was dead. Huang Feihu shouted, "You hit me with your javelin, but heaven did not want me to die." Then he attacked Chen Tong. The two of them began to fight. After fifteen rounds, Chen Tong turned and rode away.

Huang Feihu followed him. Suddenly Chen Tong turned and threw another magic javelin at him. But Huang Tianhua pointed his flower basket at the javelin. The javelin turned in mid-air and fell into the basket. Chen Tong threw more javelins, but each one was captured by the flower basket.

Chen Tong saw that the Daoist boy was capturing all his javelins. He raised his sword and charged towards the boy. But Tianhua pointed his own sword at Chen Tong. A beam of starlight flew from the tip of the sword towards Chen Tong. When it hit Chen Tong, his head flew off his body and rolled onto the ground.

"Chen Tong is dead!" shouted the Zhou soldiers. They charged towards the gate. They broke open the gate and rushed through to the other side.

Tianhua stopped and called out, "Father, I must return to Mount Green Peak to talk with my master. But we will meet again. I will see you in West Qi. Be careful!"

Huang Feihu was sad to see his son leave. But he continued with his men, riding towards the next pass. This was Chuanyun Pass and it was guarded by Chen Wu, the brother of Chen Tong.

When Huang Feihu and his men arrived at the pass, Chen Wu came out to meet them. He wore no armor and carried no weapons. "Welcome, Your Highness!" he called out.

"Greetings," replied Huang Feihu. "We have committed a crime against the king and are fleeing from Zhaoge. I am sorry to say that your brother died yesterday when he tried to stop us from passing through Tongguan Pass."

Chen Wu replied, "Your family has been loyal to the king for many, many years. But we all know that this king is a tyrant and has treated you badly. My brother did not understand the situation. He deserved his death. You may pass through with no problem. But won't you please come in and rest with us for a little bit."

Huang Feihu did not know that Chen Wu already knew of his brother's death. When he heard that his brother had died, Chen Wu was so angry that he spouted smoke from his seven orifices[1].

The men dismounted from their horses and went through the gate. Chen Wu invited them to come into the main hall and have something to eat. When they'd finished eating, Huang Feihu said, "Thank you, my friend. Now we must be going. Would you please open the other gate and let us pass."

"Of course," Chen Wu replied. "But we have prepared some wine for you. Please join us and have a few drinks." Huang Feihu could not refuse, so he and his men sat down again and drank some wine. They sat and talked for hours. Soon it was evening.

"Please don't go yet," said Chen Wu. "You have been traveling for many days, you must be very tired. We would

---

[1] This is a Chinese idiom meaning that someone is seething with anger. The seven apertures of the human head are the two eyes, two ears, two nostrils, and the mouth.

be happy to give you and your men beds for the night."

Huang Feihu was not comfortable with this, but he could not find a reason to say no. So he and his men brought the luggage inside, then they all went to bed. The men fell asleep right away. But Huang Feihu could not sleep. He kept thinking about the many years that his family had served the kings of Shang. "Who would have thought that we would now be rebels against the king!" he thought.

First watch came, then second watch, then third watch. Still Huang Feihu could not sleep. He thought, "I used to have power and wealth. Now here I am, fleeing for my life!"

Suddenly a cold wind came into the room. The candle blew out, leaving the room in darkness. A voice called softly, "My lord, don't be afraid. It's your wife, Lady Jia. You are in great danger! Your hosts are preparing a fire that will burn all of you to death. Get up and get out of there immediately! Now I must return to the land of the dead."

Huang Feihu jumped up. He woke up the others. They ran to the door but found that it was locked from the other side. They smashed the door. They saw that the other side of the door was piled high with firewood. Quickly they pushed their luggage out of the building, jumped on their horses, and left the building. As they rode away, they looked back. They saw Chen Wu and his generals running towards the building, holding burning torches.

Chen Wu saw that he was too late. He and his men jumped on their horses and rode towards Huang Feihu and his men. He shouted, "You rebel! I was hoping to kill you and your whole family. You are still alive for now, but you will not escape my net!"

The two groups of fighters came together, and they battled

hand to hand, sword to sword. Huang Feihu fought against Chen Wu. After a few rounds, he stabbed Chen Wu in the heart, killing him.

The other fighting soon ended. Chen Wu's men were defeated. Some were killed, the rest returned to Chuanyun Pass.

The next pass was Jiepai Pass, eighty *li* away. "Well, at least we won't have to fight at Jiepai Pass," said Huang Ming to Huang Feihu. "The commander there is your father, old Huang Gun."

At Jiepai Pass, Huang Gun waited for his son to arrive. He was very angry when he heard that his son had rebelled against the king and killed so many generals and soldiers. He ordered three thousand soldiers to arrest his son and the others. He also prepared ten prison carts to carry them back to Zhaoge.

Chapter 33
The Battle at the Pass

Evil ministers have evil hearts;
They bring a hundred problems and a thousand disasters

They talk about their powerful magic,
But they don't know that all their plots will fail

Yu Hua tried to succeed but failed;
Han Rong's new rank is nothing compared to my dream

Heaven's will is already set;
When I think of the naming of the gods my heart fills with
tears

Huang Feihu and his men approached Jiepai Pass. They saw thousands of soldiers waiting for them, and they saw the prison carts. "Things don't look good," said one of the generals.

When Huang Feihu rode his ox close to the gate, he said to Huang Gun, "Father, your worthless son begs your pardon, I cannot kowtow to you."

"Who are you?" asked Huang Gun.

"I am your eldest son. How can you ask a question like that?"

Huang Gun shouted, "This family has been loyal to the king for seven generations. Never have we done anything evil, never have we committed treason. But now you have left your king because of a woman. You have cut off the precious jade from your waist. You are a rebel. You have dishonored your ancestors and your father. I don't know how you can even face me."

Tears came to Huang Feihu's eyes. He could not speak. Huang Gun continued, "If you want to be a filial sun, get down off your ox. I will take you to Zhaoge. You will die an honorable death as a true minister of the king. Or if you are truly unfilial, just go ahead and kill me. Then you can do what you wish, and I will not have to see or hear any of it."

By now, Huang Feihu was crying. He said, "Don't say anything more, Father. Take me to Zhaoge now." Then he prepared to get down from his ox. But before he could get down, his younger brother Huang Ming spoke.

"Brother, don't do it!" he said. "The king is a tyrant. Why should we be loyal to a tyrant? And why are you willing to commit suicide just because of what this old man says?"

Now Huang Feihu did not know what to do. He just sat on his ox, thinking but not speaking. Huang Ming turned to Huang Gun and said, "General, listen to me. You are wrong. Even a tiger would never kill its own child. Don't you know that the tyrant killed your daughter and made your daughter-in-law commit suicide? Don't you care about them, don't you want to avenge their deaths? The ancients say, 'If a ruler is evil, the people may seek a new ruler. If a father is unkind, his sons may leave him.' "

Hearing these words, Huang Gun became furious. He attacked Huang Ming, slashing at him with his sword. Huang Ming blocked his blows. He shouted to Huang Feihu, "Brother, I am keeping your father busy. Get out of the pass now, as fast as you can."

Huang Feihu and the others rushed out of the pass. When Huang Gun saw this, he jumped off his horse. He was so upset that he tried to kill himself with his sword. But Huang Ming jumped off his horse and grabbed him. He said, "Sir, please wait and listen to me. Your son Huang Feihu has made me very angry. He has insulted me and has tried to kill me several times. I could not say anything to you, because I was afraid he would hear me. But now that he is gone, I can speak freely. I have a plan."

"What is your plan?" asked Huang Gun.

"Go quickly and catch up to your son. Tell him that I was right, and a tiger would never kill its child. Invite him to come back and have dinner with you. Tell him you will go with him to West Qi. But as soon as he comes back, have your soldiers take their weapons. You can then put them all in the prison carts and take them to Zhaoge. As for me, I just hope that you and the king will forgive me."

Huang Gun said, "Huang Ming, you are a good man. I will do as you say." He jumped on his horse and went to catch up with Huang Feihu. He called out, "My son, I have decided to come with you to West Qi after all. Please come back. We can all eat some food and drink some wine, then we will go to West Qi."

Huang Feihu did not know why his father changed his mind. But he came back to the pass. He kowtowed to his father. Then they all sat down to eat and drink.

While they were eating dinner, two of Huang Feihu's men set fire to the buildings that held all the grain. Huang Gun saw the fire and ran outside. Immediately, Huang Feihu and the others rode out of the gate. "I've been fooled!" said Huang Gun.

"Father," said Huang Ming, "I must tell you the truth now. The king is an evil tyrant. But Ji Chang is a wise and good ruler. We are going to West Qi to join up with him and his army. You are welcome to join us."

He waited for a few seconds to let the old man think about this. Then he said, "Of course, we have just burned all your grain. If you don't join us, you won't be able to pay your taxes and you will certainly be executed by the king."

Huang Gun thought about it. Then he said, "All right. My family has been loyal for seven generations. But we are all rebels now." He kowtowed to Zhaoge eight times. Then he left Jiepai Pass, taking all his soldiers and guards with him.

Huang Gun said to Huang Ming, "I hope you know that you are leading the whole Huang family to its death. The next pass is Sishui Pass. There is a magician there named

Yu Hua. They call him the seven-headed general. He has never lost a battle. If I'd taken you to Zhaoge I might have lived. But now it looks like we will all die at Sishui Pass."

They rode for about eighty *li*, and they reached Sishui Pass late in the afternoon. The commander of the pass, a man named Han Rong, blocked the gate and prepared for battle.

The next day, the magician Yu Hua came out, shouting that he was ready to fight. Huang Feihu rode forward on his ox, saying, "I will fight him."

Yu Hua had a golden face, red hair and beard, and two golden eyes. He wore a tiger-skin robe under his armor, and a jade belt. "Who are you?" he shouted to Huang Feihu.

"I am prince Huang Feihu. I am rebelling against the wicked tyrant. We are going to West Qi to join up with the sage ruler there. Who are you?"

"I am Yu Hua. I'm sorry we have never met before. Tell me, why are you rebelling against our king?"

"It's a long story. But the short story is this: the king is a cruel tyrant who does not care about the people. But the leader of West Qi is a good and wise man, and he already controls two thirds of the Shang kingdom. It is the will of heaven that the king will fall. Now, will you please let us through?"

"Your Highness, I cannot possibly let you through. You are trying to climb a tree to catch a fish[1]. You are rebelling against the king, and that makes us enemies. Dismount now. I will take you back to Zhaoge and the king can decide what to do with you. There is no way that you will get

---

[1] In other words, you are attempting the impossible.

through this pass."

"I have already gotten through four passes. Yours is the last one. Let's see if you can stop me!" And with that, Huang Feihu raised his sword and attacked. He was a very good fighter. His sword was like a silver snake coiling around Yu Hua. Yu Hua could not fight back. He turned and fled. But as he fled, he turned and raised his Soul Killing Flag. A black cloud came out of it. It wrapped around Huang Feihu and threw him to the ground. The soldiers grabbed him and took him prisoner.

Huang Gun saw this. He said, "You fool! You did not listen to me. Now these men will get the reward for capturing you, instead of me."

The next day, Yu Hua came out again, ready for battle. Huang Ming and another general rode out to meet him. They fought for about twenty rounds. Then, just as before, Yu Hua rode away. Then he turned around and raised his Soul Killing Flag. The two men were surrounded by black smoke. They fell off their horses and were taken prisoner.

The next day, two more general fought Yu Hua. Both were surrounded by black smoke and were captured. And the day after that, the last two Huang generals more met the same fate. Now Yu Hua had seven prisoners. Huang Gun was alone with his three young grandsons.

Yu Hua came out once more, ready for battle. One of the three grandsons went out to fight him. The grandson was able to stab Yu Hua in the leg, but then he also was captured.

Huang Gun could not wait any longer. The old general took off his armor, then his jade belt and his robe. He put on white robes of mourning. Then he walked with his two grandsons to the gate. He said to the guard, "Please tell your commander that Huang Gun wishes to see him."

Then Huang Gun knelt at the gate and waited.

Chapter 34
The Rebel Meets the Prime Minister

There is chaos by the side of the road,
Because a foolish king causes trouble

The king is ruled by lust and does not care about his duties;
And so the nation suffers

Generals and ministers decide to serve a virtuous ruler;
Why does Han Rong try to stop them?

Nezha stands in the middle of the road;
Be careful when he picks up his gold brick!

Huang Gun saw Han Rong coming out. Generals stood on the commander's right and left sides. Huang Gun said, "Sir, this criminal kowtows to you. The Huang family has committed many crimes, and we must be punished. But I beg you to please spare the life of my seven-year-old grandson. If you let him live, the Huang family will survive. Would you please consider this, General?"

Han Rong replied, "General, I cannot do that. I am the commander here and I must obey the law. Your family enjoyed great wealth and honor, yet you chose to rebel against the king. Now I must send all of you, including your grandsons, to Zhaoge. The court will decide who is a criminal and who is not. If I did as you ask, I would be a rebel just as much as you."

"Your Excellency," cried Huang Gun, "how can there be harm in sparing a small child? The ancients say, 'If you can help someone but you don't, it's like returning from a treasure mountain with empty hands.' I beg you to show mercy to this small child."

But still Han Rong refused. He put Huang Gun and his grandsons in prison along with the rest of the Huang family.

Afterwards, Han Rong sat down for a banquet with Yu Hua and the other generals. He said, "Yu Hua, I want you to go with the prisoners to Zhaoge. Only then will I be sure that they will arrive with no trouble."

The next day, Yu Hua took three thousand soldiers and left for Zhaoge with his eleven prisoners.

Meanwhile, on Qianyuan Mountain, the immortal named Fairy Primordial was sitting on his bed. Suddenly his heart began to beat rapidly. He did not know why. He did a divination and saw that Huang Feihu and his family were in danger.

He called for his disciple Nezha. He said, "Disciple, I see that Huang Feihu and his family are in danger. Go and help them to get past Sishui Pass. When you are finished, come back here at once."

Nezha was very happy to get this order. He picked up his Fire Tip Lance and flew away on his magic wheels to just outside Chuanyun Pass. There he waited until he saw an army coming towards him. There was a great cloud of dust. Flags fluttered in the wind, and swords shone in the sun.

Nezha stood on his magic wheels in the middle of the road and began to sing:

> *I have lived so long, I don't know my age*
> *I obey my master, I do not fear heaven*
> *No matter who comes this way*
> *They must pay me in gold*

A soldier rode up to Yu Hua and said, "General, there's a strange man standing in the middle of the road. He is singing."

Yu Hua told his men to stop. He rode forward towards the man. "Who are you?" he shouted.

"You don't need to know my name. I have lived here for a long time. Anyone who passes by must pay me in gold. It does not matter if you are a king or a common man, you still must pay."

Yu Hua laughed and said, "I am a general, taking prisoners to Zhaoge. Get out of my way if you want to live."

"Fine. Just pay me ten gold coins and you can pass."

Yu Hua was furious. He attacked the man, not knowing that he was attacking an immortal. Nezha easily blocked his sword. Unable to win, Yu Hua fled. Then he turned and waved his Soul Killing Flag. But Nezha just laughed. He waved his hand and the flag flew into his hand. He put it in his bag. "Do you have any more of these?" he laughed.

Yu Hua came back and attacked Nezha again. Nezha threw his gold brick into the air. It came down, hitting Yu Hua on the head. The general almost fell off his horse. He rode away. Nezha threw the gold brick in the air again. All of Yu Hua's soldiers turned and rode away as fast as they could.

Nezha went over to the prison carts. He looked at the tired and dirty men in the carts. He said, "I am Li Nezha, disciple of Fairy Primordial. My master saw that you were in trouble and sent me to help you." Then he used his gold brick to smash open the prison carts, freeing the men. He continued, "I will go back to Sishui Pass and open the gates. You can go through with no problem." Huang Feihu and the other men fell to the ground and kowtowed to Nezha.

At Sishui Pass, Han Rong was drinking with his generals when Yu Hua returned. "What are you doing here?" he asked. Yu Hua told him about his fight with the immortal. Han Rong said, "We must bring those rebels back to Zhaoge. If we don't, the king will never forgive me."

A few minutes later, a soldier rushed in and said, "There's a man outside the gate. He is riding on a pair of wheels. He wants to fight the seven-headed general."

"That's the man who beat me!" cried Yu Hua. They all went out to see.

"Who are you?" asked Han Rong.

"I am Li Nezha, disciple of Fairy Primordial. My master sent me to help Huang Feihu. The Shang dynasty will fall soon, and Heaven has decided that the Huang family should help the new dynasty. I am here to help them get to West Qi. Why would you act against the will of heaven?"

Han Rong and his soldiers attacked Nezha, but Nezha was as strong as a dragon and as fast as lightning. Many soldiers fell from their horses. The rest of them fled for their lives.

Yu Hua mounted his monster and attacked Nezha. Nezha blocked his blows. Then he hit Yu Hua, breaking his arm. Yu Hua turned and fled.

That was the end of the battle. Sishui Pass was now open. Huang Feihu and his men passed through the gates and continued towards West Qi. They thanked Nezha, who said, "Take care of yourselves. We will meet again." Then Nezha returned to Qianyuan Mountain.

The Huang family and their army continued towards West Qi. They climbed many mountains and crossed many rivers. They stopped just outside West Qi City and set up camp.

Huang Feihu went alone into the city. He saw that the people in the city were healthy, wore good clothes, and were polite. There was lots of food in the marketplaces. He asked where the prime minister's mansion was. A man pointed to a gold-colored bridge and told him that the mansion was on the other side of the bridge.

He walked up to the mansion gate and told the guard that he was there to see the prime minister. A short time later, Jiang Ziya came out to meet him. "Please forgive me for not riding out to meet you," he said.

"I am a refugee now," replied Huang Feihu. "I am like a bird who has lost its nest. Would you be so kind as to take me in?"

"Of course. But tell me, why did you turn against the Shang Dynasty?" Huang Feihu told him everything that happened, and why became a rebel.

Jiang Ziya said, "Our king would be happy to have you here. Please rest a while. I need to talk with him."

Jiang Ziya went to the king's palace to meet with Ji Fa. He explained what had happened. Ji Fa was happy to hear the news. He asked that Huang Feihu be brought to see him.

The next day, Huang Feihu was brought in to see Ji Fa. He said, "Your Majesty, I am not alone. I am with my father, my brothers, my sons, my sworn brothers, a thousand guards, and three thousand soldiers. They are all waiting at Mount Qi. Please tell me what to do with them."

"Bring them all to the city," replied Ji Fa. "Each will keep their old rank, with no changes." Huang Feihu thanked him. His family and his army entered West Qi City, and they all became part of West Qi.

But soon war threatened the whole land.

Chapter 35
Two Generals Join West Qi

The Huang family travels west like flying hawks;
They hope to reach West Qi, no matter how long the journey

In the silent land the army travels through five passes;
The bleeding from battles never stops

Ziya makes clever plans to save the Zhou dynasty;
But Grand Tutor Wen cannot change the king's evil ways

The army is strong but has lost its virtue;
Chao Tian travels alone through the wind and fog of war

Grand Tutor Wen was angry. He had just tried to capture Huang Feihu, only to learn that he was chasing the wind. He had been tricked by the immortal Pure Void Virtue. As soon as he realized what had happened, he rushed back to Zhaoge to protect the king and the palace.

He met with the king's ministers and told them what happened. "We don't need to worry about Huang Feihu," he told them. "There are five mountain passes between here and West Qi. The passes are guarded by loyal commanders and many soldiers. Even if Huang Feihu had wings, he could not cross those five passes and get to West Qi."

But soon, messengers began to arrive with bad news. First, a messenger said that Huang Feihu had killed the commander of Linton Pass and gotten through. Then a second messenger arrived to say that Huang Feihu had killed the commander of Tongguan Pass and gotten through that too. A third messenger reported that Huang Feihu had gotten through Chuanyun Pass. And then a fourth messenger reported that the commander of Jiepai Pass had quit his job and gone to West Qi.

Finally, a messenger came and said that Han Rong, the commander of Sishui Pass, needed more soldiers immediately. Wen said, "I told the late king that I would protect his son. But I did not think this king would be such a terrible ruler. The Grand Dukes of the East and South have risen up against the king. And now we have lost Huang Feihu. I don't know if we can win this battle, or if the dynasty will fall. However, I told the late king that I would protect his son. So that is what I must do."

He called his generals to come and discuss the matter with

him. One of the generals said, "We don't need to worry about the rebels in West Qi. There are five mountain passes between them and us. Also, we don't have enough money to fight a new war. Let's just ignore West Qi."

Wen replied, "Remember the old saying, 'When you are dying of thirst, it's too late to dig a well.' We must prepare now to fight against West Qi."

"We need to learn more," said a general named Chao Tian. "I will go to West Qi. And I will fight them if I must."

The next day, Chao Tiao, his brother Chao Lei, and 30,000 soldiers left Zhaoge. They crossed the Yellow River and all five mountain passes, then set up camp outside the west gate of West Qi City. They waited for a while. Then Chao Lei rode forward on his horse towards the gate.

He shouted, "This is General Chao Lei. I am the leader of the king's army. We do not want your soldiers to die, so I am willing to fight one man from West Qi. Who will fight me?"

General Nangong Kuo, the leader of the Flying Tiger army, rode out of the gate. He shouted, "General Chao, why have you brought this army to our city?"

Chao Lei replied, "I have come here to arrest Ji Fa. He calls himself a king, but His Majesty does not approve of this. Also, he has taken in the rebel Huang Feihu. You must go back inside, tie up Ji Fa and Huang Feihu, and bring them out to me. If you don't, you and your people will suffer."

Nangong Kuo smiled and said, "Chao Lei, your king is an evil tyrant. He cuts his ministers into little pieces. He burns them on hot pillars. He feeds them to snakes. He took his own uncle's heart and fed it to his concubine Daji. He has killed many people who did nothing wrong. But here in West Qi, my king rules with kindness and wisdom. The people love him, and they are happy. Why don't you join us?"

Chao Lei did not answer. He rode forward to meet Nangong Kuo. Two horses met, two swords were raised, and two men began to fight. After about thirty rounds Chao Lei grew tired. Nangong Kuo knocked him off his horse. Soldiers tied him up and they took him into the city.

When he was brought before Jiang Ziya, Chao Lei refused to kneel. "Why don't you ask for mercy?" asked Jiang Ziya.

"I am a minister of heaven," replied Chao Lei. "You are just a small man who sells noodles and makes baskets. Why would I kneel before someone like you?"

When he said this, the other generals in the room could not stop themselves from smiling. Jiang Ziya understood why they smiled. He said to them, "This man is telling the truth. We know that in the past, Yi Yin was once a poor farmer, but he became prime minister to the first king of Shang[1]. This is fate. Some achieve greatness early, some late, some not at all." Then he pointed his finger at Chao Lei and said, "Take him outside and cut off his head."

The soldiers took Chao Lei outside. Quickly, Huang Feihu said, "Prime Minister, please let me talk with him. Maybe I can bring him over to our side. He could be useful to us."

Jiang Ziya agreed. Huang Feihu went outside, where he

---

[1] According to legend, Yi Yin was a slave. When his master's daughter married the king of Tang, he became the king's slave. He was a good cook, so the king made him his chef. While serving meals to the king, he often offered his advice. He earned the king's trust, was named a high-ranking minister, and ruled for several years as regent after his death.

found Chao Lei kneeling on the ground and waiting for the sword. He said, "General! Look around you. Your king is on the throne now, but it is like a few cold days in the spring. You know that it will not last. And you know that our king is a good man, just like Yao and Shun in ancient days. I have spoken to the prime minister. He will let you live and keep your old rank. Please think about this!"

Chao Lei said, "Thank you. But I have insulted your prime minister. Why would he let me live?"

"Let me take care of this." Together, they went back to see Jiang Ziya.

Chao Lei knelt. He said, "I have insulted you and I deserve to be executed. I am grateful to you for letting me live."

Jiang Ziya replied, "You have agreed to join us. We are now all part of the same government. You may live. Bring your troops in now."

"My brother is still out there. Let me go and talk with him. I will try to bring him over to our side." Jiang Ziya agreed, and Chao Lei left the city.

When he got to his brother's tent, Chao Tian asked him how he managed to escape from the city. Chao Lei replied, "They brought me before Jiang Ziya. I did not kneel. I insulted him. But then I talked with Huang Feihu, and now I believe we should join West Qi. Let's go back to the city together!"

"You fool!" shouted Chao Tian. "Don't you remember that our families are all in Zhaoge? Don't you care about your parents, your wife, your children? They will all be killed."

"Then what should we do?" The two brothers talked for a while. Then Chao Lei returned to the city to meet with

Jiang Ziya. He said, "My brother is willing to join us. But he is a general appointed by the king. He wants you to send a high-ranking general to meet with him."

"That's no problem," replied Jiang Ziya. Looking at Huang Feihu, he said, "Go and see him. Bring him back here." Huang Feihu left immediately. But after he left, Jiang Ziya spoke to Nangong Kuo and two other generals and gave them secret orders.

Huang Feihu arrived at the gate of the Shang camp. Chao Tian met him. "Come in, come in!" he said, smiling. But as soon as Huang Feihu entered the camp, soldiers jumped out from the right and left sides. They grabbed Huang Feihu and tied him up.

Huang Feihu shouted and fought, but the soldiers would not let go. Chao Tian said to him, "It's just like the old saying, 'You wore out your iron shoes searching for something, then it arrived with no effort at the right time.' Now we have you. We will take you back to Zhaoge."

The two Chao brothers left the camp immediately and headed back towards Zhaoge, bringing Huang Feihu who was bound with ropes and tied to a horse. They'd traveled about thirty-five *li* and it was getting dark when they suddenly found their road blocked by two generals. One of them said, "Release General Huang Feihu at once!"

Chao Tian shouted, "How dare you!" and attacked them with his sword. They began to fight. Then the other West Qi general rode forward and began to fight with Chao Lei. The fighting went on for a while. Chao Lei became tired, so he turned his horse around and fled. The two West Qi generals captured Chao Tian, then they freed Huang Feihu. They tried to find Chao Lei, but he was already gone.

Chao Lei had escaped from the two West Qi generals, but he did not know the area and he soon became lost. He turned around several times but could not find his way. Around midnight he came to a road. On the road was a small group of soldiers carrying lanterns. In the middle of the group was Nangong Kuo.

Chao Lei tried to fight Nangong Kuo, but he was not as strong and not as good a fighter. Nangong Kuo easily defeated him. Chao Lei was tied up and brought back to West Qi City.

Just before dawn, the two Chao brothers were brought before Jiang Ziya. Huang Feihu said to him, "Thank you, prime minister! You saved my life."

Jiang Ziya said, "I became suspicious when I heard that Chao Tian wanted you to go to their camp. So I sent three generals to wait for you. Things happened exactly as I thought they would."

Then he turned to the Chao brothers. He said coldly, "You are liars and traitors. But you could not trick me. Guards, take them outside and cut off their heads."

As they were being dragged out, Chao Lei cried, "Prime minister, please wait a minute!" Jiang Ziya held up his hand to stop the guards.

"I am listening," he said.

"Prime minister, everyone knows that the king of West Qi is a good man. We would love to join you. But our parents, wives and children are all still in Zhaoge. If we join you, they will all be executed!"

"You have the heart of a wolf. Why didn't you tell me this earlier?"

Chao Lei began to cry. "We are stupid and we did not think. We should have told you."

Jiang Ziya asked Huang Feihu if this story was true. Huang Feihu said that yes, their families were still in Zhaoge and were in great danger.

"All right," said Jiang Ziya. "Chao Tian will be kept here as a hostage. Chao Lei may return to the capital with my secret instructions. He will bring both of your families back here to West Qi."

Both brothers kowtowed to Jiang Ziya. Then Chao Lei set out for the capital.

Chapter 36
The First Attack on West Qi

Heading west by imperial decree, jade split in half[1];
Flags flutter in the air throughout the long journey

Surprised to see painted battle axes turn into leopards;
Even more surprised to see ice flowers turn into Buddha's swords

Zhang Guifang captures the enemy and receives a new title;
His skills are like jewels as he fights in wind and forest

Although wise and clever he is still defeated;
Helpless against the tyrant and the will of heaven

---

[1] In ancient China, a piece of jade would be split in half and shared by two parties to document a contract, an agreement, a royal declaration, or (in this case) a declaration of war.

Chao Lei traveled for several days, crossing mountains and rivers. When he arrived at the capital, he immediately went to see Grand Tutor Wen.

"What is the situation in West Qi, General?" asked Wen.

Chao Lei replied, "First, I fought against Nangong Kuo. We fought for thirty rounds but neither of us could win. The next day, my brother fought another general and defeated him. After that there were several days with more fights and more battles. But now we have almost no food left. Han Rong has not come to help us. The army is hungry and cannot fight. We need your help."

Grand Tutor Wen said, "I don't know why Han Rong has not given you the food you need. All right. Take three thousand soldiers and bring a thousand piculs of rice back to your army."

Chao Lei did as he was told. But without telling Grand Tutor Wen, he also brought his family and Chao Tian's family with him back to West Qi. He kowtowed to Jiang Ziya and told him, "I have brought our families from Zhaoge to West Qi City. Thank you, prime minister. We will never forget this."

Three days later, Grand Tutor Wen began to feel uneasy. He did not understand why Han Rong didn't give food to Chao's soldiers. He burned incense and did a divination. From this, he learned that Chao Lei had tricked him. Furious, he sent another of his generals, a man named Zhang Guifang, to West Qi. He put a hundred thousand soldiers under his command.

Zhang Guifang and his army traveled for several days. They arrived at West Qi City and camped a few *li* outside the south gate.

Inside the city, Huang Feihu said to Jiang Ziya, "I know this Zhang Guifang. He is a sorcerer. As you know, before a one-on-one fight, the fighters tell each other their names. When Zhang Guifang learns the name of his opponent, he shouts the name and says, 'Why don't you get down off your horse?' The man falls from his horse and is captured. We must be careful not to tell him our names."

The other generals heard this but they laughed, not believing it.

The next day there was a fight between one of Zhang Guifang's generals and Ji Chang's twelfth son. The son was killed in the fight.

The day after that, Zhang Guifang shouted that he wanted to fight Jiang Ziya. Jiang Ziya said, "If you want to capture the tiger, you must go into his cave." He rode out of the city to fight Zhang Guifang. He was dressed as a Daoist, with a white robe and a long white beard. He carried two swords and rode a black horse. His generals rode on his right and left sides. His soldiers followed behind them, wearing helmets of silver and gold.

On the opposite side, Zhang Guifang waited for him. He wore white robes, silver armor, and a silver helmet. He rode a white horse. He looked like a statue carved from ice.

Zhang Guifang rode forward. He said, "Jiang Ziya, how can you rebel against your king? You deserve to die. Get down off your horse and give yourself up. If you don't, I will smash your city. I don't care if jade is destroyed along with stone."

Jiang Ziya laughed. He said, "General, you are on the wrong side. Don't you know that a good minister serves a good master? You are a loyal general, but don't close your eyes to your king's foolish ways. Here we follow the law, but your king follows evil. Take my advice. Turn around and go back to Zhaoge."

Zhang Guifang ordered one of his generals to attack Jiang Ziya. The general rode forward and blocked the attack. While they were fighting, Zhang Guifang rode forward and attacked Huang Feihu who was on his great ox. They fought for fifteen rounds. Then Zhang Guifang called out, "Huang Feihu, get down from your ox!" Huang Feihu fell down from his ox. Some of Zhang Guifang soldiers tried to capture him, but two of Jiang Ziya's men fought them off and brought Huang Feihu back to their side.

The battle continued for a while. Zhang Guifang captured Nangong Kuo and another general, then they returned to their camp. They put the two prisoners in wooden carts, to be returned to Zhaoge.

The next day, Zhang Guifang called out again to Jiang Ziya to fight him. But Jiang Ziya would not come out. He hung up a sign declaring a truce. When Zhang Guifang saw the sign, he smiled and said, "Good. Let's enjoy a short rest."

Meanwhile, Fairy Primordial was sitting in his cave when he felt something strange in his heart. He did a divination to find out what was happening. Then he told his disciple to bring Nezha to see him. Nezha arrived and kowtowed to his master.

Fairy Primordial said to Nezha, "Your uncle, Jiang Ziya, needs your help. West Qi is in trouble. They will face thirty-six invasions. Go there now and see how you can help them."

Nezha kowtowed again. Then he picked up his weapons, jumped up on his Wind Fire Wheels, and went to see his uncle the prime minister. He knelt down before Jiang Ziya.

"Who are you and where do you come from?" asked Jiang Ziya.

"This poor disciple's name is Li Nezha. My master, Fairy Primordial, has commanded me to come and serve you. What can I do to help you?"

"You have come just in time. We are being attacked by one of the king's generals, a man named Zhang Guifang. He is a great sorcerer. He has already captured two of our best generals. We have had to hang the truce sign."

Nezha said, "Uncle, it is time to end the truce. I will meet this sorcerer and take him captive."

Jiang Ziya ordered the sign of truce to be taken down. Almost immediately, Zhang Guifang called for a fight. Nezha said that he wanted to fight Zhang Guifang. "Be careful," said Jiang Ziya. "This sorcerer can make you fall just by calling your name."

"Don't worry, Uncle," said Nezha. Then he mounted his Wind Fire Wheels and rode out of the city.

He saw a large and very ugly man waiting for him. The man had a blue face, red hair, and long teeth. In each hand he held a wolf-teeth club.

Nezha said, "I don't know who you are. But get out of my way. I want to fight Zhang Guifang." The man, whose name was Feng Lin, became angry. He attacked Nezha. They fought for twenty rounds. Then Feng Lin rode away on his horse like a strong wind blowing away a leaf. Nezha chased him like heavy rain hitting a flower. Suddenly Feng Lin turned around and spat out a cloud of black smoke. In the cloud was a red ball. It flew right towards Nezha's face.

Nezha said to himself, "This is not the way of the Dao. This is sorcery." He waved his hand at the smoke and the ball, and they both disappeared. Feng Lin turned around angrily to fight Nezha. But Nezha threw his Universal Ring at the man. It hit him and broke his shoulder bone. Injured and unable to fight, Feng Lin rode slowly back to his camp.

When Zhang Guifang heard what happened, he became very angry. He mounted his horse and rode out to meet Nezha. "So," he said, looking at the man standing on the Wind Fire Wheels, "you are Nezha."

"Of course," replied Nezha. "Are you the fool who calls out peoples' names to make them fall?"

This made Zhang Guifang even more angry. He attacked Nezha. They fought for a long time, maybe thirty or forty rounds. One fought for his king and country, the other fought for the entire world. Both were very good fighters. But Nezha was an immortal. Zhang became tired. He tried to use sorcery, calling out, "Nezha, get down from your wheels!"

Nezha heard the magic words. His feet wanted to move, but he stopped them. His body did not move.

Zhang tried again and again, using the same words. Finally, Nezha said, "What a fool you are! You can see that I am not going to get down from my wheels. Why do you keep barking at me like an old dog?"

Zhang attacked Nezha again, but he could not hit him with his swords. After a while, Nezha grabbed his Universal Ring and threw it, hard, right at Zhang's head.

Chapter 37
Jiang Ziya Returns to Mount Kunlun

Jiang Ziya returns to the palace for the first time;
The mist parts before the jade tower as he approaches

Earthly dreams float away on green waters;
Green mountains watch the death of wise rulers

The army and the people meet disaster as the war begins;
Generals and soldiers die from strange magic

Their fate is to endure the investiture of the gods;
A new tower rises on Mount Qi

Nezha's Universal Ring flew through the air. It hit Zhang, breaking his left arm. Zhang was able to stay on his horse, but he could not fight, so he turned and fled. He sent a message to Grand Tutor Wen in Zhaoge, asking for more soldiers.

Nezha returned to West Qi City and met with Jiang Ziya.

"What happened?" asked Jiang Ziya. "Did that sorcerer call your name?"

Nezha replied, "I threw my Universal Ring at him and broke his arm. He called my name three times, but I just ignored him."

How could Nezha just ignore Zhang Guifang's magic? Anyone who is born from essence and blood has three souls and seven spirits[1]. When Zhang Guifang calls their name, these souls and spirits are sent away from their body, in all directions. But Nezha was born from lotus flowers and had no soul or spirit. That is why the magic could not touch him.

Jiang Ziya was worried. He did not know what he would do if the king sent a larger army. He bathed, put on clean robes, and went to see Ji Fa. He said, "Your Highness, I must go to Mount Kunlun to see my master."

"Don't be long," replied Ji Fa. "We need you here."

"I will return in two or three days."

Jiang Ziya bowed to Ji Fa, then flew to Mount Kunlun on a dust cloud. He looked around. He had not seen this place

---

[1] A person has three *hún*, the "spiritual soul" which goes to heaven and can leave the body, and also seven *pò*, the animal soul which is attached to the body and goes to earth at the time of death. These are often translated as just "soul" and "spirit."

for ten years, and everything looked new. The sun was shining. Thousands of trees covered the mountains in a green blanket. Grasses and colorful flowers filled the air with a sweet fragrance. Phoenixes flew through the sky, black monkeys rested in the trees. Blue lions and white elephants could be seen on the mountainside. It was more beautiful than heaven.

Jiang Ziya entered the palace and knelt before his master, and said, "Your disciple wishes the teacher to live forever!"

Heavenly Primogenitor said, "I am happy that you have come to see me. I have a job for you. You must go to Mount Qi and build a Terrace of Creation. Here is an important paper, it is the Feng Shen Bang[1]. Hang it up in the terrace. This will be the most important work of your life."

Jiang Ziya took the Feng Shen Bang. Then he said, "Master, please help me. A powerful sorcerer named Zhang Guifang is attacking West Qi. I am a weak disciple with no knowledge or power to use against him. Can you help me?"

But Heavenly Primogenitor said, "Must I help you with every little thing? You are prime minister now, with great wealth and great power. Your ruler is a good and wise man. You will get help from other people when you need it. You don't need my help. Now go."

Jiang Ziya got up and started to leave. But Heavenly Primogenitor held up his hand. He said, "Wait. One more thing. After you leave here, do not answer anyone who calls you from behind. If you do, West Qi will be invaded thirty-

---

[1] This document lists the names of all the mortals and immortals who are fated to be elevated to gods. It is called *fēng shén bǎng,* which is also the popular title of this book.

six times."

Jiang Ziya walked out of the palace, holding the Feng Shen Bang in his hand. As he walked, he heard someone behind him calling, "Jiang Ziya! Jiang Ziya!"

Of course, Jiang Ziya did not turn around because he remembered what his master had just told him. He kept walking. He heard the voice say, "Jiang Ziya! How can you forget your old friends? We were together in this palace for over forty years. But now that you are a prime minister, you don't even bother to talk with me anymore?"

Jiang Ziya turned around. He saw his old friend Shen Gongbao, who was also a disciple of Heavenly Primogenitor. The man wore a long silk robe and a blue scarf. There were clouds and fog under his straw sandals. He held a bright metal sword in his hand.

Jiang Ziya said, "Brother, I did not know it was you. I'm sorry if I offended you."

"What's that in your hand?" asked Shen Gongbao.

"It's the Feng Shen Bang. Master asked me to put it in a new terrace that I must build on Mount Qi."

"Tell me, brother. Which side are you on?"

"What a strange question! Our master asked me to help Ji Fa, the king of West Qi, to bring about the end of the Shang Dynasty. Now I am the prime minister of West Qi. This is heaven's plan."

"We will see about that. I am leaving right now. I am going to Zhaoge to help protect the Shang Dynasty and the king. You must help me if we are to remain friends."

"But brother, we must follow our master's orders!"

"No, I want you to protect the Shang Dynasty. Look, you are nothing compared to me. You have only studied for forty years. But I am much more powerful than you. I can move mountains and oceans. I can defeat dragons and tigers. I can fly on a crane to the ninth heaven, and I can ride on a beam of light for a thousand years."

"You have powers, but so do I," said Jiang Ziya.

"Your little powers are nothing. If you cut off my head, it can fly for a thousand miles on a red cloud. When it returns to my neck, I become whole again. Can you do that?"

Jiang Ziya laughed. He said, "Brother, let me cut off your head and throw it in the air. If you can live after that, I will burn the Feng Shen Bang and follow you to Zhaoge."

"Do you promise?"

"Of course. A man's words are as heavy as Mount Tai."

Shen Gongbao took off his scarf. He pulled up his hair with his left hand. With his right hand he swung his sword, cutting off his own head. His left hand threw his head up into the air. It flew up and up and up, until it disappeared in the sky.

A friend of Heavenly Primogenitor, the Immortal of the South Pole, was watching this. He saw the two men arguing. Then he saw Shen Gongbao cut off his own head. He saw the head flying up into the air. "Oh, Jiang Ziya," he said, "you have been tricked." Then he called to one of his disciples. "Quick. Change yourself into a white crane. Fly up, grab that head, and take it to the South Sea." The disciple did as he was told.

Then the Immortal of the South Pole came over to Jiang

Ziya. He said, "You are a fool. Don't you know that Shen Gongbao is a sorcerer? He tricked you. Your master told you not to turn around if someone called you, but you did not obey him. Now you will have to deal with thirty-six invasions."

Jiang Ziya could not say anything. He just looked at the ground. The Immortal of the South Pole continued, "I told my disciple to take his head. If the head does not return in three hours, Shen Gongbao will die. Then you will be out of trouble."

Jiang Ziya said, "Please, brother, don't do this. Daoism teaches us kindness and mercy. It does not matter what Shen Gongbao did. You must show mercy to him."

"All right," said the Immortal of the South Pole. He waved his hand. The white crane opened its mouth. The head fell onto Shen Gongbao's neck. The man opened his eyes and looked around. He saw that his head was backwards on his neck. He lifted up his head, turned it around, and put it on his neck again.

The Immortal of the South Pole said to him, "How dare you try to trick Jiang Ziya like that! Get out of here right now."

Shen Gongbao said to Jiang Ziya, "Just wait. I will turn West Qi into an ocean of blood and a mountain of bones." Then he left.

Jiang Ziya also left. Holding the Feng Shen Bang in his hand, he headed towards West Qi City. As he flew over a mountain, he saw a great sea. Huge waves crashed against the shore. Black clouds filled the sky and a powerful wind blew through the trees. Then a naked man walked out of the waves. Jiang Ziya flew down to meet the man.

The man said, "Great immortal! I have been trapped here for a thousand years. A few days ago, a master named Pure Void Virtue came to see me. He said that soon I would meet a great master and that I should serve him. Please release me from this place, and I will be your servant!"

"Who are you?" asked Jiang Ziya.

"My name is Bai Jian. I was a general under the great emperor Xuanyuan. I was killed in battle and have been trapped here ever since."

"All right," said Jiang Ziya. He held out his hand. A bolt of lightning came from each finger. The lightning flew towards the sea, releasing Bai Jian.

He said, "Bai Jian, you must come with me and serve West Qi." Bai Jian fell to his knees and kowtowed.

The two of them continued towards West Qi City. Soon Jiang Ziya saw five gods waiting to meet him. They all cried, "We are here to serve you, prime minister!"

"All right," said Jiang Ziya. "Go to Mount Qi. Start building the Terrace of Creation. This man, Bai Jian, will supervise the work. When the terrace is finished, I will come back."

The five gods and Bai Jian went to Mount Qi and began to work on building the terrace. Jiang Ziya continued on his journey back to West Qi City.

He reached West Qi City. He met with Ji Fa, but he did not tell him everything that happened, because the will of heaven must be kept secret.

That night, he ordered a night attack on Zhang Guifang's camp. The attack was a complete surprise. Nezha and the West Qi soldiers fought well. Soon they reached Nangong

Kuo, freeing him from his prison cart.

Zhang Guifang and the few surviving Shang soldiers fled to Mount Qi. He quickly wrote a report and sent it to Zhaoge, requesting more soldiers and supplies.

The report reached Grand Tutor Wen. He read it, and his eyes grew big. "What? I gave Zhang Guifang a large army, but he could not win the battle. It looks like this old man must go to West Qi and take care of this matter himself."

One of his generals said, "Sir, please think again. We need you here in Zhaoge. You have many powerful Daoist friends in the mountains. Ask them to help us!"

This seemed like a good idea. But it caused the deaths of four great Daoist masters.

Chapter 38
Four Monks in West Qi

Since ancient times the king's way has always been kindness;
Foolish war leads to defeat and death

Soldiers rush forward seeking fame;
They find only disaster and are cut off from the gods

Great skills and rare treasures, who has them?
Fighting for victory, what is real?

Better to close your eyes and sit in the mountains;
Find joy and return to your natural state

Grand Tutor Wen clapped his hands and said, "That is a wonderful idea! I have been so busy, I'd forgotten all about my old Daoist friends." Then he turned to his generals and said, "I will be gone for a few days."

He went outside and mounted his unicorn. Together they rose up into the sky. They rode on the clouds and the wind until they arrived at Nine Dragon Island in the western sea. He landed near a large cave. A young man came out of the cave.

"Is your master here?" asked Wen.

"Yes," said the young man. "He is playing chess with his friends."

"Please tell him that Grand Tutor Wen is here to see him."

The young man went back into the cave. A few minutes later, four old Daoists came out. "Brother Wen," said one of them, "it is good to see you!"

Wen said, "I have come to ask for your help. Jiang Ziya, a Daoist immortal from Mount Kunlun, has been helping Ji Fa to rebel against the king. I sent Zhang Guifang to stop him, but he could not win. I cannot go myself, because I am needed in the capital. I am asking the four of you to help me."

"Of course," they said, "we will be happy to help you. Please return to Zhaoge. We will meet you there soon."

The next day, the four Daoists flew to Zhaoge on a water cloud. The people of the city saw them and were frightened. The four Daoists were all around sixteen feet tall and quite ugly. The first one, Wang Mo, had a face as round as the moon. He wore a grey robe and a long scarf. The second, Yang Sen, had a black face, a red beard, and yellow eyebrows. He wore a purple robe. The third, Gao Youqian, had long red hair and had long fangs that stuck out from the top and bottom of his mouth. He wore a scarlet robe. The fourth Li Xingba, had a dark brown face and a long beard. He wore a golden crown and a yellow robe.

The four Daoists soon found the home of Grand Tutor Wen. Wen brought them to the palace to meet the king, who was quite frightened by their appearance. After that, the four Daoists left the city and flew to West Qi.

They found the Shang soldiers hiding on Mount Qi, about seventy *li* from the city. They were met by Zhang Guifang and Feng Lin. Both of the generals had trouble walking. "Are you injured?" asked Wang Mo.

Feng Lin told them about the recent battles. Wang Mo took some medicine from his sleeve, crushed it between his teeth, and put it on their wounds. The wounds healed immediately.

Wang Mo told the generals to bring their army back to West Qi City. Then he told Zhang Guifang to challenge Jiang Ziya to a fight.

Yang Sen gave magic charms to the two generals. He said, "Put these charms on your horses. It will stop them from being frightened when they see our beasts."

Zhang Guifang rode towards the city gate, alone. He shouted to Jiang Ziya to come out and fight him. Soon Jiang Ziya came out, followed by hundreds of soldiers. He rode a big black horse and carried a sword. He said, "Zhang Guifang, you were defeated once already. Why are you here again?"

Zhang Guifang replied, "Victory and defeat, this is the fate of a warrior. But now things have changed. Look!"

Four strange animals appeared behind Zhang Guifang. Wang Mo rode a monster. Yang Sen rode a lion. Gao Youqian rode a leopard. And Li Xingba rode a unicorn.

The horses of the West Qi army saw these strange animals. They reared up in fright, throwing Jiang Ziya and his generals to the ground. Only Nezha remained on his wind fire wheels.

The four Daoists looked down at Jiang Ziya and laughed. They said, "Get up slowly, old man!"

Jiang Ziya stood up and straightened his hat and robes. He bowed to the four Daoists and said, "Hello, brothers. Who are you, where do you come from, and what can I do for you?"

Wang Mo said, "We are four Daoists like yourself. We come from Nine Dragon Island. Grand Tutor Wen asked us to come and help you. We have three proposals for you."

"If your proposals are good, you can give me thirty of them. Please tell me what they are!" replied Jiang Ziya.

"First, your king Ji Fa must agree that he is a subject of the Shang Dynasty."

"Brother, our king has always been a loyal subject. That is no problem."

"Second, you must give away all the treasure in West Qi to the Shang soldiers. And third, you must give us Huang Feihu."

Jiang Ziya said, "I see no problem with your three proposals. Please allow me to return to the city and write a letter to His Majesty. And please thank His Majesty for his kindness towards us."

The two sides returned to their own camps. Huang Feihu said to Jiang Ziya, "Prime minister, I do not want our king or our city to suffer because of me. Please give me to them, so they can take me as a prisoner to Zhaoge."

"Don't worry," replied Jiang Ziya. "I do not plan to accept their three proposals. But we could not fight with all of our generals lying on the ground. I needed some time to think about what to do next."

Jiang Ziya bathed, then he traveled again to Mount Kunlun to see his master. Before he could say anything, Heavenly Primogenitor held up his hand and said, "I know that there are four Daoists causing trouble in West Qi. They are riding four beasts from ancient times." Then he turned to his servant and told him, "Bring my beast."

A short time later, the boy returned with the beast. It had the head of a unicorn, the body of a dragon, and the tail of a wolf. The master said, "I have chosen you to create the new gods. Now I give you my own beast, so you can meet those four beasts without fear."

Then he gave a long wooden staff to Jiang Ziya. He said, "Go to the northern sea. Someone will be waiting for you there. Protect yourself with this staff. It has a note hidden inside. If you run into trouble, take out the note and read it. You will know what to do."

Jiang Ziya kowtowed to his master. Then he took the staff, mounted the beast and flew to the northern sea. The beast brought him down on a mountain near an island in the sea. The mountainside was covered with beautiful flowers, tall bamboos and large pine trees. He could hear the sound of the sea below.

Suddenly dark clouds appeared. Then a very strange creature came out of the clouds. It had the body of a fish but a head like a camel. It had hands with sharp claws, and one foot that looked like a tiger's foot.

The creature shouted, "Jiang Ziya! Give me a piece of your flesh!"

Jiang Ziya said, "Why? We are not enemies."

"You cannot escape. Give me a piece of your flesh right now!"

Jiang Ziya did not know what to do. He pulled the note out of the staff and read it. Now he knew what to do. He said, "Do you want to eat me? Just pull this staff out of the ground. If you can do that, I will let you eat me." Then he pushed the end of the staff into the ground.

The staff grew to be about twenty feet long. The beast tried to pull it out of the ground, but it did not move. He kept trying, but he could not move it. Then Jiang Ziya held his hands up to the sky. Lightning and thunder came from each of his fingers. The beast tried to let go of the staff, but his hands were stuck. "Eat my sword!" shouted Jiang Ziya.

"Great immortal," cried the beast, "please have mercy on me! I did not know who you were. This was all Shen Gongbao's fault."

"What?" replied Jiang Ziya. "What does Shen Gongbao have to do with this?"

"Oh great one, I am Dragon Beard Tiger. I have lived here for many years by eating the essence of the sun and moon. Two days ago, Shen Gongbao came to see me. He said that you would be coming here today. He said that if I ate a piece of your flesh, I would live for ten thousand years. I was a fool to believe him. Please have mercy on me."

"I will let you live, but only if you become my disciple."

"I will."

Jiang Ziya told him to close his eyes. Then he sent a huge thunderbolt, and Dragon Beard Tiger found that he could move his hands again. He knelt before his new master. Jiang Ziya pulled the staff out of the ground, and the two of them went to West Qi City. He said to his generals, "This is Dragon Beard Tiger from the northern sea. He is my new disciple."

Days passed. Nobody came out of West Qi City to bring Huang Feihu to the Shang army. After eight days, Yang Sen said to Wang Mo, "Brother, it has been eight days. Jiang Ziya has not brought the prisoner out. Let's ask him why."

The Shang army, led by Feng Lin and the four Daoists, marched to the city wall. They shouted for Jiang Ziya to come out. Soon Jiang Ziya came out, riding his black horse. Nezha, Dragon Beard Tiger and Huang Feihu were with him.

The battle started with Wang Mo shouting and attacking Jiang Ziya with his sword. Nezha rode forward on his Wind Fire Wheels and fought against Wang Mo.

Next, Yang Sen rode forward and threw a magic pearl at Nezha, knocking him off his magic wheels. Wang Mo tried to cut off Nezha's head but Huang Feihu stopped him.

Yang Sen threw another magic pearl, this time at Huang Feihu, knocking him off his ox. But Dragon Beard Tiger ran forward and attacked Wang Mo. Quickly, Gao Youqian threw one of his own magic pearls, hitting Dragon Beard Tiger on the neck.

With three of his generals wounded, Jiang Ziya was fighting alone. Li Xingba threw a magic pearl and hit him in the heart. He cried out in pain, turned around, and fled towards the northern sea. He saw Wang Mo chasing him. So he told his beast to fly into the air. But Wang Mo shouted, "Don't you know, any Daoist can fly through the clouds!" He told his monster to follow Jiang Ziya.

As they flew through the air, Wang Mo threw a magic pearl. It hit Jiang Ziya on the back, knocking him off his beast and onto the ground. Wang Mo got off his monster. He stood over Jiang Ziya, preparing to cut off his head. But just then, he heard someone singing:

> *Soft winds blow through the willow trees*
> *Flower petals fall onto the water*
> *If someone askes me where I live*
> *My home is deep in the white clouds*

Wang Mo looked around, and saw that it was the Heavenly Master Manjusri. "What are you doing here, brother?" asked Wang Mo.

The master replied, "Dear friend, don't hurt him. I have come here to tell you that Heaven has decided several things. First, the Shang Dynasty will end. Second, a new king has been born in West Qi. Third, Chan Daoism must break the rule against killing. Fourth, Jiang Ziya will enjoy wealth and power in the world. Fifth, he will create new gods. My friend, listen to me. Go back to your cave while you can. Soon it will be too late."

Wang Mo did not want to hear all this. He raised his sword and started to attack the Heavenly Master Manjusri. But just then, a young Daoist in a yellow robe stepped out from behind the master. He said, "Stop, Wang Mo. I am Jinzha, disciple of the Heavenly Master."

Wang Mo and Jinzha began to fight, sword against sword. While they were fighting, Heavenly Master Manjusri pulled out a stake[1] from his sleeve. He threw it in the air. When it came down on Wang Mo, it held him tightly with three golden rings. One ring was around his neck, one around his waist, and one around his feet. He could not move.

Jinzha raised his sword and aimed it at Wang Mo's neck.

---

[1] Manjusri's weapon is a *dùn lóng zhuāng,* a pillar-like rod with three golden rings, and dragons wrapped around it.

Chapter 39
Jiang Ziya Freezes Mount Qi

The four immortals fight heaven for no good reason;
They use their strange skills to turn things upside down

Men come from the west with the List of Creation;
Going north, they will know immortality

How many great people have disappeared in this land;
Many evil deeds have led to those crimes

A thousand feet of snow falls in July;
You and Fei die and travel to the land of Nine Springs[1]

---

[1] The underworld is said to consist of nine wells, one after the other, giving rise to the term *jiŭquán zhī xià*, "under the nine springs."

With one blow, Jinzha's sword cut off Wang Mo's head. Wang Mo's soul left his body and flew to the Terrace of Creation.

Jiang Ziya was still lying on the ground, badly injured. Heavenly Master Manjusri poured a little bit of magic elixir into his mouth. Soon Jiang Ziya opened his eyes. He saw Heavenly Master Manjusri and said, "Brother, why are you here?"

Heavenly Master Manjusri smiled and said, "It is the will of heaven." Then he turned to Jinzha and said, "Help your uncle return to West Qi." After they departed, Heavenly Master Manjusri dug a grave and buried Wang Mo's body. Then he returned to his own home.

Jiang Ziya and Jinzha returned to West Qi. The king and all his generals welcomed them. "Where were you?" asked Ji Fa. "We were all worried about you."

"If it were not for Jinzha and his master, I would not be alive today," Jiang Ziya replied.

In the Shang camp, the three Daoist masters were very worried. They had all seen Wang Mo chasing Jiang Ziya across the sky, but Wang Mo had not returned yet. Yang Sen did a divination with his fingers. Then he cried out, "Oh no! For thousands of years our brother studied the Way, but now he has died on Five Dragon Mountain."

The next morning, the three Daoists rode to the gate of West Qi City, demanding that Jiang Ziya come out and meet them. Jiang Ziya was still weak from his injuries, but he rode out anyway, accompanied by Nezha and Jinzha.

The three Daoists shouted, "Jiang Ziya, you monster! You killed our brother. Now we cannot let you live!"

They rushed forward to attack Jiang Ziya. Nezha and Jinzha rushed to block them. The six warriors battled, sword against sword. Red clouds filled the sky. Then Jiang Ziya threw his magic staff in the air. There was a flash of lightning and a roar of thunder. The staff came down and hit Gao Youqian on the head. He died instantly, and his soul flew to the Terrace of Creation.

Yang Sen, blind with rage, charged at Jiang Ziya. But Nezha threw his universal ring at him. As the Daoist tried to catch the ring, Jinzha used his magic stake to capture him, three rings wrapping around his body. Then Jinzha cut him in half with his sword. Yang Sen's soul also flew to the Terrace of Creation.

Now there was only one of the four Daoist masters left, Li Xingba. He rushed into the fight, along with Zhang Guifang and Feng Lin. During the fight, Feng Lin was killed by one of Huang Feihu's sons. His soul also flew to the Terrace of Creation.

Zhang Guifang saw that they could not win the battle, so he returned to the Shang camp along with Li Xingba. He sent a message to Grand Tutor Wen in Zhaoge asking for more soldiers.

The next day, Jiang Ziya rode out of the city and demanded to see Zhang Guifang. The two men began to fight. One fought to protect his king, the other fought to save his country. After thirty rounds neither could win. Jiang Ziya ordered that the drums be beaten, ordering his entire army to attack. Dozens of men on horses surrounded Zhang Guifang, who fought like a wild tiger.

Jinzha and his brother Nezha fought against Li Xingba. Li Xingba could not fight both of them. He flew away on his beast.

Now Zhang Guifang was fighting alone, with all his generals dead or defeated. He knew he could not get out alive. He shouted, "My king, I cannot serve you any longer!" Then he stabbed himself with his short sword. His soul flew to the Terrace of Creation.

Li Xingba flew far from the battle. After a while he arrived at a mountain side and dismounted from his beast. Exhausted, he lay down to rest. A little while later he heard the sound of someone singing. Looking up, he saw a young Daoist coming towards him. The young man bowed and said, "Greetings, brother! Who are you and where do you come from?"

"I am Li Xingba, a Daoist master from Nine Dragon Island. I was fighting in a great battle, but our side was defeated. I came here to rest a bit."

"How wonderful to meet you! I am Muzha. My master sent me to help my uncle Jiang Ziya. My master told me that if I met a man named Li Xingba, I should capture him and bring him to Jiang Ziya."

Li Xingba laughed and said, "You foolish boy. How dare you insult me like this!" He got up and slashed at Muzha with his sword. They fought up and down the mountain side. Li Xingba was a powerful fighter, but Muzha carried two magic swords on his back, one female and one male. He shook his left shoulder. The male sword flew into the air, dropped down on Li Xingba and cut off his head. Li Xingba's soul flew to the Terrace of Creation to join the others.

Back in Zhaoge, Grand Tutor Wen received a report. He read it and learned that Feng Lin and all four of the Daoists had been killed. He immediately called for a meeting with all of his generals to discuss how to help Zhang Guifang. He did not know that Zhang Guifang had also been killed.

An elderly general named Lu Xiong stepped forward. He said, "I would like to go and help Zhang Guifang."

Wen smiled and said to the white haired general, "Thank you, my old friend. But you have lived for many years. This might be difficult for you."

The old man replied, "Grand Tutor, youth is not as important as you might think. A good general must understand the situation. He must bring together his soldiers to fight as one. He must know how to make a weak army strong. He must know when to attack and when to retreat. He must turn danger into safety, and defeat into victory. Give me a couple of good advisors and I will bring you victory."

Wen was very happy to hear these words. He said, "Wonderful. I will give you two of our king's best advisors." Then he ordered the two evil ministers Fei Zhong and You Hun to come see him immediately.

When they arrived, Wen told them, "We need your help. Feng Lin has been killed and Zhang Guifang has been defeated. You are to go with General Lu and help him turn this defeat into victory."

The two ministers were terrified. Fei Zhong said, "Grand Tutor, we know nothing about war. We are ministers, not soldiers! We cannot help you."

"Both of you are clever. You know what to do when the situation changes. That is what we need right now. No more discussion. Go now!"

Fei Zhong and You Hun had no choice, they had to agree to go. Soon they marched off to war, with General Lu and fifty thousand soldiers.

It was summer. The weather was very hot. The sky was cloudless and there was no wind. The soldiers and horses had no water. They suffered badly in the hot weather. Then a message arrived that Zhang Guifang had been killed. General Lu decided to wait before going to West Qi City. He brought his army into the forest near Mount Qi to wait for instructions from Zhaoge.

In West Qi City, Jiang Ziya heard that there was a large army camped near Mount Qi. He sent Nangong Kuo and a small army of five thousand men to Mount Qi to keep an eye on the Shang army.

The next day, they received an order from Jiang Ziya. They were to march to near the top of Mount Qi. "We will die if we try to do this!" said one of the generals.

Nangong Kuo replied, "We cannot disobey an order." They began marching up the mountain. There was no water for drinking or cooking. It was so hot and dry that the trees were dying and birds were falling dead from the sky. The Shang soldiers saw them marching up the mountain, and laughed at their foolishness.

Soon Jiang Ziya arrived with another three thousand men. And then carts arrived carrying loads of heavy jackets and hats. "What are these for?" asked the soldiers. "If we put these on, we will just die faster."

That night, Jiang Ziya went alone to the top of the mountain. He took out his sword and bowed to Mount Kunlun. Then he spoke some magic words and poured some magic water on the ground. Soon, a strong wind blew through the forest. The air began to get cool.

The Shang general Lu Xiong smiled and said, "This weather is much better for fighting!" But the wind kept blowing, and the weather kept getting colder and colder. For three days the wind blew and the weather got colder. On the fourth day it began to snow.

The Shang soldiers were wearing thin clothes and metal armor. They began to suffer badly from the cold. The elderly general Lu Xiong was nearly frozen to death. But at the top of the mountain, the Zhou soldiers put on the warm clothing and were quite comfortable.

The snow kept falling. Near the top of the mountain there was only two feet of snow, but lower down it was four or five feet deep.

Then Jiang Ziya went to the top of the mountain again. He began to recite different magic words. The snow stopped. The hot sun returned. The snow began to melt. The water rushed down the side of the mountain in fast-flowing rivers.

Then Jiang Ziya recited more magic words. The weather turned very cold. The water turned to ice. Soon, the side of the mountain was covered by a frozen sea of ice.

Jiang Ziya selected twenty of his men and told them, "Go down the mountain side into the Shang camp. Capture the officers." The Zhou soldiers went into the Shang camp. They found everyone frozen in ice. They easily captured General Lu, Fei Zhong, and You Hun. They brought the three prisoners up the mountain to face Jiang Ziya.

Chapter 40
The Shang Army Surrounds West Qi City

The four Mo brothers are called heavenly kings;
Only the Green Cloud Sword is special

When the pipa plays, soldiers die;
When the magic umbrella opens, light turns to darkness

Don't speak of how fire can burn;
Speak of how the magic fox can eat the strong

Even if you have many treasures of the world;
Once you meet Huang Tianhua, you are fated to die

When the three prisoners were brought to the Zhou camp, Fei Zhong and You Hun fell to their knees and begged for mercy. But General Lu Xiong stayed on his feet and said nothing.

Jiang Ziya ignored the two kneeling ministers. To Lu Xiong he said, "General, you must learn how to tell truth from lies. Everyone knows that your king is evil. Two thirds of the country knows this, and they now follow us. Why do you continue to act against the will of heaven?"

"There is no need for all this talk," replied Lu Xiong. "I fight for His Majesty. Now I will die for him."

Jiang Ziya told his soldiers to execute the three prisoners. Then he went back up to the top of Mount Qi and recited some magic words. The clouds disappeared and the sun returned to the sky. Soon the ice melted. Two or three thousand Shang soldiers had died in the ice, but the rest all fled back to Zhaoge.

In Zhaoge, Grand Tutor Wen did not know what to do. His best generals had been killed, and also his four Daoist friends. "Who should we send to West Qi now?" he asked.

One of his generals replied, "Grand Tutor, the situation is serious. Everyone we send to West Qi has failed. Now it is time to send the Mo brothers."

Wen agreed at once. He sent a letter to the four Mo brothers, telling them about the situation in West Qi and ordering them to go. The Mo brothers read the order and laughed. One of them said, "Why is he so worried about Jiang Ziya and Huang Feihu? This will be easy for us. It's like using a great sword to kill a small chicken."

The Mo brothers gathered a hundred thousand soldiers.

They traveled over mountains and across rivers and camped outside West Qi City.

Inside the city, Huang Feihu met with Jiang Ziya. He said, "Prime Minister, these brothers are very powerful. I was their commander when we fought at the eastern sea."

"Tell me about them," said Jiang Ziya.

"The eldest is Mo Liqing. He has a magic sword. It creates a dark wind filled with thousands of swords that kills anyone who is caught inside the wind. It also creates fire and smoke that burn anyone near it. Next is Mo Lihong. He has a magic umbrella. When it's opened, it covers the earth in darkness. When he turns the umbrella, it makes the earth tremble. Third is Mo Lihai. He has a magic pipa[1]. When he plays the pipa, fire and wind come and kill everyone nearby. And the youngest is Mo Lishou. He has a magic white fox that he carries in a bag. When he lets the fox out, it turns into a white flying elephant that eats everyone in its path."

When he heard that the Mo brothers were calling for him, Jiang Ziya was worried. But Muzha, Jinzha and Nezha all said, "Don't be afraid, uncle! Heaven is on our side!" Jiang Ziya went out the city gate to meet them.

He bowed politely and said, "Are you the four Mo brothers?"

Mo Liqing said, "Jiang Ziya, you are creating trouble everywhere. You have cut off the heads of our generals, and you don't obey the orders of His Majesty. Put down your weapons and give up. If you don't, we will destroy

---

[1] The pipa is a traditional Chinese stringed instrument.

your city."

"You are wrong, sir. We obey all of His Majesty's laws, and we have not sent a single soldier over the five passes."

"This is nonsense!" shouted Mo Liqing. All four Mo brothers rushed forward to attack Jiang Ziya. The Zhou generals fought back. The battle lasted for hours.

The magic of the Mo brothers was very powerful. The magic umbrella captured Nezha's universal ring and Jinzha's magic stake. Jiang Ziya tried to use his magic staff, but it did not work against the Mo brothers and it was also taken by the umbrella.

The battle turned against the Zhou. Fire and smoke and thousands of swords poured out from Mo Liqing's magic sword, killing many of the Zhou soldiers. Mo Lihong opened his magic umbrella, turning the sky black. More soldiers died when Mo Lihai played his pipa. Finally, Mo Lishou released his fox. It changed into a huge white elephant that killed many more soldiers. Nine Zhou generals were killed, and most of the soldiers were killed or injured. The army turned and fled back to the city.

The Shang army was pleased with their victory. There was singing and dancing in the Shang camp. The four Mo brothers met to discuss their next moves. They agreed to surround the city, attack the walls and gates, and try to capture Jiang Ziya and Ji Fa. They thought they could defeat the city in a single day.

The next day, the Shang army surrounded the city and called for Jiang Ziya to come out. Jiang Ziya did not want to fight them. He stayed inside the city and hung up a truce sign. But the Shang paid no attention to the truce sign. They put ladders up against the wall and began to climb the ladders.

The Zhou army fought to keep the Shang soldiers from entering the city. They used lime bottles[1], stone balls, burning arrows, and long spears. The Shang army tried for three days but could not climb over the walls and enter the city.

The Mo brothers told their soldiers to pull back. They decided to wait until West Qi City ran out of food and water. But after two months the city still had enough to eat and drink. They decided to try their magic weapons instead.

That night, a strange wind blew across West Qi City. Jiang Ziya became worried. He did a divination with gold coins and saw that the Mo brothers were starting to use their magic weapons. Quickly he bathed, changed to clean clothes, and kowtowed towards Mount Kunlun. Then he used powerful magic to pick up the whole northern sea and hang it above the city to protect it.

The Mo brothers began to use their powerful weapons. They used their magic swords, magic umbrella, magic pipa, and the fox. Dark clouds covered the sky, cold fog covered the earth.

But the city was not touched by the magic. At dawn, Jiang Ziya sent the northern sea back to where it had come from. The Mo brothers looked at the city and saw that it was not touched by the magic at all.

The Mo brothers did not try their magic again. They

---

[1] In the 12th century A.D., Chinese navies filled thin bottles with poison, lime and iron pickles and flung them onto opposing ships. When they broke on the decks, sailors could not open their eyes and could not fight. Sometimes the lime was mixed with explosives.

waited for two more months, hoping that West Qi City would run out of food. The city was almost out of food, it had only enough for a few more days. Even the birds and animals became hungry and left the city. But then two young Daoists came to the city. One was dressed in red and the other was dressed in blue. They asked to meet with Jiang Ziya.

"Where do you come from, and why are you here?" asked Jiang Ziya.

"We are disciples of Heavenly Master of Divine Virtue. Our master has sent us here to give you some food."

"That is wonderful. Where is it?"

One of the young men took a small bowl of rice out of his bag and held it in his hand. The generals looked at it and tried not to laugh. But Jiang Ziya told one of his aides to take the rice to the city's three rice warehouses. Two hours later, the aide returned and said, "Sir, all the warehouses are now full of rice!"

Now they had enough food to eat and enough soldiers to defend the city, but they still could not defeat the Mo brothers. Jiang Ziya waited. The Shang army continued to surround the city.

Two months later, another Daoist arrived at the city gate. He was tall and thin. He wore a long robe with a silk belt, a rising-to-heaven hat, and straw shoes. Jiang Ziya greeted him. The Daoist said, "This disciple's name is Yang Jian. My master has sent me here to help you. Tell me, where are the generals who are attacking your city?"

Jiang Ziya told him about the four Mo brothers. Yang Jian said, "I need to know more about them. Take down the sign of truce. I will meet them outside the city gates."

Some soldiers took down the sign of truce. Immediately the Mo brothers demanded that Jiang Ziya come out and fight. But Yang Jian and Nezha came out instead.

Mo Liqing looked at the tall Daoist but did not recognize him. "Who are you?" he asked.

"I am Yang Jian. The prime minister is my uncle. How dare you use your evil magic here. I will teach you a lesson. Then you will die and no one will bury your bodies!"

The Mo brothers rushed forward. Yang Jian and Nezha began to fight them. Mo Lishou released his fox. It changed into a huge white elephant. The elephant had a large mouth and teeth like sharp knives. It ate Yang Jian with one bite. Seeing this, Nezha ran back inside the city walls. He told Jiang Ziya that the elephant had eaten the Daoist.

The Mo brothers were delighted. They drank together. They decided that they would send the fox into the city to eat Jiang Ziya and Ji Fa. Mo Lishou took the fox out of the bag, released it, and told it what to do. The fox flew towards the city. But Yang Jian had made himself very small and was hiding in its belly. As the fox flew, Yang Jian reached up and squeezes the fox's heart, killing it. Then he made himself larger again. He returned to Jiang Ziya.

"You were killed in battle. How are you still alive?" asked Jiang Ziya.

"I can change my size, and I know seventy-two transformations. I can change into any animal that I wish. Just now, I was hiding in the belly of the fox. When the Mo brothers sent the fox to kill you, I killed it."

"With your great powers, we have nothing to fear!" said

Jiang Ziya. "Why don't you change into a fox, go back to
the Shang camp, and steal the Mo brothers' weapons?"

Yang Jian changed into a fox and flew to the Shang camp.
The Mo brothers looked at it. One of them said, "It looks
like our fox did not eat anyone." Then they put the fox in
its bag. They drank some wine and fell asleep. While they
were sleeping Yang Jian crawled out of the bag, changed
into human form, grabbed the magic weapons, and carried
them back to Jiang Ziya. Then he returned to the Shang
camp and crawled back into the bag.

In the morning, the Mo brothers saw that their weapons
were gone. They looked everywhere in the camp but could
not find them. Mo Lihong said, "We need those weapons to
defeat the Zhou. What will we do now?"

Meanwhile, on Mount Green Peak, Master Pure Void
Virtue called for his disciple, Huang Tianhua. He said to his
disciple, "You must go to West Qi. Help your father Huang
Feihu and your king Ji Fa." Then he gave Huang Tianhua
two hammers, a jade unicorn, and a magic javelin.

Huang Tianhua flew on the unicorn, arriving at West Qi
City. He immediately went to see his father. That night, he
gave up his vegetarian diet and ate meat for dinner. The
next day, he took off his Daoist robes. He put on golden
armor over a scarlet robe, and went to see Jiang Ziya.

Jiang Ziya saw him and said, "Young man, you are a Daoist.
Why do you dress like a soldier?"

Huang Tianhua replied, "I came here to fight the Mo
brothers, so I have to dress as a general."

"All right, but don't forget that you are a Daoist. At least,
put on this silk belt." He handed a silk belt to Huang

Tianhua, who put it on. "Now be careful!"

"Don't worry. My master told me what to do. I am not afraid of these Mo brothers at all." Then he mounted his jade unicorn and rode out of the city, with the two hammers in his hand.

Chapter 41
Grand Tutor Wen Goes to West Qi

Grand Tutor Wen leads his army out of the capital city;
The west wind comes from the setting sun

The people suffer from the king's poor leadership;
While loyal ministers lose their lives

We know the date of departure, not the date of return;
We only know the times of growth, not the times of death

The four generals follow their leader and fight in the west;
In their hearts the people remember the first king of Zhou

The four Mo brothers walked towards the gate of West Qi City. They saw a young general coming out to meet them. He was riding a jade unicorn. He wore a gold helmet and a scarlet robe covered by gold armor. He held two silver hammers.

The young man called out, "I am Huang Tianhua, eldest son of Prince Huang Feihu. I have been ordered by my king to take you all prisoner."

Mo Liqing laughed and ran towards the young man. The two began to fight, one long sword against two silver hammers. After twenty rounds, Mo Liqing threw his jade ring at Huang Tianhua, hitting him in the back and knocking him off his unicorn. He lay on the ground, not moving. Mo Liqing raised his sword to cut off Huang Tianhua's head.

Nezha saw this. Shouting, "Don't hurt my brother!" he rushed forward on his Wind Fire Wheels to fight Mo Liqing. Another of the Mo brothers rushed forward. Not wanting to fight both of them, Nezha turned and rode back to the city.

Some Zhou soldiers came out to collect Huang Tianhua's body and bring it back to the city. Huang Feihu saw the body of his son and cried. Then he brought the body to Jiang Ziya to be buried. But a young Daoist boy came to the city gate and asked to see Jiang Ziya. Coming into the hall, the boy said, "I am a disciple of Master Pure Void Virtue. He told me to bring the body of my elder brother back to the mountain."

Jiang Ziya agreed. The boy carried the body back to Mount Green Peak. There, Master Pure Void Virtue opened up the mouth of the dead man and poured in some magic elixir.

An hour later, Huang Tianhua opened his eyes.

"Master, what happened?" asked Huang Tianhua.

"You fool!" snapped the master. "I sent you to West Qi but you forgot that you were a Daoist! First you ate meat instead of vegetarian food. And then you took off your Daoist robes. What were you thinking? I only brought you back to life because Jiang Ziya needs your help."

Huang Tianhua could not say anything. He kowtowed again and again to his master. The master continued, "Now go back to West Qi and try again. This time, use this weapon." And he gave something to Huang Tianhua.

The next day, Huang Tianhua rode out again to fight the Mo generals. "I will fight you all, to the death!" he shouted at them.

Mo Liqing attacked him first. They fought for a few rounds. Then Huang Tianhua turned and rode away. As his enemy chased him, he put away his silver hammers. Then he reached inside a bag and took out a shining magic nail, seven and a half inches long. He threw it at Mo Liqing. The nail went through his heart, killing him instantly. Then the nail returned to the bag.

Next, Mo Lihong rushed at him. Huang Tianhua grabbed the nail and quickly threw it at him. His enemy had no time to move away from the nail. It went right through his heart, killing him.

Mo Lihai shouted, "You beast, I will kill you!" and attacked Huang Tianhua. But in just a few minutes he was also dead from the magic nail.

There was just one brother left, Mo Lishou. He reached into his bag to release his magic white fox. But he did not know that the fox was really Yang Jian. The fox bit his hand off. Mo Lishou screamed in pain. Quickly, Huang Tianhua threw the nail again, and the fourth Mo brother died.

With all four Mo brothers dead, Huang Tianhua returned to the city, along with Yang Jian and Nezha.

A few days later, news of the battle and the deaths of the four Mo brothers reached Grand Tutor Wen in Zhaoge. "What a demon you are, Jiang Ziya!" he said. "Enough of this. Tomorrow I will ask His Majesty to allow me to go to West Qi myself. That is the only way we will win this war."

He went to see the king, who agreed to let him go to West Qi. Grand Tutor Wen said carefully, "Your Majesty, this old minister will try to defeat the rebels and bring peace. While I am gone, I hope that Your Majesty will listen to his ministers. I will be back in a few months."

Grand Tutor Wen mounted his black unicorn. But the unicorn screamed and reared up, throwing him to the ground. As he picked himself off the ground and straightened his hat and robes, one of the younger ministers said, "Grand Tutor, this is a bad omen. Perhaps you should not go."

But Grand Tutor Wen replied, "A soldier does his job without thinking of his home, his health or his life. It is nothing to a soldier to be injured or even killed. Please say no more about this."

He got back on his unicorn, and led his army of 300,000 men out of Zhaoge. After several days they came to Yellow Flower Mountain. This was a beautiful place. The hillsides were covered with tall pine trees. Flowers made the ground look like it was made of jade and emerald. Small streams flowed down the hillsides, and birds sang in the trees.

Grand Tutor Wen ordered his army to stop and make camp. He rode his unicorn a short distance away. He looked at the mountain's beauty and said to himself, "Ah, if Zhaoge ever becomes peaceful some day, I would love to live here!"

Then he saw a man on a black horse. The man wore gold armor over a red robe and was leading a large group of bandits. The bandit chief shouted, "Who are you, and what are you doing here?"

Grand Tutor Wen smiled and replied, "I like this place. I wish I could live here, and spend my days resting and reading Daoist books. Is that all right with you?"

"You Daoist demon!" shouted the man, and attacked.

The two fought, Grand Tutor Wen using his two golden staffs, the other man using his axe. Wen was a very good fighter and he had no trouble blocking the man's blows. He stopped fighting and rode away on his unicorn. The bandit chief followed on his horse. As soon as Wen saw that the man was following him, he pointed to the ground with one of his golden staffs. A high golden wall appeared all around the man, trapping him inside. Wen stopped, got off his unicorn, and sat down to wait and see what would happen next.

Soon two more bandit chiefs appeared. As they came closer, one of them shouted, "Who are you? And what have you done to our elder brother?"

Grand Tutor Wen said, "Who? That fool over there? I asked him to give me this mountain. He started to argue with me, so I killed him."

The two men shouted and rushed at Wen. Again, Wen rode

away, then turned and pointed at the ground. One of the men was surrounded by water. The other man was surrounded by a thick forest. Happy with his work, Wen got off his unicorn and sat on the ground.

There was one more bandit chief. When he heard that his three brothers had all been killed, he flew into the air. From high in the sky he shouted down to Wen, "You are a monster! How can I let you live after you have killed my three brothers?" Then he flew down and attacked Wen with two large hammers.

Wen liked this man. He easily blocked the man's blows, then rode away. "Don't run away from me, you damned Daoist!" cried the man, and rode after him. Quickly, Wen called a local nature spirit and told him to drop a large rock on the bandit chief.

Wen walked over to the man, who was lying under the large rock. As he raised his golden staff, the man cried, "Great Daoist master, I am sorry if I offended you. I would be grateful to you if you let me live."

"Tell me your name," said Wen.

"I am Xin Huan."

Wen replied, "I am no Daoist. I am Grand Tutor Wen of Zhaoge. I was just passing through this region. Your brothers attacked me for no reason. Now, I will let you live if you become my disciple and help me defeat West Qi. If you do well, you will become a high-ranking minister. Make your decision."

Xin Huan said, "I am certainly willing to become your disciple," replied the bandit chief. "And I beg you to let my three brothers live. They will also be happy to help you."

Wen told the local nature spirit to lift the heavy rock off the bandit chief. The man tried to stand up, but he was weak and fell to the ground. Wen helped him to stand up. Then Wen said, "You should move away a little bit." Xin Huan moved away.

Grand Tutor Wen opened his hand. A great clap of thunder shot from his hand, shaking the mountain. The other three bandit chiefs were freed from their prisons of metal, water and wood.

The chiefs looked around. They saw their brother standing next to Wen. The three of them shouted, "Grab that Daoist demon!" and raising their weapons, they all rushed towards Wen.

Chapter 42
The Bandit Chiefs Join Grand Tutor Wen

Disasters come in strange ways;
Gods from heaven join the battle

Their magic is powerful but still they are defeated;
Mortals and gods are unafraid but all are injured

Once, the country prospered under the King of Shang;
But then came chaos, defeat, and a new king

Strong generals are found at Yellow Flower Mountain;
Together they travel to the land of Mount Qi

Before the three bandit chiefs reached Grand Tutor Wen, Xin Huan held up his hand. He said "Brothers, please let go of your anger. This is my master, Grand Tutor Wen."

Immediately the other three bandit chiefs got down from their horses. They knelt and kowtowed to Grand Tutor Wen. They said, "Grand Tutor, we have heard wonderful things about you. We thank heaven for bringing you to our mountain. We are sorry if we offended you."

They led Grand Tutor Wen to their camp. They told him that they did not want to be bandits, but there was so much trouble in the kingdom that they came to the mountain to seek peace.

"Come and join me," said Grand Tutor Wen. "If you help me win the battle at West Qi, you will all become ministers in the government."

"If you will have us, we are happy to come with you."

"How many men do you have?"

"Just over ten thousand."

"We will take everyone who wants to come with us. If they don't want to come, we will give them money and food and they can return home."

The men were happy to hear this. Seven thousand agreed to join Grand Tutor Wen's army.

They traveled for several days. One day they saw a stone sign at the side of the road, reading "Dragon Extinction Mountain." Grand Tutor Wen read the sign. He stopped, sitting silently for a long time.

"What's the matter?" asked Xin Huan.

"I studied with an immortal for fifty years. When I was finished with my studies, my teacher sent me down to help the Shang Dynasty. She told me, 'If you ever see the word "extinction," disaster will follow.' Now I see that word and I am a bit afraid."

The others laughed. One said, "Grand Tutor, heaven favors the good. Words have nothing to do with it. You are a great general, you will surely succeed." But Grand Tutor Wen said nothing and he did not smile.

A few days later, the Shang army arrived and set up camp just outside the city wall. Grand Tutor Wen gave Xin Huan a letter and told him to bring it to Jiang Ziya. Xin Huan entered the city, went to the palace, and handed the letter to Jiang Ziya.

The letter read,

> *Wen Zhong, Grand Tutor of the Shang Dynasty and commander of His Majesty's army, greets Prime Minister Jiang Ziya.*
>
> *You know that is a crime against heaven to rise up against the king. His Majesty has sent armies to stop you, but you refused their orders. Instead, you fought His Majesty's armies, killed his generals, and hung their heads on the city wall.*
>
> *By order of His Majesty, I have come to put down your rebellion. If you care about the people of your city, come out now and receive your punishment. If you don't, your city will be destroyed.*

Jiang Ziya read the letter. Then he said to Xin Huan, "Please give my best wishes to Grand Tutor Wen. Here is my reply: 'We will meet in battle in three days time.' "

Three days later, Grand Tutor Wen looked out from the Shang camp. He heard the roar of cannons. Then he saw a formation of soldiers coming out of the gate. They were dressed in green robes and carried four green flags. They carried swords and spears. The formation looked like a city made of iron.

At the second roar of cannons, another formation of soldiers came out. They wore red robes, carried red flags, and carried bows and arrows.

At the third roar of cannons, another formation of soldiers came out. They wore white robes and carried white flags. They carried cutlasses.

At the fourth roar of cannons, soldiers dressed in purple robes and carrying purple flags came out, led by generals wearing black. The soldiers carried axes.

At the fifth and final roar of cannons, a formation of men on horses and other animals came out. Jiang Ziya was in the center, riding his huge beast. Huang Feihu rode beside him on a five colored ox. With him were Nezha, Jinzha, Muzha, Yang Jian, Huang Tianhua, and several more generals. They wore yellow and carried yellow flags.

Grand Tutor Wen rode forward on his black unicorn to meet them. His face was pale gold, and he had a long beard. The four bandit chiefs were at his sides. They stopped a short distance from Jiang Ziya.

Jiang Ziya rode forward. He said, "Grand Tutor Wen! Please pardon me for not being able to greet you properly[1]."

Grand Tutor Wen replied, "Prime Minister Jiang, you studied for many years on Mount Kunlun. How can you be so foolish as to not understand what you are doing?"

Jiang Ziya replied, "How can you say that I am foolish? Yes, I am a disciple of Mount Kunlun. I have never disobeyed the will of heaven, and I always obey the law. We have never led an army against His Majesty, and we have never gone over the five passes. Here in West Qi, our king is a good man, and the people are happy."

"You are a criminal. You have insulted His Majesty by naming your own king. You have cut off the heads of our generals. You have taken in the traitor Huang Feihu. How dare you fight me instead of giving yourself up!"

"You are wrong, Grand Tutor. Everyone knows that the king in Zhaoge is no longer fit to rule this kingdom. A minister may leave if his king is no longer fit to rule. That is why Huang Feihu and nearly all the dukes and marquises have joined us. Are they all traitors? As for your generals, they lost their lives because they came here to attack us. Grand Tutor, you are a good man, admired by all. I don't know why you came here. Think twice before you attack us. You don't want to disobey the law of heaven and damage your reputation forever."

Grand Tutor Wen could not answer this. His face turned red. But then he saw Huang Feihu and he grew angry. He said, "You rebel, Huang! Come here at once!" When Huang did not move, Grand Tutor Wen turned to his generals and shouted, "Who will kill this traitor for me?"

---

[1] A soldier in full armor cannot bow.

Three of the bandit chiefs rushed forward. They were met by Huang Feihu and two other generals. As they fought, Xin Huan flew up into the air and came down on Jiang Ziya, swinging his two hammers. Before he could hit the prime minister, Huang Tianhua rode forward and blocked him.

Grand Tutor Wen rode forward on his unicorn and attacked Jiang Ziya. They fought fiercely. Grand Tutor Wen threw one of his staffs. It hit Jiang Ziya's shoulder, knocking him off his beast. Nezha rode forward on his magic wheels and attacked Grand Tutor Wen. Grand Tutor Wen knocked Nezha off his wheels. Jinzha and Muzha rushed forward, but both were struck by Grand Tutor Wen's magic staffs.

Yang Jian rode forward and joined the fight. Grand Tutor Wen threw his staffs but they just bounced off Yang Jian. Grand Tutor Wen said to himself, "What a powerful warrior he is!"

The battle became even more fierce. Generals on both sides all used their magic weapons. Sharp spears and arrows flew through the air. The sky grew dark. The wind blew dust and stones across the ground. The soldiers could not stand up in the strong wind, and they could not tell east from west.

The magic was too much for the soldiers of West Qi. They dropped their weapons and flags, and fled back to the city. Behind them, bodies of dead men and horses covered the ground. The West Qi army was defeated.

The Shang army returned to their camp, having won a great victory.

Jiang Ziya decided to wait a few days, then attack again.

Three days later, his army came out again. This time, Jiang Ziya was ready for the enemy's magic. When Grand Tutor Wen threw one of his staffs, Jiang Ziya used his own magic staff to break it in two.

"Jiang Ziya, you monster. How dare you break my magic weapon!" shouted Grand Tutor Wen. But Jiang Ziya attacked again, knocking Grand Tutor Wen off his unicorn. With the enemy army confused, the soldiers of West Qi killed thousands of them. This battle was a great victory for West Qi.

Jiang Ziya met with his generals. They decided to attack again, that same evening. They planned to attack the Shang camp from three sides at the same time. Meanwhile, Yang Jian would enter the camp and burn the Shang grain supplies.

But in the Shang camp, Grand Tutor Wen felt something strange in the air. He burned incense and did a divination. He saw that Jiang Ziya was planning a surprise attack that night. He smiled. Then he met with his generals and began to prepare for the attack.

At nightfall, Jiang Ziya's soldiers left the city quietly and came close to the Shang camp. Suddenly the cannons roared, and they attacked the Shang camp on three sides.

Chapter 43
Grand Tutor Wen is Defeated

Great danger comes when fighting at night;
Soldiers run away, throwing away their armor

In smoke and fire, they try to return to the path;
Their spirits drift away as they search for home

How many brave men die for nothing?
How many soldiers die in their dreams?

Who knew that Ji Li's[1] words would live so long;
They bring the gods to the northern mountains[2]

---

[1] Ji Li is a minor character in the story, a general and a disciple of Grand Tutor Wen, later killed by Nezha.

[2] The Northern Mountain is where immortals gather, ceremonies take place, and important events unfold. It is believed to be the final resting place for many emperors.

The battle was over quickly. Nezha and Huang Tianhua led an attack on the front of the camp. Huang Feihu led an attack on the left while Nangong Kuo attacked from the right. Jinzha and Muzha waited a few minutes, then rushed in to join the attack. While they were fighting the Shang soldiers, Yang Jian entered the camp and used his magic fire to burn the grain warehouse. Yellow fire rose high in the sky like golden snakes. Smoke filled the air. In the dark and smoke, the Shang soldiers could not tell friend from enemy. Grand Tutor Wen mounted his unicorn and tried to fight back, but he could not stop the Zhou army. The Zhou ran through the Shang camp, killing many Shang soldiers.

Grand Tutor Wen saw that the battle was lost. He fled back to Mount Qi with his generals, with Xin Huan circling high overhead to protect them from attack.

High on Mount Zhongnan, Master of the Clouds watched the battle from his cave. He decided that it was time to send his disciple Thunderbolt to help the Zhou. He called Thunderbolt and told him, "Go now, see your elder brother Ji Fa and your uncle Jiang Ziya. Watch out for a person with wings."

Thunderbolt opened his wings and flew quickly to Mount Qi. He saw Grand Tutor Wen and his army fleeing from the battle. He decided to attack the soldiers.

Grand Tutor Wen saw the flying man. Quickly he called to Xin Huan and told him to fly up to protect the fleeing army. Xin Huan flew up, holding his two hammers. Thunderbolt attacked with his golden cudgel. They fought in the sky three thousand feet above the ground. Thunderbolt was stronger, so after a few rounds Xin Huan flew away, defeated.

Thunderbolt decided not to chase him. Instead, he flew to West Qi City. He entered the palace and bowed to Jiang Ziya, saying, "Greetings, Uncle."

"Who are you?" asked Jiang Ziya.

"My name is Thunderbolt. I am a disciple of Master of the Clouds. My father was Ji Chang. When I was seven years old, I helped my father escape from danger at the five passes. Now my master has sent me here to help you."

Jiang Ziya brought the young man to meet his elder brother, the king Ji Fa. He greeted the king. The king replied, "Dear brother, I am so happy to meet you. Our father told me about you many times." The two brothers talked for a long time.

Meanwhile, Grand Tutor Wen gathered his army and set up camp on Mount Qi. He was very unhappy. He had lost over twenty thousand soldiers in the battle. This was the worst defeat of his life. He sat on the ground, thinking about his defeat and the deaths of so many soldiers.

One of his generals said, "Grand Tutor, do not give up hope. Don't you know, there are many holy men living in caves in the mountains. Some of them have great powers. Perhaps you could ask them for help."

Grand Tutor Wen stood up and said, "That is a very good idea! I had completely forgotten about my friends on Golden Turtle Island." He told his generals that he would be gone for a few days.

He mounted his unicorn and flew into the air. Soon he arrived at Golden Turtle Island in the eastern sea. He looked around. Huge ocean waves crashed against the shore. He heard peacocks singing, and he saw a unicorn sleeping in the grass. Deer and foxes walked through the forest. Peaches hung from tree branches. Above, white clouds floated through the sky.

He walked around the beautiful island, but saw no one. He was about to leave when he heard a voice calling out to him, "Brother Wen, where are you going?"

He turned around. It was the Celestial Lotus, a Daoist master and an old friend. "Greetings, Celestial Lotus!" he said. "I am looking for you and the others."

She said, "A few days ago, Shen Gongbao came here. He asked us to help you. So we are all working on building ten death traps. Go to White Deer Island and you will meet the others."

Grand Tutor Wen thanked her. He flew to White Deer Island. He saw his other friends there. They told him that nine of the traps were ready, and that they could leave for West Qi as soon as Lady of Golden Light finished her trap.

Soon Lady of Golden Light finished her work and joined them. They all flew to the Shang camp on Mount Qi. They met with the Shang generals and told them about the ten traps. Then they all marched the seventy *li* to West Qi City, accompanied by the Shang army.

In West Qi City, Jiang Ziya heard the sound of the returning Shang army. He climbed the city wall with Nezha and Yang Jian and looked out. They saw that the Shang camp was hidden by dark clouds and cold fog. A dozen columns of thick black smoke rose through the air. Jiang Ziya looked at this but he did not understand what was happening in the Shang camp.

The next day, Grand Tutor Wen marched out of the Shang camp and called for Jiang Ziya to come out.

Jiang Ziya came out with his generals and five formations of soldiers. He saw ten ugly Daoists standing behind Grand Tutor Wen. They all rode deer. Their faces were many colors: green, red, yellow, white and pink.

One of the Daoists, Master Qin, rode forward. He bowed and said, "Greetings, Jiang Ziya!"

Jiang Ziya also bowed, saying, "Greetings, brother. Who are you and where do you come from?"

"My name is Master Qin. My brothers and I come from Golden Turtle Island. We are Jie Daoists and you are a Chan Daoist[1]. So we are all brothers. Why do you insult us?"

"What do you mean, brother?" asked Jiang Ziya.

"You killed the four Mo brothers. Isn't that an insult?"

"Brother, you know that His Majesty is an evil tyrant and does not have heaven on his side anymore. There is a new ruler here in West Qi. And you know that the phoenix has sung on Mount Qi. You should respect the will of heaven. How can you not see the truth of this?"

"If what you say is true, then heaven wants Ji Fa to be the new king. But what of us? Isn't it heaven's will that we are here to defend His Majesty? Jiang Ziya, we should not fight, because that would be against the will of heaven. But we have created ten death traps. I'd like you to come and take

---

[1] Jie Daoism does not really exist. In this book, it is supposedly a sect of Daoism founded by Heavenly Master Manjusri. The other sect mentioned in the book, Chan Daoism, is real and is known in the west as Zen.

a look at them."

"If that is what you wish, I dare not argue."

Two hours later, Jiang Ziya entered the Shang camp. Four of his generals were with him. Master Qin led them around the camp and showed them the ten traps. They were: Heaven's Punishment, Earth's Anger, Roaring Wind, Cold Ice, Golden Light, Flowing Blood, Bright Flame, Captured Soul, Red Water and Red Sand.

"What do you think, Jiang Ziya?" asked Master Qin after they had seen all ten traps.

"This is no problem," he replied. "I know all of these, and I can defeat them all."

Jiang Ziya left the Shang camp and returned to the city with his generals. He was very worried. Yang Jian asked him, "Can you really break those ten traps?"

Jiang Ziya just sat and shook his head. "How can I? These traps are full of mystery and Jie Daoist magic. I don't understand them." He thought for a minute. Then he added, "I don't even recognize their names."

Chapter 44
Jiang Ziya's Soul Floats to Mount Kunlun

Dark magic and demons make matters difficult;
Ghosts and curses pass from ancient times to today

You don't need a flying sword of the gods to harm others;
You don't need a letter of fate[1] to find their soul

How many heroes have left this world?
If they leave, others will take their place

The will of heaven is written by fate;
A single thread of souls departs and then returns

---

[1] In Chinese folklore, *qǔ mìng jiān* ("letter of fate") is a letter or card that contains information about a person's fate or life path. A person can consult their letter of fate to see the future or understand coming events.

"Tell me about these traps," said Grand Tutor Wen, sitting in the Shang camp with the ten Jie Daoists.

One by one, each of the Daoists told him about their traps.

The first one said, "The Heaven's Punishment trap was made by my master using power from before the world was born. It has three flags, for heaven, earth, and people. This trap turns mortals to ash, and it smashes immortals into little pieces."

The second one said, "The Earth's Fury trap contains all the power of the earth. It appears, then disappears, then appears again. It has a red flag. The flag brings thunder above and fire below. No mortal or immortal can survive it."

The third one said, "The Roaring Wind trap brings magic wind and fire that was made before the world was born. Inside the wind and fire are millions of sharp swords. Mortals and immortals are cut into small pieces. None can survive."

The fourth one said, "The Cold Ice trap is actually a mountain of swords. In the middle is wind and thunder. Above is a mountain of ice like wolves' teeth. Below is a lake of ice like sharp swords. When the ice on top and the ice on bottom smash together, they kill anyone who is inside, even if they have magic powers."

The fifth one said, "The Golden Light trap is made from the power of the sun, moon, heaven and earth. Inside are twenty-one magic mirrors, each one hanging from a tall pole. If any mortal or immortal is inside, golden light comes out of the mirrors. The light turns into a stream of blood. No one can survive."

The sixth one said, "The Flowing Blood trap also contains wind and thunder, but it also has a lot of black sand. If anyone is inside, the wind blows the sand towards them. When the sand hits them, it turns their bodies into blood, killing them."

The seventh one said, "The Bright Flame trap has three kinds of fire: the fire of air, the fire of rock, and the fire that immortals make in their bellies. There are three red flags. If anyone is inside, the fires burn them to ashes. It does not matter if they are immortals who know magic, they will still die."

The eighth one, a man named Yao, said, "The Captured Soul trap closes the gates of life and opens the windows of death. It has a white flag. If anyone is inside, their soul is taken away and the person dies immediately."

The ninth one said, "The Red Water trap has a terrace inside with three gourds on it. If anyone is inside, red water comes out of the gourds like a great flood. When the water touches a person, it turns to blood and they die."

The tenth and last one said, "The Red Sand trap has three parts: one for heaven, one for earth, and one for humans. There is red sand in each part. Each grain of sand is really a sharp sword that can turn the bones of any mortal or immortal into dust. No one can escape."

Grand Tutor Wen was very happy to hear this. He said, "This is wonderful. We will defeat West Qi in just a few days!"

But Yao said, "Wait, my friends. We don't need to use all of these traps. Jiang Ziya is weak and West Qi's army is small. I can easily kill him in just twenty-one days by using my Captured Soul trap. Then West Qi will be like a snake without a head. It will die quickly."

Grand Tutor Wen and the others agreed with this plan. Yao walked over to his Captured Soul trap. He made an effigy of Jiang Ziya out of straw and wrote "Jiang Ziya" on it. On the effigy's head he put three small lamps, one for each of Jiang Ziya's souls. At its feet he put seven small lamps, one for each of his spirits. Then he recited some magic spells. He said the magic spells every day, three times a day.

After three days, Jiang Ziya began to feel weak. He could not eat or sleep. He did not speak in meetings with his generals. Everyone became worried about him.

After seven more days, he had lost one of his three souls and three of his seven spirits. He lay in bed, not speaking.

A week later, he had lost another soul and three more spirits. His eyes were closed and he slept all day. His generals began to think that Daoist magic was involved. They pulled him out of bed and brought him to a meeting, but he did not speak or open his eyes.

A week after that, Jiang Ziya lost his third soul and his seventh spirit. He stopped breathing and appeared to be dead. His generals stood over his body, crying. But Yang Jian put his hand on the body and said, "Wait! It's still warm. He might still be alive. Let's wait and see what happens."

Jiang Ziya's souls and spirits had all left his body. Because he had spent forty years studying on Mount Kunlun, that is where his last soul and spirit flew. On the side of Mount Kunlun, the Immortal of the South Pole was taking a walk when he saw the soul and spirit floating through the air. Quickly he grabbed them, put them into a gourd, and closed the gourd.

Immortal of the South Pole wanted to take the souls and spirits to his master, Heavenly Primogenitor. But he ran into another immortal, Pure Essence. Pure Essence said that he would be happy to take care of the matter. So the Immortal of the South Pole gave him the gourd.

Pure Essence carried the gourd down to West Qi City. He met with Ji Fa and said, "I came here to help Jiang Ziya. Where is his body?" Ji Fa brought him to the room where Jiang Ziya was lying. Pure Essence looked at the body. Then he said, "Don't worry, my friends. Jiang Ziya will wake up as soon as I get his souls and spirits back into his body. Now I must go to the Captured Soul trap."

Pure Essence left the city and flew to the Shang camp. He saw black smoke, cold fog and flying ghosts in the air above the ten traps. When he approached the Captured Soul trap, he saw Yao walking in circles, reciting Daoist magic words. Every few minutes, Yao stopped and used a stick to hit the ground next to the effigy. Every time he hit the ground the lamps were extinguished, but then they lit again. No matter how many times Yao hit the ground, the lamps would not stay extinguished. Jiang Ziya would not die.

Quickly, Pure Essence ran in and tried to grab the effigy. But before he could grab it, one of the other Jie Daoists saw him. The Daoist shouted, "Pure Essence, how dare you come in here!" and threw some black sand at him. Pure Essence flew away as fast as he could, then he returned to the city.

He told Ji Fa to keep an eye on the body, because he still had work to do. Then he flew back to Mount Kunlun. Seeing the Immortal of the South Pole, he said, "Brother, this is more difficult than I expected. I have to go and see our master, Heavenly Primogenitor."

But his master told him, "I am sorry, I cannot do anything about this. You must go and see my elder brother."

"Who is that?" asked Pure Essence.

"Laozi.[1]"

Pure Essence flew all the way to Mount Xuandu, the home of Laozi. It was a beautiful place. The ground was covered with colorful flowers and green grasses. He saw many immortals. Some were talking quietly, some were meditating, some were playing chess. He heard the singing of dragons and phoenixes.

He waited outside Laozi's cave for a while. A priest came out. Pure Essence told the priest why he had come. A short time later, the priest brought him in to the cave. Pure Essence entered, knelt down, and said to Laozi, "May you live forever!"

Laozi said, "Your problem has been fated by heaven. When the Daoists made the Captured Soul trap, they used my magic map of the Eight Trigrams." He handed the map to Pure Essence and said, "Here is the map. Take it and use it to rescue Jiang Ziya. Now go."

Pure Essence returned to West Qi City. He waited until the third watch. Then he flew to the Shang camp. He opened the map. It turned into a many-colored bridge made of gold. The bridge protected him as he ran across it into the Captured Soul trap. He grabbed the effigy. He flew into the air and left the camp as quickly as he could. But Yao saw him. He threw some black sand at Pure Essence. The sand

---

[1] This is the great saint known in the west as Lao Tzu, author of the *Dao De Jing* and considered one of the founders of Daoism.

hit him, causing him to cry out in fright and drop the magic map. Yao grabbed the map. Pure Essence held on to the effigy and flew back to the city.

When he returned to the city, he told Ji Fa and the generals what he had done. "I grabbed the effigy and Jiang Ziya's souls and spirits," he said, "but I lost Laozi's magic map." He opened the gourd and poured the souls and spirits from the effigy into the gourd. Then he put the gourd up against Jiang Ziya's head. He hit the gourd three times. The souls and spirits entered Jiang Ziya's body.

Jiang Ziya opened his eyes and sat up. Looking around, he saw Pure Essence. "Brother, thank you for saving my life! But how did you do it?" Pure Essence told him everything that had happened.

"How will we get the map back?" asked Jiang Ziya, worried.

"Rest for a few days, then we can talk about it," replied the immortal.

A few days later, they all met to discuss what to do next. As they were talking, Yang Jian came in and said, "We have a visitor. Yellow Dragon has arrived." They all stood up to welcome the immortal.

The Daoist master named Yellow Dragon said to them, "I have come to help you with the ten traps. Many immortals will also come to help us. But these immortals are coming from heaven and they will not enter a place like this. So you must build a clean new pavilion for them. Make it out of straw, and hang lanterns and flowers on the walls. Put clean carpets on the floor."

Within a day, the new pavilion was ready. Jiang Ziya and the generals went to the pavilion to wait for the immortals.

Soon they began to arrive. Master Grand Completion was there. So was Master Pure Essence, Yellow Dragon Immortal, Fairy Primordial, Heavenly Master Manjusri, Master Pure Void, and many other immortals.

When they all had arrived, Master Grand Completion said, "My friends, now that you are here, it is time to help the good and bring down the evil. Jiang Ziya, you must destroy the ten traps."

"What, me?" asked Jiang Ziya. "Dear brothers, I have only studied on Mount Kunlun for forty years. My powers are not strong. Would one of you do this instead of me?"

None of the other immortals wanted to take his place. But just then, they heard the cry of a deer in the sky, and the air was filled with a sweet fragrance.

Chapter 45
The First Battle of the Traps

The Heaven's Punishment trap is very dangerous;
But the Earth's Fury trap is even worse

Everything in Qin Wan's life is written by fate;
But Yuan Jiao's death comes from his greed[1]

Two immortals are killed by fire and thunder;
But three more have not been taken away yet

The ten traps have done nothing;
But names have been written on the List of Creation

---

[1] The Daoist immortal Yuan Jiao made the Cold Ice trap, and Qin Wán made the Heaven's Punishment trap.

Everybody looked up. An immortal was slowly floating down from the clouds. It was Immortal Burning Lamp, the leader of all the immortals and disciple of the Buddha himself. All the immortals came out to greet him.

"Sorry I have arrived late," said Burning Lamp. "Please forgive me. I have seen these ten traps. They are all very powerful. We must fight them. I will be your commander, and I will lead you in this battle." Jiang Ziya was only too happy to give up command of the immortals.

Just then, a messenger arrived from the Shang camp with a letter from Grand Tutor Wen to Jiang Ziya. Jiang Ziya read the letter. Then he wrote on the bottom, "We will meet you in battle three days from today." He gave the note back to the Shang messenger, who brought it back to Grand Tutor Wen.

Grand Tutor Wen looked at the Zhou camp. He saw colorful clouds and golden lanterns floating in the sky above the camp. He said, "It looks like a great many immortals have come from Mount Kunlun to help the Zhou." The ten Daoist magicians also saw this. There was nothing they could do, so they just had to wait.

On the morning of the third day, everyone in the Shang camp heard the Zhou army firing their cannons. The ten Daoists came out of the Shang camp. They placed their ten traps in a row in front of the camp.

Then the Zhou generals came out. Nezha and Huang Tianhua were in front. A dozen or more immortals and human generals were just behind them, led by Immortal Burning Lamp.

The first battle was in front of the Heaven's Punishment Trap. A Daoist magician stood in front of the trap. One of the Zhou immortals, a man named Deng Hua, rushed forward. He shouted at the Daoist, "Don't think that you are so powerful. I am Deng Hua, an immortal from Mount Kunlun!" He attacked the Daoist with his sword.

The Daoist magician blocked the sword, then turned and ran into the trap. Deng Hua followed close behind. The Daoist picked up the three flags and threw them into the air. When the flags came down to the ground there was a great crash of thunder. Deng Hua fell to the ground, dead. The Daoist ran over to him, cut off his head, and lifted it up in the air. He shouted, "You immortals from Mount Kunlun! Look what happened to your friend. Who else dares to come into my trap?"

Immortal Burning Lamp looked around. He saw Heavenly Master Manjusri. "Go and take care of that Daoist!" he shouted.

Heavenly Master Manjusri smiled. As he walked forward, he sang:

> *I dare to use my sharp sword*
> *The jade dragon cries out in fear*
> *Purple clouds rise from my hand*
> *White clouds cover my head*
> *I used to grow peaches in the jade palace*
> *I used to discuss the Dao in the golden tower*
> *But now I have left my heavenly home*
> *I've come to the human world, singing this song*

Then he said to the Daoist, "My brother, why have you brought these evil traps here to harm people? I have been commanded to destroy your trap, and so I must kill you. I'm sorry, but this is the law."

The Daoist laughed and said, "You know nothing about my

trap. You are the one who will die here."

The Daoist struck at Heavenly Master Manjusri, but his blows were blocked. He turned and ran inside his trap. Heavenly Master Manjusri carefully and slowly entered the trap. He pointed his finger at the ground and two large lotus flowers appeared. He stepped on the flowers and rode them into the trap. Then he held out his left hand. Five beams of white light shot out from his fingers. At the end of each beam of light, a white lotus flower appeared. Each flower held five golden lanterns.

The Daoist picked up the three flags and threw them into the air. They fell to the ground, but nothing happened. The lotus flowers were protecting Heavenly Master Manjusri.

Heavenly Master Manjusri threw his sword into the air. Instantly three rings surrounded the Daoist, holding him tight. Heavenly Master Manjusri turned to Mount Kunlun, bowed his head, and said, "Your disciple is sorry but he must kill today." Then he swung his sword, cutting off the Daoist's head. Then he walked out of the now-powerless trap.

Grand Tutor Wen saw what happened. He shouted angrily, "Don't leave, Heavenly Master. I'm coming for you!" But Heavenly Master Manjusri didn't even look at him. He was not afraid of the Shang general at all.

There were still nine more traps. One of the Daoist magicians shouted, "Who dares to enter my Earth's Fury trap?" A Zhou general, a mortal man, rode his horse into the trap. Strange clouds came, followed by thunder and fire. The young general was turned into dust, and his soul flew to the Terrace of Creation.

The Daoist said, "Why do you send mortals into my trap?

Killing them is too easy. Send someone with magic powers!"

Burning Lamp called another one of his immortals, a man named Kakusandha[1], to come forward. Kakusandha carefully entered the trap. When he saw the danger inside the trap, he opened a small door at the top of his head. Magic clouds floated out to protect him. He ordered his yellow-scarved genie to tie up the Daoist and throw him on the ground. The Daoist landed so hard that fire came out of his seven orifices. He was still alive, but the Earth's Fury trap was destroyed. The Zhou soldiers took him prisoner.

Grand Tutor Wen was even more angry now that the second trap was destroyed. He shouted at Kakusandha, "Don't go away, I am coming for you!"

But one of the Zhou immortals said, "Think about your words, Grand Tutor Wen. We are not fighting with physical strength, but with magical skill. You should not act like this." Grand Tutor Wen stopped, shamed into silence.

The two armies went back to their camps. In the Zhou camp, some of the immortals asked Burning Lamp what they should do next. He replied, "The next trap is Roaring Wind. But to destroy this trap, we need the Wind Stopping Pearl."

"Where do we find this pearl?" they asked.

"My friend, Woe Evading Sage[2], has it. I will write him a

---

[1] Kakusandha Buddha is the first of the five Buddhas of the present kalpa (age). He was born in India. His father was a brahmin priest. He led a family life for four thousand years and had a wife and son. Then he renounced family life, and after only eight months of study he achieved enlightenment. He lived for 40,000 years.

[2] Earlier in the story, Woe Evading Sage is mentioned as the spiritual master of Li Jing, a Shang general who was the father of the immortal Nezha and his brothers

note. Jiang Ziya, send two people to his cave. Give him my note, and I hope he will give you the magic pearl."

Jiang Ziya selected San Yisheng and General Chao Tian to go and get the pearl. They took a ferry boat across the Yellow River. They traveled for several days, finally arriving at the immortal's cave high on a mountaintop. The mountain was covered with tall ancient pines that looked like dragons.

They waited outside the cave until a young man told them they could enter. San Yisheng gave the note to Woe Evading Sage. The immortal read the note. Then he said, "Of course I will give you the pearl. But be very careful with it. Don't lose it."

San Yisheng took the pearl, then the two men rode as fast as they could. But when they got to the Yellow River, they could not find any ferry to take them across. "This is strange!" said San Yisheng. "A few days ago there were many ferries, now there are none at all."

For two days they rode up and down the riverbank, looking for a way to cross the river. They did not see a single ferry. Finally, they asked a local man where they could find a ferry. The man replied, "Recently two evil men came to this region. They were very tall and very strong. They told all the ferrymen to leave. Everyone was afraid of them, so they left. Now there is only one ferry, it's about five *li* from here. You can take that ferry, but I think it will be very expensive."

They rode to the ferry. They saw two very large men there. These two men were not using boats. They used a raft

---

which they pulled across the river using heavy ropes. Looking closely, they saw that the two men were Fang Bi and Fang Xiang. These were the two Shang generals who had saved the lives of the king's two sons several years before.

"Hello, brother!" said Fang Bi. "Where are you going and why?"

Chao Tian replied, "Would you please take us across the river? As you know, the King of Shang is an evil tyrant. We have decided to help the sage ruler of West Qi. There is a great battle going on near West Qi City, and we have a magic pearl that we plan to use to help us win the battle."

"A magic pearl?" said Fang Bi. "I've never seen one of those. Can I see it?" Chao Tian took it out of his robe. Fang Bi quickly grabbed the pearl and put it in his own robe. "This will pay for your ride across the river," he said.

Chao Tian could not fight Fang Bi, because the man was more than twice as tall as he was. San Yisheng was so upset about losing the pearl that he tried to drown himself in the river. But Chao Tian stopped him. He said, "My friend, don't kill yourself. If we die here, Jiang Ziya will never know what happened. We must return and tell him the story. Better for him to kill us than for us to dishonorably kill ourselves."

San Yisheng agreed that they should return to West Qi City. The two of them rode their horses towards the city. After a little while they came upon a large group of soldiers and carts moving slowly in the same direction. Looking closely, they saw that it was General Huang Feihu bringing grain to West Qi.

San Yisheng got off his horse. Huang Feihu got down off

his huge ox and asked him, "Where are you going?"

San Yisheng began to cry. He told the story of how they had lost the magic pearl. "Don't worry," said Huang Feihu. "Wait here, I will get the pearl back for you." Then he mounted his ox and rode away as fast as the wind.

After an hour or two he saw the Fang brothers walking down the road. When they heard him coming, the Fang brothers turned around. They immediately knelt and said, "Your Highness! Where are you going?"

"I am looking for you. I heard that you have a magic pearl. Give it to me at once." Fang Bi did not argue. He pulled the pearl out of his robe and handed it to Huang Feihu.

Huang Feihu said, "I must tell you that I no longer serve the tyrant king of Shang. There is now a sage ruler in West Qi. He rules two thirds of the kingdom. Since the two of you are homeless, you should come with me and serve the ruler of West Qi. You will be given a high rank, I'm sure."

The Fang brothers agreed. The three of them rode back and met up with San Yisheng and Chao Tian. Huang Feihu gave them the pearl and told them to return to the Zhou camp as fast as they could.

When they reached the Zhou camp, they gave the pearl to Jiang Ziya and told him the whole story. The prime minister gave the pearl to Burning Lamp.

"Now that we have the pearl," said Burning Lamp, "we can deal with this Roaring Wind Trap. We can do that tomorrow. Let's rest tonight."

Chapter 46
The Second Battle of the Traps

Immortals and Buddhas don't often complain;
Complaints bring trouble in this world

Use strength instead of wisdom, lose a thousand years of
study;
Fight, and you will pay for ten thousand kalpas[1]

How often do we look to the past with sadness;
Thinking of who harmed us long ago?

This is the day of the Investiture of the Gods;
Together we wander through the world of dreams[2]

---

[1] A kalpa is a measure of time. A regular kalpa is 16,798,000 years. The longest, a maha kalpa, is described this way by Buddha: "Imagine a huge empty cube sixteen miles in each side. Once every hundred years, you drop a tiny mustard seed into the cube. The cube will be filled before the kalpa ends."

[2] In the original Chinese poem, this line refers to *nán kē mèng*, the South Kuo Dream. This is a dreamlike world where events are not as they seem. In the classic novel *Dream of the Red Chamber* the character Xue Baochai has a dream in which she visits South Kuo and learns of the impermanence and fleeting nature of life, as and that the world is not always what it appears to be.

The next morning, one of the Shang immortals rode out of their camp, on a huge deer. He held a sword in each of his hands. He shouted to the Zhou army to come out and fight.

Burning Lamp looked around, but he did not see anyone whose fate it was to enter the Roaring Wind trap. But just then, Huang Feihu returned to the camp with the two Fang brothers. "They just joined us," said Huang Feihu. "They are good fighters."

Burning Lamp looked at them and knew their fate. But he had no choice. "Fang Bi," he said, "go and break that Roaring Wind trap."

Fang Bi was a good fighter but he had no knowledge of magic. The Shang immortal looked at him, then turned and rode his deer back inside the Roaring Wind trap. Fang Bi followed him into the trap. The immortal picked up a black flag and started waving it. A powerful wind came up. The wind turned into thousands of sharp swords. Fang Bi was instantly cut into pieces, and his soul flew to the Terrace of Creation.

"You should be ashamed!" shouted the immortal. "You sent an ordinary mortal into my trap? Send someone who knows magic!"

Burning Lamp gave the Wind Stopping Pearl to one of the Zhou immortals, a man named Merciful Navigation.

Merciful Navigation walked up to the trap and shouted, "My friend, why do you seek your own death? Your own master told you not to come here."

The Shang immortal replied, "You think your magic is stronger than mine? I don't think so. Better you should leave now and let someone else do the fighting."

Then the Shang immortal swung his swords at Merciful Navigation. They fought for a few rounds, then the immortal ran back inside the trap. Merciful Navigation followed him with the magic pearl on his head. The immortal waved the black flag. Nothing happened. The wind did not come. Then Merciful Navigation threw his magic gourd in the air. A black cloud came out of the gourd. The Shang immortal was sucked inside the gourd.

Merciful Navigation walked out of the trap, carrying the gourd. He turned it over. The Shang immortal's clothing fell out on to the ground. The immortal was dead, and his soul had already floated to the Terrace of Creation.

Seeing this, Grand Tutor Wen rode forward on his unicorn, ready to fight. But Burning Lamp said to him, "Grand Tutor Wen, why are you so angry? We have only broken three of your traps. You have seven more."

Another Shang immortal stepped forward. This was the immortal who had the Cold Ice trap. The same things happened. The Shang immortal shouted for someone to come out and fight him. Burning Lamp sent a mortal soldier to fight him. The two of them fought for a few rounds. The immortal ran inside his trap. The soldier followed. This time, the immortal waved a purple flag. A mountain of ice came down from the sky and crashed onto a pile of ice as sharp as wolves' teeth. The soldier was smashed and his soul flew to the Terrace of Creation. A Zhou immortal ran forward. Bright white light came from his fingers, melting the ice. He cut off the head of the Shang immortal, sending his soul to the Terrace of Creation.

Now there were just six traps left.

Another Shang immortal, a woman, stepped forward in front of the Golden Light trap. A mortal soldier came out to fight her. The two of them fought for a few rounds. The immortal turned and ran inside her trap. The soldier followed. The immortal pulled a rope, shaking the magic mirrors. A golden light shot out. It killed the soldier and sent his soul to the Terrace of Creation. A Zhou immortal, Master Grand Completion, ran forward. He spread out his magic robe, blocking the golden light. Then he used his magic to break all the mirrors. He threw a rock, hitting the Shang immortal on the head and killing her instantly. Her soul floated to the Terrace of Creation.

Now there were just five traps left.

The next battle occurred in front of the Flowing Blood trap. A soldier entered the trap and was turned into a stream of blood by a storm of black sand. This time, Fairy Primordial stepped forward on the Zhou side. Fairy Primordial rode into the trap on two green lotus flowers. He pointed to the sky and brought down a beam of white light that protected his body. The black sand could not touch him. Fairy Primordial threw his Nine Dragon Divine Fire Coverlet[1] at the immortal. He clapped his hands. The Nine Dragon Divine Fire Coverlet caught on fire. Nine fire dragons appeared. They wrapped around the Shang immortal and burned him to ashes. His soul flew to the Terrace of Creation.

Now there were just four traps left. Grand Tutor Wen was so angry that white light shot from his third eye and his hair stood straight up. He said to the four remaining Daoist

---

[1] This is the same weapon that Fairy Primordial used in Chapter 13 to defeat Princess Shiji.

masters, "I am willing to give up my life for my king. But I never wanted to send six of my friends to their deaths! Please, all of you, go home and leave me here. I will fight Jiang Ziya myself."

The four Daoist masters left him sitting alone. He tried to think of a way to defeat Jiang Ziya and the Zhou army. Suddenly he remembered his old friend, the powerful magician Zhao Gongming[1]. "If anyone can help me, it's him!" he thought.

He told two of his generals to guard the camp. He mounted his unicorn and flew to the mountain cave where Zhao Gongming lived. He banged on the wooden door to the cave. A young man came out.

"Is your master in? Please tell him that Grand Tutor Wen from Zhaoge is here to see him."

The young man went inside. A few minutes later, Zhao Gongming came out. He smiled and said, "Brother Wen, what brings you here? You are a wealthy and powerful man in Zhaoge. I thought you had forgotten me."

They walked together inside the cave and sat down. Grand Tutor Wen told him about the battles and the deaths of the six immortals. "I don't know what to do," he said. "Can you help me?"

Zhao Gongming replied, "Of course. You should have come here earlier. Now go back to West Qi. I will join you there shortly."

---

[1] The character Zhao Gongming appeared for the first time in this story, and later become known as *Cái Shén*, the God of Money. In Chinese folklore he can control thunder and lightning, ward off plagues and disasters, bring happiness, and chase away criminals.

Grand Tutor Wen thanked him and left on his unicorn. Zhao Gongming and two of his two disciples began walking down the mountain. Suddenly two tigers came out of the woods. One of them, a black tiger, ran towards him. "Welcome, my friend!" said Zhao Gongming. "I need your help." Then he put his hand on the tiger's neck and spoke a magic spell. He got on the tiger and together they flew through the air, all the way to West Qi.

When he arrived at the Shang camp, the soldiers were very afraid of the flying black tiger. But Grand Tutor Wen came out, saying, "Don't be afraid, my friends. This is Zhao Gongming. He's here to help us."

Then Grand Tutor Wen on his unicorn, and Zhao Gongming on his black tiger, rode out of the camp. They called to Jiang Ziya to come out and fight.

Chapter 47
Zhao Gongming Helps the Grand Tutor

There are many treasures, but don't show them to others;
Remember that they are not all the same

The dynasty is ending but still they still speak of victory;
But when they meet their enemy, they must think about defeat

One cannot ride a tiger, that is just a dream;
But one can defeat a dragon even without a plan

Sadly, the King of Shang's rule is nearly finished;
And the people closest to him cannot help him

"Come out, Jiang Ziya! Come out and fight me!" shouted Zhao Gongming.

Nezha went inside to tell Jiang Ziya about the man shouting outside. "Be careful," said Burning Lamp. "This is Zhao Gongming from Mount Emei. He is a very powerful magician."

Jiang Ziya rode out of his camp. Just behind him were Nezha, Thunderbolt, Huang Tianhua, Yang Jian, Jinzha and Muzha. He saw apricot-yellow flags fluttering, and a tall Daoist riding a black tiger. He rode forward and bowed. "Friend, who are you and where do you come from?" he asked.

"I am Zhao Gongming, from Mount Emei. You have broken six of our traps and killed six of my friends. I know that you are a disciple of Heavenly Primogenitor from Mount Kunlun. Today we will fight to see who is stronger."

Without waiting for an answer, he slashed his sword at Jiang Ziya. They fought for a few rounds. Then Zhao Gongming threw his sword up into the air. It came down and hit Jiang Ziya on the back, killing him. The others joined the fight, attacking from all sides. There were too many for Zhao Gongming to fight, so he turned and rode his tiger back to the Shang camp. He had a few injuries, but he used his magic elixir to quickly heal himself.

Jiang Ziya, however, was dead. Jinzha carried the body back to Ji Fa's mansion. They put the body on the bed. It was cold and lifeless. The face was white. Ji Fa and the others looked at the body, not knowing what to do.

Then Master Grand Completion entered the room. He said to the others, "Don't worry, it was his fate to die." He put some magic elixir in a cup of water, opened Jiang Ziya's mouth, and poured the medicine into him. Then they waited.

About two hours later, Jiang Ziya opened his eyes and sat up. "Oh, what pain!" he cried.

Master Grand Completion smiled and said, "Just rest here for a while. I will go and find out what Zhao Gongming is planning to do next."

The next morning, Zhao Gongming rode his black tiger out of the Shang camp. Burning Lamp was waiting for him. Zhao Gongming said, "Brother, we should not fight like this. Buddhists, Daoists and Confucians are all one family. Red flowers, white roots and green leaves are all part of the same lotus."

Burning Lamp replied, "Brother, we are here by the will of heaven. If you fight us, you will only make a fool of yourself. Why do you look for trouble?"

Zhao Gongming said, "Do you think I am less powerful or less wise than you? I can stop the sun and I can move the moon. How dare you think of fighting me!"

Just then, Yellow Dragon stepped forward. He said, "Zhao Gongming, you are here. That means your name is on the list at the Terrace of Creation. And that means you are fated to die here."

This made Zhao Gongming very angry, because he knew that Yellow Dragon's words were true. He threw a magic rope around Yellow Dragon and tied him up.

The other Zhou immortals rushed at Zhao Gongming, using their magic weapons. Zhao Gongming threw his string of twenty-four magic pearls into the air. While they flew through the air, the pearls gave off light of five different colors. Then the pearls came down, hitting Master Pure Essence and knocking him to the ground. Zhao Gongming threw the string of pearls into the air again, hitting Master Grand Completion and knocking him to the ground too. He kept throwing the string of pearls, and knocked down three more of the Zhou immortals.

Finally, he picked up Yellow Dragon and carried him back to the Shang camp. Grand Tutor Wen told his soldiers to hang Yellow Dragon from a tall flagpole, so the Zhou side could see him. He put a magic charm on Yellow Dragon to prevent him from escaping.

The Zhou fighters returned to their camp. Later that night Yang Jian turned himself into a flying ant. He flew across to the Shang camp and up to Yellow Dragon. He whispered in his ear, "Uncle, your disciple Yang Jian is here to set you free. What should I do?"

Yellow Dragon replied, "Just take the magic charm off me." Yang Jian found the charm and pulled it off Yellow Dragon's body. Yellow Dragon flew back to the Zhou camp, followed by Yang Jian.

The next morning, Zhao Gongming came out again, shouting for Burning Lamp. As soon as Burning Lamp came out, Zhao Gongming struck at him with his sword. Then he threw his string of magic pearls into the air. Burning Lamp was ready for this. He used his third eye to look up at the pearls. He saw them but did not know what they were. Before the pearls could come back down to the ground, Burning Lamp rode quicky away to the southwest on his deer. Zhao Gongming chased after him.

They rode for a few *li*. Then Burning Lamp came upon two men. One wore green clothes and had a black face, the other wore red clothes and had a white face. They were playing chess. They asked Burning Lamp why he was riding so quickly. Burning Lamp told them about the battle between Shang and Zhou, and about Zhao Gongming's attack.

"Oh, don't worry about him!" they said. Burning Lamp said goodbye and rode away.

A few minutes later, Zhao Gongming arrived on his black tiger. "Who are you two?" he shouted.

One of the men said, "Ah, you must be Zhao Gongming! I will tell you,

> *We live here among the beautiful clouds*
> *We grow the golden lotus in our hands*
> *We enjoy drinking wine*
> *We cook dinner over a fire*
> *We ride a dragon to see the blue sea*
> *The night is quiet, the flowers are asleep*

If you must know, we are hermits from Mount Wuyi. We are not happy at all to hear that you are attacking our friend Burning Lamp. This is an act against heaven."

Zhao Gongming shouted at them and attacked with his sword. They began to fight. Soon Zhao Gongming threw his magic rope in the air. But the man in red had a magic gold coin called the Treasure Catching Gold Coin. He took the coin out of a tiger skin bag and threw it into the air. The coin rose in the air, then came down. The magic rope followed the coin like a dog following its master. Zhao Gongming saw it fall to the ground and he cried out in anger. He threw his string of magic pearls into the air, but again, the man in red threw his gold coin and captured the pearls.

With no magic weapons left, Zhao Gongming threw his sword high in the air. The man in red threw his gold coin again, but because the sword was an ordinary sword and not magical, the coin could do nothing about it. The sword came down and hit the man in red. He died and his soul flew to the Terrace of Creation.

The man's brother shouted in anger and attacked Zhao Gongming. Burning Lamp had stopped to watch the fight. Now he returned and threw a rock at Zhao Gongming. The rock hit Zhao Gongming and almost knocked him off his tiger. Howling in pain, Zhao Gongming rode away to the south.

Burning Lamp approached the man wearing green. He said, "Sir, I am so sorry that your friend was killed trying to help me. Please tell me, what was that gold coin that the man in red threw in the air?"

The man replied, "That is the Treasure Catching Gold Coin. Here, take a look." And he handed the coin to Burning Lamp. He also showed him the magic rope and the magic pearls.

"Oh, how wonderful!" said Burning Lamp. "When the earth was first created, these pearls shone on Mount Xuandu. But then they disappeared and no one has seen them since. I am so happy to see that you have them now."

"These pearls are of no use to me. Please, just take them."

Burning Lamp thanked him. He took the pearls back to the Zhou camp and showed them to the others.

Back in the Shang camp, Zhao Gongming told Grand Tutor Wen and the others about his defeat, and how he had lost the magic rope and the magic pearls. "I must get these weapons back. To do that, I need to visit Three Immortals Island. My three sisters live there. They can help me."

He jumped on his black tiger and flew swiftly to Three Immortals Island. He came to a cave, and waited politely at the door until the three sisters came to see him. The oldest was Cloud Firmament, the second was Jade Firmament, and the youngest was Green Firmament.

They invited him to come in and sit down. He told them the story of how he lost his treasures. Then he asked for their help.

Cloud Firmament shook her head. "I'm sorry, brother, but we cannot help you. All of us were all in the room when the three religions got together and made the list of names at the Terrace of Creation. You know that the phoenix sang on Mount Qi, telling the world that a new sage ruler was born there. Now we must wait for Jiang Ziya to create the new gods. As soon as that happens, I will get your pearls back for you. But for now, we cannot help you."

 "What? You won't help your own brother?" cried Zhao Gongming.

"I want to, but I cannot. Please, go back to your mountain and wait. The new gods will be created soon."

Zhao Gongming stood up angrily and walked out of the cave. He walked about two *li* when he heard someone shouting behind him. He turned around and saw a Daoist woman. Her black hair, which was coiled on her head, was filled with a powerful magic. It was his old friend, the powerful magician named Celestial Lotus.

"Where are you going, my friend?" she asked.

Zhao Gongming told her the story. She said to him, "Are you telling me that your own sisters would not help you? Let's go back and talk with them again."

They returned to the cave together. After they sat down, Celestial Lotus said to the sisters, "You are all from the same family. How can you refuse to help your brother? You know that the Zhou now have his magic rope and magic pearls. He must get them back! Think of your shame if you don't help your brother, and someone else does. Like me."

Green Firmament said, "Sister, just give him the Golden Dragon Scissors."

Cloud Firmament thought about it for a while. Then she said to Zhao Gongming, "All right, take these magic scissors. Go to Burning Lamp. Tell him, 'Give me back the magic pearls. If you say no, I will use these magic scissors and make a great deal of trouble for you.' He will give you back the pearls. I tell you, though, you must be very careful in this situation."

Zhao Gongming took the scissors and agreed to follow his sister's command. He left the island quickly. Celestial Lotus said to him, "I will join you as soon as my weapon is ready."

Zhao Gongming returned to the Shang camp. He showed the scissors to Grand Tutor Wen and told him about his visit to Three Immortals Island.

The next morning, Grand Tutor Wen rode his unicorn and Zhao Gongming rode his black tiger out of the Shang camp. They shouted for Burning Lamp to come out.

In the Zhou camp, Burning Lamp already knew about the magic scissors. He told everyone to wait indoors, then he rode his deer out to meet the enemy alone.

Zhao Gongming shouted, "Burning Lamp! Give me back my magic pearls! If you do, I will have no quarrel with you and our fight will be over."

Burning Lamp replied, "These pearls are a Buddhist treasure. You cannot have them. Don't even dream of getting them back."

"Then there is nothing more to say," shouted Zhao Gongming. He rode forward on his black tiger. The two of them began to fight. Then Zhao Gongming took out the magic scissors and threw them in the air.

Chapter 48
The Illness of Zhao Gongming

The House of Zhou rules with the mandate of heaven;
Why fear treasure if they have heaven's blessing?

Lu Ya wrote how to shoot shadowy arrows;
Zhao Gongming cannot protect his own head

Many immortals can change their appearance;
No one believes that a cruel tyrant can survive against them

Grand Tutor Wen fights against the will of heaven;
His heart is loyal to the king, the son of heaven

The Golden Dragon Scissors was made from a pair of dragons that lived on the spirit of heaven, earth, sun and moon. When they were thrown into the air, the two dragon tails locked together. Their bodies could cut anything in two, like scissors cutting a piece of paper.

Burning Lamp saw the scissors coming down towards him. He jumped off his deer and ran away. But the scissors hit the deer and instantly cut it in two.

Burning Lamp returned to the Zhou camp. He told everyone about the magic scissors. They were all very frightened. As they were talking, a man walked into the room. He was short, with a long beard, and was dressed in a red robe. Nobody knew who he was. Burning Lamp asked him, "Who are you and where do you come from, my friend?"

The man replied, "My name is Lu Ya. I live in a cave on Mount Kunlun. I have heard that Zhao Gongming is here and that he has the golden dragon scissors. I can make the scissors useless, and I can kill Zhao Gongming."

The others listened but said nothing. They did not know if he was telling the truth or not. But they let him stay in the camp.

The next morning Zhao Gongming rode out again on his black tiger. He shouted for Burning Lamp to come out. But Lu Ya came out instead.

"Who are you?" asked Zhao Gongming.

"How could you know me? I am not a Daoist and I am not a sage. My name is Lu Ya of Kunlun Mountain. Here is my story:

I am like the clouds, my mind is like the wind

I float wherever I want to
I float on a bright moon on the eastern sea
I ride a dragon on the southern sea
I sit on a tiger in the mountains
I have no wealth, I have no power
Nobody knows my name
I do not care about long life peaches1
Three cups of wine and I am happy
I sit quietly on the rocks listening to the deer
I play chess with my friends
I write poems for heaven to enjoy
Your work of many years will be gone soon
I am here to kill you, Zhao Gongming!"

Hearing this, Zhao Gongming rushed towards him on his black tiger. Lu Ya attacked with his sword. After a few rounds of fighting, Zhao Gongming threw the scissors up into the air. But Lu Ya just laughed and said, "Ah, I knew you would do that!" He turned into a rainbow and easily escaped.

When Lu Ya returned to the Zhou camp, he said, "I know how to defeat Zhao Gongming. But I will need help from Jiang Ziya."

"Of course I will help you," said Jiang Ziya. "Tell me what you want me to do."

Lu Ya handed him a piece of paper with magic spells written on it. He said, "Go to Mount Qi and build a

---

[1] In Chinese mythology, the Jade Emperor and his wife Xi Wangmu gave their guests peaches of immortality at the annual Peach Festival. In *The Immortal Peaches*, Book 3 of the *Journey to the West* series, the monkey king Sun Wukong stole some of these peaches and ended up in serious trouble.

platform there. Make a straw effigy and write 'Zhao Gongming' on it. Put one lamp on its head and another one at its feet. Then pray to the statue three times a day, saying the spells that are on this paper. Do this for twenty-one days. Then we will kill him."

Jiang Ziya did what Lu Ya had told him. He went to Mount Qi with three thousand soldiers. They built the platform and made the effigy. Every day, Jiang Ziya walked around the effigy three times and said the prayers.

After a few days of this, Zhao Gongming began to feel uncomfortable. He felt like his heart was burning up. He walked back and forth but could not get comfortable.

Grand Tutor Wen was worried about Zhao Gongming, and wanted to let him rest. But one of the Daoist immortals said to him, "Grand Tutor, we cannot just sit and wait. How will we ever win? Now is the time for me to use my Bright Flame trap." And without waiting for Grand Tutor Wen, he rode out of the Shang camp on his deer, shouting to the Zhou to come out and fight.

The Zhou immortals heard him shouting. None of them wanted to go out, but finally Lu Ya said, "I will go." He walked out of the camp, smiling and singing a song.

"Who are you?" asked the immortal from the Shang camp.

"My name is Lu Ya. Thank you for preparing this trap. I would like to see it."

The Daoist immortal became angry and attacked Lu Ya with a sword. After a few rounds of fighting, he retreated back into the trap. Lu Ya followed him. Instantly he was surrounded by fires from the sky, from the ground, and from the human world. But Lu Ya could not be touched by fire. For four hours, Lu Ya stood in the fire, singing and smiling. Then he reached into his robe and took out a gourd. A beam of light came from the gourd and shot thirty feet into the air. At the top of the beam were two eyes. A white light came down from the eyes. It hit the Daoist immortal's head. The head fell to the ground, and his soul flew to the Terrace of Creation.

Lu Ya put the gourd back in his robe. He turned around to walk out of the trap. But then Yao, another immortal from the Shang camp, ran up to him. He had a golden face, a red beard, and long fangs coming from his mouth. His voice was like thunder. He shouted at Lu Ya, "Don't run away! Come into my Captured Soul Trap." This was a very powerful trap. It closes the gates of life and opens the windows of death. This is the trap that Yao had used earlier, when he tried to kill Jiang Ziya.

Before Lu Ya could respond, Pure Essence ran forward and entered the trap. He knew all about the trap, because he'd been inside it once before. As soon as he entered the trap he was hit by a powerful flying cloud of black sand. But Pure Essence took a mirror from his robe and held it up. The black sand turned around and hit Yao. Yao fell down. Pure Essence walked up to him and cut off his head, sending Yao's soul to the Terrace of Creation.

These two traps were destroyed, so there were only two traps left in the Shang camp. Grand Tutor Wen was worried about that. But he was also worried about Zhao Gongming, who was tired and only wanted to sleep.

Grand Tutor Wen did not know why Zhao Gongming was sleeping all the time. He did a divination with gold coins and learned that Jiang Ziya's prayers at the effigy had weakened Zhao Gongming's spirit and brought him close to death. He said, "Soon Lu Ya will shoot arrows into the effigy, and that will be Zhao Gongming's death! What can we do?"

He decided to send two of his immortals to Mount Qi, to steal the effigy. Soon after that, Lu Ya felt something strange in his heart. He did a divination and learned of Grand Tutor Wen's plan.

Quickly he sent Yang Jian and Nezha to Mount Qi. Nezha rode quickly on his Wind Fire Wheels, while Yang Jian rode his horse.

The two Shang immortals flew through the air towards Mount Qi. Looking down, they saw Jiang Ziya walking around the effigy with his head down, saying prayers and burning incense. The two immortals flew down, grabbed the effigy, and flew away like the wind.

Jiang Ziya did not see them, but he heard something. He looked up and saw that the effigy was gone. He looked around but did not see it anywhere. Just then, Nezha arrived. Nezha said, "Be careful, Jiang Ziya! Someone is coming to steal the effigy!"

Jiang Ziya replied, "You are too late! I was kowtowing just now when I heard a noise. I looked up and saw that the effigy was gone. Quick, get it back. If you don't, we all will die!"

Nezha turned and rode his Wind Fire Wheels back towards the Shang camp. Soon, Yang Jian arrived on his horse. When he heard what had happened, he knew that he could not catch the thieves. So he picked up a handful of dirt and threw it in the air. Then he sat down to wait.

Back at the Shang camp, the two immortals saw Grand Tutor Wen sitting in a chair. They gave him the effigy. Immediately, the camp disappeared, and the two immortals found that they were standing in a field all by themselves.

Yang Jian rode his horse towards them, swinging his sword. Then Nezha arrived on his Wind Fire Wheels. The fight was over quickly. The two immortals were killed, and their souls flew to the Terrace of Creation.

"Where is the effigy?" asked Nezha.

"I have it," replied Yang Jian. "When I heard that those two had stolen the effigy, I changed myself to look like Grand Tutor Wen. I told them to give me the effigy. Now those two thieves are dead and we can bring the effigy back to Mount Qi." They returned to Mount Qi and gave the effigy to Jiang Ziya.

Back at the Shang camp, Grand Tutor Wen heard about the failure of his plan. He sat down and cried. A little while later he went to see Zhao Gongming, who was sleeping in his bed. He said, "Dear brother, wake up!" Then he told Zhao Gongming about what happened.

"Oh, I am finished!" said Zhao Gongming. "Why didn't I listen to my sisters? Dear brother Wen, it looks like I will die soon. I became an immortal many years ago, during the time of the Jade Emperor[1]. Who would have thought that I would die now, at the hands of Lu Ya? After I die,

---

[1] The mythical Jade Emperor was born the crown prince of the kingdom of Pure Felicity and Majestic Heavenly Lights and Ornaments. After his father died, he ascended the throne. He was a good and wise king. He then decided to cultivate his Dao. He attained Golden Immortality after 1,750 eons of study, each eon lasting for 129,600 years. A hundred million years after that, he finally became the Jade Emperor.

please wrap up the Golden Dragon Scissors in my robe and give them back to my three sisters." He began to cry and could not speak anymore.

Now there were only two Daoist immortals left at the Shang camp. One of them had the Red Water trap. He ran out of the camp and shouted towards the Zhou camp, "Which of you will meet me at the Red Water trap?"

Burning Lamp said to Master Pure Void Virtue, "Go and break that trap." Master Pure Void Virtue stepped forward.

Chapter 49
Ji Fa in the Red Sand Trap

A single thought brings understanding, all things come to rest;
Do without doing[1], make without making, no need to worry

White jade is in my heart, most people cannot understand;
The gold of this world means nothing to me

On the rocky shore, the river speaks to me in Sanskrit;
The mountain's colors cover the cool water

Sometimes I sit by the riverside;
The moon hangs low in the sky like a fishing hook

---

[1] *Wéi wú wéi,* "doing without doing," is one of the key principles of Daoist living.

Master Pure Void Virtue raised his sword, ran forward, and attacked the Daoist immortal. The immortal turned and ran into the Red Water trap. Master Pure Void Virtue followed him.

When he stepped inside the trap, he saw that it was full of red water. He took a white lotus flower out of his sleeve and dropped it onto the water. Then he stepped on to the flower. He floated there for two hours, untouched by the red water.

The Daoist immortal knew that he had lost the fight. He tried to run away. But Master Pure Void Virtue took out his magic fan. It was called the Five Fire and Seven Bird Fan, because it produced five kinds of fire and it was made from the wings of seven different kinds of birds. The fan was so powerful that it could burn rocks to dust, and turn an ocean dry. He waved the fan once at the Daoist immortal. The immortal cried out once, then turned into red ash and died. Master Pure Void Virtue and the others returned to the Zhou camp.

The next morning, Lu Ya met with Jiang Ziya. He said, "Zhao Gongming will die at noon today. And the Red Water trap has been broken."

He took a small bow and arrow out of his flower basket and handed them to Jiang Ziya. He said, "Go back to Mount Qi. Shoot the effigy with this bow and arrows. Shoot the left eye first, then the right eye, then the heart."

Jiang Ziya returned to Mount Qi and shot an arrow into the effigy's left eye. In the Shang camp, Zhao Gongming cried out in pain and closed his left eye. Jiang Ziya shot the right eye, and Zhao Gongming cried out again. Then Jiang Ziya shot the heart, and Zhao Gongming died.

Jiang Ziya returned to the Zhou camp. When he arrived, Burning Lamp told him, "There is one trap left. It is the Red Sand trap, the most powerful and evil of all. We need someone blessed by heaven to break this trap."

"Who should we send?" asked Jiang Ziya.

"It must be our king, Ji Fa. Anyone else will fail."

Jiang Ziya sent someone to talk with Ji Fa and ask him to come to the camp. A short time later, Ji Fa arrived. "Master," he said to Jiang Ziya, "what do you want me to do?"

"Your highness, we have broken nine of the ten traps. Only the Red Sand trap remains. You are the only one who can break it. Will you help us?"

"You are all here because of your love for the people. How can I say no to you?"

Burning Lamp said to him, "Your Highness, please remove your robe." Ji Fa removed his robe. Burning Lamp used his finger to draw some magic words on the king's chest and back. After the king put his robe back on, Burning Lamp drew more magic words inside the king's crown. Then he told Nezha and Thunderbolt to protect the king when he entered the trap.

The three of them walked towards the Shang camp. A Daoist immortal rode out on a deer out to meet them. He had a face as cold as ice, a long red beard, and carried two swords. "Who will fight me?" he shouted. Then he attacked.

Nezha stepped forward and blocked his swords. The immortal turned and ran into his trap. Nezha, Thunderbolt and Ji Fa followed him. The immortal grabbed a handful of red sand and threw it at them. The sand hit Ji Fa, sending him and his horse down into a deep pit. The sand also hit Nezha and Thunderbolt, and they both fell into the pit.

Back at the Zhou camp, they saw black smoke coming up from the trap. "Don't worry," said Burning Lamp. "They will all be released in a hundred days."

Jiang Ziya replied, "But Ji Fa is a mortal man, how can he live in that trap for a hundred days?"

"Trust heaven and don't worry."

In the Shang camp, Grand Tutor Wen was deeply unhappy because of Zhao Gongming's death. Every day he walked into the trap and threw handfuls of red sand down on Ji Fa. The red sand was supposed to cause great pain. But because of the magic words on Ji Fa's body, he was not harmed by the sand.

Meanwhile, Shen Gongbao went to see Zhao Gongming's sisters on Three Immortals Island. Shen Gongbao was an old friend of Jiang Ziya and also a disciple of Heavenly Primogenitor, but he was fighting on the side of the Shang king.

Shen Gongbao told the sisters that their brother was dead, shot by Jiang Ziya's arrows. The sisters all began to cry. Shen Gongbao said to them, "Your brother told me to tell you that he was sorry he did not follow your advice."

The oldest sister, Cloud Firmament, replied, "We cannot leave this island. If we do, heaven says that we will die and our souls will fly to the Terrace of Creation. Our brother did not listen, and that's why he is dead."

But Jade Firmament said, "Sister, what are you saying? Do you have no heart? We must go and see his body, even if it means that we will die. After all, we are of the same blood."

And with that, Jade Firmament and Green Firmament flew away towards West Qi. Cloud Firmament said to herself, "I must go with them to make sure they don't get into trouble." And she mounted her phoenix and flew after them.

They heard a voice calling, "Wait for me!" Turning around, they saw Celestial Lotus. "I am going with you to West Qi," she said.

A short time later, they heard another voice calling, "Wait for me, sisters!" They turned and saw another woman, named Lady Pretty Cloud. She said, "Shen Gongbao said I should travel with you to West Qi. I am happy to meet you all! Let's go together."

A short time later, the five women arrived at the Shang camp. They told a guard to tell Grand Tutor Wen that they had arrived. The Grand Tutor came out to meet them. They all sat down.

Cloud Firmament said to him, "My brother left his home on Three Immortals Island to help you. Now he is dead, killed by Jiang Ziya's arrow. We are here to get his body and bring it home. Will you please tell us where it is?"

Grand Tutor Wen replied, "Before he died, Zhao Gongming told me, 'I am sorry I did not listen to my sisters. I have caused my own death.' Then he asked me to give you the Golden Dragon Scissors and his robe. Here they are." He handed the scissors and robe to her. Then he began to cry, and the five women cried with him.

"Show us his body," said Cloud Firmament. They followed Grand Tutor Wen to the back of the camp. Seeing the blood on his body, they could not control their anger. Green Firmament said, "Sisters, let's catch the killer and shoot him with three arrows too!"

Cloud Firmament said, "Yes, and let's not forget Lu Ya. We will kill him too. Then we will have our revenge."

The next day, the five women and Grand Tutor Wen rode out towards the Zhou camp. Cloud Firmament shouted, "Lu Ya, come out and meet me!"

Lu Ya picked up his sword and ran out of the camp to meet her. His sleeves were blowing in the wind. He bowed to the women. Cloud Firmament said to him, "So, you are Lu Ya?"

"Yes, I am."

"Why did you kill my brother, Zhao Gongming?"

"I will tell you everything, if you will listen to me."

"I will listen."

"The only path to wisdom is to follow the Dao. I studied and followed the Dao for many years, and I became an immortal during the time of the Heavenly Emperor. But your brother made a terrible mistake. He sided with a cruel tyrant. He used his magic powers for evil instead of for good. He acted against the will of heaven, and that's why heaven sent me to kill him. My friends, can't you see that this is not the place for you? Here you will only find mountains of weapons and oceans of fire. If you stay here, I'm afraid you will die."

Cloud Firmament looked down at the ground and said nothing. But Jade Firmament shouted, "You brute! How dare you tell us these lies. You killed my brother, now I will have my revenge!" And with that, she picked up her sword and rushed at Lu Ya.

Lu Ya fought back, and they battled for several rounds.

Then Green Firmament threw a magic weapon into the air. This was the Universe Muddling Dipper, a very powerful weapon. It caught Lu Ya and threw him to the ground. Green Firmament jumped on him, tied him up, wrote magic words on his body, and hung him from a flag pole.

She said to the others, "Lu Ya killed my brother with a bow and arrow. Now we will kill him the same way." Five hundred men with bows and arrows came. Arrows fell like rain on Lu Ya, but as they came near, they turned to ashes and fell to the ground.

"Sorry, ladies, but I have to go now," said Lu Ya. Then he changed into a rainbow and disappeared.

Cloud Firmament was very angry. The next day she went out with the four other women and shouted for Jiang Ziya to come and see her. Jiang Ziya came out, with disciples on his right and left. He bowed to her, saying, "Greetings my Daoist friends!"

"Jiang Ziya!" she shouted. "Yes, we are Daoists. We care nothing for the things of this world. We are only here because our brother was killed by your magic arrows. Now you must pay for what you did."

"No, you are wrong. Your brother came here against the wishes of his master, and caused trouble. He brought disaster on himself."

"How dare you say these lies!" shouted Jade Firmament. She attacked him with his sword. Jiang Ziya fought back. Huang Tianhua and Yang Jian joined the fight. Green Firmament, Cloud Firmament and Pretty Cloud Lady all rushed forward to fight them.

Chapter 50
The Yellow River Trap

The Yellow River's evil follows the Three Realms;
In this disaster even the gods will suffer

The river curves ninety-nine times to hide its nature;
Its thirty-three bays hide wind and thunder

People who study Dao speak carelessly about the heavenly garden;
Who can claim to understand the soul and the holy child?

In this situation, you must completely change your bones;
Then you'll see that dark magic does not lead to a good life

What a battle! It started when Pretty Cloud Lady threw a magic pearl at Huang Tianhua. The pearl hit him in the eyes, knocking him off his unicorn and onto the ground. Jinzha rushed forward, picked him up, and carried him away.

Jiang Ziya threw his magic staff into the air. It hit Cloud Firmament and knocked her off her phoenix. Then Yang Jian sent his heavenly dog to attack Jade Firmament. The dog bit her on the shoulder, tearing her robe.

Celestial Lotus sent a powerful black wind towards the Zhou fighters. It turned the sky dark and made the mountains shake. Pretty Cloud threw another magic pearl, hitting Jiang Ziya in the eyes.

Yang Jian fought off Jade Firmament and carried Jiang Ziya back to the camp. There, Burning Lamp gave elixir pills to Jiang Ziya and Huang Tianhua, curing them both.

The battle ended. But Cloud Firmament was angry. She had been injured by Jiang Ziya's staff, and her sister Green Firmament had been bitten by the dog.

She told Grand Tutor Wen, "Give me six hundred of your strongest soldiers. I will make the most powerful trap." Then she went to the back of the camp. She picked up a piece of chalk and drew a picture of a large building. It had many doors and windows, and there were arrows showing where to advance and where to retreat. The soldiers went to work building the trap.

Half a month later the trap was ready. Grand Tutor Wen looked at it and said to her, "Please explain how this trap works."

"It uses the powers of heaven, earth, and man. It contains

all the secrets of gods and immortals. If an immortal enters, they become mortal. If a mortal enters, they die. The trap takes away their spirits, their souls, their energy, and their life. No one can escape, not even the leaders of the three great religions."

Grand Tutor Wen liked what he saw. He rode his black unicorn out of the camp with the five women and called out to Jiang Ziya to meet him. When Jiang Ziya came out, Cloud Firmament said, "Jiang Ziya! You and I both have great powers. We both can move mountains and seas. But now I have a trap that is more powerful than anything you have ever seen. Try to break it. If you break it, we will leave West Qi and not trouble you anymore. But if you cannot break it, you will all die."

Yang Jian answered her, saying, "Ladies, we will be happy to take a look at your new trap. But please do not try to trick us when we go inside to look at it."

"Of course," replied Cloud Firmament. "We will not do anything to you, as long as you don't attack us with your dog. Now go and take a look."

Yang Jian, Jiang Ziya and the others walked into the trap. They saw a small sign reading, "Nine Bends of the Yellow River Trap." They saw several hundred soldiers carrying five-color banners. There was a cold wind and dark fog. After a while they turned and walked out of the trap.

When they were outside the trap, Green Firmament cried out, "What? Are you going to attack us with your heavenly dog again?" Quickly, Cloud Firmament threw her Universe Muddling Dipper into the air. It captured Yang Jian and threw him into the trap.

Jinzha shouted in anger and attacked Jade Firmament with

his sword. Cloud Firmament just laughed at him, threw the Universe Muddling Dipper into the air. The dipper threw Jinzha into the trap.

Muzha was next. He shouted, "How dare you take my brother!" He threw his weapon, called the Hooks of Wu, at her.

Cloud Firmament just said, "These aren't even magic!" Then she used the Universe Muddling Dipper to throw Muzha into the trap with his brother.

Next, she attacked Jiang Ziya with her swords, then she threw the Universe Muddling Dipper into the air. But Jiang Ziya was ready for her. He waved a magic yellow flag. Golden flowers came out of the flag, blocking the path of the dipper. The dipper turned over and over in the sky but could not come down.

Jiang Ziya was not harmed by the Universe Muddling Dipper. He returned to the Zhou camp. But now three men were in the Red Sand trap and three more were in the Yellow River trap. In the Shang camp, Grand Tutor Wen ordered a great feast.

The next day, the five women rode out and called for Burning Lamp. When he came out, Cloud Firmament said to him, "Burning Lamp! You have insulted us. That's why I created the Yellow River trap. See if you can break it. You should send someone with great power."

Burning Lamp replied, "My Daoist friend, don't do this. You were there when the List of Creation was made. How can you not understand what is happening here? Zhao Gongming was not destined to be an immortal, so his fate was to die."

Cloud Firmament did not reply. She threw the Universe Muddling Dipper into the air. Master Pure Essence ran forward to fight her. The Universe Muddling Dipper caught Master Pure Essence and threw him into the trap. Immediately he became like a drunken man. A thousand years of studying the Dao were turned to dust.

Master Grand Completion saw this. He said to Cloud Firmament, "How can you use your Daoist powers for evil like this?" He began to fight with Cloud Firmament. But while they were fighting, Jade Firmament picked up the dipper and threw in the air. It captured Master Grand Completion and threw him into the trap with the others.

Quickly the sisters used their magic dipper to capture nine more immortals from the Zhou side, including Fairy Primordial, Merciful Navigation and Master Pure Void Virtue. In a few minutes, all twelve immortals lost the wisdom they had gained during a thousand years of studying the Dao.

There were only two immortals left: Burning Lamp and Jiang Ziya. The sisters tried to capture Burning Lamp with the dipper, but he quickly changed into a gust of wind and disappeared. The sisters returned to the Shang camp, and Grand Tutor Wen ordered another great feast.

In the Zhou camp, Burning Lamp said to Jiang Ziya, "Our brothers will not be killed, but all of their wisdom has been lost. We cannot fight these women. I must go to Mount Kunlun and get help."

He flew to Mount Kunlun to meet with his master, Heavenly Primogenitor. But when he got there, a disciple told him that Heavenly Primogenitor was already preparing to go to West Qi. The disciple said, "Go back and prepare a place to meet him."

Burning Lamp returned to the Zhou camp. He and Jiang Ziya bathed, burned incense, and waited for their master. Soon Heavenly Primogenitor arrived. He rode in his Nine Dragon Carriage. Burning Lamp and Jiang Ziya kowtowed to him.

Heavenly Primogenitor entered the room that was prepared for him. Jiang Ziya kowtowed again and said, "Many of your disciples are in the Yellow River trap. Please, save them from this terrible fate."

Heavenly Primogenitor replied, "This is their fate and nobody can change it. Say no more." The three of them sat in silence for a long time. At midnight, a bright colorful cloud appeared in the sky. Thousands of burning lamps floated up above the camp.

The next morning, Heavenly Primogenitor said, "Now that I am here, I want to see the trap." He rode in his Nine Dragon Carriage. Burning Lamp led the way and Jiang Ziya followed behind. When they got to the Shang camp, a disciple shouted, "Cloud Firmament! Come out and meet Heavenly Primogenitor."

Cloud Firmament came out, with her sisters on her left and right. They bowed to Heavenly Primogenitor and said, "Uncle! Please forgive us for our rudeness."

"It is my disciples' fate that they suffer. But still, even I do not go against the will of heaven. Why do you ignore heaven's will?"

Then without waiting for a reply, Heavenly Primogenitor rode his Nine Dragon Carriage into the Yellow River trap. His carriage floated two feet above the ground on a colorful cloud. He looked around and saw his twelve disciples lying on the ground. Their eyes were closed. "Ah," he said to himself, "they could not let go of their desire. Now they have lost everything."

Just as he turned to leave, Pretty Cloud threw a magic pearl at him. But the pearl turned to dust before it reached him. Cloud Firmament saw this. Her face turned pale but she said nothing.

When Heavenly Primogenitor returned to the Zhou camp, Burning Lamp asked him how the twelve immortals were doing. He replied, "They have lost their divine flowers, and their divine gates are closed. They are just mortals now."

"Can you rescue them?"

"I must consult with my elder brother." Then he smiled and looked up towards the sky. "Ah, here he comes now."

They all went outside to meet Laozi. As the master came down from the sky, Heavenly Primogenitor said to him, "I know that you will be here to help me throughout the eight hundred years of the new Zhou Dynasty."

"Here I am," replied Laozi, smiling. Then he asked, "Have you looked at the trap yet?"

"Yes. It was just as we thought. I have been waiting for you."

"You should have destroyed it, no need to wait for me." Then the two of them sat in silence for the rest of the day and all night.

The next day, Laozi said to his younger brother, "Let's go and break the trap. We should not stay in the red dust of this world[1] any longer than we need to." Heavenly Primogenitor agreed.

Heavenly Primogenitor rode his carriage and Laozi rode his blue ox. A red fog appeared, and the smell of incense filled the air. Together they went to the Yellow River trap.

Laozi called out, "You three sisters, come out and meet us!"

The three sisters came out from the trap. But they did not bow and they did not greet their visitors.

"How dare you!" said Laozi. "Even your master would bow when meeting us."

Green Firmament replied, "We have our own master. And since you don't show us any respect, we will not show you respect."

Laozi said, "Well, you are a brave little beast, aren't you?" Then the three sisters turned and walked into the trap. Laozi and Heavenly Primogenitor followed.

What will happen inside the trap? And what will become of the three sisters and the immortals trapped inside? If you want to know, you will have to read the next book.

---

[1] Red dust (hóng chén) refers to the bustle and activity of human affairs. It comes from a poem "Ode to the Western Capital" by Ban Gu, a writer and historian of the Eastern Han Dynasty. It refers to the flying dust raised by horses and carriages on busy roads.

About the Authors

Jeff Pepper is President and CEO of Imagin8 Press, and has written dozens of books about Chinese language and culture. Over his long career he has founded and led several successful computer software firms, including one that became a publicly traded company. He's authored two software related books and was awarded three U.S. patents.

Xu Zhonglin (1567 – 1619?) was a Chinese novelist who lived during the Ming Dynasty. He is believed to be the original author of *Investiture of the Gods*. The only direct evidence for his authorship is an original copy of the book in the Japanese Library of the Grand Secretariat, which is inscribed with the words "edited by Xu Zhonglin, the Old Recluse of Mount Zhong."

www.ingramcontent.com/pod-product-compliance
Lightning Source LLC
Chambersburg PA
CBHW060426310726

48977CB00001B/60